W. Catton Grasby

Teaching in Three Continents

Personal Notes on the Educational Systems of the World

W. Catton Grasby

Teaching in Three Continents
Personal Notes on the Educational Systems of the World

ISBN/EAN: 9783337405502

Printed in Europe, USA, Canada, Australia, Japan

Cover: Foto ©Andreas Hilbeck / pixelio.de

More available books at **www.hansebooks.com**

TEACHING IN THREE CONTINENTS

PERSONAL NOTES

ON THE

EDUCATIONAL SYSTEMS OF THE WORLD

BY

W. CATTON GRASBY

SYRACUSE, N. Y.
C. W. BARDEEN, PUBLISHER
1895

PREFACE.

The observations and inquiries with which this book deals were made for the sake of the information, and not with any view of publication.

Last year, I found myself able to indulge a cherished wish to renew and extend my acquaintance with some of the chief countries of Europe, and to make an extended visit to America, to which continent the attention of Australians is being more and more directed.

The people of the United States are essentially Anglo-Saxon. The circumstances which have altered, developed, modified—in other words, made them Americans—have been similar to those influences which are giving distinctive characteristics to Australians. It is profitable for every Australian to study American history and institutions, if he would understand his country's destinies. English folk in new countries are untrue to their origin if they do not, untrammelled by traditions, with all the advantages of new, rich, and boundless fields of enterprise, progress faster than their relations in the Mother Land. An investigation proves that such is the case, but to a less extent than might reasonably be supposed. It also shows that development, following the line of least resistance, does not always take the expected course.

Although I have not been actively engaged in Educational work for some time, my interest in the subject is an ever-increasing one, and the study of the development of Public Education in America, where the conditions of life have been in so many respects similar to those which surround us in Australia, has been of particular interest.

The comparisons I was able to make, as a result of my observations in Australia, America, and Europe, proved so interesting to the many educationists I met on both sides of the Atlantic, that I have yielded to their wish to publish them; and I have found the task of collating this summary of my conclusions with respect to some of the prominent progressive educational questions of the day a very pleasant, although it has been a hurried one.

Wherein the book deals with debatable questions, I have not hesitated to state my opinions, draw inferences, or make deductions, although perfectly aware that some will prove more or less erroneous. Just which, I do not know; or, of course, I would not express them. A man in a lifetime cannot compass truth; but just as an instantaneous photograph is a true representation of a person at a particular time, although special conditions may render it not typical—if, for example, it should exhibit him yawning—so these impressions are a representation of things as I saw them, but may be only one of many phases which a more extended experience would reveal. Should a reader fail to recognise this, and so misjudge, he alone is to blame. A man who waits until he is sure, will probably die waiting, or will prove a bigot ; and I would rather make a thoughtful error than be guilty of an unreasoning correctness, and lose an opportunity of stating a conviction which may help in the slightest degree the solution of a problem.

I would beg to tender my warmest thanks to the very great number of ladies and gentlemen who have placed me under a life-long debt of gratitude for the very many instances of courtesy and open-hearted kindness in the three Continents. The world is large, as it need be, to hold all the human fellowship therein contained. The world is small. It takes but twenty days to pass from Australia to the Great Republic—a Republic drawing yearly closer to the parent who, in the inexperience of young motherhood, drove her from her breast, to show the world what grit is in the good old Saxon Stock. A brief week of rocking on the bosom of Britannia's protector, and the grand Mother Land is reached, hallowed with the traditions of Old Time, where Socialism jostles Conservatism, becomes acquainted, and finally, claiming brotherhood, is jostled in turn. In thirty days, and the traveller may again be treading the soil of the "New Land of the Golden Fleece," the Sunny South, England's fairest and brightest daughter, soon, I believe, to receive the blessing of her parent, whom she will not love the less, that she will obey the natural law in the evolution of nations—that Separation must precede Federation.

My thanks are particularly due to Dr. Harris, United States' Commissioner of Education at Washington; to the various officials connected with Education on both sides of the Atlantic; and especially to Mr. George Ricks, B.Sc., of London, for kindly seeing this book through the press.

W. CATTON GRASBY.

ADELAIDE, SOUTH AUSTRALIA.

INTRODUCTION

TO

THE AMERICAN EDITION.

IT gives me pleasure to introduce to my countrymen this comparative study of our school-system in connection with those of other nations. It is profitable to see ourselves through the eyes of others. In the attempt to justify our motives and our modes of procedure before the court of public opinion to which we always appeal, we are obliged to purify our motives and reduce to a consistent theory our methods. Criticism has its value, even when it proceeds from the most unsympathetic sources. When from friends it is easiest to assimilate; when from enemies, it requires a greater effort on our part to separate the reasonable from the unreasonable. But all criticisms, whether from friends or enemies, are wholesome reading if they help us to see a deeper ground that explains our differences from our neighbours, or on the other hand, if they goad us forward to better methods of procedure.

In this book, we have the rare opportunity of seeing our Educational System as it appears to one of our large-minded cousins from the opposite side of the world. The various branches of the Anglo-Saxon family—at home in

Great Britain and widely scattered in Colonies round the world—are all engaged in working out the problem of local self-government. Different surroundings afford occasion for different devices, but each community profits by the experiments made by the others. Thus, within the past four years, many of the States of our Union have adopted the Australian ballot law. Doubtless this is but the beginning of mutual help in the solution of our greatest problem—the problem of purifying the suffrage system from demagoguery.

We can be sure of a generally friendly treatment of our institutions from our kindred beyond the sea, for they are obliged to sympathise with our tendencies and aspirations, even if they condemn our means of realising them.

In the matter of schools and education, we find in the German theory the deepest contrast to our own. The reform led forward by Pestalozzi and Fröbel, and carried out into practice by the pedagogues of the German States, is a perpetual challenge to the educational methods of other nations. The Romanic and the Anglo-Saxon nations have always laid more stress on prescription than the Germanic nations have done. They have taken pains to fill the memory of the child with the prescribed conventionalities of intelligence, and have laid more stress on obedience to external authority in the matter of behaviour.

The German theory takes for granted without the slightest question the docility of the pupil. The German pupil belongs to a knowledge-loving nationality. Hence the German theory of education makes prominent the self-activity of the child as the supreme object of education. It repudiates foreign constraint, either in conduct or in intellect. It condemns memorising, as a process of enslaving the intellect to prescribed items of information and opinion. It condemns the strict discipline of schools, as producing mechanical habits of obedience to the will of others.

Hence it happens that the German school, at least theoretically, lays all stress on the process of awakening the pupil's mind intellectually. Critical alertness, and individual power to test and verify the statements of others, as well as to undertake works of original investigation—these are the supreme objects of German pedagogy.

Students of ethnology are aware, however, that nations differ in respect to their bent of mind. While the Germanic nations are knowledge-loving, the Anglo-Saxon nations love adventure and the exercise of will-power. The precocious English or American child exhibits an amount of restlessness and caprice, which compels his teacher to divert a large amount of nervous energy from the work of pure instruction, to the work that is called discipline or government of the school. The child with precocious directive power, and correspondingly small love of knowledge for its own sake, is very difficult to manage in the school. I take it that this explains why it is that in English-speaking countries, the work of intellectual instruction is always prone to degenerate into requiring that work of the pupil which chiefly exercises the memory alone.   Memorised work may be tested with the least possible trouble—the least possible distraction of the mind from the work of controlling and disciplining the school.

For the last forty years, however, throughout English-speaking countries there has been the tradition of Pestalozzian methods in the air, and the loud and oft-repeated cry for reform of our methods of instruction.   Finally, with the Fröbelian Kindergarten, now being widely adopted in our cities, this reform has taken root in a practical manner, and is bound to effect a change in the methods of instruction in all the grades or standards above it.   Notwithstanding this, our schools will continue to lay more stress on the discipline side than on the side of intellectual instruction, so long as the idiosyncrasies of our people remain what they are.   Stated in a language less technical, the English and American school is founded on the idea that moral education is more important than intellectual.

In view of this trend of educational management, the very intelligent criticisms of Mr. Grasby will be read with profit by all our teachers and school directors.

W. T. HARRIS.

Bureau of Education,
    Washington, U.S., 1891.

CONTENTS.

CHAPTER I.

PUBLIC PROVISION FOR EDUCATION.

UNITED STATES OF AMERICA.

CHAPTER II.

PUBLIC PROVISION FOR EDUCATION (*continued*).

CHAPTER III.

HOW WORK IS TESTED.

CHAPTER IV.

THE NEW EDUCATION.

KINDERGARTEN, ETC.

CHAPTER V.

THE NEW EDUCATION (*continued*).

TECHNICAL EDUCATION, ETC.

CHAPTER VI.

THE NEW EDUCATION (*continued*).

SCIENCE TEACHING.

CHAPTER VII.

TEACHERS AND THEIR TRAINING.

CHAPTER VIII.

SUPPLEMENTARY MEANS FOR TRAINING TEACHERS.

CHAPTER IX.

MORE ABOUT TEACHERS AND EDUCATION.

CHAPTER X.

SCHOOLS AND SCHOOL-HOUSES.

CHAPTER XI.

ORGANISATION OF SCHOOLS.

CHAPTER XII.

EXTRA-OFFICIAL EDUCATION WORK.

CHAPTER XIII.

PRIVATE MUNIFICENCE IN AMERICA.

Teaching in Three Continents.

CHAPTER I.

PUBLIC PROVISION FOR EDUCATION.

UNITED STATES OF AMERICA.

Knowledge of Political and Social Conditions necessary to proper under-
standing of School Systems.—Summary of Political System.—General
Appreciation of Value of Education.—Reason for Absence of National
System, and of Compulsory Laws.—Educational Work of National
Government.—Bureau of Education.—Grants of Land.—Smithsonian
Institution.—Education in Southern States.—General Statement of
American System of Education.—Kinds of Schools.—State Super-
intendent.—County Superintendent.—City Superintendent.—School
Government in Massachusetts.—The District System.—Tendency to-
wards Centralisation.—School System of Michigan.—Organisation of
Schools in Washington D.C.

THE national motto, "One out of Many," aptly describes
the composition of the Great Republic of America—many
states, but one nation ; freedom, diversity, competition, but
unity.   A commonwealth of commonwealths, it is in some
respects different from all other republics.   For some years
after the close of the Revolutionary war, each of the thirteen
colonies carried on its own government almost independently of the rest.   There was indeed a loose union ; but it
was rather a source of trouble than anything else.   The
people who had fought for freedom were afraid of a central
government, lest it should again bring upon them the evils

B

from which they had escaped. When finally the United
States became a reality by the adoption of the constitution,
it was only because this remarkable far-seeing composition
most clearly defined the exact privileges which they gave
up by joining the Union. They retained all powers not
thus expressly and voluntarily abrogated. It may be interesting to notice the slightly different principle pursued in
the Canadian Dominion, where the powers and privileges of
the provinces are defined, all else being referred to the
Federal Parliament. The Republic has limited the power
of the superior legislature; the other has defined that of
the subordinate. To what extent, if any, this has to do
with the very marked difference the visitor notices on going
from the States to the Dominion, I could not, if it were my
province, say; but the difference exists. It is said that an
Englishman feels at home when he crosses the St. Lawrence.
The citizen of the sister Union says it is like stepping
back a few years to visit among the " Royal Americans ";
but his opinion is not impartial, and the Canadian is not
backward in retaliating respecting " Americans," as he
oddly enough calls the citizens of the United States.

The same idea is carried through all the gradations of
government. Just as the States have full powers in all
directions not defined in the Constitution, so they permit
their own sub-divisions or counties to manage all affairs not
affecting the interests of the State as a whole. In the
same way the city, town, or township forms a third unit of
self-government, with powers only definable by saying that
the interests of the higher powers must not be infringed.
For the purposes of Education, the ordinary political unit—
the township, is sub-divided into districts, of which I shall
speak later. So freely does the American citizen interpret
this principle of the limitation of the greater, and the freedom of the lesser, that liberty would soon turn to licence
were it not that, after the novelty has worn off the

consciousness of power is the surest foundation for forbearance and consideration for others, and constitutes the difference between the showy military order of Germany, and the less regular, but superior, spontaneous self-government of England and America.

It is by contrasts we learn, by comparisons we understand; but perfectly fair comparisons cannot be made between institutions of different people in different lands. The American, or, indeed, any school system, cannot be understood except in connection with the spirit of the country. America is more democratic than England, but the Federal Government is more Conservative. It is Socialistic in asserting that everyone is equally a citizen, and in the eye of the Government he cannot be more. Its success depends more than any other on the higher and nobler instincts of man; yet its papers are full of denunciation and ridicule at the frequent and gross political corruption. It is admired and laughed at in turns. As in England, sovereignty is vested in the people; stability is secured by a system of overlapping of authority. The people elect a President, and give him greater power during his term of office than is enjoyed by many despotic monarchs. He can veto a Bill passed by both Houses of Congress; but Congress can pass it over his head by a two-thirds majority: yet if it be opposed to the Constitution, it is annulled by the Supreme Court, which, without exaggeration, is probably the first Supreme Court in the world. The President is restrained by Congress, Congress by the President, and both by the Supreme Court. Thus, before any vital change can be made, the Constitution, the pride and boast of every American, must be amended. Any desire for change which is persistent enough to outlast the time necessary to do this must be very deep-seated, and not a passing whim, or the result of a panic.

The greater the power vested in the people, the greater

the need for their education. No better example of this
exists than the related and corresponding progress of education, and the extension of the franchise, in England. The
leaders of the labour organisations recognise it, and attribute
all their success in the late struggles to Mr. Forster's Education Act and Board Schools. The illiterate remain ciphers
in society ; or become the dangerous tools of unscrupulous
and designing politicians. Americans know best what they
have suffered from this cause. None see it more clearly
than did the founders of the Republic. I quote expressions
of Washington and Jefferson elsewhere. Referring to them,
Boone says: "The sentiment was no forced one, nor
exotic. It was familiar to the best men in every state and
station : to John Adams, Madison, and Rush ; to lawyers,
statesmen, and clergymen. It was so general, that the
memorable saying of Chancellor Kent that 'the parent who
sends his son into the world uneducated defrauds the community of a youthful citizen, and bequeaths to it a nuisance,'
was not more a mere personal opinion than an expression
of widespread public faith"; and Dr. G. S. Hall said : " In
the United States he who does not send his child to school
(which he should do for the same reason that he pays his
taxes or fights in the time of war) must be regarded, in
a peculiarly insidious sense, an enemy of the State."

When such widespread and decided opinions were held
by the framers of the Constitution of a country without a
satisfactory compulsory law, or, in fact, *any national system
of education at all,* the omission must be by design for the
carrying out of a principle. This I believe to have been
the conviction that *education should be undertaken for its own
sake,* and when this was not sufficient, on account of a healthy
public opinion. The majority of the *American-born* citizens
were, and are, imbued with this spirit ; and this has been
the chief hindrance to satisfactory compulsory laws. The
wish has been to have education valued for the additional

power and opportunities it gives; and to a great extent the effort has been successful. Many who are not open to the higher influence, nevertheless send their children to school, because the failure to do so entails a loss of respect from their fellows; and no true American can resist this potent power. Unfortunately, the hordes of low-class foreigners who annually flock to the country do not understand, and care not for one motive more than another. They go to America for freedom—a state they have not been used to; and they mistake freedom for licence.

One of the best examples of the appreciation of educational advantages is the prominence given to school facilities in advertisements wishing to "boom" a western settlement. I do not mean it to be understood that the advertisers themselves are actuated by benevolent motives, and wish to benefit their fellows; but they, more than any class, know exactly what will attract the American people. When out West, I collected a number of splendidly illustrated and beautifully printed advertisements of Western settlements. One's first thought, if he is not well aware of the art of the land agent, is that in the wonderful West—and it is wonderful—Paradise has had the multiplying powers of the Australian rabbit. Among the chief attractions are the school facilities. Plates are usually given of—in the words of the advertisement—"elegant school-houses," showing that any new settler taking up his abode in the district will not have to deprive his children of that "inestimable boon, the dearest and most highly-prized advantage of the American citizen, free public schools." To what extent, if any, the engravings participate in the prophetic spirit which enables the agent to see in a dry and dusty plain boundless smiling fields, yellow with waving corn, blooming gardens, and fruitful orchards, I am unable to say; but in the few cases where I had opportunities of testing their correctness, I was surprised to find that, while the surroundings (although quite possible with irrigation, labour, and time) were more or less imaginary, the public schools were really built, on a lavish scale, quite out of proportion to the present requirements. It is a frequent saying that the "best building in an American town is the school-house." Like other sayings, it frequently is only relatively true.

The Federal Government of the United States has assisted education in three ways :—

1. In 1785 it was ordered that in all new States thereafter to be added to the seventeen then existing, a special appropriation of one-sixteenth of the public land should be reserved for the purpose of supplying a School Fund. Of the twenty-five States since admitted, a number have sold the lands to provide the initial expense of school-houses ; but many still derive considerable funds from this source.

2. In 1867 the National Government founded at Washington a central Bureau of Education. It is a section of the vast Department of the Interior, and costs, according to the last report, $51,000. It has no authority ; but is charged with collecting information and statistics concerning home and foreign education, and circulating them for the benefit of the nation. Unfortunately for the completeness of its reports, it has no authority for enforcing the production of statistics or other information. This is not felt to be such a drawback in America as it would be elsewhere, on account of the love of publicity inherent in the American people, and their fondness for publishing elaborate and splendidly printed reports, which they distribute with characteristic liberality. Thus, although the figures cannot be depended on to the same extent as an English matter-of-fact blue-book, they are approximately correct ; and the annual report of the Bureau (a volume of some 1,200 pages) is a most valuable compilation of collected and original matter—not only to educators in America, where the diversified systems

render such a work particularly valuable, but in other lands where they are freely distributed.

The Bureau also publishes frequent reports and monographs on special departments of educational work. These are distributed without stint throughout the country, and must be productive of much good. In addition, it gathers, for additions to its bulletins, or for the use of Congress, numerous reports respecting the educational systems of foreign countries. Indirectly, its influence must be very great. The present Commissioner is the Hon. W. T. Harris, A.M., LL.D., who was formerly superintendent of the public schools of St. Louis, where he was the means of introducing Kindergartens in connection with the schools throughout the city. He has the reputation of being America's foremost writer on the Philosophy and Psychology of Education ; and the usefulness of the Bureau is expected to be largely increased under his direction.

There is a very fine pedagogical library connected with the Bureau, in which are to be found all standard works bearing on education, and a very large and valuable collection of pamphlets and reports. Sufficient material is also stored away to furnish a splendid museum of educational appliances, illustrative of the school architecture and appliances in use in various parts of the world. Efforts are being made to induce the National Government to appropriate funds for a new building, when the Pedagogical Museum will be properly housed, and will prove of great value.

The *Smithsonian Institution* does not come strictly within the scope of my remarks; but its great influence on the general education of the people, and the example it affords of the liberality of the people of the United States in the free distribution of reports, makes it desirable that its work should be mentioned. Its foundation is due to the bequest of James Smithson ; and probably no man ever gained for himself such a memorial at such a comparatively small cost.

James Smithson was an Englishman of noble descent, a graduate of Oxford, with, as far as is known, anti-democratic tendencies, who had never visited the United States. He died early in the century, leaving his fortune to the people of the United States "to found at Washington, under the name of the Smithsonian Institution, an establishment for the increase and diffusion of knowledge among men." The object of the extensive organisation—a mere fraction of the cost of which is provided by the bequest of the founder—is original research and publication.

It is also the curator of the adjoining National Museum. Every public library throughout the world receives the publications of this Institution, under the title of "Contributions to Knowledge." But the unique feature about its operations is that it is a sort of international knowledge exchange. It has agents in London, Paris, Leipzig, and Amsterdam, through which it distributes the publications of all the American learned societies ; while, on the other hand, academies and learned societies in Europe send over bundles of their publications to be distributed by the Institution according to a list sent by each society.

There have been spasmodic efforts to found a National University at Washington; but the movement does not gain ground rapidly. It was George Washington's great wish, and will, no doubt, at some time be an accomplished fact ; and, when it is done, it will be worthy of the people, the city, and the nation.

Previous to the civil war, I believe, no slave-holding State possessed a free school system. Since then all but two have adopted new constitutions, which include articles providing for free public schools, in some cases quite as liberally as the Northern States ; but, unfortunately, they cannot be carried out on account of the lack of funds ; and unless the Blair Bill becomes law, great progress may not be expected for some time.

It was believed by the Northern States, where great importance had always been attached to education, that the lack of public schools in the slave States was one of the chief causes of the rebellion. This belief, that the lack of education lay at the root of the greatest disaster that has fallen on the Republic, has had an important bearing on the inclusion of articles relating to education in the newer States. In fact, so minutely has the North Dakota Convention gone into details with regard to the school lands, that one is ready to agree with the writer who thinks that "the framers of the State Convention have no confidence whatever in the good sense, judgment, and honesty of future legislation."

Unless they are specially mentioned, my observations must not be taken to refer to the Southern States. While great progress is being made, education in the South is, apart from the fearful ignorance of the coloured population, in a backward condition. Taking the whole population of the Southern and South-Western States, illiteracy is increasing at a greater ratio than the population. It is on this account that the advocates of the Blair Bill wish the Federal Government to apportion about 80,000,000 dollars, from the surplus in the National Treasury, among the most illiterate States in proportion to the percentage of illiteracy; which money shall be chiefly devoted to actual education, not the building of elaborate school-houses. It is almost certain that this will shortly be done, and the threatening danger averted; and thus another precedent in favour of the National Government concerning itself directly with the education of the States will be established.

Consideration of this subject affords a very good instance of how very misleading general statements may be, although in themselves correct. Roughly speaking, it may be said with truth that in two-thirds of the States education is in a more or less low condition. Perhaps even stronger language might be used—Americans certainly speak more forcibly. These States, however, contain little more than one-third of the population ; and if out of this number there be taken all those belonging to the numerous centres where the school systems are very efficient, and the children of those well-to-do people whose training is well looked after, but a comparatively small proportion of the total white population will remain. There are enough and to spare to justify Americans in using all the vigour of expression at their command to arouse the people to remedy the evil ; but not enough for outside writers to conclude that the language so used applies to the people in general.

Of the mass of the coloured people I do not intend to say much. I shall speak of a few schools in their place, and will only remark here that the conviction forced itself on my mind that the difficulty with regard to these unfortunate people, instead of having been solved by the war, was only changed into a new and more perplexing problem by the amendment of the Constitution ; an amendment that gave them legal rights of equal citizenship with the whites, which the latter in many cases endeavour to prevent them from exercising.

According to the last census and the present estimates, then, one-third of the States contain approximately two-thirds of the population. It is to this small portion—about one quarter of the area of the whole country—that I refer when making general observations. These may or may not be correct with reference to the rest of the country. If I included Alaska, the proportion would be smaller. Another comparison may be interesting. The total area of the States with which I deal is about equal to that of Queensland, the third in size of the Australian colonies ; and the population, roughly speaking, is somewhat greater than that of the British Isles.

Although the systems of education in the States differ in

minor points, and sometimes have very distinctive features, there is sufficient similarity to enable me to make a general statement, after which I will give one or two examples of fairly typical systems in greater detail.

The period of free attendance is usually from five or six to twenty or twenty-one years of age. The period of elementary education generally extends from six to fourteen, the first four years being spent in the *Primary School* or Department, from which in the ordinary course the pupil passes at the age of ten to the *Grammar School* or Department. The terms Primary School and Grammar School are commonly used, even when the two departments are under the one roof. In some places, on the other hand, the lower classes are spoken of as the Primary Grades, and the Senior as the Grammar Grades. The use of the term standard in the English sense did not come under my notice. Free secondary education is provided by all the States under consideration in the *High Schools*, which take the pupils after they have graduated from the Grammar School. I shall speak of these schools in another chapter.

Each State has its central educational authority, generally a Board with a practical secretary or superintendent; but sometimes merely a superintendent. The powers of this central authority vary greatly; generally the practical working of the school system is left to the committee or School Boards of smaller administrative areas, each State being divided into counties, and each county into "townships," these being sometimes again divided into districts. Or the county may be directly divided into districts, as in the case of California.

The constitution of these Boards or Committees varies greatly. The elective system largely predominates, and the *personnel* of the Boards is subject to frequent changes. The cities, beyond supplying statistics, are usually independent of any outside authority. In California each city or incorporated town, unless sub-divided, forms one school district.

School Superintendence.

The school superintendent is a peculiarly American development. He has no prototype elsewhere. The word itself is one of which the people are fond, and is used in many connections not usual in England. This is another example of the difference in meaning and use of the same word in the two great English-speaking lands. The oft-used word " captain," designating one in command of a ship or a mine, is generally discarded. The master of a ship becomes a commander, and he of the mine a superintendent; and, just as the chairman of the board of directors becomes the president, so the office of manager in England becomes superintendent in America; in addition to which, it is used in connection with education to designate an office which is unlike any in England or Australia. The student of American education will find at least four kinds of superintendents mentioned; but no exact statement can be made as to the appointment or duties of each. There are State, County, City, and Town Superintendents, supervising more or less directly the schools of the political divisions of the same name. All the States of which I am speaking have State superintendents, in most cases supplemented by a Board of Education, of which he is, *ex officio*, a member and executive officer. The chief functions of the Board are— (1) The distribution and management of the school funds derivable from lands, and of the legislative appropriations for education. (2) The supervision, directly or indirectly, of the training and examination of teachers. The superintendent and his Board may, in many cases, be termed the political head of the school system; and in some instances the political aspect predominates to an extent detrimental to the best interests of the schools.

County Superintendents.—All the charms of variety are to be found in connection with the appointment and duties of the County Superintendent. In thirteen States he is elected by the people. In other places the appointment rests with the Governor, State Superintendent, or County Board of Education. As the various officers having the gift in their hands are elected, the one under consideration is influenced in the second degree by the vote of the people. The duties of a County Superintendent vary as greatly as his mode of appointment. In some States he is chiefly concerned in business affairs; but usually he has to visit and inspect schools, criticise the management and teaching, direct and counsel the teachers, and hold examinations for teachers' certificates. He has generally been a teacher; and in some States—California, for example—a teacher may contest an election for the office while in charge of a school, which he gives up if elected. One of the important duties of the superintendent is to hold institutes for teachers, of which I speak more fully elsewhere.

City Superintendents.—Perhaps because I did not understand the full significance of the remark, I was frequently inwardly amused at what appeared to me an absurdly extravagant use of dignity on the part of City Superintendents in large cities, when they informed me " that the city of —— is quite independent of the County or State Officers of Education. It manages its own affairs with as little reference to the State Superintendent as if it were in another State, only furnishing him with certain statistical and other information required by law." City Superintendents are often among the foremost educators of the country, and the schools under their care are equally a credit to themselves, and to the splendid cities over which they preside. At the same time, the superintendents, holding lofty ideals and considering that the fine work which has been done, is but treading on the threshold of the possible, with the frankness of their nation, freely exhibit and court inspection of the indifferent equally with the good. They know that in comparison with others they have little to fear; but in contrast to the attainable the position is humiliating. Merely putting forward the latter comparison; depreciating the excellencies, lest the object of improvement should be defeated; wishing to rouse the people to a sense of the need for continued progress; they sometimes use language which leads to a false opinion being formed by outsiders. This is equally true with regard to the authorities in England and Australia. Before legislation or reforms are possible in self-governing countries, the public must be educated. The means taken to attain this end will be different, according to the peculiar conditions of the people. Unless due regard be paid to this fact, one is apt to attribute many of their actions to those causes which give the drum its value, or to which the pebbly brook owes its murmuring.

Massachusetts.

Mr. J. W. Dickenson, Secretary of the Massachusetts State Board, in reply to my question, "What are the special features of your school government?" said :—

"The State Board collects statistics, attends to the appropriation of money, provides and works normal schools, and exercises a control over all the schools of the State. The latter, however, is more by moral force than anything else.

"Each town and district, as a centre or unit of the commonwealth, is called upon to elect a school committee to look after the education of the district. These committees provide schools, and conduct them as they like within the law, which is very elastic. This Board has five agents, who visit the various towns and school districts, and after doing so, call the committee together, and discuss the state of the schools and make suggestions. The committee may or may not accept and act on the advice; but they generally do, and the visits are productive of much benefit. The agents also hold institutes in suitable centres all over the State."

The District System.

The district system, the extreme of decentralization, was the outcome of the reaction against monarchism, and has given character to American schools and to the people. The interest of every citizen was thereby enlisted in all public affairs. Every resident was supposed to understand the business of the district, the affairs of which were regularly discussed at the annual meeting, when the officers for the year were elected. The schools received their due share of attention, the control being vested in the school committee.

Possessing many advantages, the system was open to evils. As a rule, the best men would be elected to the school committee, and as their intelligence was above the average of the community, it would be their desire to raise the general standard of knowledge. Unfortunately, ignorance is generally not self-conscious; and thus the control would sometimes become vested in men who were apt to agree with the farmer—

" There ain't no great good to be reached
  By tiptoein' children up higher than ever their fathers was teached."

They did not know how to properly value a teacher, and were not enlightened, even if rich enough, to pay liberal salaries. Like all small communities, they had party disputes; and energy, which should have been given to education, was devoted to quarrelling. Instead of the best teachers being appointed, the "schools were taught" by those who could secure the greatest influence, or work for the least pay. No doubt the committee generally considered they were appointing the best teachers, but they were not good judges, and apt to agree that—

"Whatever is done as to readin', providin' things go to my say,
  Shan't hang on no new-fangled hinges, but swing in the old-fashioned
    way."

Education is either solely a family duty, or it is a State concern. That it is a matter of importance to the State is agreed; and being so, its management should not be left to small communities. If this be done, the portions of the country most needing education will be left without it for two reasons :—

(*a*) Want of Funds.

(*b*) Want of Inclination.

The poorer districts need the greatest educational care; but the people are as unable to regulate as to provide it : this was amply proved in many places.

In addition, the plan tended to cause the erection of many small schools where one large one would be more economical and efficient. This wasteful plan still exists; but other reasons are assigned for it. In one town I visited there is one Grammar School, the upper floor of which is devoted to a High School. The building is a new and handsome one, as well adapted to its purpose as the American schools usually are. In the same town are some six primary schools. It would be infinitely better to have one central establishment; but when I asked several people why such was not done, I received the reply that in the severe winters it is impossible for the small children to travel the distance most would have to do if the plan of having one large central establishment were adopted. This is a reason which cannot be lightly dismissed. As I was there on a lovely autumn day, it had not struck me.

The town is following the general tendency to centralization seen everywhere in the States under consideration. The principal of the High School, in which there are only between forty and fifty pupils, is also superintendent of the other schools of the town, having an assistant to help him with his school, and take charge when he is away.

This is again illustrated by Mr. Stockwell, Superintendent of Schools, State of Rhode Island; who, during an address before the Rhode Island Educational Association, at which some seven hundred teachers, and twice that number of friends were present, said :—

"Legislation of the State has followed the onward sweep of the world, which is tending towards centralization. Rhode Island is taking the power out of the hands of town committees, and placing it where it can be looked to do its work." Indeed, I found a growing feeling in all the Northern States in favour of centralization, better supervision, and a more careful attention to compulsory education.

The unit of government in school affairs is being altered and enlarged; and at the same time brought more into harmony with, and more directly under the control of, the State Boards. More uniformity, a better class of men as managers, less party influence in the appointment of teachers, and consequently a better class of teachers, greater economy in management, and altogether a more advanced condition of education, is, I think, rightly expected as the outcome of the movement.

Michigan State System.

The educational organisation of Michigan is a combination of the District and Town systems, the former predominating. It may be taken as a type of many. The State is divided into counties, which are again divided into smaller divisions, known as "townships," consisting of

c

several school districts, each of which has its School Board of three members—a moderator, a director, and an assessor. The duties of the Board are—to build school-houses, employ teachers, and decide for what length of time the school shall be open. This formerly depended on how much money could be raised, and the smallness of the sum necessary to hire a teacher.

Each township has a Board of three trustees or directors, whose main duty is to regulate boundaries of school districts, and visit schools. The County Board of school examiners consists of two members, elected by the chairman of the township Board of Inspectors; and a secretary, who is, *ex officio*, a member, elected by these two, acting with the County Judge of Probate. The secretary of the County Board visits, or causes his assistants to visit, each school of the county at least once a year; counsels with teachers and School Boards as to the courses of study and discipline; makes suggestions with regard to school buildings and grounds, heating, ventilation, &c.; promotes the improvement of schools and the elevation of the character and qualification of teachers and officers; and receives the reports of the township inspectors. In addition, the secretary holds two regular, and not more than six special examinations for teachers annually. Certificates of three grades are granted, and are good for one, two, and three years respectively. Second- and third-grade certificates can be used only in the county in which they are granted, while those of the first grade have been made valid throughout the State. At the two regular examinations, the State Board of Education sends out sealed uniform questions to be used throughout the State. This Board consists of the Superintendent of Public Instruction, and three other members, elected for a term of six years. It has the entire control of the State normal school, grants State certificates good for ten years anywhere in the State, and prepares the questions to be used by the County Board secretaries.

The State Superintendent of Public Instruction nominally has general supervision of all the public schools and State educational institutions; collects and tabulates the school statistics; and makes an annual report to the Governor. He organises and visits teachers' institutes; appoints instructors for them; and delivers lectures on educational subjects. He is general adviser of county superintendents, to whom he addresses from time to time circular letters giving advice as to the best manner of conducting schools, constructing school-houses, furnishing the same, and procuring and examining competent teachers. He has further to make such rules and regulations as may be necessary to carry into effect the provisions of the Education Acts; be legal adviser of all school officers; and, when requested, give his opinion in writing upon any question arising under the school laws of the State. He has power to enforce the supplying of returns, reports, and any other requisite information from all authorities controlling educational institutions.

The District schools are known as "ungraded schools," (that is, they have pupils of more than one standard in a room, under one teacher), and are often poor. Many are only in session for a few months of each year. The teachers are frequently poorly paid; and consequently are sometimes but ill qualified for their work. On the other hand, they are often able and bright, and are using the school as an opportunity for self-education, and to obtain means to provide for college expenses. Many of America's great men and women have been District teachers, and their influence must have been good. The men and women trained under these conditions are an example— although, I believe, not as good as those of Iceland—of how education may be carried on without schooling. With only from three to six months of attendance during the year, under an untrained and often comparatively illiterate teacher, in a school lacking all appliances—without even a blackboard—a lamentable condition of ignorance would be naturally expected. But pupils, at all events, learned to read. With this power, the long cold winter, a supply of books (and it is somewhat astonishing what books are to be found even in the back country), and the American fondness for lectures, an unexpected state of things is brought about.

Above the Grammar School is the High School, which only admits pupils who have a grammar school certificate; or, as the Americans say, have "graduated" in a Grammar School.

A High School course extends over from three to five years, and usually provides for at least two courses of study: the one a preparation for the university, the other having a more direct bearing on commercial life. The High Schools, like the lower grades, are free. In Michigan there is an arrangement by which High Schools desiring recognition from the university are visited and examined by a committee of the "faculty"; and if approved, have their graduates admitted to the university without further examination. This last link towards connecting the lowest and highest departments of the school system is in operation in California, and some other of the newer States.

For the purpose of providing professional training, a Free State Normal School is provided, which sends out about one hundred students annually. This does not nearly supply the demand for trained teachers; and there is a large number whose only training is obtained by reading and observation, or at the Teachers' Institutes.

This State also has a State Agricultural College to promote its agriculture; and the Michigan Mining School to foster the mining industry. Liberal provision is also made for the blind, deaf, and dumb. Dependent children are provided with a home and educational advantages; and youthful criminals are instructed in the State Reform Schools.

The criticism which first rises naturally to one's lips, is that all this system, and the acknowledgment on the part of the State of the necessity of education as a guarantee of well-being, is useless, if the parent of a child is unwilling to take advantage of the means provided. There is no compulsion for those who would injure the State by bringing up children in ignorance.

The lack of training on the part of the teachers is another weakness; and associated with this is the poor pay they as a rule receive; but of these points I shall speak elsewhere.

Washington, D.C.

The organisation of the school system here has peculiar features. Education is under the direction of a Board appointed by the three commissioners in whom the Government of the Federal District of Columbia is vested. There are two systems of schools; the one for white, the other for coloured children. The schools of both sections are of the usual three classes:—Primary, Grammar, and High Schools, each system being under its own superintendent. The coloured pupils follow the same course of study as the white, and there appeared to be very little difference in the character of the work; but the pupils in the coloured classes are older than those in the corresponding grades in the schools for white children. I was much surprised to find many pupils very nearly or quite white in the coloured schools; but learned that, being associated with coloured people in their homes, they would not be allowed to attend with white children, even did they not choose to be with their young coloured friends.

The schools for white children are divided into six districts, each under a supervising teacher, who takes much of the work which usually falls to a principal.   In fact, it is in this point that the chief peculiarity of the city's organisation lies.   Each teacher works independently of the principal, being responsible to the supervising teacher.   The principal teaches a class—an unusual thing, as far as I could learn in the parts of America which I visited—and only differs from the other teachers in being responsible for the building, the playground arrangements, and any outside business which may have to be transacted with parents, and so forth.

The coloured schools have the same organisation, there being two supervising teachers.

Result examinations have been abolished for about four years, and the change seems to have given great satisfaction. The course of instruction is carefully laid down by the Board ; and the superintendent and supervising teachers see that it is carried out.   They make such frequent visits to the schools, at which they test the work in any way they see fit, that they are able, they say, to ensure much more systematic, regular, and careful teaching than when the work was chiefly tested by an annual examination.

"There is a compulsory law; but it is not enforced, because there are not sufficient schools to accommodate all the children."   I quote the words used to me, for it seems incredible that the city of "magnificent distances," and more magnificent buildings; the city wherein is built, at a cost sufficient to provide schools for twice the population, the monument in honour of the justly revered Washington, who, in his farewell address, gave the injunction to his fellow citizens, to " Promote as an object of primary importance institutions for the general diffusion of knowledge"; the city where probably the largest deposit of coin in the world is stowed like potatoes in the treasury vaults, and where money to any amount can be found for party purposes ;—that this city cannot afford sufficient to build school-houses ! The Superintendent of Education, in discussing what is to be done for the numbers of children who do not attend school, has to say : " In the first place, ample provision should be made in comfortable, well-lighted, and ventilated buildings where they could receive full attention through the full school day, instead of for two or three hours in the morning or afternoon." It is odd, I think, that in the only little spot of Federal ground : bearing, too, the honoured name of Columbia ; in the national city, grand in its proportions, with marble edifices, its palatial and sumptuous offices unsurpassed by those of any capital in the world, the just pride of over sixty millions of " the freest people under the sun," there are not sufficient school-houses to accommodate the children ; and that it permits the Bureau of Education to be the worst accommodated of any Government department. To disregard the fervent wishes and wise admonitions of noble men, while employing the sculptor's art to perpetuate their memories ; to march in triumphant procession and listen to fervid orations in honour of their doings on the fourth of July, and for the remaining three hundred and sixty-four days pay no heed to their advice, is so unlike the usual practical wisdom of the American people, that such an exception as this is the more remarkable.

CHAPTER II.

PUBLIC PROVISION FOR EDUCATION
(continued).

ENGLAND :—Former Neglect of Elementary Education.—Work of Voluntary Schools.—Effect of the Act of 1870.—The Education Department.—Favourable Comparison of England with United States in Provision for Elementary Education.—Voluntary and Board Schools, how managed and supported.--Powers of Managers.—Comparison of Board and Voluntary Schools.—The Science and Art Department.

SCOTLAND :—Similarity between English and Scotch Departments.—Modification of Examinations.—Result Payments.

FRANCE :—How Controlled.—Council of Education.—Departments.—Academies.—Three Grades of Inspectors.—Primary Instruction.—Secondary Instruction.—Normal Colleges.—Special Schools.

GERMANY :—Control by Government.—Classes of Schools.—Scope of each.

AUSTRALIA :—Similarity in all Colonies.—Methods of Administration.—Centralisation.—Summary of School Systems.—New South Wales.—Victoria.—South Australia.—Queensland.—New Zealand.

ENGLAND.

UNTIL quite recently, while there existed in England extensive provision for the education of the few, the many were almost totally neglected. Culture on the one hand ; ignorance, and consequent degradation, on the other. The great richly-endowed foundation schools of the sixteenth century provided for the rich and influential an education leading to the world-renowned Universities of Oxford and Cambridge — institutions whose origins are lost in the darkness of the Middle Ages, whose colleges are memorials of the religious fervour or munificence of men whose histories are now legendary ; but whose precincts were hedged round by tradition, so that only the rich or influential could gain access to their unique culture and learning.

Just as exclusive in their sphere were lesser institutions for those lower down in the social scale ; but the masses were to a large extent left in ignorance. The credit for changing this unsatisfactory state of things must be given to the religious denominations, particularly to the Church of England, which even now has more children in its schools than are to be found in those of any other organisation. In addition, the Wesleyans, the Roman Catholics, and the British and Foreign School Society :—all must be mentioned as assisting to prepare the way for the wisest and greatest legislative measure of the past twenty-five years, Mr. Forster's Education Act of 1870. By it provision for the accommodation of all children was made obligatory on the people of the various cities and districts ; and attendance at school became compulsory on the part of every child.

I shall not attempt to state the estimate which some educators and statesmen with Socialistic tendencies made to me, of the influence of this act of legislation. Probably in no other country, France not even excepted, has such a change been made in the education of the mass of the people during the last twenty years. At the present time the English people are better provided with elementary schools than their cousins in America ; and no group of American States can be taken, containing an equal population, where such a large majority of the whole school population of, say from six to thirteen, are attending school and receiving the rudiments of knowledge. Every child is provided with the means of instruction, and compelled to attend.

The result of the work of the Education Department is causing a social revolution in England. If the character of the teaching is too mechanical, if the chief aim of the teacher is to earn as much money as possible for his managers, it must be remembered that this cannot be done without at least giving the pupil the ability to read and write. Of course the schools are not nearly so good as the friends of true education wish. Much remains to be done, and undoubtedly it will not be long ere a still greater change will have taken place. Free education will shortly be an accomplished fact; the partial absorption of the voluntary schools by the School Boards will necessarily follow, and further facilitate the abolition of what have been the cause of so much evil—result examinations, and "grant payments." "Write 'Grant factory' on three-fourths of our schools" said an educator to me.

Before being long in England, I formed the opinion that the chief function of the Education Department is financial rather than educational; and I cannot do better than quote the sentiments of a gentleman whose intimate knowledge of the Department rendered his words of great weight with me. In the course of a conversation in which the difficulties caused by the rival influences of the various voluntary school societies were touched upon, he said: "The Department had never made full use of the provisions of the Education Act, simply from the lack of some one at its head in the earlier stages of its existence, who could have taken up the educational side with as powerful, determined, and comprehensive grasp; and could have initiated the working of the Act with as much tact, skill, and diplomacy as the founder displayed in passing it through the intricate mazes of Parliamentary procedure, party feeling, and the natural objection of the English people to change. Mr. Forster performed his part, and executed the statesman's mission with success; but there was no one to do the still more difficult work of practical educator on a scale hitherto untried."

My informant did not however wish me, nor do I wish

others, to under-estimate the splendid work which the Education Department has done. It is the interpreter of the law; it decides what must and what may be taught; it formulates regulations for the working of elementary day and evening schools, as well as training colleges for the efficient training of teachers; and it employs a large staff of Inspectors to see that the requirements of the law are being carried out, and that the schools are efficient. It distributes, too, the immense annual vote from the Public Treasury for the support of elementary schools, and generally exercises supervision over these schools, in consequence of being able to grant or withhold funds to the average extent, roughly speaking, of half the annual cost of maintenance. The other half of the cost, as well as the school buildings, fittings, and appliances, has to be provided by local means; and the organisations—be they School Boards elected by taxpayers, or managers appointed by a particular section of the people—which provide the school-houses and the remaining half of the maintenance, have ample scope, outside certain well-defined limits, for materially varying the character of the schools. These limits are intended to constitute a minimum of central control and departmental interference, sufficient to ensure a proper use being made of the Imperial vote.

The schools are known as (1) *Voluntary Schools*, which have been built, and are partly supported by voluntary subscriptions. These are under denominational control. (2) *Board Schools:* viz., schools built and supported by money raised by local taxation, and controlled by elected School Boards.

Out of 4,688,000 pupils in the elementary schools, 2,154,000 are in the schools known as *Voluntary*, provided by, and under the control of the Church of England; 1,780,000 are in *Board* schools; 330,000 attend schools under the *British School Society*, or other undenominational control; 248,000 are in *Roman Catholic* schools; and 174,000 belong to *Wesleyan* schools. The schools here spoken of correspond more nearly than any other in England to the Public School of the United States and Australia; but are in many respects very different, chiefly from the fact that they are provided expressly for the poor, and in many cases are attended by no other class. I shall say more on this point elsewhere.

The above figures are quoted, because it is only by a consideration of the influence of these opposing interests that the student of English elementary education can attempt to estimate the difficulties of the Education Department, and find any excuse for the system of examinations which, it is pleasant to record, are being much modified, and which, it must in fairness be stated, were not so much due to the Department as to the peculiarly difficult problem which it has had to solve. It has to administer a vote of over three million pounds sterling of the public revenue in such a way, that the interests of the State shall be promoted to the best advantage among a number of opposing parties, each anxious to obtain as much as possible from the Government. This it has done by means of a complex system of grants, perfectly bewildering to the stranger, who for the first time hears how the schools are supported. The responsibility of recommending the amount of these grants rests on Her Majesty's Inspectors, who make a greater or less number of surprise visits to a school during the year, and annually, at a stated time, carefully examine each pupil in reading, writing, and arithmetic, and hold class examinations in such other— if any—subjects as might be taught. The new Code provides for very important modifications of the system of individual examinations, following much the same course as the Scotch Education Department.

The employment and payment of teachers, provided

that they have the qualifications fixed by the Education
Department, the charging of fees within the law, teaching
of subjects outside those required by the Department, and
religious instruction, are left in the hands of local authorities.
The schools in different parts of England, in consequence,
vary greatly with regard to the accommodation provided,
and the salaries paid to teachers ; and, consequently, the
character of the education given varies greatly. Even in the
same town this may be very noticeable, sometimes in
favour of the voluntary schools ; but as far as I could judge,
the Board Schools are generally superior. The denominational schools have to raise funds by voluntary contributions
from friends ; who, being ratepayers, have to contribute to
the support of the Board Schools. This is often a sore
point of contention. The School Boards, with the tax-
levying power at their backs, are able to build handsome
school-houses according to modern and approved patterns,
replete with every convenience ; and, by offering good
salaries, attract the best teachers in the country. The
teachers in the neighbouring voluntary schools feel it hard
to have to compete with those who are thus more favourably
circumstanced.

The churches acted nobly and liberally, in providing
schools when the English Government was neglecting its
duty in this respect. They would do more nobly now,
were they to hand over all their schools to the School
Board, or rather to the public, to be provided for from one
common fund, thus relieving the country of the greatest
difficulty in connection with elementary public education.
I could not help sometimes concluding, when visiting the
poorer voluntary schools, that it is possible to pay too
dearly for the privilege of teaching a Church catechism,
a Roman dogma, or a Methodist creed. To struggle, for
no other purpose than to keep open schools which are
veritable barns compared with the adjoining well-built,

well-ventilated, well-fitted school-houses; with appliances
that are poor and woefully out of repair: where the ventilation, lighting, and seating are opposed to all laws of
health, modern science, or common sense: where the
teachers are badly paid, and over-worked, is hardly worthy
of the high standard and practical nature of the nineteenth
century churches. Happily, such schools are the exception.
As a rule, excellent work is done in voluntary schools.

So much has been said and written about cramming for
result examinations in order to earn grants, that the
belief is prevalent outside of England that the teachers
receive the money thus earned. This is only indirectly
true. The Education Department has nothing to do with
the payment of the teachers. All sums earned by the
schools are paid to the managers, be they School Boards
or Voluntary Committees, who distribute them in connection
with funds derived from other sources, as they have
occasion. I believe that all the larger School Boards, and
also the managers of the more important voluntary schools,
pay their teachers fixed salaries.

It must be clearly understood, with reference to any
comments I may make regarding the mechanical teaching
and lack of intelligence observed in English schools, that I
attribute the chief blame to neither teachers nor pupils;
but to the administrators who, professing to undertake the
work of Education, not only allow, but enforce, a condition
of things which, however great an improvement it may be
on the disgraceful state of twenty years since, is unworthy
alike of the people of England, and of nineteenth century
civilisation. The School Boards find it necessary to obtain
every possible pound from the Department, to save local
taxation. The managers of voluntary schools must do the
same, to avoid the obnoxious task of collecting subscriptions. Neither members of School Boards, nor voluntary
managers, are usually practical educators; and naturally

consider a high percentage, and a good report from the inspector, a guarantee of good work on the part of their teachers. The good grant which follows is a more tangible expression of satisfaction. Many good teachers, who only use the soundest and most educative methods of teaching, always earn the highest grants, and receive the best reports; but it is easily possible to obtain the same tangible result in a less satisfactory manner; and while the shortest road is often neither the easiest nor most commendable, it is the one which usually commends itself to the majority.

It is, therefore, a source of much gratification to the friends of true education, that the Education Department is making a new and commendable endeavour to ensure education as well as instruction, by giving an increased grant on average attendance, and attaching more importance to the manner of teaching, than on the ability of the children to reproduce facts at the annual examination.

The Science and Art Department.—There is no doubt that the foreigner's estimate of English education suffers on account of the complicated system. For example, the work of the elementary schools in connection with the Science and Art Department does not appear in the reports of the Education Department; and yet it forms a distinctive and very valuable feature in connection with many of the schools. Drawing has hitherto been under the control of the Science and Art Department, and although over eight hundred thousand elementary school pupils have been receiving systematic instruction, no reference to this important work appears in the Education report. In consequence of this, I have met foreign educators who were under the impression that no attention was paid to it. In future, it is to be a compulsory subject in the schools. The large classes of ex-seventh pupils in connection with some of the School Boards are not recognised by the Education Department. By teaching two or three science subjects, the managers are able to earn sufficient grants from the Science and Art Department to pay all expenses, and thus continue the education of these pupils at the ordinary small fee.

The Science and Art Department gives aid to schools of art, and art classes, science schools, elementary schools, and training colleges, and affords instruction in its various ramifications of junior and advanced classes to an aggregate of nearly one million pupils. Its influence in other ways is also widespread. By the Normal School of Science, the Royal School of Mines, the magnificent museums at South Kensington and Jermyn Street, the National Art Training School, the system of loans to schools and museums, and in many other ways, does it exert a far-reaching and powerful influence on the education of the people.

SCOTLAND.

Scotch Elementary Education is under the control of a Department similar in its organisation and working to that presiding over the English schools. Scotland is decidedly ahead of England in her school legislation. Her schools are now free in all the lower standards, and in some places altogether. Under the new Code of 1890, again, the system of result examinations has been so modified, that many of the evils under which English schools labour will be absent in the future from Scotland. The Department has felt its way very carefully in this matter. For three years no individual examination has been required in the lower standards, and the effect has been so satisfactory that " My Lords have decided that the time has now come when efficiency need not, in every case, be tested by individual examination ; and when the experiment of giving greater freedom of organisation to the managers of schools may fairly be tried.

"Where my Lords are satisfied that the aim of the school is good, and that its methods are well adapted, and successfully pursued, towards realising that aim : where, further, your inspection convinces you that the intelligence of the children is kept in full activity, and that the training given them places them in possession of the essential branches of elementary education, and trains their faculties in such a way as to prepare them practically for the duties of life, my Lords will not require you to carry the individual test further than may be necessary to a safeguard against inefficiency."

The Department has also considerably curtailed the list of specific subjects, and given managers the option of submitting a syllabus of any subject which they deem specially suited to the requirements of their schools ; and they have been given a wide option with regard to elementary science, and manual instruction.

FRANCE.

The French system of public education is controlled by the Minister of Instruction and Fine Arts, who is assisted by a Council—of which he is president—composed of members of the Council of State, of the Institute, Army, Navy, Catholic Church, and nine lay members. This council prescribes the course of instruction in all public schools established, new Lycées, and Communal Colleges, and generally governs the education of the land. The country is divided into eighty-seven departments. The departments are divided into seventeen districts, or " Academies," in each of which there is an Academic Council, under the direction of the Minister of Public Instruction, which has charge of the affairs in the Academy. Each department also has a " Departmental Council," composed of the Préfect, as president, the Academy inspector of the district as vice-

D

president, four councillors elected by their colleagues, the director and directress of the Training Colleges, two masters and two mistresses chosen by the teachers in the Department, two primary inspectors nominated by the Minister, and two representatives, one clerical and one lay, of the private schools. These councils supervise the internal working of the schools of their departments, and forward reports to the Minister of Instruction. Every commune also has its local board, with the mayor at its head, which supervises both the public and private schools.

The inspection of the schools is attended to by three classes of inspectors :—

1. Inspectors-General, of whom there are several, to act as advisers to the Minister.

2. Academy inspectors, who, besides acting as vice-presidents of the councils, and inspecting the schools of their district, supervise the private schools, arrange for the examination of teachers and training colleges, and receive the reports of the visits of primary inspectors.

3. Primary inspectors, who report to the Academy inspector within fifteen days of a visit to a school :—

(*a*)   Upon each teacher.

(*b*)   Upon the work being done in each class.

They also preside over teachers' conferences, and during July examine all children being taught at home. They must have had a training equivalent to that of an English University man, and have been engaged in teaching for at least five years prior to appointment.

Public instruction is divided into three grades : primary, secondary, and higher.

Primary instruction is free and compulsory between the ages of seven and fourteen years. Every commune must support at least one primary school ; but in the case of thinly populated communes the consent of the Minister may be given to allow several to combine for the purpose.

Aid from the national funds is only given to communes which are unable to support the whole cost of their schools.

Secondary education is given in the Lyceum or Communal College.

Higher education is given by the "faculties" of law, medicine, theology, science, and literature.

Two normal schools are established in each Department, one for male and one for female students ; and there is a superior normal school to prepare teachers for lycées, communal colleges, and all schools above the primary. These schools are in charge of the State. I do not know of another country where this wise provision for the training of secondary teachers exists. Germany, with all her thoroughness in primary education, has omitted this ; and England knows nothing of the kind.

One of the special features of French education is the great number of special schools. I can only name a few ; but there is hardly an industry which has not its special school. There are schools of telegraphy for Government employés exclusively, schools of manual apprenticeship, schools of road and bridges, schools of forestry, schools of master workmen in mines, schools of political science, and so forth. Those having a bearing on elementary education will be dealt with elsewhere.

GERMANY.

While England and the United States each claim to be the most perfectly self-governing country in the world, and dispute over the amount of liberty or licence enjoyable under their particular forms of rule of the people by the people, Germany undisputedly presents the best example of a governed people. The German educational system has received great attention for a longer period than any other ;

and it embodies many excellent features. In the absence of result examinations; in the systematic thoroughness of the work; in the sound psychological basis of their course of study; and in the training and professional standing of their teachers, the Germans are in the advance guard of educational progress.

The education is entirely in the hands of the Government, being under the supervision of a Minister of Public Instruction, assisted by School Boards in their various provinces. The names of the German schools are confusing; but under different titles they may be said to be of three classes.

In the Primary school the attendance is compulsory from the age of seven to fourteen years. Secondary education is carried on in a Gymnasium, or a " Realschule." The former gives prominence to Latin and Greek, and especially aims at preparation for the University and professional life. The latter pays great attention to modern languages, mathematics, and natural sciences, aiming at special fitness for the ordinary business callings. The courses of study differ in both classes of schools in different parts of Germany. Forming a kind of sub-division, intermediate between the primary, or people's schools, and the gymnasia, are the Bürger Schools for boys, and Higher Young Ladies' Schools. These two classes of schools appear to give a primary education of a somewhat better character than the people's school, and carry on the work of instruction for several years longer.

German Universities are so well known, that I only refer to them as receiving large subsidies from the State.

AUSTRALIA.

There is a general agreement in the methods of administration of Elementary Public Education in the chief

Australian Colonies. In New South Wales, Victoria, South Australia, and Queensland, centralization is highly developed; and, under the present conditions of the country, to attain the maximum of economy and usefulness, must remain so. The scattered nature of the population in the major part of each colony renders local government of a school system—requiring, as it does, the greatest intelligence, experience, and freedom from party considerations—not only wasteful and unsuitable, but injurious to the best interests of the object in view. The superior character of the educational facilities in the thinly-populated districts of Australia is one of the most noticeable and commendable features in connection with the colonial school systems. Probably no other thinly-populated country is so well provided with good schools.

The following general statement of administration is in the main equally applicable to each colony:—The system of Public Instruction is managed by the Education Department of the Civil Service, at the head of which is an Inspector-General, on whom depends the working of the Department; and, through his assistants, the carrying out of the legislation on education. This officer acts under, and is responsible to, the Minister of Education, who has full control over the whole system, and is alone responsible to Parliament (of which he is a member), and the country. He is a member of the Cabinet, and the *personnel* of the Minister therefore changes with each change of Ministry. In the Minister is vested all school property; and the appointment and dismissal of teachers is nominally in his power.

The grouping of the population of New Zealand round a number of well-defined centres, often somewhat difficult of access the one from another, has naturally led to the adoption of the opposite system of management by local Boards of Education. Excepting in Tasmania and Western

Australia, whose united population does not exceed two hundred thousand, all the colonies agree in enacting that elementary education up to a certain standard shall be compulsory, and in carefully carrying out the law. They are also agreed that religious teaching shall form no part of the official programme ; and, moreover, shall not be given during school hours.

There are, excepting in South Australia, but slight differences in the courses of study and methods of teaching, English example being followed. South Australia, on the other hand, has during the last few years made a departure ; and, like the most advanced American centres, has formulated a course of study on the German plan— retaining, however, in common with the other colonies, the English plan of result examinations as the chief means of testing the work.

School-buildings do not differ materially, being constructed with special reference to the method of organisation followed. Although they are well built, commodious, and often handsome structures, in which great attention has been paid to light and ventilation, they are not of the modern type of the more recent Board Schools of London and other large English centres, and are far from being as convenient as American school-houses.

The pupil-teacher system is in operation in all the colonies ; and is, no doubt, one of the causes operating to prevent the adoption of the single class-room plan in constructing the buildings. The system found so necessary and successful by the London School Board of allowing the young apprentices to teach only a short time each week, and of taking the responsibility of their literary studies out of the hands of the teachers, and carrying on the teaching in pupil-teacher schools, has not been adopted. The first step in the movement has however been taken in many centres, where the pupil-teachers are gathered on Saturday mornings for special collective teaching.

On the Australian Continent, Victoria and Queensland have free elementary schools, while New South Wales and South Australia charge all who are able to pay nominal fees of a few pence per week. Curiously, not only are there two colonies in favour of each plan, but the population of the two pairs is very nearly the same. New Zealand, however, has adopted the principle of entirely free elementary education, and there is a decided tendency towards the principle in South Australia, so that I am safe in saying that Australia as a whole is in favour of free, compulsory, and secular public elementary education.

While New South Wales does not admit the principle of entirely free instruction to all alike, she has established a system of public high or secondary schools, open to all who have passed through the elementary schools, at the same nominal fees. She thus connects her primary system with the university.

Each colony has much to learn from the others, as well as from the older systems of England and America; while the latter might with equal advantage take lessons from their younger cousins of the Sunny South. For example, New South Wales and South Australia would do well to adopt the free system of Victoria and Queensland; Victoria and South Australia would make their systems more complete, and more worthy of their democratic pretensions, were they to follow the mother colony, New South Wales, in establishing secondary schools with nominal fees; or, more desirable still, free to all who have completed the course in the elementary schools. The other colonies might with decided advantage adopt the splendid course of study followed in the South Australian schools, than which I know of none better in the English language. Again, all would do well to relegate examinations to their proper sphere of useful assistants, instead of tyrannical masters. After England, Australia is the stronghold of examinations. Australians are not equally slaves to the system that the English elementary schools are; but the percentage of results, the number of passes, still remains the chief standard of public judgment on a teacher's work.

Again, England is doing her best to get rid of the evils of the pupil-teacher system; but there is, so far as I am able to judge, no general conviction in Australia that it is a weakness. Invented by Messrs. Bell and Lancaster as an emergency means of providing a substitute for proper assistance, which at that time it was impossible to obtain, it has become so much a matter of course to have young, inexperienced pupil-teachers bungling in their attempts to teach what they themselves, in the nature of things, do not—cannot—understand, that it is now asserted that the pupil-teacher system is the only effective mode of training teachers, and the only practicable plan of working schools at reasonable expense.

Apart from the exceptions mentioned elsewhere, the Governments of South Australia, Victoria, and New Zealand do not provide for secondary education.

The Australian Universities are not State institutions in the same sense as those of the newer Western States of America; but the various Governments have provided largely towards founding and supporting them, a considerable portion of the revenues being drawn from the Public Treasury. The degrees entitle the holders to the same rank, title, and precedence as those of the Universities of the United Kingdom.

New South Wales.

The public system of education of New South Wales includes five classes of schools.

1. *Public Elementary Schools*, intended to provide the best primary instruction to all children, without sectarian or class distinction. These in the main correspond, so far as the scope of the work is concerned, to the Board Schools of England, and the Primary and Grammar Grades of America.

2. *Superior Public Schools*, established in towns and populous districts, where larger numbers give scope for more perfect classification, and division of labour. In addition to the work of the first class, these give lessons in the higher branches of education: *i.e.*, Latin, Mathematics, Elementary Science, and so forth.

3. *Evening Schools*, in which the object is to instruct those who have not had the advantage of Primary Education.

4. *High Schools for Boys.*

5. *High Schools for Girls.*

The course of study in the High Schools is such as will complete an ordinary education, or prepare students for the University.

The fees are not to exceed threepence per week per child, or a total of one shilling for one family; and the children of parents unable to pay this are admitted, without distinction, free. This small fee is charged less for revenue, than in the hope that it will lead to a better appreciation of the school privileges. There is a strong feeling, on the other hand, that the people would take even greater pride in their schools if they offered the boon of education freely to all, without distinction of any kind, and that for the paltry sum gained it is a pity to put aside this great principle. The advocates for and against are thus seen to be actuated by very similar motives; and it only remains a matter of time for the colony to adopt Free Education, as Victoria has done.

Attendance is compulsory for seventy days each half-year, for all children between the ages of six and fourteen.

The schools are supervised by a staff of inspectors, who make visits of inspection at uncertain times, and hold annual examinations on the year's work; the tabulated results form the chief basis of judgment on the teachers' work.

The University of Sydney is supported from three sources of income :—

(1) An annual vote from the Public Treasury; (2) Revenue from Endowments; (3) Fees from Students.

It has cost in buildings and endowments some £300,000, part of which was provided by private munificence, and part by the Government. In addition to the above, there is a bequest of over £200,000, left by Mr. J. H. Challis, which is just available for University purposes.

Victoria.

In Victoria the term *State School* is used in the same sense as Public School is in New South Wales and South Australia. Attendance is free and compulsory between the ages of six and fourteen for at least sixty days each half-year—subject, of course, to the usual exemption on account of attendance at a private school, ill-health, etc. The work of supervision is similar to that in New South Wales. It should be noticed, however, that although the schools are free, fees may be charged by teachers for giving instruction in subjects other than those fixed by law as compulsory subjects. The Government makes no provision for secondary education; but it is well provided for by private corporations, many of which are controlled by the religious bodies. As in New South Wales, the University has three sources of revenue :—(1) An annual vote from the Public Treasury; (2) Income from Endowments; (3) College Fees. Private munificence has also been largely devoted to the erection of magnificent buildings. "Wilson Hall," for example, cost some £40,000, and Ormond College about £35,000.

South Australia.

The public system of education in this colony is under similar management to that existing in New South Wales and Victoria. The Education Department is under the direction of the Minister of Education, who is responsible to Parliament and the country for its efficient working. The work is, however, carried on by the permanent head, who is a practical educator, as well as a scholar of high standing, with the title of Inspector-General of Schools. With him virtually rests the appointment and removal of teachers, although the power is nominally vested in the Minister of Education, whose confirmation is needed in all cases.

The compulsory law provides for the attendance at school of all children between the ages of seven and thirteen, unless the compulsory standard is passed earlier, for at least thirty-five days each quarter. As in other portions of Australia, appeals to the law are seldom needed, although the Act is strictly enforced.

There are two classes of elementary schools.

1. *Provisional Schools.* — Frequently held in rented buildings by untrained teachers. They are intended to supply elementary education in the outlying districts, where the population is too small to warrant the expense of building a school, and paying a trained teacher. The course of study is the same in character, although not so wide as that given in the public schools ; and as great care is exercised by the Department in only employing persons of sufficient educational attainments, and the numbers of pupils are but small, the character of the work is highly satisfactory, as evidenced by the reports of the inspectors.

These schools to some extent correspond to the back country rural schools of America, in size, character of pupils, lack of training on the part of teachers, and such points; but they differ in that they are open for the same time each year as the city schools—viz., forty-six weeks—are subject to the same supervision, have to present their pupils for similar examinations, and the teachers are not subject to the worrying influences of a local committee, who may dispense with their services, or refuse to pay their salaries in case of dispute. The teachers are encouraged to improve themselves, and if they do good work are sure of permanent employment.

2. *Public Schools.*—Schools under certificated teachers are called Public Schools. The fees payable are fourpence or sixpence a week; but anyone unable to pay this is admitted free, and supplied with the necessary books. Books, excepting copy- and drawing-books, for use in school, are supplied to all pupils. The Department is preparing and publishing a series of special school books. When these are sold, a trifle over cost price is charged.

The secondary education of boys is left entirely to private enterprise; but the Department annually provides a number of scholarships, of the value of twenty pounds, to the best pupils in the public schools. The law provides for the establishment of "Advanced Schools"; but hitherto the work has been so well carried out by the existing schools that the necessity for these "advanced schools" has not arisen.

The Education Department has acknowledged its obligation with regard to the secondary education of girls by establishing, in the face of much opposition, a central Advanced School. Originally intended to form a link between the Public Schools and the University, it has been an institution affording, for those who are able to pay for it, an education of a character not obtainable elsewhere. Like the Leeds Higher Grade School, and unlike the High Schools of New South Wales (leaving out the question of fees), the standard of admission has been made lower than was intended; and being able to pass the upper standard of the Elementary School is no longer insisted on. Since it is only available for a section of the community, it cannot be considered an integral part of the Public School system. The fees are twelve guineas a year, so that—apart from a few of those who have received scholarships for exceptional merit at the Public Schools—the poorer people are excluded from availing themselves of it. Notwithstanding the splendid work it has done in raising the standard of female education in Adelaide, and the fact that the fees are sufficient to carry on the work without cost to the country, the opposition it has met with has prevented the extension of the experiment.

It must be admitted that such schools are opposed to the principles of Democratic Australia. They are bitterly denounced by the friends of the private establishments with which they compete, and do not enlist the sympathies of the mass of the people. It is the duty of the State to provide secondary as well as primary education; but it must be done on the same terms, and in the same way, as in South Australia and in a few of the English School Boards. It should not be left to the haphazard of private enterprise; but as the only firm basis of the argument for their establishment is the welfare of the State, the whole community as nearly as possible should be able to avail themselves of the provisions. This is one of the great features of the American system of education. The State must for its own safety establish elementary schools, that the mass of her citizens may be enlightened, and have the means of constant improvement in their hands. This is now everywhere recognised.

What we call secondary education cannot be given to all, and it is hardly possible to conceive of a state of society where, for many reasons, it could ; but it is not the less necessary and important that the State should endeavour to obtain the greatest possible benefit from its best minds, whether they belong to the poor or to the rich. This it can only do by providing the means for their education. All else must depend on the individuals themselves. America recognises this, so does New South Wales ; South Australia and Victoria do also ; but in an unsatisfactory manner, by giving scholarships to a few. When explaining our systems to friends in America, I frequently heard the remark : " Australians appear to do more for the few but less for the many than we do "; and I could not but grant that the indictment was true.

The University of Adelaide is similar in character to those of Melbourne and Sydney.

Queensland.

Like the colonies already described, Queensland possesses a good system of compulsory, free, and secular education, of which she is justly proud, and to which she pays great attention. She differs from the other colonies in requiring the people of a district to provide a portion, to the extent of one-fifth, of the cost of the school-buildings. Secondary or "Grammar" schools, are assisted by grants from the public funds to the extent of two-thirds of the cost of construction and maintenance.

New Zealand.

The colony is divided into thirteen educational districts, which are again divided into school districts, each under an Education Board. The teaching is secular and free. The funds are provided by statutory grant of £3 15s. od. per annum for every child in average attendance, there being additional votes for scholarships, training of teachers, &c. In other particulars the schools resemble those ot Australia, and do not differ greatly from the Board Schools of England.

CHAPTER III.

HOW WORK IS TESTED.

The Need for a Test.—A Difficult Problem.—Plans followed in Germany
and France.—Methods adopted in the United States.—Discussion of
Result Examinations in England and Australia.

THE problem how to test the work of the teacher is one
of the most difficult in connection with a public system of
education. Where a large number of men and women are
employed, there must be some means adopted for securing
the proper performance of the work for which they are paid.
The difficulty is how to secure this end, without interfering
with the work and individuality of those teachers who do
not require supervision.

The English Education Department has depended
almost entirely on yearly examinations as a means for
deciding the amount of assistance to be given to the school
by the central authorities. The result has been an ex-
emplification of the text—"Unto him that hath shall be
given." The schools in poor districts most in need of help,
where the enlightening and elevating influences of education
are most needed, have had to carry on work at less cost than
more favoured districts. State aid should be given equally
to all ; but if it is to be unevenly distributed, let the poorest
have the most.

In Germany the authorities estimate the teacher's work
chiefly by ascertaining how he teaches. Examinations are
used, and used frequently ; but it is to test present work,
not the ability of the pupil to retain isolated facts for long

periods of time. The pupils may be examined at any time in any portion of their work; but I could learn of no general examination of all pupils in all subjects with a tabulated statement of the result.

A good deal of examining and inspecting is done in Paris, and, I fear, not a little cramming is the result.

In the United States each town has its own method of testing the work of the teachers. It chiefly rests with the superintendent and his assistants. Result examinations as understood in England, where the greatest drawback is the fact that the amount of money allotted to a school depends on the examination, are, as far as I am aware, unknown. When examinations are held at a definite period annually, they are for the purpose of promotions, not for publication of percentages and payment of grant.

The following are a few notes I collected on how pupils are promoted :—

Indianapolis, Indiana.—"The pupils are promoted twice each year. They are examined by printed questions, prepared by the superintendent of schools. All who pass a creditable examination on these questions are promoted without further question. All pupils who fall low in the list, but whose daily work has been satisfactory to the teacher in charge, and to the supervisor in immediate charge of said teacher and pupils, are passed on the recommendation of these two persons—the greatest stress being placed on the teacher's estimate as being the more definite and intimate."

Chicago, Illinois.—"In primary and grammar grades, promotions are made by the principal, with or without special examination, at his discretion. From grammar to high school pupils pass on the recommendation of the grammar principal. The superintendent holds a supplementary examination for those not recommended."

Brooklyn, Long Island.—"Semi-annual examinations,

E

promotions, and gradations are the rule. The superintendent may at his option prepare the questions for the examination of all the grammar grades, but he *must* prepare those for the graduation examinations. Promotion is based solely on the record of scholarship for the term and at examination combined."

Boston, Massachusetts.—" Promotions are made half-yearly. Principals are responsible for promotion from one grade to another in their own schools, but the questions for the promotion from the primary to the grammar, and from the grammar to the high schools are prepared by the supervising officers. The instructor's record of the pupils' work is a factor in promotion. Changes of grade not involving promotion to a higher department may be made on any Monday throughout the year."

Philadelphia, Pennsylvania.—" At the time of my visit a long discussion was brought to a close by deciding that the superintendent may dispense with examinations for promotion, and depend on the estimate of the class teacher as to the progress and fitness of the pupil, only examining in the case of dispute."

Washington, District of Columbia.—With reference to examinations, the Principal of the Normal School at Washington writes me :—" ' Ranking by per cent.' is well nigh forgotten here, though not so very long ago it was important. We are glad to forget. Frequent tests—oral and written—are given by the supervising teachers, but the formal examinations, deciding promotions, are not held. Teachers promote pupils by the exercise of their judgment, after having ' summered and wintered ' them. All the year the pupils are being ' measured,' not more by the number of facts they can get and keep than by the power of their mental grasp in new lines. Teachers feel the added responsibility and dignity, and unprepared pupils are not sent on. If the teacher of the next grade thinks such has been done, the supervising teacher has the power to decide. *We like the system.*"

San Francisco, California.—" Yearly written examinations have been dispensed with, and all promotions are made by the principals and class teachers, subject to appeal to the superintendent on the part of parents dissatisfied with the non-promotion of their children."

In *Toronto, Canada,* the superintendent adopts the plan of having a certain number of questions on each subject drawn up by several well-known teachers. These are sent round sealed to all the schools on a given day, and in the presence of the pupils opened and distributed. All pupils in a given grade have the same questions. All the papers on a given subject are corrected by one principal. No results are published.

Cincinnati, Ohio.—The superintendent says : " An impression prevails that written examinations have been wholly dispensed with in Cincinnati schools. This is an error. The written test is no longer made the *basis for the promotion of pupils*, and it no longer occurs at stated times, but it is continued as an element of teaching, where its uses are many and important. It is so distributed throughout the year, and comes without previous notice."

Mr. Aaron Gove, Superintendent of Denver, Colorado, the most English of American superintendents I met, is not at all satisfied with many points of the American plan of managing education. He would like more centralisation and less of the elective principle ; but considers the change made by abolishing result examinations years since, as being entirely beneficial.

Annual examinations form the principal test of work in the Australian schools, and are the chief, often almost the sole basis of promotions. The results are tabulated and the percentage of passes in each subject is published. This

E 2

percentage is supposed to be a correct measurement of the efficiency of a school, is published in the records, and on it depends directly or indirectly the teacher's position. In Victoria, a large proportion of the teacher's salary directly depends on the percentage of possible passes obtained. That is to say, the teacher is paid according to the results he obtains. He is a servant of the Education Department, and directly suffers if his percentage falls. I mention this particularly as a contrast to the English system, where the grant of the Education Department depends on the result of the examination, but where the payment is made to the managers or School Board as the case may be, the Education Department taking no cognisance of the teacher in the matter, he being a servant of the managers and out of the Department, although having to be approved by its officers.

In South Australia the teachers are paid a bonus for successful teaching, as judged by the percentage gained, varying from sixteen to twenty-four pounds per annum. This bonus is the same for all teachers irrespective of their status or regular salary, and may form from six to twenty-five per cent. of the teacher's income. Should a school obtain less than sixty per cent. of passes, the bonus is deducted altogether, and may then be considered a fine of sixteen pounds for unsuccessful teaching. In the case of teachers of small schools, or junior assistants, the fine may amount to one-seventh or more of the total salary; and it may happen in the case of an assistant whose particular class has done well, that he may suffer this loss through the failure of the rest of the school to secure the required percentage. So dominating has the examination become, that the average teacher is ever either worrying about the coming ordeal, or suffering a reaction because it is over.

In New South Wales the examination may take place at any time, and extends over the work of the six months previous. It is more oral than that of Victoria, and less individual than that of either Victoria or South Australia. In New South Wales no result payments or bonuses of any kind are made. Each teacher is paid a fixed salary from the public treasury according to the size of his school and his classification. His promotion depends on his success as a teacher and his attainments. His success as a teacher is judged by the percentage of passes and his special mark for skill. The latter is dependent on the impression he is able to make on the inspector and the percentage of passes obtained.

The Victorian examination bears the greatest resemblance to the system followed in England.

In New South Wales a different plan is followed, characterised in the first place by a much greater fulness. In the second place—and here it also differs from the course followed in South Australia—no record is kept, and in most cases none is attempted, of the individual pass or failure of each pupil. The inspector conducts his examination and awards a percentage of marks according to a scale for excellent, good, and so forth. The teacher takes a considerable part in the examination. The inspector examines a selected number haphazard, and the teacher a selected few, presumably of the best, the work being done orally and in class. A peculiarity of the examination is the marks given for "attention," "mental effort," and "mental culture." This is a responsible part of the inspector's work, being an attempt to estimate not only the result of the teacher's work so far as the acquisition of facts is concerned, but the success of the methods of instruction pursued as educative processes.

In South Australia the inspectors have to visit the schools twice each year, once for a preliminary or "surprise visit"—the surprise, not infrequently, being on the part of the inspector at finding everything evidently prepared in expectation. As a rule teachers know, to within a few days,

when to expect him, and acquaint one another when he is
in the neighbourhood. At this preliminary visit he is to
observe the school in its ordinary condition, note the
methods of instruction followed, criticise and offer suggestions on the general work of the school, and report on
the order, moral tone, discipline, and so forth. About one-
fourth of his time is spent in making these visits ; the remaining three-fourths being devoted to examinations. These
take place at stated times in each school, and are the most
important events in the year to pupils and teachers. On
them depend the promotion of the pupils, the status, and,
to a large extent, the prospect of promotion of the teachers.
The system employed is the most elaborate of any with
which I am acquainted, and there is probably even more
value and importance attached to the examination than
where the money consideration involved is much greater.

Each pupil is individually examined in reading, spelling,
writing, arithmetic, language, drawing, and, for girls, needlework in addition ; and the marks obtained by each pupil
are recorded and kept. From one-quarter to one-third of
the total marks obtainable are given for arithmetic. In addition class examinations are conducted in geography, history,
poetry, special and moral lessons, singing, and drill. Marks
are also awarded for discipline and order. In reading one
mark is given for a bare pass, and another for expression
and an intelligent knowledge of the subject-matter. One
mark is given for spelling as tested by dictation, and a
second for a properly kept book, in which throughout the
school year the spelling has been taught by transcription
and dictation. In writing one mark is allotted for a finished
copy-book, and one for a piece of transcription done during the examination. In drawing a mark is given for a
finished book, and one for an exercise performed during
the examination. From four to six marks are given for
arithmetic—that is, from twice to three times as many as

for reading, writing, spelling, language, or drawing. The examination in this subject includes a mental and a written test, and the marks are divided between the two kinds of work.

I will make an exception, and add a set of questions in arithmetic for the fourth class, or compulsory standard, which it is necessary for pupils to pass before being exempt from attendance at school.

Out of the five problems to be worked on paper or slate, at least three must be accurate in result, neat in execution, and *correct in method according to the idea of the inspector.* Questions in mental arithmetic must be answered promptly, and three answers out of four must be correct.

Example of questions set for fourth class pupils in South Australia.

Mental arithmetic :—

(1.) My draper's account amounted to £55 10s., but I received $2\frac{1}{2}$ per cent. discount : what was the actual amount I paid ?

(2.) Find cost of a gross of exercise books at $4\frac{1}{2}$d. each.

(3.) How many square yards in a paddock one mile square ?

(4.) Take one-eighth from one-half, and what is left ?

Slate or paper arithmetic, forty-five minutes allowed :—

Class IV.

(1.) A rectangular garden, 20 yards by 12 yards, is to be covered with 6 inches of manure. How much will it cost at 4s. 3d. a waggon load of 2 cubic yards ?

(2.) What will 138 men earn in a week, if 89 men earn £153 10s. 6d. ? (unitary).

(3.) If a watch is set right at 9 o'clock on Monday morning, and loses 2 seconds every hour, what time will the watch show when it is really 9 o'clock on the Monday following ?

(4.) A man bought 100 acres of land at 45s. an acre ; spent £45 in fencing, and £230 in buildings. At what price must he sell the whole land so as to gain 5 per cent. ?

(5.) A ton and a half of potatoes are divided equally among 24 poor families. How many stones will each get ?

The following is the approximate value attached to the various subjects as shown by the percentage of marks awarded for each. The calculation is based on the maximum marks obtainable in an ordinary mixed school, under normal conditions of classification. About thirty-one per cent. of the total marks may be obtained for arithmetic, fifteen for reading, thirteen for spelling, fourteen for writing, fourteen for drawing, nine for language (this does not really show the importance attached to this subject, there being a special allowance for work in the junior part of the school), and four per cent. for needlework. In addition to the marks thus obtained, an allotment of not more than five per cent. of the maximum thus obtainable may be added at the discretion of the inspector for the class subjects.

The labour entailed in conducting an examination with the exactitude and detail required by the South Australian Education Department, is only equalled by the maturity of judgment necessary to make the whole affair anything more than a troublesome mechanical procedure. Probably, and I make this statement with due consideration after careful observation, no body of inspectors and teachers in the world have worked harder or with greater exactitude than those of South Australia.

The English teacher complains, with justice, that the Education Department cares nothing for methods, and merely applies a mechanical test for results. The New York city teacher considers herself degraded to a mere machine by the way the superintendent has laid down methods by which every detail of the school work is to be taught. She complains that all individuality is crushed out by the working of a mechanical system. She not only has a given number of facts to teach, but a manual telling her exactly how she must teach it.

The city of New York must not be taken as an example of the system followed in the United States generally. It is the result of the extreme application of a method found very effective elsewhere. Some writers have fallen into the error of considering that the same judgment of the schools of the United States may be formed from the schools of New York as may be in the case of England from the Board schools of London.

The English authorities estimate the value of a school by what they consider the results, while those of New York do so by the way in which the teachers carry out the directions of the Teachers' manual. Speaking generally of America, it may be said that the machinery and methods are more valued as means of judging the work of the teacher than are the measurable results obtained.

In South Australia the attempt is made to attain both these ends. The department directs precisely what shall be taught, lays down rules as to how it is best to teach it, and tests the results more minutely than any other educational authorities with which I am acquainted. The usual criticism passed by American teachers on the South Australian code, was to the effect that the examination seemed to be too exacting. In England, on the other hand, the first expression on the part of teacher or inspector who examined the course of study, was to the effect that it seemed to leave the teacher no choice of either methods, books, or anything else. To some extent both the criticisms are correct. That they are not so to a greater extent is due to the unusual qualifications of the Inspector-General of Schools, whose capacity for work is only equalled by his love for the cause of education. Exemplifying that characteristic of many who themselves are actuated by most unselfish motives, he refuses to credit the majority of teachers with possessing any of that love for work for its own sake which is the controlling power in himself.

As a matter of fact, I never heard a hard-working enthusiastic teacher complain that the *methods* laid down in the course of study in any way hampered his work; but probably the teacher is not to be found who has not more or less complaint to make about the method of testing his work by an examination. If the methods are right, as they believe they are—being confined to general principles which admit of sufficient variation in detail—then it is contended that the examination is wrong, for it is impossible by it to test the methods employed. Moreover, the methods laid down are not rigid rules, but suggestions, and any teacher who can show a better way, or one more adapted to his particular requirements, is at liberty to follow it.

My observations confirm my previous conviction as to the evils of the result examinations, and prove my contention that they are not necessary to secure the best value for the public money expended.

Teachers who have learned to work for no other object would, no doubt, do little for a time if they were suddenly abolished; but they should gradually be made unnecessary, because they do not test the genuine work of the teacher. They are not a true measure of the pupil's intelligence, and very often not of his knowledge. They are detrimental to the intellectual, moral, and physical well-being of the children, and they are the cause of a certain amount of dishonesty in various forms on the part of pupils and teachers, though as often from omission as commission.

Carried on at great cost of money and effort to secure reasonably, if not thoroughly honest work from lazy or dishonest men—for it would be manifestly absurd to spend so much money and effort unless it be to secure a proper performance of duty, and it is always admitted that the conscientious worker is better without the worry of outside interference—it fails in its purpose, while it tends to make a well-intentioned but somewhat weak teacher dishonest.

But I would not dwell on the dishonesty caused, because that is not the most important of the objections to the system of Examination to test results.   The greatest evil of all, is the false view which is created of the use of the school.   It has created the idea that education consists in the knowledge of a few facts, and the ability to perform a few mechanical operations, rather than the power to think, and the love for the acquisition of knowledge.

CHAPTER IV.

THE NEW EDUCATION.
KINDERGARTEN, ETC.

Conceptions of Education.—Cry for Practical Education.—Terms used.—Scope of Work.

KINDERGARTEN.—Conceptions of Term.—Nature of Fröbel's Idea.—Means of Attaining it.—The Primary Grades of the United States.—Language Lessons.—Classes for Foreigners.—Course of Study in Receiving Class, San Francisco. — Want of Sympathy between Kindergarten and Primary Classes.—Infant School of England described.—No True Kindergarten connected with English Public Elementary Schools.—The American Kindergarten—Philadelphia, Toronto, San Francisco, St. Louis Kindergartens described.

THE USE OF PICTURES.

DRAWING and FORM-STUDY. — United States ahead of England.—Massachusetts System.—System of New York State.—Supervisors.—Private Enterprise in Training Teachers.—Form-Study.—Language Lessons.

"THERE is nothing new under the sun" is a much used aphorism, sometimes aptly expressing a truth, frequently hiding a falsehood. I am using the term "New Education," not because I like it, but because I found it in common use, and it appears to be the best available. The New Education is new only in a sense; but in that connection it is new enough. There is nothing in regard to which educators or educationalists differ more than in the meaning they attach to the word "Education," and the means they would adopt to secure it for the young. I suppose it has always been so; but at the same time there has been a dominating idea in each age, and among every people.

To the Athenian, for example, education meant mental

and physical beauty—"a beautiful soul in a beautiful body" —and his chief means of attaining that ideal were, perhaps, gymnastics, music, and philosophy. Eloquence was the surest means of success in public life for a Roman— eloquence and debating power, in his idea, constituted the highest education. In the ages of æsthetic Christianity, the monastic idea prevailed that man was an utterly depraved, untrustworthy being, and education accordingly consisted in stifling and uprooting all natural instincts; scourging the body that the soul might grow; destroying the house that the tenant might be happy in the ruins. During the period of the Renaissance, education became synonymous with classical culture, and a knowledge of the literatures of Greece and Rome in the original tongues. This idea, modified and broadened so as to include modern literature, and later still, to embrace science, gives the prevailing conception of higher education in this latter half of the nineteenth century.

But with this in itself I have nothing to do at present. All such conceptions were, in their realisation at all events, chiefly confined to a few; but they have always supported a wider field of training which, less distinct, followed the same laws, and in its turn supplied its controlling parent with its vivifying power. But it is only of late years that education has extended to the whole people, and it is only since it has done so that the great development of educational thought has taken place—a development corresponding to the spread of the teaching of the newer, the more ennobling revelation of the rise of man, and confidence in his destiny. New and old are but relative in their meaning; and, however old the idea may be, we are only beginning to practically put into operation the established conception that education is no longer to be considered a war against nature, but an alliance with her : not the suppression of inclinations, not training by what is distasteful and disagreeable, but the nurturing, the developing of those loves and likes which so early manifest themselves in childhood—fostering of the good, that the evil tendencies may not have room to grow.

With the movement towards basing the training of young people on the principles of psychology, has grown up another, originating in the opposite wish to make education more practical, a more real fitting for the active duties of life, which the pupils will be called upon to fulfil when earning a livelihood. These two apparently antagonistic movements are largely in harmony. They are, in fact, related conclusions, the one resting on empirical, the other on theoretical basis. No position can be stronger than that one based on scientific reasoning and demanded by practical experience. Either might err; the two, never.

This movement is variously known as Technical Education, Practical Education, Industrial Education, Whole Education, Utilitarian Education, Hand-and-Eye Education, Manual Training, the New Education, and by many other names. Its various advocates do not agree either in their reasoning or their demands; but this is neither to be wondered at nor altogether deplored. It matters little by what name it is called, if the children get it; and get it they will, if their teachers have the wisdom to guide and the will to work. That which is passing away has done its work; let us bow our heads in reverence before its departing spirit, and prepare to give it decent burial, raising over it the inscription, "Served its appointed time, and died hard."

It is not my purpose to enter into the theory of modern education, but to record my observations with regard to some of the attempts being made to put it into practice.

Science teaching will receive separate consideration. I propose in this place to compare the various conceptions of Kindergarten, form study, and drawing, various schemes of handiwork, hand-and-eye training, Sloyd, manual instruction, cookery and needlework, for elementary and intermediate schools; with technical, and industrial, and manual training for higher schools. These are undoubtedly the most warmly debated topics in educational circles. The terms are used in a way which leads to much confusion; but there are certain clear ideas round which the opinions may be grouped. These are somewhat broadly indicated by the arrangement I have adopted above. In dealing with the subject I have hesitated which of two courses to adopt. I might have taken the whole subject as dealt with in England, where the industrial idea predominates, and then pursue the same course with respect to America, showing how the same work is advocated more from an educational point of view; or, as for the present purpose seems preferable, I may treat each division as a whole in reference to the various countries I visited.

KINDERGARTEN.

The American conception of the word Kindergarten differs very much from the idea ordinarily conveyed by the same word in England, where, probably, no word is more frequently used in connection with the progress of education. Yet I did not find one true Kindergarten in connection with an English public elementary school. I saw an abundance of so-called " Kindergarten work," but not a Kindergarten. In America, both in Canada and the United States, I saw many.

After making a statement like this, it becomes necessary to recall the origin of the term and its significance. Such an inquiry may or may not prove anything with regard to the actual value of the teaching; but it will show that the term Kindergarten as used in English schools, has very little of the meaning attached to it by the founder. The occupations are an essential part of the Kindergarten system, but do not constitute it.

The idea apparently held by most infant teachers, and certainly by members of School Boards, and others whose interest in schools and school work is in the highest degree pleasing and beneficial, is that the Kindergarten is the preliminary stage of preparation for industries, and the beginning of manual work. In its way it serves both these ends. If children are to be prepared to become artisans and manufacturers, the Kindergarten is the best beginning, because it gives the elements of industry from their starting point in nature. But this preparation is but incidental. It is equally beneficial without this ulterior object. In the true Kindergarten, such as its founder contemplated, the industry of the child is a means. It does not attach value to the things made, but to the making of things. It is the experience gained in applying natural laws for making the inward thought appear in outward form. The paper mat, a drawing, or a piece of fashioned clay, is, or should be, the expression of an idea, which under the patient industry of the child has taken form outside the mind. The child expressed this very prettily when she told her mother during a chat about her school, that in drawing "you had to think and think and then put a line round your think."*

And so, in my visits to Kindergartens and to infant schools, I did not wish so much to see the stores of pretty things which had been made, as to see why and how the children made them. If a mat be considered merely as a pretty *thing* to be made, it is worthy of a place in the school for little children ; and the infants' schools are therefore to be commended for introducing the *busy work* misnamed Kindergarten. But the mat must not be considered merely as a thing to be made ; that is only incidental. True, it

---

* A fact.

must be made; but only as a means of awakening the inventive faculty, of utilising thought through the hands, to again stimulate thought.

It is necessary to draw a clear distinction between the *message of Fröbel*, with regard to education as a whole, which will be applicable to the requirements of children of all ages for some generations to come, if they do not, as his enthusiastic disciples assert, "prove the principles on which true education will be based for all time"; and the *system he worked out* for the early education of childhood, which is known as the Kindergarten.

Fröbel's message is general, and is rather distinguished, as philosophy must be, by the absence of "methods." It is a gospel of love and unity, of harmony of nature, of common sense; and therefore concerns the whole life of man in all his relations, social and individual. Indeed, much is not new, but it is a clearly applicable statement of what is old.

The way in which a certain branch of knowledge shall be taught is manifestly dependent on one's ideas of the nature of the particular study, which ideas are seldom or never alike in two generations.

Fröbel's writings are generally conspicuously free from references to methods and branches of study, but are full of the loving spirit which must pervade every successful method which has for its object the liberating of the eternal, life-giving forces of the human mind.

With regard to the Kindergarten, the case is somewhat different. He did elaborate a system; not rigid it is true, but not the less a system of harmonious development of the child in its first searches after knowledge. Recognising the child as a bundle of possibilities bound by three relationships—to God, to nature, and to his fellow-man—each involving necessities and duties, each capable of successful realisation, each subject to the possibility of failure, he set

F

himself to develop a theory of child-education. The result
was his Kindergarten, complete in itself for the conditions
for which it was formulated. The threefold object is never
lost sight of. It is to be a complete world in miniature, a
child garden, where the pupil will grow by itself through
nature, but under the fostering care of the human gardener,
who will keep back the undesired, and allow the good to
grow in its own way. It was to take the child from the
nursery, and introduce him into a community of his equals,
in which the usual incidents of child-life are constantly
taking place. These little difficulties have to be adjusted,
and in the adjustment he obtains experience that has much
to do with the formation of character. He must respect
the rights of others as well as assert his own. The chief
end and aim of a Kindergarten is to lead a child to love
that which is good and true, and to do it by the utilisa-
tion of those energies which are most pleasing and
agreeable.

To accomplish this aim, he considered that a child must
pass through the same series of steps or stages as the
human race in its upward progress. In other words, the
way God has conducted the education of the human race
must be the pattern whereby we should endeavour to
educate the child; but if we proceed aright we may spare
the child the details of experiment. Much of his system is
based on the motto, " *Often may a symbol teach, what thy
reason cannot reach.*"

He held that, "just as the savage has his fetich, as the
people of antiquity in a higher stage of culture personified
their ideas in the form of their gods and various allegories,
as even the Christian Church does not attempt to make
itself understood without symbols ; so the deepest need of
childhood is to make the intellectual its own through
symbols or sensuous forms." Children should therefore
first read the only book God gave humanity in its child-

hood—the world in which man lives, the works in which He has manifested His divine thoughts.

" School is the effort to acquaint the pupil with the true nature and inner life of things, and to bring him into a consciousness of his own inner life and nature, and to acquaint him with the real relation of things to each other and also to mankind, to the pupil himself, and to the living ground and self-conscious unity of all things."

The means for the accomplishment of this high aim are contained in his remarkable book " The Mother Play and Nursery Songs," with regard to which he often said, " I have here laid down the fundamental ideas of my educational theory : whoever has grasped the pivot idea of this book understands what I am aiming at "; and the Baroness Marenholtz, who more than any one else has been Fröbel's interpreter to the world, says, " The keynote of the book is the analogy between the development of humanity from its earliest infancy, and the development of the individual." That is to say, the fundamental ideas of Fröbel's system are symbolism, analogy, the *unity of life.*

The world is a great schoolroom of the human race ; all objects of nature are God's gifts to man for his education. These he symbolised by a few elementary forms in which are expressed all the properties common to material things, and which he termed *Kindergarten gifts.*

Again, he held that the whole education of man comes through activities which are conditioned upon material things. The race has so developed, each individual so develops ; hence he was never tired of saying that children must *learn by doing.* Therefore the *Kindergarten occupations* correspond to the activities of the greater world of grown people, and the games abound in representations of animal life and of the phenomena of the external world.

Fröbel said :—" The worth of my Kindergarten material is found exclusively in their application—that is, in the method in which I use them.   But this method consists in the application of the law of contrasts and their connections. *The whole meaning of my educational method rests upon this law alone."*

I have dwelt thus lengthily on what is in itself a very interesting subject, solely that I may not be misunderstood in references I make to the excellent but misnamed " Kindergarten methods " in elementary schools, and in connection with manual training.

Primary Classes of the United States.

In no respect do the English and Australian elementary public schools differ from those of the United States and that portion of Canada which I visited, more than in the accommodation and method of teaching adopted for the younger children.   The infant school of England and Australia has, so far as I am aware, no representative in America.

In the greater number of the United States the schools are free for pupils from six to twenty-one years of age. Occasionally this varies.   In Connecticut, for example, it is from four to sixteen, and in a few States it is from five to twenty-one.   On admission the pupil enters the primary grade, the room for the accommodation of which does not vary greatly from those devoted to other classes.   The children usually have exceedingly comfortable single desks and seats suited to their age, the blackboards are fixed nearer to the floor, and there is not infrequently a greater or less supply of pictures.   The methods of teaching are adapted to the age of the pupils ; and prominence is given to exercises and songs.   The methods of teaching vary considerably in different schools, cities, and States, depending largely on the opinions held by the ruling spirit, who is generally the superintendent.   They also vary a good deal from those most frequently inculcated in English training colleges and practised in the schools. This necessarily follows from the fact that the requirements are different. In most of the States, for example, children do not deal with numbers higher than ten before they are seven or eight years of age ; but they perform any operation involving no higher number, first with objects and then mentally.

Language Lessons.

Again, great importance is attached to the language lesson, which is, I understand, unknown as such in English schools. These are to supplement all other lessons, and are probably the foundation of that faculty of ready expression and correct speech among the mass of the American people.

To what extent the origin of this excellent custom is due to the need for dealing with the children of foreigners, I cannot say. In schools attended by new arrivals in Boston very little else can be done for some months. I visited several, where whole classes were unable to speak more than two or three words of English. The treatment of these children is worthy of notice. They are gathered into schools and placed in the primary classes—of course irrespective of age—under experienced and capable teachers, who are unable to speak any language other than good English. Perhaps it was unnecessary for me to have said " capable teachers," for one can hardly imagine any but a capable teacher taking charge of forty boys of all ages and nationalities—Italians, Russians, French, Germans, Poles, Austrians, Polish Jews—unable to understand her, or she them, except by signs. The mode of procedure which proves so successful, is worthy of imitation by some who profess to teach French and German in English and Australian schools. These sometimes succeed —but that is through no fault of theirs. Usually they manage to create an utter dislike for the language they are supposed to teach by cramming a few unintelligible declensions ; but any knowledge of the language they seldom give. Grammar —which is created after a language—is placed by these people first. I must not digress further on this point. The teachers in these schools for foreigners teach their pupils English as a child learns it. The names of the most familiar things are taught first. The teacher holds up a hat, and making the pupils watch her mouth, she says, "This is a hat," several times, and they repeat the sentence. "This is a hat, this is a book, this is a slate, this is a pen," if she has the article in her hand; or if she points to it, " that is a desk, that is a coat," and so forth. Then she sends one child for a hat, another to bring a slate, a third to pick up a pen, and so on.

The written language is taken at the same time as the spoken, and reading follows later. The principle followed is that nothing but good, clearly enunciated English shall be heard by the pupil, and all sentences must be complete. He writes nothing he cannot speak, and must speak all he can write. By the time these boys and girls have been at school a year or two, they are able to both speak and write fluently. Some make very rapid progress. I saw an Italian lad who entered the ungraded class not knowing a word of English at ten, passed through the eight grades of primary and grammar school by the time he was fourteen, and graduated fifth in his class for the high school. I heard his brother, who was doing equally well, and several others, read from a piece of English poetry, with good expression and correct pronunciation. "This is the way we try and make Americans of the scourings of Europe, which our Government ought to prohibit from landing here," said one of the masters to me after I had spent some time in the school.

In the primary grades of ordinary schools, the attention paid to language is a most noticeable feature. In addition to the regular Language Lessons, in connection with which pictures are largely used—some of the publishing houses selling special sets for this purpose—every oral lesson is supposed to be a language lesson. The children have to answer questions and make statements in the form of complete and correct sentences. I will quote a typical course of study in language for the receiving class of the San Francisco schools.

PRIMARY GRADES.

" Course of Study, Receiving Class. Language :—

" Have familiar chats in pleasant, conversational tone, to enable pupils to gain freedom of expression.

" Require complete statements from pupils in reference to their names and addresses, and about things which they see and do.

" Require reproduction orally, of short stories read or told to them by the teacher.

" Memorise short gems of prose and poetry.

" Name the parts of the body, as head, arms, &c., and their positions as to right and left.

" Teach the organs of sense and the location of the same.

" Teach the names of the days of the week."

The children entering the class for which the above directions are given would be from six to seven years of age.

It is not unusual to find such instructions as the following in the manuals published for the use of teachers. These are again taken from the Course of Study for the schools of San Francisco, and apply to the receiving and first primary grades :—

" *Music.*—Singing and playing symbolic songs and games, motion songs and other songs, as prescribed in Kindergarten work.

" *Physical Exercises.*—Have physical exercises every half-hour, with windows and doors open, using arm movements and breathing exercises.

"*Oral Instruction.*—Teach the name, production, and use of surrounding objects. Hold familiar talks about such animals as the cat, the dog, the cow, and the horse; also about parts of the human body, and the senses.

"*Morals and Manners.*—Teach self-control, and independence by encouraging true effort. Teach the value of cleanliness, industry, punctuality, politeness, honesty, obedience, and patriotism.

"*Kindergarten Instruction.*—Apply the principles of the Kindergarten Instruction in teaching all subjects, as: (1) Proceed from the known to the unknown, (2) Proceed from the whole to the parts, (3) Learn to do by doing.

"All Kindergarten work under the direction of the special Kindergarten teacher.

" Use the six coloured worsted balls, the sphere, the cube, and the cylinder, the coloured sticks, the rings, and the tablets for observing lessons to develop ideas of :—

" *Colour.*—Red, orange, yellow, green, blue, and purple.

"*Form.*—Sphere, cube, and cylinder, and from these surfaces, faces, edges, lines, squares, and the like. All new terms and all new shapes to be taken from the object.

"*Motion, Position, Arrangement, Location.*—Roll, slide, top, bottom, etc.

" *Prominent qualities and objects.*—Rough, smooth, hard, soft, and the like.

" *Size.*—Large, small, long, short, and the like.

" *Occupation Work.*—Sewing, weaving, paper folding, and clay modelling to supplement work with solids, tablets, sticks, and rings, and to work out ideas, gained through the use of these solids, etc.

" *Modelling.*—Solids in clay, and a few simple objects based on the type forms.

This programme, together with reading, writing, and arithmetic, constitutes the "course of study" for the primary grade of San Francisco, and, except that there is more " Kindergarten " than usual, may be taken as typical; but from what I saw, I am inclined to think that " Busy work " would be a better name than " Kindergarten work."

Usually the teachers begrudge the time they have to give to the subject. Examples of mats, embroidery, paper folding, and clay modelling were always to be seen; but the replies of teachers outside a few special schools convinced me that the teachers do not yet understand it. They would use the words of one who, when asked what she considered the influence of the work on the pupils, said : " It is in the course of study, and I teach it." She was also not alone in her opinion that if " Kindergarten work " is to be taken, it should be before school age, *i.e.*, before six, for after that age all time is needed for reading, writing, and arithmetic. The primary teachers do not usually consider the so-called Kindergarten anything more than manual training or busy work. The same may be said of most of the primary grade teachers whom I saw at work. In fact, some of the strongest opposition to true Kindergartens comes from the primary grade teachers.

So far as my observation extended—and I paid considerable attention to this point—I have little hesitation in saying that there is as little of the true spirit of Kindergarten in the primary grades of the schools of the United States as in the English infant schools.

Perhaps it can hardly be otherwise. A watch case is of no use without the works, and if Fröbel's system be complete it cannot be divided. It must be taken as a whole or left alone. When a primary or an infant school teacher understands the principles, laws, and symbolism of the Kindergarten, she will not attempt to tack on a part of the means therein adopted, but she will use the principles in other ways. Mrs. Mary H. Peabody not inaptly says :—

" The Kindergarten as a thing complete in itself cannot be extended. As a form of training preparatory to the school, it is organised for and adapted to the youngest children, and as a form of instruction, with its occupations, games, and exercises limited to their working capacity, it cannot be used as a mere repetition in older classes. But while thus leaving the form, we still have to consider the underlying principles, elements, methods, and spirit of the

Kindergarten, for these, if natural and true, will serve as a point of contact between the Kindergarten and school which is always seeking for natural methods, and often ground upon which schemes of education may be wrought out ; and so we have before us the true substance of the Kindergarten, the school as it is, and the possible union of the two upon the basis of a natural method of education."

English Infant Schools.

The English or Australian infant school usually consists of a large oblong room, with one or more class-rooms attached. Usually one of the latter is a small room with a gallery, known as the "babies' room," in which are children from three years of age. The large room is usually provided with—

(*a*) A gallery on which all the pupils can be massed for singing and other united exercises, and very pretty and beneficial they are. The pretty and educative active songs of the infant schools are often identical with the symbol songs of the Kindergarten ; but they are disjointed units instead of being parts of a whole.

(*b*) A large open floor space used for marching, and in the better schools for games such as form such a prominent feature in the Kindergarten. The large amount of work necessary for the examinations prevents full use being made of this part of the room.

(*c*) A portion, sometimes terraced, sometimes with level floor, seated with dual desks for writing. In the more recently built English infant schools, the desks have adjustable tops, so that they can be made flat for "Kindergarten work" or sloping for writing. They are marked out in one-inch squares, the same as a Kindergarten table.

The best schools are provided with pianos, which have usually been paid for by subscription, or with money raised by concerts. Many which have no piano have a small harmonium for marching purposes.

It would be impossible to speak too highly of some of the infant schools I have visited ; but many appear to have no higher ideal than the examination. I frequently left schools, feeling pained at what I had seen of little dots of children, whose young bodies and tender, budding minds are alike unfit for close and continued attention, having to spend more than half their time on backless forms, sitting in one cramped position of "attention" for more than thirty or forty minutes at a stretch, under fear of severe penalty, preparing for examination. Classes of fifty in charge of inexperienced girls, who "don't mind teaching if they could only keep the children quiet ; but they are *so restless.*" I several times hastily excused myself and hurried out into the street, unable to longer bear the sight of mites of babies "from two to three years of age" learning to write, read, and do addition sums involving hundreds! In one babies' room where this was going on, the pupil-teacher of the second year was in charge of fifty children, and said she had eighty towards the close of the year. She said, "she had to spend most of her time at reading, writing, and arithmetic, but they had singing *several times a week.* They also made wool balls and did Kindergarten sewing. I asked what the Kindergarten was for, and she replied, "Ah, they got better marks at the examination if they did Kindergarten."

In another school, the mistress, in reply to a remark I made about the babies doing sums and writing, said, "Yes, I like to have them in as soon as possible, for I find that those children who commence at from two to three years of age make 'splendid fivers,'" which I found meant, would pass the required examination at five without trouble !

I believe it is not long since the English Parliament passed a Factory Act prohibiting the employment of child labour; and I read while in London of prosecutions of theatrical managers for employing children of tender years. The next need will be, if England retains her result system, an Infant School Act to ameliorate the condition of the poor little things who are supposed to be under a process of beneficial education!

I have spoken of two extremes. The greater number of infant schools are intermediate between the two classes I have mentioned. They are usually much more liberally provided with pictures than the primary schools of the United States. The teachers appear diligent and hard-working, according to the standard set before them. They are very anxious that a visitor should see how well the pupils write, the kind of sums they do, hear how they recite selections of suitable poetry, and mark their proficiency in reading. The mechanical part of all these exercises is splendidly done. The work is all very desirable at the proper time, and for doing it the teachers are paid, or rather, it is the means by which the success attending the efforts of the teachers is judged. They may therefore be considered to fulfil their duties when they attain the ends fixed by the authorities. They do more than the minimum required; but it is on the same lines, and is rather a matter for regret than commendation. They work conscientiously according to their light, and if the light is too often of the nature of twilight, the blame must be largely attached to the authorities. Of course, not altogether so: we cannot blame a man for not seeing the true beauties of a landscape through blue spectacles, but we can for putting on the spectacles.

An account of the English infant school would not be complete without reference to the noble work of the women who conduct these schools in the poor districts, which are not usually seen by visitors. The tender motherly care which the children receive in these schools must be one of the most humanising influences at work in the great cities; but I did often wish that they would not further deaden the small spark of sensitiveness remaining in the breasts of the forlorn creatures, by wishing to show off the wretchedness and raggedness of the barefooted unfortunates in much the same way that a dime museum proprietor shows off his abortions and " curiosities." " This way, ladies and gentlemen, and I will first draw your attention to the curious freak of nature, the armless girl, who sews, knits, and plays the piano with her feet. You will "—and so forth, says the showman. In the same way some of these well-intentioned and, at heart, kind and sympathetic teachers, would call upon the most woebegone child in the room to stand and step out, while she pointed out the marks of his poverty loud enough for the pupils to hear, and in as matter-of-fact manner as a man might discuss the "points" of a horse at an agricultural show. In one school where this was done in several rooms, the mistress also made two comfortably dressed boys stand out, while she explained that they had been as miserable as the others, but she had obtained clothing for them from friends. I consider such treatment positively cruel, whatever the motive may be. It is certainly unnecessary to point out marks of poverty to an Australian : it is one of the first things which strike him in Europe. I well remember my first experience in this respect nine years since. Things become noticeable by contrast, and the contrast between Australia and England is prominent enough in this respect.

Would it not be well to make the salaries of the teachers of the schools in the poor parts of every city, higher than those prevailing elsewhere, and make the positions dependent on special qualifications ? Children everywhere require the best of teachers, but the need is especially urgent in the case of the poor little beings almost without homes. It is apparently in this respect that the Maternal Schools of Paris excel ; they feed and clothe as well as teach the children.

Granting the correctness of my observations, I have sufficiently proved my statement that the Kindergarten as understood by the founder and his followers does not exist in connection with English public elementary schools, and that the work known as Kindergarten is misnamed, inasmuch as it is not, if it was ever intended to be, in keeping with the idea of Fröbel's leading principle of analogy, or the unity of life. But I would again repeat that this has nothing to do with the value or otherwise of the work known as Kindergarten. In fact, I may state—for repetition in such a matter is useful—that the influence of even the small amount of *Busy Work* or *Manual Instruction* which I saw in the Infant Schools must be in the highest degree beneficial ; and I can further add, that I think the adoption of those principles of education which are common to all true plans of education, is doing much to revolutionise the work of the schools.

The genial and able clerk of an important School Board, whose kind assistance in furthering my investigations I shall always gratefully remember, informed me that his Board had sent a teacher to Germany for three months to study the system (in St. Louis, Toronto, and other places, two years' study and practice are required in order to qualify for the position of director of a Kindergarten), and they had also brought over a German lady teacher to instruct their teachers in the system. His experience, and it agreed with that of most men who had studied the subject, was that the Germans were not practical enough. Fröbel was not practical. His system was all theory ; it would never get results. His ideas about symbolism and all that were altogether ideal. The English people had reduced Kindergarten to practice. Just so, and the reduction has been thorough. The resultant system is as complete, as the solemnisation of a wedding with the bride absent.

The Kindergarten was never intended as an associate of

a system of teaching the conventionalities of learning, and is as much out of place there, as a Mississippi river boat on the stormy Atlantic. What it was intended to do, and what its advocates claim it will do, is thus summed up by an English lecturer : " What the Kindergarten has to show are happy, healthy, good-natured children ; no proficiency in learning of any kind, no precocity, but just children in their normal state. The Kindergarten rejects reading, writing, ciphering, spelling. In it children under six years build, plait, fold, model, sing, act ; in short, they learn in *play* to work, to construct, to invent, to relate and speak correctly, and what is best of all, to love each other, to be kind to each other, to help each other."

This aim I believe is attained in some private Kindergartens in England, although I did not see them ; but I visited infant schools whose teachers fully understand the aim, and would gladly carry it out if they had the opportunity. They have made those principles, which Fröbel did not invent, but clearly demonstrated, their own, and applied them in their work as he did in his Kindergarten. These teachers stated that they would like the " Babies' Class " made a Kindergarten, and then proceed by a natural transition to the work, which they now have to enforce at an age when it is detrimental to the future wellbeing of the children.

The American Kindergarten.

What I have indicated that the most advanced English infant school teachers would like to do, is being done in " sixteen States and twenty-five cities " of the United States, as well as in, at least, one city of Canada. Fröbel expressed the opinion that " the Kindergarten could only have its full development in America, where the national principle is self-government; in perfect freedom, but according to law." However this may be, it was introduced early into the United States by his pupils, who founded private Kindergartens.

It is not my intention to trace the history of the movement, which is typical of the manner in which reforms are almost invariably initiated in the schools of the United States, and as a few moments' thought will show, of other countries as well.

The first Kindergartens struggled against great drawbacks. Ladies of means were attracted by the value of the principle, and provided funds for establishing charity Kindergartens, while others became popular for the children of well-to-do parents. About 1870, Miss Blow, an enthusiastic Kindergartener, offered to train a teacher and direct a Kindergarten in connection with one of the schools of St. Louis, to show the adaptability of the system as a preparation for ordinary school life. After several years, the Superintendent of Schools, Dr. Harris, now United States Superintendent at Washington, succeeded in inducing his committee to accept the offer, and the school was established in 1873, with an average attendance of forty-two. A gradual extension of the system has taken place since then. At the time of my visit there were fifty-three Kindergartens, taught by one hundred and thirty-one paid and sixty-five unpaid teachers, with six thousand two hundred pupils enrolled, and an average attendance of three thousand eight hundred pupils.

In Boston, the progress of the Kindergarten movement has been chiefly due to the charity of Mrs. Quincey A. Shaw (daughter of Professor L. Agassiz, the Naturalist). In 1887, she started four schools at her own expense, next year she opened fourteen more ; all were free, and in connection with schools situated in districts inhabited by the labouring classes. In a few years she had established thirty schools, which she supported at an annual cost of nearly ten thousand pounds. About a year since she handed them all over to the School Board, free of expense, on condition that the Board would work them. Not only has the Board adopted those so generously provided, but, having thus affirmed the principle, it is establishing Kindergartens as rapidly as possible in connection with the other schools. It must be understood in connection with this movement, that hitherto there had been no provision for the training of children of the age taken in the English infant school. The Kindergartens, therefore, of which I am speaking, take the place of the two first years of English infant school life.

Philadelphia has largely adopted the public Kindergarten as a sub-primary preparation, having in 1887 taken over twenty-five schools established in conjunction with the public schools by a private society, formed for the purpose of showing the School Board their value as an addition to the school system. The Superintendent objects to the name Kindergarten, although they are arranged on Fröbel's plan, because it makes them appear as something separate from the public system, instead of being an integral part of it. He suggests the term " Sub-Primary." Public Kindergartens are being rapidly established and incorporated into the public school system in a great number of States, and will complete the gradation of American schools.

In Toronto, Canada, true Kindergartens are being established as quickly as possible in connection with all the schools. A number are already in operation, and are being used as a training-ground for Kindergarteners for the new Kindergartens. A training-class is also in operation. Two years' training are required to qualify a teacher to take the position of director. A year is spent in a Kindergarten as voluntary assistant, or in a training-class. If a student is serving as a voluntary assistant, she must attend lectures several times a week on the theory of the gifts, occupations, and games. At the end of the year she must pass an

G

examination in practical work, after which she is eligible
for the position of paid assistant.   Paid assistants meet
once a week for instruction in Fröbel's principles, etc., by
the Supervisor.   At the end of the year, on passing an
examination in the theory and symbolism of the gifts,
songs, etc., and satisfying the examiners with regard to
ability for practical management, the teacher becomes
eligible for the position of director.

Mention should be made of the success of the private
free Kindergarten in San Francisco under the presidency
of Mrs. Sarah B. Cooper, who for nine years has, with
the aid of generous ladies of the city, established over
thirty schools.   Many persons of wealth have been induced
to study the system and its work for themselves, and,
becoming convinced of its value, have generously given
money for the support of free Kindergartens.   One
wealthy lady has given over 40,000 dollars for this object,
supporting eight schools, two of which she has under
her direct supervision.   There are at present over 3,000
children attending these free Kindergartens.   The children
are too young to be admitted to the public schools, their
ages ranging from two and a half to six years, and would
otherwise be receiving vicious training in the streets.   In
the Kindergarten they are taught habits of cleanliness
and industry, and become familiar with the customs and
usages of well-ordered lives.

It is said that the influence of the Kindergarten is very
noticeable when the children enter the public schools.
They take a good place in the primary classes, and usually
progress more rapidly.   This is becoming, I believe, so
apparent, that it is the cause of the growing desire to
establish Kindergartens in connection with the public schools,
as an integral part of the system.

The teachers of these Kindergartens are veritable missionaries, for, like their sisters in St. Louis and Boston, they

work in the homes as well as in the schools. If necessary, they feed and clothe the poorer children, who, in consequence, present anything but a disconsolate appearance to the visitor. "These ladies are often called upon to settle family disputes, to advise perplexed mothers, and to protect some of their little flock from the severities of drunken mothers, and the neglect of besotted fathers. When we reflect upon the conditions of such homes, we must bestow unstinted praise upon the women who thus go into them, to carry out their educational work with little children."

The general plan of American Kindergarten rooms is as uniform as that of the English infant school rooms; but just as the latter vary in details, elaborateness of finish, and furniture, so do the rooms for Kindergarten. They usually lack one feature of the ideal Kindergarten—that is, the small plots of ground where the pupils may plant seeds or cuttings, water, watch, and tend them, and enjoy for their own the product in the form of the resultant flowers. This want is to some extent supplied by the use of flower-pots and window-boxes. In St. Louis the Kindergarten, although associated with the public school, is usually more or less detached. Not unfrequently it is held in a room specially built in the playground, quite apart from the regular school. Such was the case with the first I visited. Others are attached to the main buildings, but have separate entrances. In this, convenience and economy are seen to have had the same influence as in the determination of the English infant school.

In some cases Kindergartens are conducted in assembly or other convenient hired rooms. I visited one held in a fine, airy, well-lighted room over a beer saloon. This was in the quarter of the city chiefly occupied by German citizens, which constitute a considerable proportion of the population of St. Louis. To those who understand German customs, this will be quite sufficient to explain that no comparison must be made between a Kindergarten over such a beer saloon, and an infant school over a London public-house bar or " gin palace." Still, it was explained that the arrangement was a temporary one of necessity.

The accommodation usually consists of a large rectangular room, generally lighted on two or three sides, with convenient cloak-rooms and lavatories, and plenty of cupboards for the storage of new and used material.

Three hours a day are considered sufficient for a child to attend a Kindergarten ; consequently, the same rooms are generally used for two sets of children. Some teachers work both morning and afternoon, but, as a rule, a different staff is employed for the afternoon Kindergarten. The rooms are invariably well built and nicely finished, being painted in unobtrusive, soft, harmonious colours. This will apply to nearly all the schoolrooms of the United States which I saw. They are always clean, always bright, always harmonious.

At the commencement of the school year, when the pupils first enter the Kindergarten, the walls are merely decorated with a few pictures. At the close, they are frequently literally covered with decorative devices made by the children. I was sometimes shown designs which it was intended to work out during the year, all the work being done by the children ; the controlling idea being, that when the pupil first enters the Kindergarten there is sufficient novelty in all the surroundings to thoroughly exercise his powers of observation. To add more would distract him. As he becomes familiar with his surroundings, his constructive powers are exercised in adding new variety and charm to his school home. The exercise is educative in many ways, not least in that it shows him how the combined efforts of himself and neighbours at dissimilar work produce a complete and harmonious result—the law of which Fröbel was so fond.

The furniture consists of small bent wood children's arm-chairs, such as are used in nurseries, and small tables, each table to accommodate two children. The surface of each table is marked into squares of one inch, to guide the children in many of their occupations. In some cities large tables are used to accommodate ten or twelve children, but the St. Louis teachers advocate the small ones as being more convenient. A few minutes are sufficient for the children to move their own chairs and tables to the sides of the room, leaving the floor clear for games and exercises. The floor is usually marked with devices to assist in carrying out the games.

One of the strongest arguments used by Dr. Harris, in advocating the establishment of Kindergartens, was the benefit they would be to the children of the poorer districts of the city, where it was found that pupils usually left school at ten years of age. Without a compulsory law, the period of school influence could only be extended by drawing the children into school earlier. I therefore visited several of the Kindergartens in the most disreputable parts of the town. The surroundings tell their own expressive tale of the condition of the people, among whom the Kindergarteners are veritable missionaries. In one of the Kindergartens near the river, for example, the supervisor informed me that the director and her assistants had provided many of the children with the clothes in which I saw them, and that the difference in the children since the establishment of the Kindergartens was marvellous. I do not doubt it. The teachers spend the last week or two of vacation in going round to the houses, and helping the mothers to get the children ready for opening day ; and thus are able to exercise beneficial influence on the homes in other ways, besides caring for the children. In this Kindergarten were about seventy children, under a director, a paid assistant, and two unpaid assistants or " novitiate teachers."

While I was watching the "work" proceeding in its ordinary way, a pigeon flew through the open window, and appeared much frightened at finding itself in a Kindergarten; but the children went quietly on with their play-work. Presently the bird settled on a window-sill and allowed the director to catch it. The pupils were then gathered quickly and quietly round her, and joined in a conversation about the pigeon. It was evidently not the first time that the director had had a live bird or other animal for the subject of a lesson. It was surprising how quietly the pigeon took all the stroking and petting, even feeding out of the children's hands. This incident gave me a clearer insight into the work of that Kindergarten than all else I saw. The bird knew it was among friends, and the children talked and acted as though they were in sympathy with nature. After a short time spent in chatting and playing with the pigeon, it was allowed to fly up into a window, where it remained until I left. The teacher then proposed that as a bird had come to see them, they should have a bird song and game, which they did.

I visited several coloured Kindergartens—that is, Kindergartens for negro children—and highly interesting they proved. The singing was particularly good, the negro aptitude for simple melody being, no doubt, accountable for this result. The directors and teachers, as in all coloured schools, had more or less negro blood. Frequently the trace was so slight, that outside the United States it would probably not be recognisable; but so strong is the feeling there, that such would not be allowed to teach in a school for white children! The coloured people have "equal rights of citizenship;" they are as well provided with schools, which are as well built, as well furnished, and more liberally supplied with teachers; but they must not attend the same schools as their white fellow-citizens. I was unable to detect any difference in the work of the two classes of Kindergartens. All are under one supervisor, and a liberal departure from custom has been made in allowing the coloured and white Kindergarteners to attend the same lectures on the method and practice of Fröbel's system; and I saw a number of coloured teachers present to hear an address I was invited to give before several hundred Kindergarteners, on a comparison between an Infant School and a Kindergarten.

Every Kindergarten is provided with a piano—it is an essential. They are sometimes the property of the school authorities, but more frequently are rented by the school at from two to four dollars a month. The practice of hiring out pianos appears to be much more frequent in the United States than in England, and they are much more frequently a part of the ordinary school furniture than in England.

The Kindergartens of St. Louis are under the management of a supervisor, to whom I am indebted for very great assistance in thoroughly understanding the working of the system, the largest and most complete in the United States. Her time is spent in visiting the various schools, and in giving special preparation to the paid and unpaid assistants, who are learners. In this latter, she is assisted by one of the ablest directors, who receives an extra salary as normal instructor in programmes and occupations; and unless appearances are more deceptive than usual, a particularly wise selection has been made.

The system of training has been arranged not on account of its perfection, but for reasons of economy.

The average cost of *tuition* per pupil in the public schools of the United States ranges from twelve to twenty dollars for the year of two hundred days. The cost of tuition in the St. Louis Kindergarten is given at six dollars. Sixty pupils entitle the director to a paid assistant, and one additional is appointed for every thirty pupils; but the present degree of success would never have been attained if no other assistance had been given.   As a matter of fact, an equal or greater number of unpaid assistants are always found in the Kindergartens.   Many—indeed, I believe the majority—never follow teaching as a profession.   Young women of at least seventeen years of age, who have had a good education, and are not dependent on their own efforts to earn a livelihood, enter the Kindergartens for the sake of the training they obtain.   By their aid, the children are divided into classes of ten or fifteen for the gifts and occupations, joining under the trained teachers for the higher work.   These voluntary assistants meet once or twice a week for instruction in the theory and symbolism of the system by the supervisor and her assistants.   After one or two years of this work, they may enter for the first examination, after passing which they are eligible for the position of paid assistants, but still have to continue the outside study.

This system has been of great value to the young women of the town.   Hundreds of young women have thus obtained education in those valuable matters relating to the early training of children.   The culture and thought derived from the study and discussion of Fröbel's ennobling teaching, the knowledge and experience of child nature and development, are such a peculiarly fitting and invaluable preparation for the high and responsible duties of wife and mother, that many young women gladly enter the Kindergartens who would not otherwise engage in teaching.   " It is useless to expect social regeneration from persons who are not themselves regenerated," and the St. Louis authorities consider that in thus disseminating the principles of Fröbel, they are adding very greatly to the value of the public school system.

The plan I have just described has a very serious drawback.   No city has adopted Kindergarten so extensively as

St. Louis: yet in no city I visited are the primary and grammar school teachers so opposed to it. It is a system within a system, and not a part of a comprehensive system. The Kindergartener thinks her mode of training perfect, and denounces primary methods which she does not understand. The primary teacher knows nothing of Kindergarten except that " the children who have been in Kindergarten are so inquisitive, won't sit still and listen, want to know the reason of everything, and don't know any more of reading and writing than those who come straight from home." Do they learn more quickly? I repeatedly asked ; and the reply was generally a reluctant admission that they did in anything that required thought, but not in remembering. That they learned arithmetic more quickly was nearly always admitted. The object of the primary teacher's work is "to teach to read, write, and do sums." The Kindergarten does not do that ; therefore, she says, the Kindergarten is not practical : it is a waste of money and time. These antagonistic forces are represented on the School Board, and there is a constant fear lest the enemies should prevail, and displace the Kindergarten from the school system.

Philadelphia, Boston, and other cities, are avoiding this danger by a proper system of training their teachers. Before a normal student can take up the study of a speciality, she must graduate in the usual general course. The Principal of the Boston Normal School remarked during a chat on this subject : " I am becoming more and more convinced that each subject should be taught by special teachers with special fitness and training ; but the special training must *first of all* be based on *general training.* By this means the teacher will first see the relation of all the subjects to one another, and will not try to subordinate all others to his special study. Take Kindergarten teachers, for example. We give a general training in Kindergarten principles in our general course ; but the ordinary student

is not fit to be a Kindergartener. She knows enough of
it to see its objects, tendencies, and methods, and this
will show her whether she has a taste and fitness for it. If
she has, her special training is based on her general. She
no longer thinks the Kindergarten is the ideal and only
mode of teaching, and does not look on all other teachers
as enemies to her system. On the other hand, the primary
teacher does not look on the Kindergarten as a fad of a
few specialists. She gives it its place and the Kindergarten her sympathy ; and is able to take advantage of the
Kindergarten training of the child when it comes under
her care."

THE USE OF PICTURES.

As a rule, the English Board schools are very much
better provided with pictures, than the American, or even
the Australian. Sometimes their gaudy colouring and
imaginary character suggests that their educative value is
not great; but, generally, their influence must be very
beneficial, although in some cases appearances, supported
by conversations with the teachers and talks with the children, would indicate that they are not made to serve to
the greatest possible extent the purpose for which they were
bought. Here again the false principle of the Education
Department is to blame. The standard is fixed. Reading,
writing, arithmetic, must be taught. Inducement in the
shape of additional money grant is held out for the teaching
of grammar, geography, object lessons, and so on. In
the majority of cases the teacher would gain no extra credit
—I do not refer to money, which is, in this case, a secondary consideration—were he to use them to the best advantage. The attitude of the authorities is wrong ; the
blame is with them, not with the teachers. I think that
the following quotation from a little work by Mary E. Burt,
of Chicago, will apply in this case.

"The most natural thing a man can do when he is trusted, is to try to rise to the level of the occasion. If he does not reach the standard, he will reach in the direction of it. If he does not reach it the first time, he will reach more nearly to it the second. Every time the ideal is put before him he will reach a little closer to it. I do not mean the faith that pretends to believe, but 'keeps an eye open' to make sure, as some teachers trust their pupils ; but the absolute faith that God has in man. The most natural thing a man can do when he is suspected, is to lower his standard of action to meet that occasion. Let a child or man think that you suspect him of being capable of intentional wrong, and he is very likely soon to justify you in that opinion."

I believe there are many School Boards with wise, broad-minded men controlling their affairs—men who, grasping the true scope of elementary education, seek to carry their ideal into practice, and use every means to make the schools serve their legitimate purpose. In their schools, earning the merit grant is considered a necessary evil, not an end. I also had the pleasure of meeting, outside such boards, many teachers with a nobleness of purpose, a depth of conviction which no false legislation could affect. The good of the children is to them the first aim ; "results" a necessarily important but secondary consideration.

Considering the unsurpassed character of American books and printing in general, and the elegance and comfort of the school-rooms, I was continually surprised at not finding more pictures in the schools of the United States.

In San Francisco, teachers pay considerable attention to providing pictures for composition and other exercises. For the former purpose the illustrated papers are largely utilised. In several schools were good pictures of Queen Victoria, the Emperor of Germany, Mr. Gladstone, Prince

Bismarck, and other famous personages, as well as of noted places, all of which had been the subjects of composition exercises.

They are utilised in various ways. For example, the teacher takes a picture, say, of Prince Bismarck, and gives a biographical sketch, or tells a story about the subject of the picture, which the pupils reproduce. The same may be done with an ordinary sketch from life, an illustration of some scene in a foreign country, with or without a sketch of the picture. The practice thus given in some schools has produced a facility for sketching quite noteworthy, and shows clearly that drawing from copies is useful in its place. I found that from this exercise some had developed the power of illustrating a story told them with capital original sketches. I saw this kind of work in many schools, and had the pleasure of looking over the ordinary class exercises. Trained in this way, and with plenty of blackboard practice, the teachers often show a wonderful power of illustration with a few lines of chalk; in fact, American teachers are more ready with chalk and blackboard than any I have met.

Another exercise in frequent use in many parts of the United States, as well as in San Francisco, is, placing a picture before the pupils, and, without any explanation, ask them to describe it and put the story it tells into words. I consider this exercise a very valuable one when used in its proper place, and was more than once struck with the powers of observation and description developed by it.

I am aware that it is not always wise to form conclusions from what one sees during an ordinary visit. Some teachers—I believe and hope they are few—consider that pictures and maps are best kept in portfolios, or rolled up, except when they are required for direct use. This usually means that when they are required for reference they are not available. So far as the maps are concerned, there are two reasons for their not being displayed. In the first place, they are usually mounted on spring rollers, so that they fold out of sight in a neat case ; and this being fastened to the wall, the map is always available by pulling it down in the same way that a modern window-blind is unrolled. When no longer needed, it is allowed to wind itself up again. In the second place, every school-boy or girl has one of the profusely illustrated, and splendidly printed combined atlases and geographies, always ready for reference. Consequently wall-maps are comparatively rare. When a large map is required for class-teaching, the teacher's handiness with the chalk, and the large available blackboard space, quickly provides one to illustrate just what is wanted. I noticed that coloured chalk was generally available for this and similar purposes. It was not unusual to find a well-drawn map of the particular State in which the school was situated, on the blackboard of a junior room.

In the newer schools of Philadelphia I noticed that the rooms not unfrequently had very bold large maps illustrative of the special geography of the classes which occupied them, painted in oils on the walls. Sometimes these were imitation relief, and the effect was very good. Occasionally I found enthusiastic teachers with large maps in bold outline, on which they had fastened the products of the different countries in their proper place. One teacher, who must have gone to considerable trouble in thus preparing a map of the world, and, with her pupils, was reasonably proud of their joint work, when she saw me look at it, apologised for Australia being so bare. She remarked with perfect truth that the geographies said very little about Australia, and she had no means of obtaining the products of the country.

In England the schools appear to be usually well provided with large bold prints illustrative of natural history and geography.   They are generally either German productions, or English editions of German pictures.   Knowing the fondness of the Americans for German ideas on education, I was almost as surprised that these prints were not more frequently seen in the schools of the United States as that pictures should be so little used.

The schools of South Australia are usually well supplied with maps and diagrams by the Education Department; and, in addition, the teachers are encouraged to add pictures.   The Department has adopted a plan with respect to maps which is worthy of imitation.   Geography is a necessary subject of study in all schools; but the wish of the authorities is that the memory should be burdened with few names of places; but that the teachers should endeavour to give their pupils as realistic an idea as possible of what the country is like, the kind of people who live there, what articles they produce, and so forth.   In furtherance of this object, a series of wall maps have been prepared in the Government printing office, in which it has been the endeavour to combine attractiveness of appearance with bold and striking outline.   Only such details are inserted as it is necessary to teach.   The course of instruction states, under the head " General Principles " :—

" The object of the lessons in geography is to give the children a fair general knowledge of the world in which they live.

" It is too often the custom to require the learning of a great many names of capes, rivers, mountains, etc., which are entirely devoid of general interest.   Every teacher should lay it down as a fundamental rule never to teach the name of any place unless he is prepared to associate it with some fact of interest.

" Every school will be supplied with (1) a compass, (2) a globe, (3) the requisite maps, (4) such diagrams as may be necessary.

"Teachers are strongly recommended to form for their own use a small collection of pictures, which will be found of the greatest use in giving intelligent and lasting ideas as to the various parts of the world. Old numbers of the *Graphic, Illustrated London News*, and other periodicals, will be found useful, and Messrs. Cassell publish many excellent illustrated geographical works."

Relief Maps are most frequently seen in Paris, where the ordinary printed map is now out of date. When relief maps are not used, they have a process of representing the relief surface on the flat paper which is very effective.

Definition maps are common in English schools, and some are very good representations of the features of land and sea. These are not nearly so frequently seen in the schools of the United States; but, instead, the primary rooms in many cities are provided with large combination modelling trays and tables, about four feet by three feet, made of stout light wood, the tray being about three inches deep and lined with zinc. It is so arranged that it can be used flat when the pupils stand round, or raised at a convenient angle for pupils to see from their places. Provided with a supply of fine, clean sand, this becomes a most useful aid to good teaching. In some cities these trays are found in every room, and the visitor not unfrequently finds a class or a section of a class standing round, all engaged in a united effort at making a relief map of Europe, the United States, or some other continent or country. This plan of modelling maps in sand is in use in South Australian schools, but the convenient trays are absent.

In London I came across a kind of relief definition map superior to everything else I have seen; but its weight and expense will prevent its general use. It was a model in cast iron, about four feet square, on which every geographical definition could be represented. By pouring a bucket of water the sea was formed; by a little arrangement with a can of water placed at an elevation, and a thin rubber tube, the rivers were set running ; a candle underneath would make an active volcano, and a few grains of powder an eruption.

DRAWING AND FORM-STUDY.

It often occurred to me that the value of the drawing, which I inspected as an adjunct to manual training no less than as an item of the greatest educational value, was in very different—sometimes directly opposite—proportion to its "show value," often curiously called "artistic merit."

The elementary schools of the chief centres of the United States are in drawing as distinctly in advance of those of England, as the average English school-girl is ahead of her American cousin in her skill in needlework.

Drawing in most of the English public elementary schools appeared to me to be most unsatisfactory. Neither has a poor system been followed generally, nor a good one partially. When the subject was taught at all, it consisted, in the lower grades, of a little copying of figures composed of right lines on slates ; in the intermediate, a little freehand and mechanical copying on paper ; in the higher classes, the same, with a little drawing from simple models. It could not by any charity be considered an educational, much less an art course. A few School Boards, notably Birmingham, were to some extent exceptions. But as I believe drawing is to be made compulsory, and in other respects placed on entirely a new footing, it would be manifestly useless to enter further into a discussion of the subject here, or to transcribe the notes of work I saw. If the gentlemen directing the Science and Art Department can see their way to do it, they have all the knowledge, and are not lacking in the desire, to make the teaching of drawing worthy of England.

The progress made by the United States has been due, I believe, to the work initiated by Walter Smith, whose name I found to be honoured from the Mississippi eastward. He was imported from South Kensington by the State of Massachusetts twenty years since, when it was determined to make drawing a fundamental feature in the education of the people. As sketched out by Mr. Smith, it was on English lines, especially valuable as leading to art education. It had features which did not suit the American mind; and Mr. Smith, able and strong, a master of his business, with conscious knowledge of his power, would not bend; and, in consequence, met with much opposition. The unbending rigidity, akin to stubbornness, of the Englishman, is not the surest or most direct means of attaining an end in America. The aphorism of Franklin—" He who will bend his head will save himself many a hard knock "— is largely followed by American public men everywhere. If it is not, they cease to be public men. The American likes to take the shortest course to the end he has in view ; but the direct road is not always the best, and if it has objections, he will not wear himself in breaking them down, but will go round : but, to quote the Western expression, " he gets there all the same." When a proposal is met with opposition, showing to his quick mind that he is doomed to defeat, he does not take the defeat: he withdraws—he goes round. As likely as not, it is not the reality, but what is imagined to be such, that people oppose. He " introduces his proposal in another form, and people are delighted ; and instead of having his purpose defeated, and himself being relegated to the adornment of obscurity," he accomplishes his end, and is rewarded with the plaudits of his former opponents. This is not always beneficial, or conducive to the best type of character ; neither is stubbornness, which is the opposite characteristic.

Walter Smith's unbending adherence to the one course

H

which he believed would answer the purpose for which he had been taken to America, and perhaps a not too pleasant way of asserting his convictions, cost him his health; but the work he did for his adopted country will never be lost. Such is the substance of what I heard of him in many places, and probably he did his work in the only way possible for him. That work has been modified very much, but formed the nucleus, out of which has been evolved various systems of form study and drawing for primary and grammar schools, of the highest educational value.

Industrial drawing is a required study in all the schools of Massachusetts.

(*a*) Because of its educational value.

(*b*) Because of its industrial value.

The State Board issues an excellent course of study, which includes modelling in clay, paper-folding, and kindred occupations. "Throughout the course, models and objects should be constantly used, for correct ideas of things can only come from observing the things themselves. The forms should be observed by both eyes and hands, and the knowledge thus gained should be spread in three ways —by Language, by Drawing, by Construction. Language means the expression of knowledge by words, either oral or written; Drawing the expression of knowledge by lines, representing the forms; Construction the expression of knowledge by forms : that is, by making the forms themselves."

Several other States, as well as many cities, publish courses of study, proceeding on the same general principles. In very few if any progressive centres, is drawing taken as a subject of study in itself. It is almost invariably associated with form study. The introduction to the course of study adopted in 1888 by the State of New York very concisely expresses the views generally very elaborately enunciated by the various superintendents in discussing the subject.

" The term Drawing very inadequately expresses the nature of the study it is desirable to have taught in the schools under the name. When the subject was first introduced into the schools, it was very properly called drawing, inasmuch as the work of the pupils consisted principally of drawing from printed copies; and the instruction was devoted mainly to the training of the hand and eye in copying. As the study has developed, however, under the influence of educational methods, the character of the instruction and work of the pupils have entirely changed.

" The study of form, as observed in models of type-forms and in objects, has taken the place of the study of printed copies; and the instruction has been broadened so as to include the cultivation of the observing powers by the study of things on the one hand, and the expressive powers, through drawing and language on the other; Drawing, however, beyond the elementary work, being the principal means used in expressing form-knowledge and its applications.

" Thus it will be seen that Drawing is only a feature in the important study of form; while in the application of form-knowledge, both in education and in practical life, it becomes the principal means for expressing thought. Hence the proper title for the study is form-study and drawing, and not drawing alone."

The syllabus which was adopted by a conference of principals of normal schools and teachers of drawing, with the Hon. A. S. Draper, State Superintendent, is arranged in accordance with the ideas expressed above, and is divided into two parts. The first, or elementary part, is devoted to gaining a knowledge of the properties of forms, from models of type-forms, and from objects based on them. In this division it is intended that the aim shall be to develop the pupils' powers of observation, and to give training in the means of *expressing thought* in regard to form, through *drawing* and *language.*

H 2

In the second division, the study of form in objects is still continued; but it is now the aim of the instruction to give expression to this form-knowledge, and to make application of it, mainly through drawing. In this division the course of study prepares broadly for general education, and for practical life.

The plan is nearly always followed of placing the teaching of drawing of a town or city in the hands of a supervisor, with or without assistants, according to the size of the place. Under the direction of the supervisor, the work is carried out by the ordinary teachers. At stated times, generally one evening a week, or on Saturday mornings, the teachers have to meet at a central school to receive instruction in the work to be taken, and to discuss the progress being made. The supervisor spends his or her (most of the supervisors are ladies) time in going from school to school, giving lessons, and testing progress. The plan appears to work well, and was spoken of as thoroughly satisfactory by all the superintendents whom I questioned on the matter.

Although the general and prevailing principles are the same, each supervisor has her own peculiar ideas; consequently, there is considerable variety to be found in the work from different centres. In one, modelling in clay is prominent; in another, paper-folding and cutting, and modelling in cardboard, is highly valued. Some supervisors prefer books; others will not allow them to be placed in the hands of children, but use either separate sheets of paper, or drawing pads. In one thing all are agreed, viz., in the use of plain paper. *I did not see slates being used for drawing anywhere in the United States*, and only once did I see paper ruled in the small squares so common in Germany in the primary classes. In all the leading States —under every progressive supervisor, in fact, as far as my observation extended—wherever drawing is a special subject, the old plan of commencing to draw straight lines is discarded. The first model studied is the sphere; and a circle, being its representation on paper, is the first figure drawn.

I admitted while in the United States the *educative* value of the course of study taken; but I carefully refrained from expressing an opinion as to its comparative value as *drawing*. After what I saw in Europe, I have now no hesitation in saying that the system I saw followed in Providence, Springfield, Chicago, St. Louis, and many other cities, is the best plan for *elementary schools* which I have seen. With regard to higher work, I as carefully wish it to be understood that I express no opinion any way. I would however remark that my observations appear to indicate that in individual cases—limited, however, by the personal influence of the teacher—other methods will produce much better results as far as power of representation by drawing is concerned.

The features of the plan of form-study and drawing, which appeared to me to be most in its favour as applicable to elementary schools, are :—

1. It can be taught right through the schools by the ordinary teachers, under the guidance of a qualified supervisor.

2. It is distinctly educational, being based on sound psychological principles.

3. It does not stand as a subject by itself, but is in harmony with and can be taught in connection with other studies.

4. It is attractive and popular with the pupils.

5. It produced as good or better average results in freehand and mechanical drawing, as any other system I have seen in general operation.

I believe that not a little of the success which has attended the progress and development of this system of form-study, and drawing, has been due to private business enterprise.   In fact, it is sometimes difficult for an occasional observer to decide whether business or education is the chief aim.   A little inquiry will generally dispel any illusions ; but it is nevertheless true that in America, as well as in England, there are publishing houses (not those who appropriate English copyright) which, while ensuring financial success, touch nothing which has not for its object the progress of the world.

The Prang Educational Company, for instance, is a business concern, and on that account should, strictly, be excluded from these notes ; but it is also an educational factor in the Progressive movement of education, and as such should be noticed.   As a business concern, I presume the wish is to sell as much material as possible ; but in the ordinary way of business they would not do this, because it is only those who make true education their aim in the teaching of drawing, who will use their books.   They have first of all to create a demand, by training teachers who understand the true principles of Progressive education, and, in consequence of the special nature of their training, consider that the Prang method fulfils these conditions.   The system is called Form-Study and Drawing.   Much of it would be termed by English teachers Kindergarten work, or hand and eye training. While it has a special aim in itself, it is interwoven with and cannot be separated from, the rest of the school work. In fact, it is part of a system of education which refuses to be marshalled into regiments and companies, each under its own leader, and capable of individual movement and action.

In its working it is very elastic, allowing great play for the individuality of the teacher, or the peculiar conditions of the locality ; so that, although I found the principles everywhere the same, the practice was modified under each supervisor.

The Company has several systems of Instruction for teachers wishing to introduce a system of Form-Study and Drawing—of course hoping that those thus instructed will bring about a greater use of their material. One of the most successful plans is the " Prang Normal Drawing Class for Home Study and Instruction by Correspondence." The students, scattered all over the country, are supplied with the manuals of study, models, clay, &c., and each week have to work the required number of exercises and forward them to Boston for criticism, together with questions, and so forth. I saw a number of exercises as they came in, and others ready to go out again. They varied in quality, but generally were very good. The plan the Company prefer, however, is for the student to attend the normal class, held in their rooms in Park Street, Boston. I had the pleasure of being present at several of the meetings, and as I had already seen much work under this or kindred systems in various cities, the meetings were more than usually interesting. The students work through the course of study, each one taking her turn as teacher, the remainder acting the part of pupils and performing all the exercises, *answering each question in a complete sentence*, as they are taught to insist on their pupils doing, making each model in clay, fingering the wooden models, drawing on paper and blackboard, acting, in fact, *as if they were children.* This is found even more difficult than conducting the lesson ; but is insisted on by the director of the class, who believes that teachers will only properly understand the steps of the lessons and the difficulties of the children they will have to teach, by actually going through the process themselves, though of course much more quickly.

At the close of each lesson a general discussion takes place. This discussion is a distinctive feature in American education. It is attempted in England and Australia, but not with the success that is reached in America. All know how difficult it is to get pupils to talk and question freely on a lesson ; and a corresponding difficulty is found in dealing with adult students.   In the case of boys and girls, the influence of the old maxim, " Children should be seen and not heard," has not yet departed ; and consequently, in the older country boys and girls are to a greater extent expected to listen to the wise words of their teachers in respectful silence, and " understand these things when they grow older."   One lady started a discussion by asking the question, which she had evidently thought over before :— " Suppose a teacher who has mapped out her work, during a lesson finds that she will either have to assist the pupils more than she thinks is wise, by telling them what they should discover for themselves, or only give part of her lesson. Should she let the pupils take their time, or help them ? "   The result arrived at was :—" Let the child take his time; for if his mind be developed his capacity will increase, and the apparently lost time will be made up later ; whereas, if he be told, his power is weakened. A programme is for the *help* of a teacher, not to be his master."   They did not take into consideration an inspector and the dread of a " result examination," with its efforts at making pupils advance in an unbroken line, like a company of soldiers !

At one meeting the subject of Language Lessons in connection with Form-Study was discussed. I have referred elsewhere to the importance which is attached by American teachers to the need for cultivating the faculty of expressing one's ideas in suitable language, and its influence on the people at large. Every visitor notices the superior conversational powers of the average American over the corresponding Englishman. *This is not due to accident or climatic effect, but is the result of careful training.* The polished eloquence of the exceptional Englishman is unequalled ; but how few really good speakers there are ! The exceptional Englishman is, maybe, superior to the exceptional American; but the average American is a far better speaker than the average Englishman. As the aim of education is to do the best for the greatest number, the superiority of the Americans in this particular, granting the correctness of my observation, is proved; and I do not think that any one who has attended a number of American meetings, either general or political, and is able to compare them with similar assemblies in England, will be likely to disagree. This is not only my own experience, but that of many with whom I have compared notes.

Mr. Clark, the manager of the Institute, in impressing upon the students the great importance of the Language Lesson, stated that American children entering school usually have some two hundred words at their command, although the number is sometimes as great as six hundred. The teachers should carefully note new words used by various children, and use these in the Language Lessons to record and impress them; for when a pupil discovers a word its use is natural and spontaneous, and it is wise to give all the benefit.

At another meeting the same subject came up for discussion in another form. The subject under consideration was the mental development of children. Of course, the old methods of education came in for their usual share of condemnation; and I must digress here to say that it is surely possible to inculcate good ideas of education, without absolutely condemning all other conceptions as more or less incorrect. That they are so considered should, contrariwise, rather teach us that the one just then advocated as infallible may possibly also be less perfect than it seems! It is to some extent a matter of opinion whether "old educators seemed to have no definite ideas as to why they insisted on certain studies; but hoped, like the man who fired at a flock of birds with a scattering gun on the chance that some might be hit, that in some unknown way the child's mind would be developed." I am, I hope justly, considered to be in favour of what is termed "the New Education," because I think that both methods and means of education must change with the continually changing conditions of men and nations. As with any statement of religious ethics, or of philosophy, so with the enunciation of the principles of education. They are true only for the time, condition of thought, and development of the people who make them; and can only be rightly understood in their relation to the conditions under which they existed. But the wiser course is not to condemn the old system, under which the grand and great men in times past grew to be intellectual beacons, and by which we have grown to be what we are prone to consider ourselves—not only the latest, but the greatest and best development of civilisation; but to devote our energies to preventing people from attempting to make them still serve under a new condition of things. Whether that condition is an improvement does not affect the argument. It is the only possible condition until a new one is brought about.

However, having relieved himself and amused his hearers with his short tirade against the old, the president gave one of the nicest little expositions of our new idea of mental development which I have heard. It was not new, but splendidly put. I cannot reproduce it, as his use of the blackboard—one of the strong points of the American teacher—formed one of the most valuable features. Briefly, he argued that the brain receives its stimulus through the senses being aided by the secondary stimulating faculties—memory, imagination, and will; and expresses itself chiefly by two agencies—the tongue and the hand. If information be poured into the brain, it soon becomes surfeited; but set the faculties of expression to work, and a current naturally flows to replace the drain.

The teacher should therefore merely *provide* knowledge ready for assimilation, but place himself on the " expression side " of the child, and draw out ; because what is expressed through language or by the hand must enter by the senses, and be enriched by the secondary agencies—memory, imagination, and will. If mental activity is employed in giving out, there need be no fear but that the assimilating faculties will be suitably employed.

A prominent feature of drawing, as taught in the schools of the United States, is the large amount of blackboard work. It is no uncommon sight to enter a room, and find all the pupils standing round the room drawing on the blackboard. This, of course, is only practicable where the custom is to have continuous boards round the room—a custom, by the way, which I consider worthy of imitation. This practice of blackboard drawing has an important bearing on the power of illustration possessed by American teachers.

CHAPTER V.

THE NEW EDUCATION (*Continued*).

TECHNICAL EDUCATION, ETC.

English Conceptions of Technical Education.— Sloyd.—Liverpool Experiment.—City and Guilds of London Institute Experiment.—Mr. Ricks' Scheme of Hand and Eye Training.—Dublin Experiment.—Manual Training in America.—Definition.—Who shall Teach it?—Account of Various Experiments.—New York City.—Washington, D.C.—Springfield.—The Manual Training School.—Course of Study, St. Louis.—Public Free Manual Training Schools —Industrial Training in Paris.—Course of Study.

SEWING.—Better in England and Australia than in United States.

COOKERY.—How Taught in London.—In United States.—Fittings of a School.—The Washington Experiment.

PEOPLE in England talk as freely of technical education as those in the United States do of manual training. If multitude of speech were associated with clearness of conception, I would omit this chapter, merely referring my reader to the next man he meets who "takes an interest in Education."

Some of the conceptions of technical education prevalent in England may be summarised :—

1. "Technical education is the preparation of young people for some trade or industry." This is consistent and intelligible. Among those who hold this opinion are the supporters of the many excellent technical schools, of which those at Bradford, Manchester, Huddersfield, Stockport, and many others I visited, may be taken as examples, but of which I shall not further speak.

2. Many use the term to mean a certain amount of

science teaching and handiwork in connection with ordinary schools; but especially with secondary schools. To this class, too, belong those who desire the introduction of "technical education" into the public elementary schools, and the majority—although not the *chief advocates*—do so because of the influence they believe it will have on the industries of the country. In fact, it is apparently the exception to find an article written or a speech delivered on the subject without some reference being made to the industrial progress of Germany in consequence of the attention she has paid to "technical education," and the absolute necessity of England taking up the subject vigorously, if she wishes to maintain her position as the premier manufacturing country of the world. I cannot help thinking that many of these would do well to consider, whether it is tool work or head work which has enabled Germany to take the position she has. I think not a little of her progress is due to the fact that, as a rule, she only teaches tool-work as a means of giving an all-round training, leaving the special avocation entirely to look after itself. The toy and lace making of South Germany do not affect my argument. It is not in these that she has affected England. There are not wanting many advocates who, while not forgetting the influence on industries, base their plea for the introduction of tool-work into schools entirely on educational considerations.

3. There is a large class of people whose ideas of technical education are more limited, and who confine the meaning to special day or evening classes in the arts and sciences underlying manufactures, supplementary to apprenticeship in mills or workshops. The German continuation school to a large extent forms the pattern on which these would establish their classes. To a considerable extent the technical schools in manufacturing towns answer this

purpose ; and, perhaps, still more extensively is the end served by the evening classes held throughout England in connection with the Science and Art Department.

4. In addition to these fairly clear conceptions of technical education, there is a large residuum of people who are ever ready to express an opinion on the subject ; but whose thoughts are as obscured as St. Paul's in that most novel of experiences for an Australian—a London fog. They have a hazy indefinable idea that it includes all that I have already indicated, and much besides; that it will make mechanics and factory hands of the whole population, and that it is impracticable, meddling with " natural laws " of supply and demand, and altogether a dangerous thing, to be avoided as revolutionary.

The Technical Instruction Act of 1889 defines : " Technical instruction as instruction in the principles of science and art applicable to industries, and in the application of special branches of science and art to special industries and employments. It does not include teaching the practice of any trade. Subject to this reservation, it is held to embrace all subjects for which grants are made by the Science and Art Department, and any other instruction which the School Board, Town Council, or other local authority which carries out the provision of the Act considers suitable to the circumstances of the district, with the sanction of the Science and Art Department."

A separate definition is given of " Manual Instruction," which is held to include the use of tools, and modelling in clay, wood, or other material.

The progress made in Manual Instruction in England has not been great ; but a number of very interesting experiments have been carried out under different names by various authorities ; but more particularly by enthusiastic and progressive teachers who have been to Sweden to study the system of Slöjd, or Sloyd, at its head-quarters at Nääs.

There are fifteen or more teachers under the London School Board who have been trained at Nääs, and I had the pleasure of seeing some of the results of their enthusiasm in experimenting with classes in their particular schools. In 1889 these teachers held a conference, and presented a report to the School Management Committee of the School Board for London, which is too lengthy for inclusion here, but it may with advantage be summarised.

The aims are :—1. To instil a taste for, and love of work in general. 2. To inspire respect for rough, honest bodily labour. 3. To develop independence and self-reliance. 4. To train to habits of order, exactness, cleanliness, and neatness. 5. To accustom to habits of attention, industry, and perseverance. 6. To train the eye in the sense of form. 7. To promote the harmonious development of the physical powers. 8. To give general dexterity of hand. They discuss the methods, deciding that the " eighty-five exercises " are carefully graded, form a complete analysis of the system, and contain all the principal manipulations used in woodwork. They consider that the system lends itself to an easy and practical application of drawing as taught; but think that the "models" will need revision before finally settling on a course for English schools. At the same time they think " it will be dangerous to alter the Nääs course, which has taken so long to build up, excepting on the results of experiments made by those who are thoroughly alive to its educational principles."

They think the pupils should be boys, beginning the work between the ages of ten and twelve years; that the classes should not exceed twenty pupils to a teacher ; and that there should be at least one lesson of two hours each week.

The professional teacher is considered the best instructor, and that artizans as manual training instructors are failures, lacking aptitude for teaching.

I cannot even mention all the experiments I inquired into, deeming it preferable to speak in greater detail of one or two. The Liverpool branch of the National Association for Promoting Technical Instruction conducted an extensive experiment, in which a large number of teachers assisted. The exercises taken were wood-carving and fret-work, and the experiment was considered of sufficient range to permit of generalising from the results obtained. The leader in the matter was Professor Hele Shaw, of the Walker Engineering College, who is an enthusiastic advocate of the educational value of manual training.

At the close of a lecture given before a large attendance of the members of the Liverpool Teachers' Guild, Professor Strong occupying the chair, it was resolved, on the motion of Mr. Shaw, that, accepting the definition of technical instruction given in the Technical Instruction Act—

" 1. Technical instruction should not be given as part of the curriculum of elementary schools ; but that the teaching of science, and manual instruction (combined with cookery and laundry work for girls) should form part of the instruction of all elementary schools.

" 2. That 'Kindergarten Work' should be introduced into all elementary schools.

" 3. That *Trade Schools* should not be established at the expense of the State or municipality.

" 4. That every facility should be offered for obtaining instruction of all kinds after ordinary school hours for the lowest fees ; and that boys and girls below a certain age should be encouraged by a judicious system of rewards to attend voluntary classes after leaving school."

I have quoted these resolutions in full, because I consider that they express the views of a much wider constituency than the important guild which adopted them.

An extensive experiment is in operation under the joint

management of the City and Guilds of London Institute and the School Board for London, the former body finding the money, the latter the accommodation and pupils. Six centres have been fitted up, and the instruction placed under the direction of two trained masters, and two practical mechanics as assistants. The instructors were carefully selected, the teachers having a knowledge of tools as well as being fond of using them, the carpenters having apparently an aptitude for teaching. Selected boys from schools within a radius of about a mile from a centre, spend one morning or afternoon a week at the manual instruction room.

I attended some of the classes, and was quite satisfied that if the lessons I saw given were fair specimens, the work is decidedly educational. On the walls of the work-rooms are hung German lithographic pictures of the most useful timber trees, and some excellent manual training diagrams, published by Messrs. Cassell & Company. Each class contains from twenty-four to thirty pupils, who are accommodated at large benches, six or more boys being at one bench. There is a set of smaller tools for each boy, and a few sets of larger tools for common use.

The committee, in their syllabus, state as general principles :—1. The aim must be educational rather than industrial. 2. The scholars must be given an intelligent knowledge of the principles which underlie their work. 3. Working drawings to scale of every exercise must be made. 4. All bench work must be done to exact measurement, and every piece of wood be correctly lined before being cut or planed. The simple instruments, try square, rule, and compass are used, and the drawings are made in isometric projection.

In the Vittoria Place centre I watched a demonstration lesson on the "Bridle joint." The principle was first explained by means of models, and a free use of the blackboard.

I

The way the demonstrator handled his subject proved him
to be an adept in the art of teaching. When the boys
understood the new principle involved in the new exercise,
in its relation to what they had already done, he proved
himself to be equally, at home with his tools, and very
quickly made the joint he had explained and drawn, the
whole time keeping up a running series of comments and
questions upon the work. Previous to his engagement by
the joint committee, this teacher had been a carpenter and
joiner, but had qualified himself for teaching under the
Science and Art Department by attending evening classes.
With a supply of such men, the question of manual instruction would be solved. I saw other men teaching equally
well, particularly at Brighton and Manchester.

I think the latest, most complete, and most extensive
experiment in manual instruction for the elementary schools
has been conducted by Mr. George Ricks, B.Sc., the Senior
Inspector under the London School Board. After conducting a number of experimental classes, he formulated a
comprehensive scheme, or series of schemes, which have
been published by Messrs. Cassell & Company in two
handsome fully-illustrated volumes, under the title of
" Hand and Eye Training."

Mr. Ricks is well known as the author of a number of
works on practical teaching, his methods being always
educational. If the teacher will not go to the trouble to
work out his own lessons, let him by all means have books
in which the methods are sound. In his books, Mr. Ricks,
leaving the more general discussion of the science of
pedagogy for others, endeavours to show the teacher,
—anxious to do more than earn a grant—how to put into
practice the soundest of the principles theoretically discussed by others.

The following summary, taken from the Introduction
to " Hand and Eye Training," shows the scope of Mr.

Ricks' scheme, which has been adopted by the Bristol and other School Boards, and is being introduced gradually, under his supervision, into all the London Board Schools.

SUMMARY OF SCHEME OF HAND AND EYE TRAINING.

By MR. GEO. RICKS, B.Sc.,

Senior Inspector of Schools under the London School Board. (Taken from his work on the subject, published by Messrs Cassell & Co.)

For Children from 7 to 10 Years of Age.

1. Paper-Folding, Cutting, and Mounting (First Series).
2. Drawing, Cutting, and Mounting.
3. Building with Kindergarten Bricks, Cubes, &c., and Drawing the Plans and Elevations of structures built.
4. Clay-Modelling.
5. Drawing and Coloring.

For Pupils from 10 to 14 Years.

6. Drawing and Coloring to be continued.
7. Clay-Modelling for those showing special aptitude.
8. Paper-Folding, Cutting, Mounting ; Designing in Form and Color (Series II.).
9. Drawing and Cutting Geometric Forms, &c.
10. Modelling in Cardboard, &c.
11. Bench-work in wood.

Note.—It is not intended that *all* this should be taken in the same school ; but that one or two courses should be selected most suitable to special needs.

I spent several very interesting days in the Dublin Schools. I cannot say that I learnt much likely to prove of value elsewhere, for what is suitable in one place is not so in another ; and the conditions under which the Irish teacher labours do not exist elsewhere. The schools of Dublin are worth visiting, if only to see the happy Irish nature show itself in school. The boys' department of the model practising school of the National Training College consists of a very large room, with several class-rooms opening from it.   The large room has seats in the middle and open spaces at each side, where the pupils stand round their teachers in groups.   Each teacher stands with a long cane in his hand, and the noisy din of the school is frequently interrupted by the sound of the forcible contact between the shoulders of some boy and the cane.   A boy makes a mistake, forgets his turn or does not pay attention, and down goes the cane. The utmost good-nature prevails ; a teacher soundly scolds and thrashes a boy one minute, and the next joins in the hearty laugh of the class at some outburst of the native wit of the boy who was thrashed.   The elder boys have manual instruction in a roughly fitted-up shop in the playground. The class is conducted by an assistant master of the school, who has a taste for carpentry.   The boys buy the wood and make what they choose ; or, as often happens, cut up the wood in attempts at making what they would like. They call it Slöjd work, and " enjoy the time spent in the shop better than that in the playground."   After what I saw, I should prefer to say they enjoy playing with tools better than at football.   Of the educational value I will not express an opinion.

I spent an hour in the same shop watching the Training College students at their manual training work ; or, as it is called, the wood-working department.   The men spend three hours a fortnight at the work.   The classes consist of from eight to fourteen students, and are conducted by a practical mechanic.   The object is to qualify teachers for doing any odd job about a school : "to mend an easel, solder a gutter, glaze a window, patch up a desk, fix up a hat-rack, put on a hinge, repair a roof, or any other repairs which may be needed about a school where a tradesman is not available."

The male students of the Training College also have lessons in farming, and have to attend a course of practical instruction at the excellent model farms at Glasnevin, so that they may give instruction in practical farming on the small farms found in connection with many of the Irish country schools.

The female students, in the same way and for the same purpose, have instruction in dairy-work. These efforts at making the National Schools a means of raising the character of the agriculture of the country by introducing improved methods of farming and dairy-work are in the highest degree commendable, and I think likely to be very beneficial.

Besides dairy-work, the female students all take lessons in cookery, and the results of their experiments appear on the college table.

Manual Training in America.

The visitor to the United States hears comparatively little about technical education. When the terms technical and technological are used, it is in connection with advanced schools for mechanical engineering, architecture, chemistry, or other branches of applied science. The most noted of these is the Massachusetts Institute of Technology at Boston, which claims to have been the first of its kind to establish physical laboratories for the proper teaching of natural philosophy. It was the first to adopt the Russian system of training in practical mechanics, from which have developed the Manual Training Schools so common in the United States. The nearest equivalent to these schools in England is the Technical School in Finsbury, under the City and Guilds of London Institute; though this institution differs very greatly from an American " Manual Training School."

The term industrial school is used to designate schools with a most confusing variety of objects, from a reformatory to a trade school; but to these I will not refer.

"Technical Education," in the opinion of many, is to save the industries of England; "Manual Training" is advocated in the United States with as much enthusiasm, and frequently with as little regard for the proper balance of a perfect education ; but from a different standpoint.   "Put the whole boy to school" was a very happy expression made use of by Dr. Woodward, the apostle of the Manual Training movement, in seeking to have it recognised in its proper place as a part of a related whole, not as an appendix tacked on to the usual school course.   But many talk as though "the whole boy" consisted of the manipulative powers of the hands.   They cannot hold more than one idea at a time, and as Manual Training has been embraced, they can consider nothing else.   I think, however, that the definition adopted by the New Jersey Committee on Manual Training, and which is due to Dr. N. Murray Butler, fairly expresses the idea of the great majority of advocates in the United States.   *"Manual Training is training in Thought Expression by other means than gesture and verbal language, in such a carefully graded course of study as shall also provide adequate training for the judgment and the executive faculty.*   This training will necessarily include drawing and constructive work ; but experience alone can determine by what special means this instruction may best be given."

So far as the Secondary or High Schools are concerned, the second portion of the definition is now superfluous.   It appears to be generally admitted by progressive men that the St. Louis, Toledo, Cleveland, Chicago, Baltimore, Philadelphia, and similar Manual Training Schools, solve the problem of what the Secondary School adapted to the requirements of the present day should be ; but discussion still continues in unabated vigour over the introduction of Manual Training into the Grammar and Intermediate Grades.   The proposition that Manual Training is necessary in order to make the curriculum of the school complete, appears to be admitted as proved, but of what it shall consist and who shall teach it, are still debatable points.

Of course, there are teachers who are firmly anchored to the past; who, living in the midst of progress, are quite oblivious to it, and unconscious of the prevalence of new ideas. I occasionally found teachers, who, when asked whether any experiments in Manual Training were being tried in their schools, replied—"Oh, yes; we have calisthenics, and musical drill." On one occasion, a principal, after reading my card of introduction, and welcoming me with characteristic American urbanity, said—"I see you are particularly interested in Manual Training; as there is a class at the work now, perhaps you would like to see it." I accompanied him to the playground in the basement, and found a fine class of boys going through a series of dumb-bell and other physical exercises! It is only fair to add that such teachers are exceptional, as was the English teacher who was surprised at finding a native-born Australian white.

A man cannot teach what he does not know; but because he knows, it does not follow that he can teach. Hence the difficulty in regard to Manual Training. A man may be a first-class mechanic, but the school has no use for him unless he be a skilful teacher. Unless the instructor can control boys, and understands the pedagogical principles governing the presentation of facts—or, what is the same thing, has that intuitive power possessed by a few people of presenting a fact in the precise way most intelligible to the uninitiated—his ability to perform all operations with tools is useless in the school, where it is the making, not the thing to be made, which is to be the dominating idea. It is not the less true, that the mere understanding of the principles involved is not sufficient. Manual Training becomes an education, only in the hands of such teachers as the one I have spoken of in connection with the Vittoria Place experiment, when teaching ability and executive skill are properly combined. If a choice has to be made, however, it is better to have a good teacher with poor manipulative power, than a good mechanic, but a bad teacher.

After all, those who have more faith in Manual Training, than in history and grammar, as a means of making education more complete than it has been, must not look to manual training, but to the teachers. Systems are merely the skeletons upon which the teacher builds the shapely, rounded forms of beauty; and, breathing into them the breath of life, they become educative because he is in them.

Did we but recognise it, pedagogy is the noblest of professions, and the teacher is the greatest of artists. The sculptor fashions marble, the teacher children's minds; the painter with consummate art transfers to canvas ideals of beauty which become the treasures of nations, the shrines of art at which all worship; but the teacher, working on surface more delicate than photographer's plate, may imprint pictures of ideal manhood on noble souls, which may prove the regenerating influences of the world. The musician wakens strings to life, the teacher ideas: the one thrills the crowd, the other quietly sets thoughts vibrating which, thrilling through the human soul, shall roll on through the ascending ages in ever widening circles, and time only can show the end, the good God their value.

Such teachers may not be, frequently are not, in schools. A school hedged round with regulations, is no place for many men, and should not be for children. A man with vigour of purpose must not be hemmed in and hampered with regulations. To do so is as purposeless as to chain up a locomotive with the steam on—whatever happens, the desired result is not attained. This is good theory: at present not fully practicable.

I saw many good and successful experiments; but there is a very great difference between an experiment, carried out by a competent enthusiastic conductor, and the ordinary conditions, where funds may be ill-supplied, and those with whom success or failure rests indifferent. It is only when an experiment is carried out on a sufficiently extensive scale, and under normal conditions, that it becomes valuable. I consider the Manual Instruction experiments in Washington and New York cities are most in accord with these conditions.

In New York City a system of form-study and drawing similar to those I have described is in operation. To this —which includes clay-modelling, paper-folding, making models in paper and cardboard—is added a series of wood-working exercises, selected from different systems being tried elsewhere. The whole of the work is done in the school. A few workshops have been fitted up; but I believe that there has been opposition to this, not only on account of the expense, but because it is supposed to partake of the nature of trade teaching. By the time this will be published, I understand the earlier stages will have been established throughout all the schools. With regard to the work itself, I will say little. What I saw was being dealt with—as, indeed, most of the work in New York appeared to be—in much too mechanical a manner; it was the nearest approach to the English preparation for examination which I saw. New York city claims to have the most perfect system in the States. I will not dispute the superintendent's word; but I have not always found that education and "system" go together, although there must be system in education. At all events, it is not wise on the part of a visitor to allow himself to form conclusions concerning the schools of the United States from what he sees in New York city. The teachers have not the freedom they have elsewhere.

The plan adopted in Washington, D.C., differs considerably from that of New York. Prang's system of form-study and drawing has been in operation for some years. This, of course, includes clay-modelling, paper-folding and cutting, and such exercises. Complementary to this, the authorities have instituted a series of wood-working exercises similar to those being tried by the City and Guilds of London Institute in conjunction with the School Board.

The system of establishing "centres" has been adopted. The first vote was small, and was entirely spent in providing tools and appliances. As in the case of the kitchens, any available rooms have been utilised for workshops. They are not always the best adapted to their purpose; but as the work is said to succeed under present conditions, it would be the more certain to do so if it were taken in suitable rooms adjoining the schools. In two districts, all the pupils of the seventh and eighth grades take the work; in the remaining portions of the city about seven-eighths of the senior grammar grades take manual training, it being at present voluntary. This I consider a strong argument, and worth more than the assurance of many principles. The classes are conducted by practical mechanics, and vary in size from twelve to twenty, according to the accommodation. Each class has two hours' work, and the conductor takes three classes a day. When the manual training comes after or before school work, fifteen minutes are allowed for the pupils to pass from the shop to the schools, which are not in any case more than from half to two-thirds of a mile away.

For the High School pupils special shops have been provided, one fitted with benches and wood-working tools, and one with six forges, eight wood-turning lathes, three engine lathes, vices and tools complete, the motive power being provided by an eight horse-power engine. The first year High School pupils take wood-turning and pattern-making (they have had simple wood-working in the grammar school). The second year pupils have forging and a little moulding, while the third year pupils take machine tool-work.

I asked Dr. Lane, principal of the splendid High School, in which were some fifteen hundred pupils: "After the experience you have had with reference to this matter, and the comparisons you have been able to make between the lads who take manual work and those who do not, what effect, if any, do you consider the manual work has on the literary? Does the fact of their having to be out of the school for so much time each week, engaged in an entire change of occupation, by distracting their attention and decreasing the time to be devoted to academic work, cause the latter to suffer?"

"No. I consider it is a decided help to them. They come back as though they have had so much physical exercise together with mental stimulus. The exercise does not tire—it refreshes. It is optional with pupils whether they take the manual course; but if they elect to do so, they must continue, unless excused for some special reason. About forty per cent. of pupils take manual training."

In a number of cities and towns shop-work, or manual instruction, has been introduced into the High Schools in much the same way as at Washington. The school committee of Springfield, Massachusetts, for example, have incorporated three years' course of manual work into their High School with excellent results. They are also experimenting upon a plan for placing tool-work into the Grammar grades. Their system of form-study and drawing does not differ from those described elsewhere; in fact, Prang's books and models are used to some extent; but the enthusiasm of the supervisor has made it one of the most complete I examined. The supervisor of drawing and director of manual training, with the aid of the superintendent and several liberal citizens, are endeavouring to add to the form-study a graduated series of exercises in wood, suitable for all ages, and which can be introduced into all schools without fresh buildings, or any great outlay. The work I saw being done was interesting, but it is too early to offer an opinion as to present success.

Very many towns are experimenting in the same way, and I have no doubt but that a visitor a few years hence will see tool-work an ordinary adjunct to every grammar school.

The Manual Training School.

I have spoken of the Kindergarten; of the splendid systems of Form-Study and drawing which in a great measure correspond with several series of work in Mr. Ricks' excellent system of Hand and Eye Training; of the efforts to add to this tool-work in the grammar grades, and of the addition of shop-work to an ordinary High School. It now remains to give a brief account of the Manual Training School proper. Had I dealt with the question historically, I should have had to discuss the Manual Training School after the Kindergarten, for in the evolution of the complete system of manual instruction the Kindergarten came first, the Manual Training School second, and both have been pursuing their ever-widening spheres of useful work; while in pedagogic circles, and to a certain extent among the public, the educational mind has been disturbed and otherwise beneficially excited over the problem how to connect the Kindergarten with the Manual Training School.

The first Manual Training School was established through the liberality of several wealthy citizens of St. Louis, as a department of the Washington University of St. Louis. Dr. C. M. Woodward, the present director, is responsible for the name, and for much of the success of the school. From the beginning all have insisted that the incorporation of workshops is purely for educational purposes, and does not tend more to prejudice a pupil to a mechanical occupation than the study of Latin does to make him a lawyer or doctor. "Put the whole boy to school" is a saying of Dr. Woodward's which has assumed crystalline form, and is heard through the length and breadth of the United States.

The school has an endowment of thirty thousand pounds, which provides scholarships for seventy pupils; in addition to which, there are upwards of two hundred who pay from thirteen to twenty-four pounds sterling a year for tuition.

The motto of the school is, "*The Cultured Mind, the Skilful Hand;*" and it may be interesting to quote a few sentences from Dr. Woodward's account of the school in his work on Manual Training :—

"The business man may be narrow, but so may the scholar; and, in either case, the narrowness results not so much from the necessities of the case as from the character of the man."

"Hitherto, men who have cultivated their minds have neglected their hands, and those who have laboured with their hands have found no opportunity to cultivate their brains."

"No attempt is made to cultivate dexterity at the expense of thought. An exercise with tools or books is valuable only in proportion to the demand it makes on the mind for intelligent, thoughtful work. In the school shops the stage of mechanical habit is never reached. The only habit actually acquired is that of thinking. No blow is struck, no line drawn, no motion regulated from muscular habit. Such a limited training cannot, of course, produce a high degree of manual skill."

Nevertheless, I saw some cart-loads of really accurate work done in the ordinary exercises.

As a rule, pupils are at least fourteen years of age on admission, and must have graduated from a grammar school, or be able to pass an equivalent examination. The course of study extends over three years; and, as it is fairly typical of very many schools which have been established on the model of the St. Louis School, I will insert an outline of the study.

ST. LOUIS MANUAL TRAINING SCHOOL.

COURSE OF STUDY.

First Year.

Algebra, to Equations.   Arithmetic, completed.
English Language, its Structure and Use.   History of the United
    · States.
Latin Grammar and Reader may be taken in place of English.
American Classics.
Zoology.   Physical Geography.   Botany.
Drawing, Mechanical and Freehand, from objects.   Penmanship.
Tool-work—Joinery.   Wood-carving.   Wood-turning.

Second Year.

Algebra, through Quadratics and Radicals.   Geometry begun.
Chemistry.   Experimental Work in the Chemical Laboratory.
English Composition and Literature.   Rhetoric.   English History.
Latin (Cæsar) may be taken in place of Rhetoric and History.
British Classics.
Drawing—Line-shading, and Tinting, Development of Surfaces, Free-
    hand Detail Drawing, Isometric Projections.
Tool-work—Forging: Drawing, Upsetting, Bending, Punching, Weld-
    ing, Tempering; Pattern-making, Moulding, Casting with Plaster,
    Soldering, and Brazing.

Third Year.

Geometry continued through Plane and Solid; Reviews in Mathematics,
    Mensuration.
English Composition and Literature.

Political Economy. General History.

French or German may be taken in place of English and History, or in place of the Science Study.

Physiology. Elements of Physics. Students who have taken Latin, and who intend to enter the Polytechnic School after completing the course in this School, will take History in the place of Physiology.

Book-keeping.

Drawing—Brush-Shading, Geometrical Machine and Architectural Drawing.

Tool-work—Metal work with hand and machine tools ; Filing, Chipping, Fitting, Turning, Drilling, Planing, Screw-cutting, &c. Execution of projects.

THE DAILY PROGRAMME.

The Daily Session begins at 9 a.m. and closes at 3.30 p.m., thirty minutes being allowed for lunch. Four hours per day are devoted to recitations, study, and drawing, and two hours are given to tool instruction and shop work.

Owing to the decided success of the St. Louis School, several others were established on the same lines and in the same way : that is, by private subscription. These schools, like the parent establishment, charged fees to all but those holding scholarships. The great fundamental principle of American education, however, is that it must be free ; and it only required to be thoroughly demonstrated that the Manual Training School was a requirement of the age, to cause several of the progressive School Boards to establish free Manual Training Schools as part of the public school system. Philadelphia, Baltimore, and Toledo are examples. These may be termed Manual Training High Schools. I have already shown how other Boards have dealt with the matter.

Industrial Training in Paris.

Although I have a quantity of material, it is not my intention to write more than a few lines on manual instruction, or industrial training, in the schools of Paris. To do more than simply refer to the extensive nature of the work would require a volume to itself. Nowhere has so much been done towards a general introduction of tool-work into elementary schools; and nowhere did I see such an abundance of excellent work.

The object of the schools is to specially fit the pupils for particular callings. To this end different districts have their special trade schools, to which pupils may be transferred after completing the elementary school course. For example, in the quarter of the city devoted to cabinet-making I visited an apprenticeship school where the literary work of the pupils was still further advanced; but most of the time was devoted to learning the trade of cabinet-maker. In other districts are numerous schools devoted to other trades.

The following programme of Manual Training for the Primary Schools of Paris will indicate the comprehensive character of the work :—

Special Equipment to carry out Full Course :—

1. WOODWORK SHOP.—Eight to 12 benches about 4 ft. 6 in. long, 2 ft. 6 in. wide, and 30 to 34 inches high (each bench accommodates two boys) ; four turning lathes ; suitable tools.

2. WORKSHOP FOR IRON.—Eight to 12 vices, forge, anvil, and ordinary tools.

The following is the programme worked out by the School authorities for Manual Training in Primary Schools :—

Manual Exercises intended to develop the children's skill of hand.

I. ELEMENTARY CLASS.

In operation in nearly all the Schools. Work done in ordinary Class-rooms.

[Seven and eight years old. One hour per day.]

Elementary Exercises in Freehand Drawing, Symmetrical arrangement of Forms, Cutting out pieces of Colored Paper and applying them upon Geometrical Forms, Exercises in Coloring, Cutting out Geometrical Forms in Cardboard, Representations of Geometrical Solids. All these exercises to be done first on squared and subsequently on plain paper.

Small Basket Work. Arrangement of strips of Colored Paper : (1) In Interwoven Forms. (2) In plaited Patterns.

Modelling ; Reproductions of Geometric Solids and Simple Objects.

II. INTERMEDIATE CLASS.

Chiefly performed in Class-rooms. Not so general as I.

[Nine and ten years old. One hour per day.]

Cutting out Cardboard Patterns, Construction of Regular Geometric Solids, Construction by the Pupils of Cardboard Models covered with Colored Drawings or Colored Paper.

Small Basket Work ; Combination of Plaits ; Basket Making.

Objects made of Wire ; Trellis or Netting ; Wire Chain Making.

Combination of Iron and Wood : Cages.

Modelling Simple Architectural Ornaments.

Object Lessons : Principal Characteristics of Wood and the Common Metals.

III. UPPER CLASS.

In operation in about one-third of the Boys' Primary Schools.

[Eleven and twelve years old. Two hours per day.]

Drawing and Modelling ; Continuation of the exercises in the preceding Class ; Repetition of the Ornaments previously executed, in the form of Sketches, with dimensions attached to them ; Drawing the requisite Sections for this purpose ; Reproducing the Sections as Measured Sketches ; Study of the various Tools used in working Wood—Hammer, Mallet, Chisel, Gimlet, Centre-bit, Brace, Screwdriver, Compasses, Square, Marking-gauge, Saws of different kinds, Jack-plane, Trying-plane, Smoothing-plane, Files and Rasps, Level.

Theoretical and Practical Lessons in the above.

Planing and Sawing Wood ; Construction of Simple Joints.

Boxes Nailed together, or Jointed without Tacks.

Wood Lathe ; Tools used in Turning ; Turning Simple Geometrical Forms.

Study of the Tools used in Working Iron—Hammer, Chisel, Cutting-tool, Cold Chisel, Squares, Compass, Files, &c.

J

Theoretical and Practical Lessons concerning them.
Exercises in Filing, Smoothing, and Finishing Rough Forgings or
Castings (Cubes, Polygonal Nuts).

———

The Practical Work in the Shops in Primary Schools is to be followed
by Gymnastic Exercises, in accordance with the Specialised Programme.

Sewing.

Sewing is better and more extensively taught in England
than in America. Needlework is a compulsory subject
throughout the country, being taught by the ordinary
teachers. The same applies to the Australian public
schools, where the sewing, like that of England, is, as a
rule, of excellent character.

Where sewing is taught in the United States it is usually
of a much more elementary character, and is generally
taught by special teachers.

Much attention is paid to sewing in Australia, the instruction being usually given by the regular teachers. It is
a matter of opinion whether the work of the English or
Australian girls is the more praiseworthy.

Cookery in England.

I consider that the teaching of cooking is much more
general in England than in the United States. I know of
no large town or city in the Union where all the girls or the
higher grammar grades are taught; but in the London
Board Schools, all girls over eleven years of age, without
regard to standard; and all girls in Standard IV. and upwards, who are ten years of age, are required to attend each
year at least twenty out of a course of twenty-two lessons
in practical cookery at one of the centres. The plan
followed is to build cookery class-rooms, technically called
" Centres," in the playgrounds of suitable Schools, in which

pupils from all Schools within a convenient distance from the "Centre" may receive instruction. There are now nearly seventy centres, while others are in course of construction.

A "Centre" consists of (1) a stepped class-room, about twenty-one feet by eighteen feet, containing a demonstration counter, a gas-stove, a kitchener, an open-range stove, a dresser, and necessary appliances for teaching plain cookery; (2) a scullery; (3) a cloak-room; (4) a lavatory. A class consists of thirty pupils. The work is carried on by three superintendents, and fifty-eight instructors. Four courses of lessons are given during the year. Children who do not attend Board Schools are allowed to attend the classes on payment of four shillings for a course of twenty-two lessons. Nearly twenty-four thousand pupils receive instruction in a year. The dishes made are sold to teachers, and children for lunch.

The fittings of the centres are, in common with the school fittings in England, plain and strong, with little attempt at elegance. [The education of the perceptions of the beautiful is much neglected in England. Strength and durability are all very well, but beauty should not be neglected. The Frenchman and Italian cannot help being more artistic : he is surrounded by forms of beauty.]

In Liverpool, each school has a room provided with a gas-stove, a kitchen-range, and a dresser with appliances, and the instructor visits from one school to another.

Cookery in the United States.

Where cooking is taught to pupils of the public schools of the United States, the cookery schools are usually fitted up with characteristic provision for convenience and comfort. One lesson taught—and there is no doubt but that it is well taught—is that a kitchen need not be an ugly place. In

J 2

no city or town I visited did I find the subject taught on a comprehensive scale, as in London, Liverpool, and other English cities. More is taught in a superior manner, to a selected number of pupils. In a few towns—Washington, for example—it is taken by the majority of the girls in the two upper grades of the grammar school. In Philadelphia I only found one cookery school—a very elaborate one—in which some two hundred pupils, selected from the grammar schools near, receive lessons. A school of six hundred pupils will send twenty pupils, those being chosen who can best afford time from other work. This has proved so successful that it is intended to make the teaching general, and no doubt the thoroughness which has characterised the rest of Superintendent MacAlister's work will be applied to this subject. All the normal students have had lessons in cooking for some years past.

In fitting up a cookery school, provision is nearly always made for each pupil, or, failing that, for every two pupils to have a small gas-stove, on which all operations involving only boiling, frying, and stewing can be performed. The classes, I believe, never exceed twenty, and I only found that number once. Sixteen is the usual number, and two are always occupied as " kitchen-maids for the day," to wash, scour, scrub, and generally do the work which, in the London " centres," is done by paid help. The position of " kitchen-maid " is a popular one ; the girls are always ready to take their turns, and the tidy and the slovenly house-keeper foreshadows herself in her work on these occasions. The teachers were fairly unanimous in the opinion that fourteen pupils were as many as could be properly looked after in practical work. In this they agree with English teachers of the subject ; for although the classes in London consist of thirty pupils, the work is so arranged that only half that number do practical work at once. The order of procedure was stated to be :—First, a demonstration by the teacher; second, one-half of the class take notes, while the other half have forty minutes' practice; third, the sections change places.

A similar plan is followed in New York city; but in other places the classes are kept down to the number to be accommodated at practice work. Two arrangements of demonstration tables are used. The first consists of a long horse-shoe-shaped counter, with fourteen or sixteen gas-stoves, and places for the same number of sets of kneading and mixing boards and necessary appliances. The teacher's table is placed between the "heels" of the counter. The cooking-range for general work is placed at the side of the room, round which are placed the dressers, with such utensils as are only occasionally used, supplies, and so forth. A cabinet of specimens of the common articles of food and special articles used in cooking is not unfrequently included among the appliances. The plan most preferred is to have a number of small tables to accommodate two or four pupils, instead of the long counter; otherwise, the fittings are the same.

In Washington, D.C., the plan of establishing "centres" has been adopted, and about five-sixths of the seventh and eighth grade girls of the grammar schools, and the majority of the high school girls, take the lessons. The following syllabus of the work for the grammar schools will illustrate the mode of dealing with the subject generally followed in the United States :—

COURSE IN COOKING OF THE WASHINGTON (D.C.) SCHOOLS.

First Year (Seventh Grade).

BOILING: A.—Talk about Cooking, to discover what it is, how it affects food materials, and what is needful for Cooking ; heat—natural and artificial ; fuel—wood, charcoal, coal, gas ; give directions for making a fire and make one.

Teach boiling by means of experiments : (*a*) Heat a cup of

water, noting the change in temperature from time to time ; note simmering and boiling. (*b*) Compare, by boiling, fresh and salt water with respect to density ; experiment with eggs and blocks of wood ; discover that it takes longer to boil salt water than it does to boil fresh water. (*c*) Put a piece of fresh meat into boiling water for a short time ; note the result to meat and water ; cut the meat and note the result ; show the effect to meat and water of cold water on meat (this requires some time) ; cut the meat and note the result ; boil the water. (*d*) Break an egg into boiling water and another into cold water ; note the results ; boil the cold water with the egg ; draw inferences ; hot water hardens albumen ; to retain the nutriment in the article boiled, put the article into boiling water and boil ; to have nutriment mix with the water, put the article into cold water and boil. (*e*) Make beef tea ; have the meat prepared for the first class, after which let each class prepare meat for the succeed-ing one.

Boil meat to prepare the same for food. Boil meat for broth. Make jellied soup stock. Teach which parts of meat (beef, mutton, and lamb) are used for soups. Show economy of making stock. Teach the pupils how to distinguish between fresh and stale meats (appearance, smell, &c.). Poach eggs.

B.—Experiment with salted and smoked meats : Put salted meat into cold water ; then show that the water is salty by tast-ing it and by testing its density. Whence comes the salt, what it is, where found, how prepared for market.

C.—Experiment with starch and flour : (*a*) Cut a potato into thin slices and soak it in cold water. Pour off the water ; show that starch is a fine powder found in grains and vege-tables ; show starch cells in potato—microscope. (*b*) Pour cold water over some starch, mix, and let it stand for a short time ; stir again and pour on boiling water ; stir and note the result. (*c*) Pour boiling water over dry starch ; stir and note the result. (*d*) Make like experiments with flour ; draw conclusions. (*e*) Dip a potato into boiling water ; note the result. (*f*) Pour boiling water over oatmeal ; note the result ; draw conclusion.

Make Blanc Mange. Corn-starch ; from what and how obtained, how prepared, substitutes. Make a Roux ; plain, egg, and caper sauces. Boil rice and potatoes and mash ; boil beets, onions, and squash. Give directions for preparing and cooking other vegetables. Make either vegetable soup or celery purée. Boil oatmeal (cracked wheat, cerealine). Boil rice and make rice custard. Boil coffee and cocoa, steep tea. Coffee, cocoa, tea; from what and how obtained; properties and value of each.

D.—Utensils used in boiling. An intelligent study of the materials from which the utensils are made.

STEWING.—Experiment with tough meat and vegetable acids, such as lemon-juice and vinegar. Compare tender and tough meat before and after soaking in the acid. Show where in the animal tough pieces of meat are found. Explain why they contain so much nutriment, and show their value as food. Make a beef stew. Make an Irish stew without dumplings. Braise a calf's heart, or smother a piece of beef. Haricot mutton. Stew fruit (apples, prunes, &c.). Make " bubble and squeak." Pepper, butter, substitute, from what and how obtained ; use and value in cooking.

BROILING.—Broil a steak (beef or veal) : (*a*) Compare results obtained with those obtained by putting meat into boiling water. (*b*) Names and positions of best steaks. Broil chops, mutton, lamb, or pork : (*a*) Positions of chops. (*b*) Lard and oleomargarine ; from what and how made ; use, value, how to select different kinds of meat by appearance ; toast bread ; utensils used in broiling.

BAKING.—Experiment with yeast, soda, cream of tartar, sour milk, and baking powder : (*a*) Mix soda and cream of tartar with cold water ; show the presence of carbonic acid gas (lighted taper). (*b*) Pour water over baking powder ; show the presence of gas. (*c*) Mix soda with sour milk ; show the presence of gas and that the milk is sweet. (*d*) Mix baking powder or soda and cream of tartar with flour ; moisten and make a dough ; put one-half into a hot oven immediately ; allow the other half to remain exposed to the air for a short time, then put it into the oven ; note the difference ; cause of difference ; draw conclusions. (*e*) Make yeast ; talk about the yeast plant or germ ; from what and how obtained ; proper temperature necessary to the growth ; what is caused by the growing ; fermentation—microscope ; show presence of carbonic acid gas in yeast ; mix yeast with a little flour and note the result.

Make white bread and rolls with potato yeast : (*a*) Kneading, length of time, motion, &c. (*b*) Compressed yeast. (*c*) Flour ; from what and how obtained ; kinds ; properties and value of each ; processes ; make biscuits (baking powder) ; make muffins (soda and cream of tartar) ; make corn-bread (soda and sour milk) ; make Graham gems.

Roast meat : (*a*) Compare the appearance of roast meat with boiled meat. (*b*) Best pieces for roasting. (*c*) Basting. (*d*) Solid and rolled roasts. Give, incidentally, the arrangement of oven dampers ; kind of fire necessary for baking, and proper temperature of the oven.

Second Year (Eighth Grade).

BOILING.—Review facts learned about boiling, and obtain a definition. Boil mutton : (*a*) for the broth, (*b*) for the meat ; make caper sauce. Boil fish ; make egg sauce. [Note.—Give directions for selecting and cleaning fish.] Raising, slaughtering of animals, and packing of meat ; means of preserving ; principal cities for this industry ; markets. Boil corned beef and cabbage ; boil cauliflower ; make egg sauce ; make apple dumplings and sugar sauce ; make roly-poly pudding and sauce ; make soft custard ; make salad dressing ; make potato salad.

STEWING : Oysters : (*a*) stewed, (*b*) scalloped ; chowder ; make a fricasse of beef, or stew beef with carrots ; make a white stew and a pot-pie.

BROILING : Broil a shad, a herring, or any other fresh fish. Broil a salted mackerel, or any other salted fish. Broil a smoked fish. Broil a slice of ham. Broil oysters.

BAKING.—Review facts learned about carbonic acid gas, fermentation, and heat for baking ; make white bread, Graham bread, and brown bread ; stuff and bake a fish.

Make cake : (*a*) Cookies : Spices : from where and how obtained ; their properties and use in cooking. (*b*) Ginger snaps. (*c*) Dover cake. (Note.—Citron ; from what and how made.) (*d*) Sponge cake. (*e*) Jelly cake. Make pies : (*a*) Pie paste. (*b*) Apple pie (peach, rhubarb, &c.). (*c*) Lemon pie (custard, &c.). Make puddings : (*a*) Bread. (*b*) Cottage pudding. (*c*) Sago, rice, or tapioca ; Sago, tapioca, rice ; from what and how obtained ; how prepared for market : bake apples and potatoes.

FRYING.—Experiment with fat : (*a*) Show that pure fat will not boil. (*b*) Show that fat containing water boils. (*c*) Show the proper temperature of fat for cooking by putting pieces of dough or a little of beaten egg into it at different times (before it is hot enough, when hot enough, and when burning) ; note the difference and draw conclusions. Show the economy in the use of eggs in kettle-frying ; scramble eggs ; make an omelet ; make griddle-cakes ; make fritters. (*a*) Batter. (*b*) Salsify, parsnip, corn, &c. (*c*) Apple, oyster, clam, &c. ; make doughnuts (raised by yeast); make crullers (raised by baking powder).

It is worthy of remark—as a coincidence, if nothing more—that in Washington, where cookery lessons are given to a larger proportion of pupils than in any other city I visited (unless it be New York), the appliances and accommodation in general are the least expensive and elaborate. The share of the first appropriation of five thousand dollars for manual training and cookery was not, as is too frequently the case, spent in building one elaborate school, but in fitting up ten centres in any suitable rooms which were available, or could be hired. The accommodation in several of the centres consists of two rooms in a cottage. In one are placed the cooking range and other appliances for practical work ; in the other a large mixing table, consisting of a movable top resting on trestles.

Each teacher conducts three classes a day, each class varying from fourteen to twenty, so that a teacher gives instruction to from two hundred and seventy to three hundred pupils a week.

These centres were fitted up at a cost of from two hundred and fifty dollars each; and, for children of moderate means, appear better suited for their purpose than the more elaborate kitchens. The work being done, as in other cities, was essentially practical, and the cooking of a plain and inexpensive character, though not the less good on that account; but the children in the Washington schools had to work with precisely the same appliances as they would have at home.

The successful introduction of cookery into the Washington schools was due to the benevolence of a lady who was impressed with its importance, and who established a school for teachers and such pupils as could attend out of school hours. She could not take more than a small proportion of those who wished to attend; but she proved the practicability of teaching the subject, and providing teachers who could take charge of it; these being first, teachers; and secondly, cookery demonstrators.

CHAPTER VI.

THE NEW EDUCATION (*continued*).

SCIENCE TEACHING.

General Remarks. — Official Science Teaching disappointing. — Science Teaching in England.—Science Teaching in the States.—Science Teaching under the English School Boards.—Mechanics. — Methods of Instruction in Liverpool.—In American Schools.—St. Louis.—Middletown. — Boston. — New York College. — South Australia. — Other Australian Colonies.

IN Chapter XII. will be found several accounts of genuine science teaching carried on out of school hours by enthusiasts, for the love of the subject. Of course, teachers cannot separate such teaching from their regular school work ; but here I wish to confine myself to what is done in the ordinary course of the day's programme, as an integral part of a regular course of study.

It was the desire to acquaint myself fully with what was being done towards the general introduction of Science Teaching and Manual Training into elementary schools, which chiefly prompted me to take the present trip round the world. I have for some years advocated the necessity for greater attention being paid to the study of science ; but always insisted that in the elementary school there should be no attempt made to associate Science with Examinations.

The nature of my advocacy may be gathered from the following quotation from a paper contributed to the *Education Gazette* five years since :—

" We should train the senses and deductive powers of the mind by a practical, systematic, but, at the same time, essentially elementary study of natural science.   Nothing need be said to prove the value of science in daily life.   Here a little chemistry is useful ; there physics proves of service ; at one time physiology is required ; at another, some knowledge of natural history is of immense advantage.

"At first, indeed, one is almost frightened at the mass of information apparently requisite ; but if we look into the matter carefully, we find that in our daily life *only* the fundamental facts and the simplest principles are necessary.   Common salt need not be called sodic chloride.

" I think something may be done now by substituting regular courses of science lessons of the character indicated, instead of 'special lessons.' Some teachers do this with great success.   Others, just as anxious to benefit the children, give highly interesting experimental lessons on chemistry and physics ; but with questionable success so far as scientific training is concerned.   The wonder of the children is excited rather than their faculties developed.   The want of success may be due to the lessons not being simple enough, and in consequence breaking the cardinal law of science—'proceed from the known to the unknown.'

" Any branch of science (chemistry, physiology, natural history, or geology) might be taken ; but the *manner of teaching*, and not imparting a technical knowledge of the science, should be the chief aim in all the lessons ; or, stated in another way, give ideas and develop reason, not teach facts.

" By natural history is not meant detached lessons on animals, plants, and insects (these, of course, are included) ; but general ideas of the animal and vegetable kingdoms ; their chief divisions and why divided ; their points of semblance and contrast, mutual interdependence, &c.   The subject is a most fascinating one to children, and can be made essentially practical, by calling in the aid of such examples as are to be found everywhere.   By fastening a bit of muslin over a pickle bottle half full of water with a number of eggs and larvæ of the mosquito, means may be provided for illustrating its threefold life, and the impromptu aquarium will be a source of interest for weeks."

Since this was written, courses of science lessons have been added to the curriculum of the South Australian schools.

In so far as "official" science teaching is concerned, my inquiries have been very disappointing.   By official teaching, I mean that which is undertaken in obedience to the requirements of an official course of study. In the first place, much less progress has been made towards the systematic introduction of the subject into schools than I had expected; and in the second place, where it has been attempted, the results are far from satisfactory. This is, of course, nothing more than might be expected. When the feeling of a country becomes so strongly in favour of an addition to the school course, the department having control of education formulates its plans, devises a long series of rules whereby the new machinery is to be fixed in the education—or rather the teaching mill—and, amid the plaudits of the advocates, sets it going. The instruction factory having been got into working order, it becomes necessary to test its work to see whether value is being obtained for money expended. What article is being produced? In this there is frequently displayed a maturity of judgment and soundness of reason fully equal to that of the child, who three times a week pulls up the plant from his garden to see whether it is growing.

The "practical" members of School Boards, and the unpractical officers, frequently cannot see the difference between hiring a man to build a wall, and hiring one to educate a child. In the one case, at the end of a given time a calculation can be made of the number of hours' work, the quantity of bricks, lime, sand, and so forth used; and with tape and rule a few minutes will suffice to tell how much wall has been built; and an inspection will show the quality of the work, which, if satisfactory, entitles the man to his wages. In the other case, the inspector calculates how many lessons have been given, what subjects have been dealt with, what facts should have been learned, what words will best convey the full signification of a fact, in what order the facts should lie in the pupil's mind; and then proceeds with his absurd "test" to find out whether science has been taught.

I am strongly of opinion that in fully three-fourths of the American schools in which I saw so-called science being taught, the pupils were, to a large extent, being simply loaded with indigestible facts of science, instead of being educated through it.   That the lessons are frequently "experimental" makes little difference.   The process may be likened to being told the length, breadth, height, weight, quantity, and kind of materials used in a cake made by someone else, instead of having all the fun of weighing and measuring the ingredients, mixing, baking, and then sharing with friends the resultant dainty.   The first process is not without benefit, and is, probably, an improvement on the old grind at classics.   I consider this proved by the fact that pupils *like* the lessons, which is more than can be said of their Latin.   The memory is exercised as much, the reasoning powers more, while the experiments performed by the demonstrator at least excite wonder and admiration, which may lead to useful results later.

If possible, the case is still worse in England, where success depends on the number of pupils who can pass an examination and earn the special grant.   I know that the one can be done, while the other is not left undone ; but it is not too much to say that the two ends are to a very great extent opposed to each other.   The grant must be earned, or the opportunity of teaching at all is lost ; therefore it is made the chief end in view, and education suffers.   A man tried on a plant the experiment of finding how little water he need give it to keep it alive.   He was astonished to find that it would exist almost without his aid, by drawing its supply from unconscious sources, and rashly asserted that water was unnecessary ; until he saw one of the same species planted at the same time, but properly nourished.   It was with difficulty he recognised that they were the same.   It is not, how little is necessary to prevent death ; but how much to ensure the most vigorous life.

To this generally adverse criticism there is a reverse. There are numbers of schools, and a few systems of schools, where the controlling spirit is an enthusiast, who imparts his spirit to teachers and pupils, until the subject is rather instilled than taught, rather breathed than learned. Such teaching is never undertaken for the purpose of preparation for examination; not but that it would serve that end better than the method usually followed, but because the scope of work required for an ordinary examination is altogether too great to be properly learned in the time allowed for it. If science is to be taken in elementary schools, it must be for its training. The practical utility is so great, that this may well be allowed to take care of itself. The value of the teaching is proportionate to the degree in which an intimate knowledge of the details of the subject itself is subordinate to a grasp of the general principles.

It must not be understood that I underrate the value of teaching chemistry, physics, physiology, or any other branch of this great subject, even as I saw it being carried on; but rather that a very poor use is usually made of time and means. A method which may be good in a University, where the professor is dealing with men whose age and training should be a guarantee of some degree of maturity of mind, may be very unsatisfactory when adopted for boys and girls. This, and the fact that far too much is attempted, are the chief causes of lack of success. In response to the great outcry for science in schools, laboratories have been fitted up and much money spent in apparatus, to the material benefit of the manufacturers and dealers. The pupils have perhaps learned a number of hard names, and seen a variety of pretty experiments performed, and may have performed a number of experiments themselves; made oxygen and burnt iron wire in it; possibly have burnt themselves and been the wiser for it. Nevertheless, the experiments carried on at considerable cost have failed in the purpose intended. The pupils are little better able to understand the great world around them than they were before; and the knowledge gained will not materially help them if they should have to take up the subjects for special purpose. No attempt has been made to teach what is of most use as education; and a partial failure has resulted from attempting what is unsuitable or impossible to mere children. On the other hand, harm has frequently been done by *supposed* success. The boy leaves school with conceited notions of his accomplishments, and a certificate wherewith to practise fraud on his fellows.

There is an ancient aphorism which says, he who knows one truth knows all truth. All such truisms, are after all only half truths, and form the best possible debating ground. Is truth divisible into sections? Can anyone know all truth? Who is sufficiently free from error to decide what is truth? I will leave these and many other questions. One partial meaning may be, that when the perfectly genuine truth-seeker has placed his mind in the condition for accepting truth, and becomes conscious of one little glimmer, that glimmer serves as a light to guide him on his ever-satisfying, but never-ending search; or, limiting the meaning, when a fact becomes thoroughly understood, it renders many more knowable. It is a standard by which others may be measured without error. In science, many studies lead to but one end : therefore a thorough study of one is preferable to a skimming of many. At the same time, the proper study of one must be preceded by a knowledge of the principles of all. Natural history, astronomy, chemistry, philosophy, all lead to the same cycle of truth; but the facts of each, or of all, may be known, and the truth remain a sealed treasure. The facts are the skeleton; essential, but to ordinary humanity uninteresting, dry, and valueless. The dry bones must live; and, living, become the poetry of Nature.

An encyclopædia is valuable as a book of reference. The ordinary man, busied with the cares of life, wants his facts assorted, distributed, arranged. The specialist needs his catalogue of scientific names and descriptions, and the more condensed these are the better. His work in itself advances life but little; but he gives the fact, and the utilitarian, with his empirical intuitive knowledge of the science of men, seizes it, and gathers in a fortune. The same fact may be taken by the poet, who builds upon it his ideal, and all admire the lovely resultant imagery. The entomologist spend hours upon the study of the wing of a fly; he dissects, mounts, examines, draws, disputes over the twentieth part of an inch in its length, and is so wrapped up in such details that beauty is unnoticed, and the insect becomes to him something to examine and classify. The ornithologist may see in a new bird a specimen to be shot, sketched, stuffed, and mounted, with a sufficiency of chemicals to keep it from the ravages of insects. A chemist may value a new material merely as something to be analysed, to be weighed, dissolved, burnt, or otherwise resolved into its elements. It is not these men who directly influence the ethics of humanity. I do not depreciate the work of the specialist, neither are any words of mine required to show the importance of his efforts to humanity. In fact, everyone should be a specialist in something; *but we should not attempt to make specialists of children.* If natural history be the means by which we seek to introduce our pupils to Nature, we would do well to take as our model not the collector, but the naturalist, who makes friends with Nature, communes with her, tells her his secrets and receives hers in return, gives her himself, and has her for the giving. Such were Audubon, Agassiz, and many of the poets. Such an one is John Burrows. Nature told them her secrets, for she recognised them as her children. As Longfellow so beautifully sings of Agassiz :—

K

> " And Nature, the dear old nurse, took
>   The child upon her knee,
>   Saying : ' Here is a story-book
> '   Thy father has written for thee.'
>
> " ' Come, wander with me,' she said,
>   ' Into regions yet untrod,
>   And read what is still unread
>   In the manuscripts of God.'
>
> " And he wandered away and away
>   With Nature, the dear old nurse,
>   Who sang to him night and day
>   The rhymes of the universe.
>
> " And whenever the way seemed long,
>   Or his heart began to fail,
>   She would sing a more wonderful song,
>   Or tell a more marvellous tale."

A crystal was a poem of life to Ruskin ; and Charles Kingsley made paving-stones and roof slates tell the life-history of our planet. To Hugh Miller a quarry was a romance of growth, life, convulsion, and decay ; while the helpless worm, for which Cowper pleaded, found in Darwin one to whom it could tell its life purpose, more wonderful than romance. This life of Nature in Nature is the knowledge which will be of greatest value to the people, for in itself it is ennobling, and from it is developed the practical study of the specialist.

This almost indescribable knowledge, or rather love for knowledge, can be cultivated ; and, where imparted, is loved. I have seen it working its elevating powers in Australia, in America, in England. One interprets it through his chemicals in the school-room, another among the flowers in the garden, another in the quarry, others in the fields among the butterflies, or in the woods making friends with squirrels, or perhaps use all in turns. Nature's laboratory is always open, and no manufacturer exercises a monopoly over apparatus. I have just come across an address delivered by Professor Huxley at Manchester in 1887, in which occurs this passage :—" The other matter in which we want some systematic and good teaching is what I have hardly a name for, but which may best be explained as a sort of developed object lesson. Anybody who knows his business in science can make anything subservient to that purpose. You know it was said of Dean Swift that he could write an admirable poem upon a broomstick ; and the man who has a real knowledge of science can make the commonest object in the world subservient to an introduction to the principles and greater truths of natural knowledge. It is in that way that your science must be taught if it is to be of real service. Do not suppose any amount of book-work, any repetition by rote of catechisms, and other abominations of that kind, are of value for our object. That is mere wasting of time. But take the commonest objects, and lead the child from that foundation to such truths of a higher order as may be within his grasp."

Never can such teaching be given for a grant, or any reward other than the pleasure of doing, giving, and exercising. Nature is always just, though exacting ; often cruel to those who oppose her knowingly or unknowingly, yet generous to those who are so to her. Her laws are wide-reaching : she is a gentle servant or a hard taskmaster ; a merciless tyrant or a generous friend ; just as she is treated. She will not yield her secrets for a salary, or allow children to learn to love her that their teachers may earn a merit grant. They who seek her for the love they bear her, nevertheless find treasures not the less welcome because unsought. " Seek ye first the kingdom of heaven, and all these things shall be added," is expressive of a wider, broader, more significant meaning than is frequently assigned to it.

This chapter already contains too much theory; but that is because I found so little good science teaching to record. This may be a hard statement to make, after travelling round the world in search of information on this precise point. As a matter of fact, however, I have rather learned what to avoid than what to advocate for adoption. I have not seen a comprehensive course of rudimentary science—I use the word science here apart from its meaning in college, because I have no other word to express the kind of teaching I have indicated—in satisfactory operation in any large system of English-speaking schools. I have a number of excellent courses of study on "General Knowledge," "Common Objects," "Elementary Science," "Physiology and Hygiene," and so forth, and I sometimes travelled long distances to see them in operation; but I have found that it does not follow that because a certain town, city, or district, has a reputation for general education, or with regard to some special feature, that, therefore, its schools are superior to those of its neighbours. The fame of its presiding genius, peculiar circumstances leading to its being well advertised, or other fortuitous circumstances, may give it a reputation, while the equally good, but more quiet, modest, hard work of its neighbour may be unrecognised, and remains unknown to the pedagogical world.

Generally, where experiments have been tried on a large scale, their best purpose has been destroyed by the absurd wish to see "results" in a few months. The fact that the results have been highly beneficial under existing circumstances, proves that if the subject could be taught in a suitable manner—for example, on the lines advocated by Professor Huxley—there would be no subject in the school course more educative, more popular, and at the same time more practically useful in after-life, than the scientific treatment of common things.

The generally increasing interest in the subject, the expense which authorities are occasionally willing to bear, and the awakening desire to educate for the life of the pupil, not for the result immediately attainable, lead me to hope and believe that the day is not far distant when what I have written on this subject will be erroneous and out of date.

Since writing the preceding, I have read for the first time the report of the School Management Committee of the London School Board on this subject. My remarks had no particular reference to London ; but an extract from the report will show how they apply even to the excellent schools of that great city, where I saw some really fine science teaching. It illustrates, too, how a measure of success is often the surest ground for general dissatisfaction, when a comparison is made between what is thus shown to be possible, and the ordinary, but no longer satisfactory work :—

" Perhaps of all subjects, the greatest progress has been made in the teaching of geography, and the least in that of elementary science. This is curious, because the latter subject can be made intensely attractive and instructive to children. Probably the reason lies in a want of knowledge on the part of the teacher, and a somewhat vague syllabus not answering well to examination requirements.

" Teachers are unanimous in according to object lessons a high place among the subjects best calculated to awaken the reasoning faculties of children, and to develop an interest in their work generally ; but this theoretical unanimity is, unfortunately, not the only point on which they agree, for they are practically unanimous in either not taking any definite course of lessons, or in giving them in a perfunctory and slipshod fashion. Even in schools where special attention is paid to object lessons, their *raison d'être* appears to be not so much ' to induce to observe, or to encourage to compare and note resemblances and differences,' but, as is sometimes said, to promote a better attendance on Friday afternoons. The teacher who makes such a statement utters an unconscious satire on his teaching, and acknowledges that one factor in bad attendance is the dryness and wearisomeness of the lessons. There can be no doubt that object lessons, apart from their utility in other directions, brighten school life, and encourage children to take a deeper interest in their work. They are apt, however, to take the form of lessons, in which certain definite facts are imparted, instead of lessons in which the children are taught to think and acquire the power of gaining information. This arises mainly from two causes :—

"(*a*) Lists of lessons are apparently drawn up at random. There are no connecting links, and care is not always taken to supply the information in the order necessary to its being understood. The lessons present a number of facts for the consideration of the children, without the preliminary knowledge which may be requisite. Underlying principles are ignored, and the statements of the teacher, as to reasons and causes, are simply presented for acceptance on faith. A lesson on the pump, for instance, would be given without a preliminary explanation and illustration of the weight of the atmosphere and the pressure of fluids ; a lesson on the electric light without any allusion to the difference between conductors and non-conductors ; and the notion of the electric current would be given in such a way as to be misleading. The children are taken into the domain of fairyland, as it were, and see, or are told, wonderful things ; but this is not the scientific training which should be the aim of object lessons.

"The lessons are not prepared. The teacher depends for his facts on knowledge picked up at random, perhaps never verified, and generally incomplete ; and for his method he trusts to devices on the spur of the moment. The consequence is, that the lesson frequently turns on points already well known to the children, as that the cow is a quadruped; or on certain formulæ that have been adopted apparently as adaptable to most things, as that the object under consideration is opaque or transparent, that it is rough or smooth, &c."

Several English School Boards have adopted a peripatetic plan of teaching science to boys, and domestic economy to girls. I first saw the system in operation in Liverpool, where I understand the method was first adopted with great success, owing to the enthusiasm of the Demonstrator. The subject first taken for the boys was mechanics. Birmingham, London, Leeds, and other cities have adopted the same plan. I believe there are between eight and nine thousand boys receiving instruction in mechanics in the London schools. The plan is similar to the supervisor system found so useful in the United States.

An enthusiastic and able scientific teacher is appointed to take charge of the instruction in a certain number of schools. A laboratory is provided for him in a convenient centre, which is supplied with a complete set of apparatus for the illustration of the subject selected. A course of lessons is drawn up and a time table arranged, so that the Demonstrator can conveniently get from one school to another without waste of time; but a whole morning or afternoon is usually spent in one school. The Demonstrator prepares his day's work in his laboratory, packing the apparatus required for his illustrations in suitable boxes, which a boy conveys to the school in a handcart. A few minutes suffices to set up the apparatus in a class-room, into which the regular teacher brings his class, and remains with it during the demonstration, taking notes of the lesson for recapitulation. Between each visit of the Demonstrator the regular teacher recapitulates the lesson, often improvising apparatus wherewith to impress a principle not thoroughly grasped during the regular lesson. When a teacher shows by his knowledge and interest that he is capable of taking charge of the subject, he is allowed the use of the apparatus to give the lessons without the attendance of the Demonstrator. There are now a number of teachers in Liverpool who thus relieve the special teachers of work in particular schools, and enable them to devote more time to children less highly favoured. In addition to the work in the schools, the science master conducts special classes for pupil teachers, who attend at stated times at his laboratory ; so that he is doing a double work in teaching science to the present school children, and training teachers who will be able to teach the subject themselves in a few years.

As an introduction to the special lessons under the science master, a carefully prepared course of experimental object lessons has been drawn up, with elaborate notes on the method which *may be employed*, for the guidance of teachers. The apparatus required is such as anyone can procure and make at a cost of a few pence and a little time ; and the lessons, if carried out after the manner of the method suggested, cannot fail to have a very valuable educative result. The titles of some of the lessons are suggestive of the methods employed, such as—The Senses and their Use; Classification of Substances; Classification into Solids, Liquids, and Gases; Action of Water on a Solid placed in it; Evaporation of Water for Recovery of Dissolved Matters; the Pressure of the Air ; and so forth. Mr. Hewitt, the special master, among his suggestions, says : " The lessons should be largely of a conversational character, the children being permitted and encouraged to take as large a share as possible in the work." I will insert the syllabus of Study in Mechanics.

MECHANICS.

SYLLABUS.

1st Stage.—Matter in three states ; solids, liquids, and gases. Mechanical properties peculiar to each state. Matter is porous, compressible, elastic. Measurement as practised by mechanics. Production of a plane surface. Measurement of length, time, and velocity.

2nd Stage.—Matter in motion. The weight of a body, its inertia and momentum. Measures of force. The work done by a force. Meaning of the term "energy." Energy may be transferred, but cannot be destroyed. Modern notions as to the nature of heat.

3rd Stage.—The simple mechanical powers, viz., (1) the lever; (2) the wheel and the axle; (3) pulleys; (4) the inclined plane; (5) the wedge; (6) the screw. Liquid pressure; the hydrostatic press; liquids under the action of gravity. The parallelogram of velocities. The parallelogram of forces—examples commonly met with.

Method of Instruction.

This subject is taught, as far as possible, by means of special experimental demonstrations, supplemented by lessons given by the teachers in the respective schools.

The first stage is taken up by the boys in the fifth standard, the second stage by those in the sixth standard, and the third stage by those in the seventh standard. In the first stage a demonstration is given weekly, in the second stage fortnightly, and in the third stage monthly.

In every case there should be a careful revision of the subject matter of a demonstration before the time for the next succeeding demonstration. This recapitulatory lesson should, whenever possible, be given by a teacher who was present at the original demonstration, and who will, therefore, be able to refer to the experiments then shown. In addition to these recapitulatory lessons, it will be necessary in the second and third stages for the teachers to give independent lessons on certain portions of the subject in those weeks when there is no demonstration. Since the knowledge of the children is tested, at the inspection of the school, by means of a written examination, every opportunity should be taken to exercise them in expressing their ideas in writing.

The Liverpool Board, finding that the experiment with regard to mechanics has proved so successful, have adopted a course of study, which, for want of a better name, is called chemistry. The object is to give such knowledge of things as will serve as a preparation for the study of chemistry at a later stage, and will either enable boys to take up the study of the subject for the Science and Art Department with intelligence and profit; or be in itself a source of mental training, and useful instruction in those fundamental principles of things which will enable them to take a more enlightened view of the surroundings of daily life.

Having entered thus fully into the nature of the work in Liverpool, I need not attempt to describe that carried on in other places on the same general plan.

Where science is taken for the boys in the way outlined, domestic economy is usually provided for the girls by a similar plan of itinerant teachers. Some of the courses of lessons are excellent, and I am sorry that the frequency of the directions for "preparing for examination" points to the prevalent idea that instruction is only beneficial when it leads to an immediate measurable result. That quickness of growth, associated with rapidity of decay, is not confined to mushrooms, appears very frequently to be lost sight of.

It is the custom of the superintendents of American schools to publish manuals in which are laid down, in exact detail, the work of each grade. The course of study then becomes a work, or the method of teaching with definite application. In the case of partially trained teachers this is highly beneficial, and as no good superintendent thinks of confining teachers to the methods laid down, the plan is a commendable one. Many of the school laws of the State have provided that lessons in physiology, hygiene, and the effects of alcoholic drinks shall be given in all the schools. Generally, I consider that the effect of these lessons is highly beneficial, although they are sometimes given to comply with the law instead of for the purpose intended. Occasionally a school committee will select a text-book, about which nothing can be said in praise, and which is not worth the space to condemn. When a teacher follows such a book slavishly, the effect is apt to be an addition to that narrow-minded-ness and bigotry, which certainly needs no special training in most natures.

In speaking of Cook County Normal School, I gave a short account of the way natural history was there taught in an indirect way, apart from set lessons; and in my remarks on Natural History Clubs will be found further details of similar teaching. I witnessed similar excellent work in various schools; and from several incidents am inclined to think it is more frequent than I at first imagined. The teacher who manipulates an electric machine, to the amusement of his pupils; or makes them learn a tabulated list of the strata of the earth's crust, under the delusion that he is teaching science, rarely fails to inform the visitor of his doings, although he may thereby write himself down as an ass; but the gentle lover of Nature, who from day to day instils into his pupils a love and know-ledge of Nature and her laws, possibly never thinks, or at all events, does not tell others, he is teaching science.

On one occasion, I visited a school to see some work in drawing, which I had heard was praiseworthy. After satisfy-ing myself on the matter which had caused my visit, I sought for information on other points. In each of the rooms I had noticed sundry specimens of shells, preserved crabs, butterflies, dried flowers, boxes in which were cocoons, and so forth, and therefore remarked to one of the teachers that I was pleased to see that she taught natural history, and wished to know whether the pupils were fond of it. With evident surprise, she informed me that they did not teach natural history at all! After a little chat, I asked about the specimens in the room, and what she did with them. I found that they were nearly all brought to the school by the children, so that they might talk with her about them. It appeared that the principal was very fond of natural history, and had succeeded in interesting her pupils and her teachers in the subject without giving it a name. Each spring the pupils bring to school the first specimen of every wild flower that they find open. The date is recorded and compared with last year's record, and then the specimen is examined and talked about.

It is not my intention to enter into further details of this most desirable means of education. At present it appears impossible that it should be otherwise than exceptional. I will give one or two examples of how many of the superintendents plan out the work for their teachers.

The course of instruction in natural science for the schools of St. Louis, requires that oral lessons on plants and animals be given in the first and second grades; that physiology and hygiene be taught with the text-book in the third, fourth, fifth, sixth, and seventh grades; and that oral lessons in physics be given in the eighth grade. In the first, second, and eighth grades, the maximum time for one recitation shall be set apart each week for giving these oral lessons in natural science. In the third, fourth, fifth, sixth, and seventh grades, two recitations shall be given each week in physiology and hygiene.

A large selection of topics is given for each school year, from which the teacher will select such as she can best clearly illustrate and explain. She must not take any more than she can properly teach during the quarter.

I will not quote all, but will insert the topics for the first and sixth years as fairly typical.

FIRST YEAR OR GRADE: PLANTS OR OUTLINES OF BOTANY.

First Quarter.—Flowers; their structure, colour, perfume, habits, and shapes. Inasmuch as the pupils of this grade enter school in the spring or early fall, their first quarter's work can be illustrated directly from the garden.

Second Quarter.—Leaves, fruit, seeds ; shape, uses, sap, decay.

Third Quarter.—Buds, roots, their purpose ; stalks and trunk, bark of plants, wood.

Fourth Quarter.—Circulation of sap, what is made from sap, shape of plants, etc.   Review of topics taken during year.

SIXTH YEAR OR GRADE : PHYSIOLOGY AND HYGIENE.

First Quarter.—How we live ; how the body is covered ; what the hair is ; how to keep the hair healthy ; thinning and greyness of the hair ; why the body should be clothed ; how the body should be clothed ; hygiene of the skin ; something to find out ; how bodily motion is directed ; bodily organs must act in harmony ; how the nerves are distributed ; nerve matter ; the brain.   .

Second Quarter.—How bodily motion is directed ; the spinal cord; the ganglia ; sympathetic system ; use of the nerves ; direct nerve action ; reflex action ; sympathetic action ; habit and training ; exercise of the nerves ; rest of the nerves ; how alcohol affects the nerves ; effect on the mind ; how tobacco affects the nerves ; hygiene of the nerves ; something to find out.

Third Quarter.—How the mind gets ideas and expresses them ; sensations ; the taste as a sentinel ; flavours; odours ; sound ; the ear ; care of the ear ; light ; need of light ; the eye ; structure of the eye ; muscles of the eye ; action of light ; care of the eye.

Fourth Quarter.—How the mind gets ideas and expresses them ; the voice ; speech ; care of the voice ; hygiene of the organs of special sense ; something to find out ; stimulants ; narcotics.

The following extracts give the general principles of the method to be adopted in dealing with the course :—

" The teacher must not consider herself required to go over all the topics assigned for any given quarter. She must not attempt to do any more than she can do in a proper manner. If it happens that only the first two or three topics are all that can be dealt with profitably, the teacher must not allow herself to undertake more.

" In case the teacher finds that the topics of any given quarter are not arranged in such an order that she can take them up to the best advantage, she is at liberty to change that order ; but she must not proceed to the work of a new quarter, or to any portion of it, until she has first given ten weekly lessons on the quarter's work she has begun.

" No more than ten lessons should be given on the work laid down for a quarter. When these have been given, proceed to the work of the next quarter, whether the topics of the quarter in hand have all been considered or only a very small portion of them.

" The course is arranged with reference to method rather than quantity or exhaustiveness. If only one topic is thoroughly discussed in each quarter of the first year, some very important ideas will be gained of the science of botany.

" The question will be asked : Why not reduce the number of topics under a given subject to the number that can be actually discussed by the teacher ?

" The answer is : (1) A selection of topics from a comparatively full enumeration is best left to the individual teacher. (2) The exact number of topics that can be profitably discussed by teachers will vary with their capacities ; moreover, it will vary from year to year, as teachers become familiar with the course ; hence it is necessary to have a variety, and to have topics enough for the most rapid classes. (3) It is, moreover, important to keep before the teacher a full outline of the subject, so as to prevent the (very common) tendency to treat a theme in its narrow application only, and to omit its general bearings."

I think the following course of study prepared for the use of the teachers of the town of Middletown, Connecticut, and included in the Teachers' Manual for 1888, deserves to be quoted in full, not only on account of its value in itself, and as an illustration of the detail with which courses of study are elaborated; but also, and more particularly, because it is drawn up in accordance with the scheme of the American Society of Naturalists, as adopted at their meeting held in New Haven in 1887.

Its compilation is due, I believe, to Professor William North Rice, Ph.D., LL.D., the chairman of the Middletown Board of Education.

COURSE OF STUDY IN NATURAL SCIENCE FOR SCHOOLS OF MIDDLETOWN, CONN.

GENERAL PRINCIPLES.

The object of elementary lessons in natural science is two-fold : to train the observing powers, and to give information. The former should be especially emphasised in the Primary grades, and the two made about equally important in the Grammar grades.

Before entering school, most children spend a large portion of their waking hours out of doors in close and sympathetic contact with Nature, seeing, feeling, handling, smelling natural objects. Curiosity is the incentive. This unconscious study of Nature should not, as too often happens, cease when children enter school. Natural curiosity, so active in the young, should be stimulated and directed, not repressed and killed. Such repression has often caused children to hate school. Their hours in school should be their happiest, because there they should find, not only many of those natural objects that arouse and attract their attention; but also a wise, sympathetic teacher to inspire and guide them in the exercise of their rapidly developing powers.

The teaching should be chiefly objective. Large, well-defined pictures may be used, whenever it is impossible to obtain the real objects; but it should always be borne in mind that the best pictures are poor substitutes for the objects themselves. ·

In the lower grades, the teacher should studiously avoid the use of technical terms, whose meaning is unknown to children. The chief object here is, not to teach science, but to train to close and accurate observation, and to stimulate a keen interest in Nature. In no grade should special emphasis be laid upon technical terms and classifications, though somewhat more attention may properly be given to them in the Grammar grades. All classifications should, so far as possible, be the result of observation and comparison on the part of the pupils. Let the teacher stimulate, direct, suggest, and name. Happy the teacher and fortunate the pupils, if, in this delightful work, the teacher judiciously combines speech and silence. An occasional talk, however, by the teacher on the subject before the class is both proper and desirable. Such talks should furnish information beyond the reach of the pupils' observation.

Every lesson should be carefully prepared. Aimless and irrelevant conversations are profitless. Allow and encourage the freest expression of what the pupils see. Encourage the pupils to collect and bring in specimens. Elicit, by judicious questions, a description of what they have brought. Give them additional information. If necessary, postpone the subject till the next day, and learn something about it.

NATURAL SCIENCE.—GRADE I.

PHYSIOLOGY.—Regions of the body—head, trunk, limbs. Details of external parts. Uses of external organs. Hygiene of the skin—bathing.

ZOOLOGY.—Lessons on common mammals, *e.g.*, cat, dog, horse, cow, rat, squirrel. Let the pupils observe, compare, and describe these animals, as regards their external aspect and habits. Compare these animals with ourselves. Tell stories illustrative of habits of these and other mammals.

BOTANY.—Lessons on common plants. Teach pupils to distinguish root, stem, leaf. Compare leaves of different plants, as regards general form, margin, venation. Require pupils to draw and describe leaves of many plants.

NATURAL SCIENCE.—GRADE II.

PHYSIOLOGY.—The framework of the body. Bones, joints, muscles. Exhibit anatomical diagrams. Teach the pupils to find in their own bodies some of the bones, which can be easily felt through the skin. Emphasise importance of correct attitudes, while framework of the body is rapidly growing and taking shape. Warn against stooping shoulders and crooked backs. The teeth—their forms and uses. Emphasise importance of thorough mastication. Necessity of cleaning teeth.

ZOOLOGY.—Lessons on mammals continued. Special study and comparison of limbs of mammals. Let the pupils find the elbow, wrist, knee, and ankle in the cat, dog, horse, cow, rat, squirrel, and any other mammals of which specimens or pictures may be at hand. Thus teach them the idea of homology, though the word should not be used. Compare teeth of common mammals, and lead pupils to recognise adaptation of different kinds of teeth to different kinds of food. Teach pupils to recognise degrees of resemblance between animals. The cat and the dog resemble each other more than either resembles the horse or the rat. Develop idea of classification. Lead pupils to recognise character of carnivores, ungulates, rodents. Most of the mammals with which the children are familiar are included in these three orders. But tell them about monkeys, and kangaroos, and other very different forms of mammals, that they may not suppose that all mammals are so included.

BOTANY.—Different kinds of stems—woody and herbaceous, exogenous and endogenous. By study of numerous examples lead pupils to recognise that exogenous stems usually bear net-veined leaves, and endogenous stems usually bear parallel-veined leaves. Distinguish deciduous and evergreen trees. Let the pupils make lists of each.

NATURAL SCIENCE.—GRADE III.

PHYSIOLOGY.—Elementary ideas of digestion. Why do we eat? All parts of the body are made of the food which we eat. Food is made into blood, and blood made into all the materials of the body. But our food is mostly solid, and it must be made liquid before it can get into the blood. Different substances dissolve in different liquids— *e.g.*, salt in water, camphor gum in alcohol, iron filings in dilute sulphuric acid. Show these experiments. Body itself must make liquids which will dissolve food. Put lump of sugar in mouth. Mouth fills with saliva, and sugar is dissolved. This illustrates secretion of digestive fluids. But meat will not dissolve in saliva. What does become of it? Show anatomical plate of stomach, and tell about gastric juice. Teach (with use of anatomical diagrams) outlines of anatomy of digestive organs. Show, by experiment, how much more quickly powdered salt dissolves in water than lumps of rock-salt. Teach importance of thorough mastication. Show gizzard of turkey and explain its use. But we have no gizzard, and hence must not swallow our food whole, as the turkey does. Wholesome and unwholesome foods. Alcohol.

ZOOLOGY.—Lessons on common birds—*e.g.*, robin, hawk, hen, duck. Let pupils compare these with each other and with mammals. Compare feet and bills of different birds, and show adaptation to habits. Continue lessons on homology of limbs. Let the pupils find elbow, wrist, knee and ankle in birds. Is the bat a bird? Talk on instincts of birds, shown in periodical migrations and in nest-building.

L

BOTANY.—Lessons on flowers. Select plants with perfect and somewhat conspicuous flowers. Teach the pupils to recognise sepals, petals, stamens, pistils. Let pupils describe and draw the parts in a variety of flowers. Study polypetalous flowers first, afterwards monopetalous flowers. Cut open the ovary in large flowers, and show the ovules. Develop the idea that the parts of the flower are altered leaves.

NATURAL SCIENCE.—GRADE IV.

PHYSIOLOGY.—Circulation.   When food has been made into blood, blood must be carried to all parts of body—function of circulation. Show by anatomical plates the outlines of anatomy of circulatory apparatus.   Let the pupils find some of their own veins, and feel pulsation of heart, and of arteries in wrist and temple.   Respiration. Show difference between inspired and expired air by experiment with lime-water.   Burn a candle in a jar, and show that the air in the jar affects lime-water like expired air.   Carbonic acid always formed when carbon burns—*i.e.*, when carbon unites with oxygen.   Carbon in body and in food.   Carbon burns—*i.e.*, unites with oxygen all over the body. Body runs, like a steam-engine, by burning carbon.   Object of respiration—introduction of oxygen and removal of carbonic acid.   Anatomy of respiratory organs.   Hygiene of respiration—dress, ventilation. Respiration in aquatic animals.   Show gills of fish, and respiratory movements in living fish.   Fish breathes air dissolved in water.   Show presence of such air by warming a beaker of water, and so forming air-bubbles.

ZOOLOGY.—Lessons on common reptiles, amphibia and fishes—*e.g.*, turtle, snake, frog, perch, pickerel, eel.   Let pupils observe, compare, and describe.   Continue study of homology of limbs.   How many of these animals have two pairs of limbs like those of mammals and birds? Notice external covering of these animals.   Their bodies are cold. Why?   Respiration of fishes.   Is the whale a fish?   Metamorphosis of amphibia, as shown in changes from tadpole to frog.   Teach characters of the three classes—reptiles, amphibia, fishes.   Characters possessed in common by mammals, birds, reptiles, amphibia, fishes.   Subkingdom vertebrates.

BOTANY.—The pistil of a flower develops into a fruit.   Different kinds of fruits.   Seeds.   Show the embryo in beans, and other large seeds.   Plant seeds in pots, and show growth of plants from seeds. Cycle of growth, reproduction, death.

NATURAL SCIENCE.—GRADE V.

PHYSIOLOGY.—Nervous system.   Analyse the series of actions when a boy put his hand on the radiator and finds it too hot.   Nervous system, a telegraphic system in the body.   Brain the central office. Afferent and efferent nerves.   Anatomy of the nervous system. Hygiene of the nervous system—stimulants and narcotics.

ZOOLOGY.—Study the lobster.   Lead pupil to recognise jointed external skeleton, distinct regions of body, jointed limbs.   Trace similarity of structure in feelers, jaws, and accessory jaws, nippers, legs and other appendages, including the caudal fin.   Cut off edge of carapace on one side, and show gills.   Contrast articulate type of structure, as shown in lobster, with vertebrate type, as shown in animals previously studied.   Compare diagrams of nervous system in vertebrates and articulates.   Compare with the lobster, the crab and the sow-bug. Teach pupil to recognise the common characters which unite these animals in the class crustacea.   Study angle-worm as illustrating articulate type in much simpler form—body not differentiated into regions, no jointed appendages.   Talks on useful animals.

BOTANY.—Study more obscure and difficult forms of flowers than those examined in Grade III.   Flowers densely aggregated, as in sunflower, dandelion, daisy.   Imperfect flowers, as in willow, oak, chestnut.   Flowers with open (gymnospermous) pistil, as in pine, spruce.

NATURAL SCIENCE.—GRADE VI.

PHYSIOLOGY.—Briefly review work of previous grades.   Special study of the eye.   Anatomy of the eye.   Illustrate formation of image on retina by use of a large lens.   Hygiene of the eye.   Injury of eye by use of light too strong, too feeble, unsteady or improperly placed. Cultivation of near-sightedness by bad positions in reading and writing.

ZOOLOGY.--Study common insects, as the bee, butterfly, fly, beetle, squash-bug, dragon-fly, grasshopper.   Compare these animals with lobster, sow-bug and angle-worm, and recognise in all these the common characters of articulates.   In insects, note the characteristic division of body into head, thorax, and abdomen.   Compare wings of insects, as regards number, form, venation, texture.   Show scales from wings of moth and butterfly under microscope.   Examine the mouth-parts of those insects which are not too small.   Supplement observation with pictures. Under lens examine eyes of insects.   Explain their peculiar structure.

Metamorphosis of insects. Catch some caterpillars in the fall, and keep them in boxes in the school-room. Some of them will probably survive, and appear as moths or butterflies early in the spring. Talks on injurious animals. Show how some animals are useful by destroying injurious animals—*e.g.*, insectivorous birds.

BOTANY.—Distinction between flowering and flowerless plants. Examples of flowerless plants—ferns, club-mosses, horse-tails, mosses, lichens, fungi, sea-weeds. Show fructification of ferns. Show that the distinction of root, stem, and leaf, so obvious in nearly all flowering plants and in ferns and others of the higher flowerless plants, vanishes entirely in fungi and sea-weeds.

MINERALOGY.—Study crystalline form, cleavage, colour, lustre, hardness, of some of the minerals common in the vicinity of Middletown—*e.g.*, quartz, feldspar, mica, hornblende, garnet, tourmaline, beryl.

NATURAL SCIENCE.—GRADE VII.

PHYSIOLOGY.—Senses of hearing, smell, taste.

ZOOLOGY.—Study the river mussel. Direct pupil's attention to shell (with its hinge, ligament, mantle impression, and muscular impressions), mantle, gills, palpi, mouth, foot, adductor muscles. Compare this animal with the oyster and the clam. Note that the former has only one adductor muscle; while the latter has the mantle lobes united, forming a sac which is continued posteriorly in the breathing-tubes or syphons. Examine some pond-snails. These will be found to resemble the preceding in their flabby unjointed bodies, destitute of internal skeleton ; but will be seen to differ in having a distinct head with feelers, and a spiral univalve shell. Examine shells of some of the sea-snails. Lead the pupils to recognise characters of lamellibranchiata and gastropoda, as classes of the sub-kingdom mollusca. Contrast the mollusca with the vertebrata and articulata. Give some talks on corals, sponges, and other animals lower in the scale than molluscs. Do not let the pupil suppose that the classes he has studied comprise the whole animal kingdom. Talks on geographical distribution of animals. Give a little idea of geological succession of animals.

BOTANY.—Geographical distribution of plants. Uses of plants. Relation of plants to animals.

GEOLOGY.—Gravel, sand, clay. Show that these result from the disintegration of pre-existent rocks. Erosion, transportation, and deposition by water. Study gutters and puddles for illustration of action of aqueous agencies. Conglomerate, sandstone, shale. Show that these result from consolidation of gravel, sand, clay. Visit Portland quarries. Other rocks are sediments not merely consolidated, but crystallised by action of internal heat. Study specimens of gneiss and mica schist. Contrast their texture with that of sandstone and other sedimentary rocks. Still other rocks have come up in molten condition from interior of globe—*e.g.*, lava, trap. Talks on volcanoes.

NATURAL SCIENCE.—GRADE VIII.

PHYSIOLOGY.—Review nutritive functions, using elementary text-book. Illustrate subject with a few dissections.

PHYSICS.—Elementary text-book. Illustrate with experiments, as much as practicable.

In many places when I asked whether science was taught, I received the reply, "No; I should like to teach science, for I was very fond of it at college [or normal school, as the case might be], but we have no apparatus, and the Board of Education will not go to the expense of fitting up a room and providing it." They referred, of course, to physics and chemistry. I believe those teachers were usually in earnest; but they had been badly taught, and were under the impression that teaching physics and chemistry consists in manipulating certain expensive apparatus. It would appear that very many of those who take short courses of chemistry or physics in expensive laboratories, are unable to conceive of either subject existing anywhere outside a laboratory with curious brass instruments and numerous glass vessels.

A teacher who is unable to improvise the greater part of the apparatus needed for all the science necessary in an elementary school, is not a fit person to be trusted with expensive and elaborate apparatus. One who can properly teach the fundamental principles of chemistry and physics to boys and girls is independent of the manufacturer ; and if he cannot teach, no manufacturer will enable him to do so. Of course, while a good teacher can do without apparatus, there is no doubt but that he will do still better with it. I am not merely theorising; I am but stating the result of many observations, and I will give two examples of what I mean.

In a magnificent school in Boston, where I spent a very pleasant afternoon, and heard some good teaching in other subjects, I listened to a "science lesson" given by the principal to the eighth grade boys and girls. He had a very convenient demonstrating table, and large cases of first-class chemical and physical apparatus at hand. Here is an outline of the lesson (?) The pupils were seated with large note-books and pencils, when the master called out, "Put down : To make red light, you take nitrate of strontium in a saucer and add alcohol; then you warm the saucer and set light to the alcohol, when it burns with a red flame. Now watch me do it." Without further comment he performed the experiment, and smiled with evident satisfaction when the flame burned red, and the class cried, "Oh! isn't it pretty!" He then prepared several other coloured flames in similar fashion, after which he said, " Put down the word 'Attraction,' and take careful and full notes, making a sketch of each experiment as I perform it. The first kind of attraction is called magnetic attraction, which, as you know, points to the north. I will take this needle-magnet, and when I hold another magnet near, the needle is attracted, showing a law of which we will have to speak by-and-bye. Draw the experiment. Now write down ' Electrical Attraction,' which is the next kind we will take, according to the order of the book. I take a glass rod and rub it with a silk handkerchief, and when I put it near this pith ball hung on a silk thread, the ball is first attracted and then repelled. Now draw a picture of the experiment. Now write ' Cohesion ' as the next kind of attraction. Everything is made up of molecules. I take a piece of wood, and I cannot pull it apart; but if I take a rope of sand I can do so, because the sand has no attraction. This force is called cohesion. Now I put a globule of mercury on a glass plate, and put another plate on top—draw a picture of the experiment—and you see the mercury spreads out flat. Now, when I take off the plate, the cohesion of the mercury draws it up into a heap again. Here are two sheets of glass which I will wet and put together. Now, you see, I can hardly separate them again except by sliding one off the other. That is cohesion. Now put down 'Adhesion.' When chalk sticks to the blackboard, that is adhesion. Now put down 'Capillary Attraction.' I will hang this piece of blotting paper on a hook and let the end dip in water. You see the water is drawn up. That is capillary attraction. If I dip this stick into a bowl of mercury, you see none sticks to it, because there is no adhesion. When I put the stick into water they adhere." He then took out a set of tubes for showing capillary attraction, and holding them up said, "You see these tubes. Some are larger than others. Now, if I were to take some coloured water in a basin, and put the ends of these tubes into the basin, the water would rise up a good way in the smallest tube, but hardly at all in the largest. Make a drawing of this." He did not perform the experiment, but took another piece of apparatus for illustrating the same property of liquids, and said, " You see these two sheets of glass? They are so fixed that the edges to my left are joined, but those to the right are open about half an inch. Now, if I were to put this into coloured water, the water would rise a long way up on the closed side, and form a curve facing the other way. You will read about it in your books, and you have seen the glass and know what it is." When he had proceeded thus far, I concluded I had written sufficient, and did not take further notes. Apart altogether from the accuracy of his statements, I think it would be difficult to find an example of greater disregard of all sound principles of teaching. That man, though principal of one of the finest schools in the best parts of Boston, when supplied with the best appliances, could not teach !

By way of contrast, I cannot do better than refer to the work at the New York College for the training of teachers, where all the apparatus used is made by the Science Master, or the students themselves. Lamp-chimneys, pickle bottles, preserve jars, canned fruit tins, laths, bits of elastic from old boots, scent bottles, glass rods and tubes, sealing-wax, and such-like inexpensive articles, are made to serve the purpose of illustrating all the principles of science needed. The aim of the enthusiastic teacher is to get the pupils to think about things, and understand the principles ; the scientific wording can be obtained from books if needed. I cannot give the outline of a lesson, because I did not take notes, and prefer not to trust to memory. I was too much interested in watching the work to attempt to write down what took place, and as a matter of fact, such lessons can-not be put on paper. It is the aim of the college to show the students how to teach, and how to make the apparatus for themselves.

I saw excellent science demonstrations being conducted in several high schools, but of these it is not my intention to speak. The laboratories are usually finely and conveni-ently fitted, so that all the pupils can engage in experimental work. My experience is not sufficient to enable me to express an opinion as to whether the use of text-books is abused ; but I may say that I usually found that students worked at the laboratory-table with a book open in front. Thus, if they were testing for a given salt, they would have the book, with directions as to what tests they should apply, open on the table for constant reference.

In the schools of South Australia, slow but steady

progress is being made towards a general systematic teaching of that introduction to scientific thought, which I have indicated is about all that can be at present made compulsory in the way of science in elementary schools. When the last course of study was drawn up some years since under the head of *Special Lessons*, the following instructions were given: "These are to take the place of the object lessons hitherto given, which have been of comparatively little use from the want of a definite plan. A programme of lessons suitable to each class is to be prepared by the teacher, and submitted to the inspector; and for this the courses given below are to be considered merely as suggestions. It is, however, expected that at least. one General Lesson and a lesson on the principles of morality will be given in all cases each week, and that the fourth and fifth classes (equivalent to the sixth and seventh of England and the seventh and eighth grammar grades of the United States) will receive instruction in the duties of a citizen based on the text-book 'Laws we Live Under,' issued by the Department. The text-books for object lessons used up to the present time are unsatisfactory; the lessons are too pretentious. 'Ricks' Object Lessons' will be found a good guide for *Method*.

"Special lessons should never be allowed to degenerate into mere explanations of terms.

"*Suggested* courses of lessons.

"Lessons on animals illustrated by pictures.

"Lessons on plants, illustrated by specimens and pictures.

"Lessons on manufacturing processes, illustrated by specimens and pictures.

"Lessons on elementary physics, if the teacher possesses suitable apparatus for illustration.

"Lessons on the human body, if properly illustrated."

Under these regulations much progress was made, and

many teachers developed a taste for genuine science in consequence of their endeavours to make it interesting to their pupils. The Department did not supply apparatus; but sold it to teachers for only a portion of the cost. Altogether the result was satisfactory, although, but for the yearly result examinations, I believe much greater progress would have been made.

In 1886 the Technical Education Commission appointed by the South Australian Parliament reported, among other things, that instruction in elementary science should be given in the higher classes. The reference made to the subject by the Inspector-General of Schools, Mr. J. A. Hartley, B.A., B.Sc. (Lon.), in his next report, is worthy of being quoted in full :—

"It is somewhat doubtful how far another recommendation of the Technical Board can be carried out, viz. :— That 'instruction in elementary science should be given to the children in the higher classes.' The obstacle to be feared is the want of knowledge on the part of the teachers, and their consequent dependence on text-books. It is unfortunately true, that it is very easy to teach so-called science in such a way, as to make the whole business a pretentious sham ; and many text-books lend themselves to this deception. Such a book consists of a logically arranged summary of results expressed in strictly technical language. If it should fall in the way of a person who has no first-hand knowledge, he may draw up imposing notes of a lesson, the hard words are duly written on the blackboard, and committed to memory by the children, who will astonish the unwary visitor (if he comes soon enough) by the facility with which they will reproduce this parrot knowledge ; but within a week or a month all will have disappeared from their memories as completely as did the chalk from the blackboard when the lesson was over. For more than twenty years the leaders of scientific thought have been vigorously proclaiming against instruction of this kind, and a great change has resulted in the Universities and the better class of secondary schools; but, so far as I know, primary schools have not yet succeeded in teaching science satisfactorily. There are exceptions, of course, to the rule, and some are to be found in this colony. A teacher takes an interest in nature; he is an enthusiast with the microscope, a student of mineral specimens, fond of physics or chemistry; such a man carries his pupils along with him, and they receive impressions in their young days which may last their lives. All men of this class are sure to teach science, and to teach it well; and the more severely they are let alone by the Department, the better for everybody. There is an intermediate class who will probably teach the subject well with a little assistance; lastly, there are a certain number who are as deaf and blind to the attractions of science, as some scientific men are to those of literature. I hope I am not overstating the case, but the greatest caution will be required if the Department is to avoid falling into the error referred to, of mistaking the appearance for the reality, knowledge of words for knowledge of things. We intend to make an earnest attempt, and time alone can show whether it succeeds or fails."

Since then much progress has been made both with regard to supplying the necessary training to teachers, and in giving systematic instruction in the schools.

I will quote from the report made by the Inspector General of the Colony of Victoria, and the Principal of the Melbourne Training College, Messrs. Main and Topp, who spent some months in 1888 in making a comparative investigation into the work of the public schools of the colonies of New South Wales, Victoria, and South Australia:—

" Elementary science is now taught in the three colonies in the higher classes, and in the lower classes object-lessons are prescribed as an introduction to science teaching. In

New South Wales physiology is first taken up, then physics ; and, in the highest class, lessons in physics are generally given in boys' departments, and physiology is again taken up in girls' departments.

"In our (Victorian) schools the course is more logically correct, though perhaps not so suitable for children. The earlier part of the course consists of the general properties of matter, laws of heat, etc.; this is followed in the next class by the physical principles on which common machines depend, and in the highest class the laws of living things are to be explained.

" In South Australia teachers are allowed to choose any science for which they have a taste, provided that a systematic course is given. In one school magnetism and electricity are taken ; in another, chemistry ; in another, geology, mineralogy, and so on.

"The attainments of the children in this subject were very varied.

" In all the colonies, we found in many cases that the pupils had merely learnt a few definitions by rote, while in other schools the children had a really intelligent grasp of scientific principles and of the experimental method.

" The method of examination in this subject is open to criticism. In the other two colonies, as in England, the examination is oral, partly by the teacher, partly by the inspector ; in Victoria the examination is written, and consists in giving three brief answers to as many questions."

CHAPTER VII.

TEACHERS AND THEIR TRAINING.

General Comparison.—Comparison of Methods of Training.—English System gives prominence to Practice.—American more Educational.—English Teacher studies Methods.—American, Principles.—Causes of Difference between American and English Teachers.—English Pupil Teacher System.—Training Colleges.—American Normal Schools.—High School Course and Normal Course.—Prominent Characteristics of English Teachers.—Prominent Characteristics of American Teachers.—Normal Schools.—Philadelphia.—Cook County Normal School.—Nature-Teaching.—Newspaper Cyclopædia.—Washington Normal Schools.

GENERAL COMPARISONS.

"The principle of Co-operation is fundamental in a republic; it is the soul of both its individual and constitutional life. Social friction and the free interchange of experience presuppose a degree of equality; and equality, in turn, incites to combination. The individuality is strong in proportion as he takes to himself the experience of all; each is increased as he gives to all."—BOONE.

THE United States is the great home of association. The instinct and capacity for government is very strong. It is facetiously said, that if three Americans have the same object in view, they form an association, of which one is president, another secretary, the third treasurer, and all are equals. This great tendency—I might say power—must not be lost sight of in comparing the teachers of America with those of England. I find the few English educators who have paid any attention to American schools, invariably lay great stress on what undoubtedly is one of the weaknesses of the Republic—the lack of training on the part of teachers. The great difference lies in the fact that an

English teacher, having gone through the period of pupil-teachership and training college course, is considered to be trained ; and certainly the majority leave the college with the idea that they know how to teach well, and if the cold, unsympathetic authorities would but give them the chance, they would regenerate the teaching world. "Unwise" authorities do not give them the opportunity, and things are not reformed. The ardour of freshness gives way to indifference. They often do not teach as they have been taught to do, except when a visitor is present, who is considered important enough to cause them to rouse themselves. The outcome of this feeling is seen, in the little interest taken in the science or ethics of education afterwards. If they read books or papers on education, it is chiefly those which show real or imaginary short roads to 100 per cent. Consider the small number of educational papers in England, the scarcity of pedagogical libraries, the weakness and insignificance of the teachers' guilds of England, compared with the educational literature, the State, county, city, or even school pedagogical libraries, and the great flourishing Teachers' Associations and Institutes of the chief States of the Republic. The American teacher more frequently studies Herbert Spencer, Fröbel, Horace Mann, Pestalozzi, Payne, Sully, and Fitch, while his English cousin prefers works bearing on "How to Gain 100 per cent. in Arithmetic," "How to Prepare for Examination," "Practical Aids to Teaching," etc.

I would not be misunderstood here. It must not be thought that I believe all, or even the majority, are the great readers of the books I have mentioned—or that there are not a large number of English teachers who read the science of education just as much as Americans—but that a larger *proportion* do so in the Republic than in the Kingdom. And it must be remembered that I am generalising from teachers as I saw them, and from the books which I found they owned, or which were most widely advertised and talked about, as well as from those numerous points of indirect evidence which perhaps have even greater influence on the judgment, but cannot be stated. Many of our most correct impressions are frequently formed from evidence of that indescribable character which refuses to be put on paper. The much-laughed-at "woman's reason," "I know because I do," is not so illogical as it seems; being but another way of saying that the knowledge is rather the effect of intuition, or the unconscious result of accumulated experience, than of a definable reasoning process. I came into contact with only a very small fraction of the vast army of about 400,000 American, or the smaller body of English teachers; but I think those I met were representative.

It must further be remembered here as elsewhere, when comparisons are made, that a lady or gentleman whose social relations would cause the idea of teaching in an English elementary school to be considered derogatory, would consider it a perfectly natural thing to take an appointment in an American public school. According to the English idea, the social status of teachers is higher in America. English teachers appear to frequently discuss the politics of education, or, more correctly, questions relating to status, etc., and I heard a good deal in London about attempting to send a teacher to the House of Commons at the next election to represent their interests. Nevertheless, educational questions, both of a theoretical and practical nature, I believe, form the chief subjects considered in the meetings, which are usually only attended by the teachers of one class of schools, and not at all by the public. There are exceptions to this—notably the Teachers' Guild of Liverpool, the largest in England, I was told—of which I shall speak elsewhere.

The National Education Association of America is the

largest organisation of education in the world, and annually crowds an opera-house for a week with thousands of teachers and educators of all grades, to discuss the psychological basis, no less than the practical bearing, of the most prominent educational proposals. The individual States hold meetings, which are often large; even the small State of Rhode Island can attract nearly one thousand teachers for three days once a year—two special holidays being granted for the purpose, the railway people giving free passes or reduced fares, and the hotels making special rates—to discuss the " live " questions of the education of the day from the practical standpoint of educators. One of the most interesting features of the meetings is the fact, that an equal or greater number of citizens of the city and the neighbourhood, where the Association meets, will sit and listen to the papers and discussions. Could the teachers, say of Huddersfield and district, or even of Sheffield, Leeds, or Manchester, engage a town-hall for three days a year, and fill it with teachers of Board schools, voluntary schools, private schools, academies, colleges, School Board members, managers, and friends of education generally, to carry out such a programme of "*Exercises*"—using the Americans' term for the items on such programmes—as the Rhode Island Institute of Instruction prepares annually—an example of which will be found in the chapter on " Supplementary Means for Preparing Teachers "? In America direct and personal interest in education is not confined to the minority—it is the few who do *not* take an interest in the schools. The opposite is the case in Australia, and I believe to a still greater degree in England.

The difference between English and American schools and teachers must be attributed to a great variety of causes; but perhaps the chief may be summarised and briefly stated to be—difference in the social status of both teachers and pupils; difference in character and degree of the training of teachers ; difference in social and political conditions of the two countries, and the consequent differences in school government ; varying methods of testing school-work ; different character of discipline, again largely due to varying social conditions, together with the arrangement of the school-houses. Or, more briefly still, the differences are due to the fact that the American public school is provided for all sorts and conditions of children, who can be attracted by the inducements of fine buildings, cheerful and bright surroundings, and free instruction, and who are attended and taught by the sons and daughters of rich and poor—professional, clerical, and industrial citizens alike ; while the English elementary schools are expressly provided for the children of the poor and indigent, who, either from social status or lack of means, could not attend the more expensive private schools. This broad statement is, of course, subject to modification. Many of the rich and exclusive Americans do not send their children to the public schools ; and many English people who could afford to pay academic fees wisely send their children to the Board schools. I was given to understand that these are constantly increasing. They are above the petty class prejudices which so retard the progress of reforms in the grand old Mother Land ; and, seeing that Board schools give a better elementary training than private institutions, consider it no disgrace to give their children the advantage of what they by their school-rates assist to provide.

METHODS OF TRAINING.

England.

The majority of English elementary teachers receive a systematic training ; the majority of American teachers have no such preparation. The English teacher, commencing at

M

fourteen or fifteen, has three or four years' apprenticeship, and following that, two years in a training college. When special training is given in America, it consists of a High School course, and one or two years' special Normal course. The dominating feature of the English training is practice, or experience; of American, study and science of teaching. The English system is a development of the special conditions of the country at the time of Messrs. Bell and Lancaster; the American is based on German methods—as indeed many other prominent features of American schools are.

One of the ablest of the School Board clerks whom I had the pleasure of meeting in England, said during a chat we had on this subject, "I must confess that the German system of training makes better students; but ours produces better teachers. The English method certainly fails in giving us cultured, educated men, who are life-long students for the sake of knowledge; but the English schoolmaster *can teach*, and that is what we want." I did not agree; but were I to admit his conception of what constitutes teaching, I would at once grant his conclusions. Or I might grant the correctness of his statement; but submit that not "teaching," but education, is the chief aim of a schoolmaster, and that training a pupil to find out one fact in such a way that he thereby gains the desire as well as the power to obtain more, is a better result than "teaching" facts sufficient for 100 per cent. at the result examination. It may be our disagreement was probably more from a failure to understand one another, than from actual diversity of opinion.

A contrast somewhat more in detail may be interesting here. "A pupil teacher is a boy or a girl engaged by the managers of a public elementary day-school, on condition of teaching during school hours under superintendence of the principal teacher, and receiving instruction out of school hours." The period of apprenticeship is usually four years, but may be reduced to two provided the candidate is old enough, and can pass the corresponding examination. The minimum age is fourteen years, so that their term of service may not be completed before eighteen.

" At the close of their engagements they may become— (*a*) Students in Training Colleges, (*b*) Assistant Teachers, (*c*) Provisionally Certificated Teachers." I cannot give any estimate as to the proportion of ex-pupil teachers who enter the training colleges, or what number are employed as assistants ; but I believe the proportion of the latter is not great.

Nearly all of the most proficient pupil teachers, on completion of their course, at the age of from eighteen to twenty, enter one of the excellent training colleges. The fees are merely nominal, and include board and residence in college ; but each institution makes its own terms. They are all, like the schools, under private management, being supported by the funds of the educational societies and Government grants, which depend on certain requirements being complied with. The chief of these are the annual examinations of the Education Department and the reports of Her Majesty's Inspectors. The grant may amount to £50 a year for each male, and £35 a year for each female student, but must not exceed 75 per cent. of the cost of the institution. The course of study is—(*a*) Academic, (*b*) Professional—including both the science and practice of teaching. There are always practice, or " Model " Schools, in connection with the colleges.

If the student satisfactorily passes the final examination, he receives a provisional certificate, which is replaced by a full certificate if the inspector reports favourably on his subsequent work in the school to which he may be appointed.

M 2

Thus, under the English system, the teacher begins his special training at the close of the elementary school course, steps out of the senior class to be junior teacher in the same school, and in many cases at once takes charge of a class of forty pupils. He commences to earn money for professional work during the period when the character is unformed, and the mind least stable. In most cases, the whole day is spent in teaching under most difficult conditions, with one or two other classes in the same room. In the evening, what little energy is left is to be used in preparing themselves for the next examination. Strenuous efforts are being made by several School Boards to improve this state of things, to provide time for study, and relieve the strain of teaching the whole time.

From this it will be seen that not only does the English teacher receive his training free; but is able almost to support himself while doing so. Those who take up the work of teaching intend to continue at it. A full certificate cannot be obtained until a year or two after leaving college —or, say, at twenty-two years of age; but when received, is good for life. This gives security and permanency, but has the disadvantage of allowing and encouraging the feeling that, the certificate having been earned, effort may cease; and the teacher not unfrequently crystallises into a grant-earning machine. Desire for promotion, love of study, and other influences, are powerful enough to stimulate all the better men and women to continuous effort. The permanency and security of the teacher's position in England seemed to me to be much greater than in America, where they are usually only engaged for a year at a time, although the average length of service in the city schools shows that the re-engagement at the beginning of each year is a mere formality in most cases.

It is more difficult to make a concise statement with respect to the training of American teachers. There is considerable variety in details under the different authorities. The minimum age at which a person may be employed as a teacher is generally eighteen years ; in some places— Chicago, for example—it is nineteen. Graduates of Normal Schools are usually at least a year older. At the time when the English pupil-teacher is passing her candidate's examination, the American pupil is "graduating" from the Grammar School. She then enters upon a three or four years' High School course, frequently—or rather, generally —with no adaptation to the work of teaching. It is simply an academic course preparatory to the University. At eighteen she graduates, and then takes a special course of one or two years in the Normal Section. As she has already graduated in academic subjects, this time is spent in the study of the science and history of education, and practice-work. Literary work is only taken in connection with the theory of teaching. The schools are all free, but students usually have to provide books, so that it is necessary for the parents of an intending teacher to support her until the age of eighteen to twenty. The custom of having residential colleges is not followed. I shall presently give more detailed accounts of three Normal Schools, which I believe will give a clearer idea of the American system than a lengthy general statement. It will be conceded, I think, contrary to established notions, that the English authorities are more liberal than the American. While the one provides means of training free, the other provides for the support of the intending teacher from the elementary school age.

The American Normal graduate is ready for active work at about the same age as the English Training

College student; and we can to a certain extent compare their qualifications for the high duties they have to perform.

The special feature of the English teacher is technical skill in practical teaching; that of the American, an educated and cultured mind. The time one has spent in teaching or learning to teach, the other has spent in study. The one has all along been subject to the influences of a narrowing occupation, and now oftentimes considers himself well-nigh perfect in his art; the other has been under the influences of a liberal training, is well versed in the principles of education, has had little practice in teaching; but is fully conscious of the fact, and therefore ready to take advantage of every means to compensate for his lack. A conscious ignorance is often better than a self-satisfied knowledge. The one is a continuous antidote against itself, the other the mother of pedantry and prejudice. The social conditions of England make the attainment to the position of schoolmaster, one which many teachers and their friends look upon as sufficient progress in the social scale to warrant the assumption of airs, which often afford considerable amusement to visitors used to democratic surroundings and ideas.

So far I have endeavoured to confine myself to the small proportion of American teachers who have had a special training; but so far as I was able to judge, the line of demarcation between the teachers who have had a special and those who have only had an indirect training was imperceptible. The conclusion was irresistible, that the excellence of American teaching is the result of those supplementary, casual, indirect means which I, in common with the majority of others unacquainted with the conditions of country and people, was inclined formerly to depreciate.

The general impression left on my mind may be summarised :—

1. The special and systematic training of teachers,

especially of men, while excellent and thorough in some centres, is decidedly weak in many places and deficient generally.

2. The average American teacher maintains better discipline with less force; is a superior educator, but less an adept than her English compeer in filling the pupil's head with facts.

3. The conditions of the States are very different from those of either England or Australia. Indirect influences so generally modify the expected condition of things, the interest in and acquaintance with the public education is so widespread and keenly felt, and the teachers are usually so bright and progressive, that a much smaller amount of special training produces an equal degree of competency.

The thought occurs, when reading the severe comments of Americans on the poor teaching in the schools of the States, that either their ideal must be so high, that what I considered good, by comparison with work done elsewhere, is very much below their conception of possible excellence; or, perhaps more likely, with all my care not to confine myself to the show schools recommended by the authorities and friends of education, who, of course, very properly wished to give me as favourable an opinion as possible, I may not have seen average schools. That the first hypothesis is true I am convinced. I am equally willing to admit the likely possibility of the second; but I do not intend to modify the descriptions of what I did see, and the conclusions to be drawn therefrom, on account of what it might have been possible for me to find had I searched for the bad. The comparisons between different systems being made on the same basis, the conclusions are still just. As a sample of the florid language which has led me to make these remarks, I will quote a few lines from the editorial columns of the April number of *Education* :—

" Untold thousands of children in our oldest and most

cultivated States get little help from the kind of country school which is their only seminary; kept by a green girl or bumptious boy, in defiance of all sound principles of elementary education. And even in our great cities, and oftener in our large towns, the graded schools are honey-combed with incompetents, mental and moral, who muddle the work for a year and baffle the wisdom and energy of the ablest superintendent." Probably this, like patent medicine, should be taken with discretion.

AMERICAN NORMAL SCHOOLS.

Philadelphia.

The Normal School for the training of teachers, like many other points of the American system of education, follows the German rather than the English plan. When I state that I found each successive institution I visited differed somewhat from those I had previously inspected, it will be understood that uniformity does not reach the stage of monotony. Besides many private Normal Schools, there are three classes which may be termed public institutions. These are the State, County, and City Normal, and each derives its designation from the authority under which it has been established. State institutions are to be found in the Eastern, Northern, and Middle North-Western States, as well as in California.

County Normal Schools are generally similar to the above; but are provided to supply the needs of a more limited area : while the school systems of cities, being perfectly independent of the State in which they are located, prefer to make their own arrangements for the training of teachers. The pedagogical chairs of some of the Universities will come under the head of private means.

The Normal School usually admits pupils at from fifteen

to seventeen, after they have passed through the Grammar
Grades, and takes them through a four years' High School
course. During the last year or two they are instructed
in the science of teaching, and have a certain, though
usually small amount of practical work in the attached
practice-school.

A few insist on a higher standard for entrance, only
taking as students graduates of a High School, and spend
more time on practical work ; while in other cases the High
and Normal Schools are combined. Philadelphia may be
taken as an example of the latter. This institution is of
large proportions, there being, I was informed, about 2,200
pupils in attendance at the time of my visit. This number
of course includes the practice departments, consisting of
two model Kindergartens of about fifty pupils each, and
between five and six hundred boys and girls in primary and
grammar grades. The first three years of the Normal
School would be more correctly called the Girls' High
School, as the course of study is similar to those pursued in
the High Schools of other cities, and corresponds with the
Boys' High School of Philadelphia itself. Pupils have to
pass an examination before entering the school. As a rule
candidates must have graduated in a grammar school a year
previously and have spent one year in the post-graduate class.
I had the pleasure of questioning one of these post-graduate
grammar school classes on several subjects, including the
United States Constitution, and concluded that if they
exercise their reasoning powers as logically and clearly on
ordinary occasions, the Normal teachers have good material
on which to work.

The course extends over four years, during the last of
which those who have elected to graduate in the Normal
class spend the greater portion of their time either at
practice work, or in studying the science of teaching. Six
weeks are spent in the practice school with one class.

During the first two the student observes, during the second fortnight she assists the regular teacher, and for two weeks takes complete charge of the class under the eye of the critic teacher. I heard the principal of the Kindergarten Normal Training Department lecture to fifty students on "How to show the Children the way Seeds Grow." It was one of the many treats I had in the schools.

She supposed that the children being Kindergarteners would be unable to read or write; but simply to see, do, and reason. They were to see the seeds from day to day sprouting on moist flannel, porous earthenware, or damp sand. Each child would see his own seeds swell and burst as the first and then the second sprout began to show. He would watch the growth, and find some having two seed-leaves, and some only one. This and much more was to be shown in the most simple and natural way. The children were to be trained, educated, or rather were to be put in the position to do this themselves under tender guidance. The theory exactly agreed with the practical work I had so often been delighted with in the American Kinder-gartens.

No inspector goes once a year to endeavour to measure off the amount of intellectual development made by the child-flowers in the child-garden. They grow, but you cannot say just where they have increased. Every part of the plant develops, and you see it is not the same as a month before; but you cannot say just where the difference is, for it is everywhere. So with the child.

The Normal students have a course of cookery; but not with the idea of each student teaching it, for although the subject is included in the Philadelphian schools it is taken by special teachers. It is rather a part of the school course, which also includes the theory and practice of music, and the history and psychology of education.

I was particularly struck with the importance attached to giving every student a knowledge of the theory of Kindergarten, together with six weeks' practice in the methods. In this, Philadelphia, Boston, Cook County, and many other Normal Schools, are surely guarding against the weakness of St. Louis, where the Kindergarten in itself has made the greatest headway. The principle is becoming everywhere more and more admitted that, while the first portion of a child's education should be Kindergarten pure and simple, no time can be fixed when it may be said that Kindergarten must give way to other methods. This is the mistake in St. Louis. The better institutions try to turn out Kindergarteners who shall understand the after-education, and primary and grammar teachers who understand Kindergarten.

The attention given to physical exercises is a very noticeable feature in the Philadelphia, as in many other American High Schools.

Another feature of this, as of other Normal Schools I visited, is that it contains an excellent library with a regular librarian constantly in attendance. I invariably found that these libraries were well used. The rooms are well provided with tables and comfortable chairs—but this follows as a matter of course, for seats are always made for comfort in America—and I often found all occupied. The building and its fittings are palatial.

The "recitations" (oral lessons or lectures) which I listened to during a somewhat lengthy visit, were excellent; and the practical results of the demonstrations in cookery were eminently satisfactory, and an eloquent prophecy of good dinners in some future homes.

I believe not one-third of the pupils who enter the school, graduate in the teachers' class, and probably many of those do not teach. It may be interesting to show the course of study.

COURSE OF STUDY IN THE GIRLS' NORMAL SCHOOL, PHILADELPHIA.								
A Fourth Year.	History of Education.	Mental and Moral Science in their relations to Education.	Methods of Teaching.	Philosophy and method of the Kindergarten.	Drawing; with instruction in methods of teaching this study.	School Organisation and Management.	Modelling in Clay. Instruction in the Gifts and Occupations of the Kindergarten.	Music.
	English Language and Literature.			Mathematics.	Science.	History.	Drawing.	Sewing.	Music.
B Third Year.	Literature. Theme Writing. Reading of English Classics.	Elocution.		Higher Arithmetic; including Mensuration, Principles of Accounts and Book-keeping. Geometry.	Chemistry. Natural Philosophy. Astronomy. Human Physiology and Hygiene.		Drawing.	Sewing.	Music.
C Second Year.	Rhetoric. Theme Writing. History of the English Language; including the study of the derivation, formation, etc., of words. English Literature. Reading of English Classics.	Elocution.		General Review of Arithmetic. Geometry.	Zoology. Geology. Natural Philosophy.	General History.	Drawing.	Sewing. Cooking.	Music.
D First Year.	Grammar. Composition. History of the English Language; including the study of the derivation, formation, etc., of words. Reading of English Classics.			Algebra.	Physical Geography. Botany.	History and Civil Government of the United States. General History.	Drawing.	Sewing.	Music.

1. Physical Exercises throughout the first, second, and third Years. 2. Laboratory Work in Chemistry when possible. 3. Laboratory Work as far as possible in Physics. 4. Drawing to include the Treatment of Geometric Drawing, Construction, Decoration, Representation, and Object Drawing.

One of the most interesting of the public institutions for the training of teachers, which I visited, was Cook County Normal School, at Chicago, under Colonel F. W. Parker. Its interest lies in the fact that the Colonel holds decided views, and has splendid opportunities of putting them into practice. The building is not of the most modern American type; but is fairly well adapted to its purpose. The establishment, besides the Normal School proper, contains a Kindergarten, and all grades of Primary, Grammar, and High Schools, so that the future teachers become acquainted with every part of the school course.

Some of the students take the High School course before the Normal; but the majority are attracted from more distant parts, often from other States, by the colonel's fame as a reformer. The Faculty are all men and women of advanced views, and established reputations as teachers; so that the school is looked on as a hotbed of Radicalism even in the West, where new ideas take root like European weeds in Australian fields.

I paid a number of visits to the school. One special feature, I noted, is the attention paid to science, the teaching being thoroughly experimental and practical, with a view to its being taught to pupils not as facts, but as an education in observation, and love for nature.

The institution possesses a fine Natural History Museum, which bears distinctive evidences of being well used; but more interesting still were the small collections of specimens in each room.

The primary grades were under a lady happily possessed of one of the most wonderfully expressive faces I have seen. Kindness, power, and tenderness were equally shown; and her manner of dealing with the children was so diversified that she apparently treated no two children alike, although

there were perhaps forty in the class.   In the room of the
first grade was a cage with a pair of squirrels, whose antics
were most interesting.   They belonged to the children, who
were able to tell me, in their own pretty way, very much of
the habits and life of these forest economists. On the teacher's
desk were several tumblers upside-down, enclosing cocoons
of various kinds which had been spun in the room ; while on
the table were boxes with caterpillars feeding on *fresh leaves*
of the tree or bush on which they were found.   These had
been brought in by the children, who were only allowed to
do so on condition that they bring a regular supply of fresh
food.

I had a favourable opportunity of judging the lady's
mode of dealing with these specimens ; for one morning
a child brought in a caterpillar on which were a number of
tiny cocoons.   This was passed round for the children to
look at.   The majority said they had seen the same
kind of caterpillar ; but they were puzzled by the white
silky egg-like attachments, although several said they
looked like cocoons, about which they had evidently had
some talk.   The teacher then told, in the form of a simple
story, how, "while the caterpillar was feeding quietly on a
bush, a little fly came flitting along ; and, seeing the soft
leaf-eater, settled on him ; and, with a sharp weapon made
for the purpose, pierced a number of holes in the poor
caterpillar's back and sides, and in each laid a tiny egg.
Then she flew away—perhaps to do the same to another
before she died.   The caterpillar, perhaps, never felt
her ; but in a short time the tiny eggs hatched, and out
of each came a small grub.   These fed on the flesh of the
poor caterpillar, which ate more and more ravenously ;
but only to feed the grubs, which, after they had grown
to their full size, came out and spun the small silk cocoons,
and went to sleep inside.   You see, the poor caterpillar
looks very sickly compared to this one having no cocoons ;

but as Nellie has brought some leaves, we will put him in this box, to see what becomes of him and his load of cocoons." The children had from time to time supplied information, and now several were eager to carry the story further, and anticipated the result of the experiment by saying that the sleeping grub or chrysalis in the little cocoon would change into the same sort of tiny fly as the one that laid the eggs in the caterpillar. This was noted, and the specimen put aside to see whether the speculations would prove to be correct, and, if so, that the appearance of this wonderful little fly might be noted.

That this took place as an ordinary occurrence I am sure, for no one knew I would be there; and the pupils appeared quite used to the kind of discussion, and very greatly to enjoy it.

I need hardly say that the intelligence of these children was wonderful, even for America. I have omitted to mention that the new words used in the chat were written on the blackboard, and impressed on the minds of the pupils. This is, indeed, part of the system of reading followed. The children learn to read scrip first by the look-and-say method ; and their writing proceeds hand-in-hand with the reading, the process being the real thing, the written symbol of the thing, reproducing the symbol on the slate. The Colonel's pupils would be behind those of an English Voluntary, or Board School, at an examination in reading, writing, and arithmetic; but in intelligence, mental activity, general knowledge—or, in other words, in education—the English children would be far inferior.

The mode of teaching drawing is different from any-thing I saw in operation elsewhere, although the principle is not novel, having been advocated by more than one writer on education. The children, instead of drawing lines, or even objects, with pencil, are provided with

paints and brushes, with which they try to reproduce
simple objects, such as leaves, fruit, etc. Drawing was
on the time-table for the second day of my visit, and I
saw three classes endeavouring to produce pictures of
cucumbers. The children had all brought cucumbers,
which first served as the subject for the day's observation,
or object lesson. There were large cucumbers, small, long
green, curly yellow, smooth, rough—all shapes and sizes:
every variety seemed to be represented. One lesson which
I listened to was being given by one of the staff, and I
have seldom heard a better. In another room the class
was divided into groups of six or seven, each under a
student. I passed from one to another. Many of the
groups were teaching their teachers; others were being
lectured to; others were giving and receiving knowledge
in a way to delight anyone able to appreciate true teaching.
After chatty lessons on the things themselves came the
drawing. It is difficult to decide as to the value of this
exercise. The pupils were unmistakably interested, and
that is saying much. There was no difficulty in deciding
what the majority of the pictures were meant for; a few
were very good, while some might have represented many
things, but it would require the imagination of an American
newspaper interviewer to imagine that they were intended
for cucumbers.

It was interesting to note that the little children showed
as great—if not greater—an aptitude for this work as the
normal students, for whom I should mention there was in
addition a good course of clay modelling and drawing from
model and cast—in fact art-work.

Unlike most American schools for the training of
teachers, a residence hall constitutes part of the establishment, affording accommodation for the students from a
distance. The school is free to residents of Cook County,
Illinois; but others have to pay tuition fees. The library

has between six and seven thousand volumes, and there is a library for the children of nearly two thousand volumes.

The tuition fees above mentioned are devoted to the purchase of books and apparatus. There is a novel feature of the library which deserves special description. It is called the Newspaper Cyclopædia, and is worthy of imitation, especially in England and Australia, where the newspapers —although heavy and lacking in the bright, racy, not to mention the sensational character of American—are, as a rule, more reliable and of a higher literary merit. It originated in the ordinary newspaper scrap-book, which in Mrs. Parker's hands assumed such proportions that a fresh plan had to be adopted for keeping the extracts in such a manner that they might be accessible and easy of reference. At first a series of pigeon-holes was employed, each numbered and devoted to a given subject, the clippings being mounted on sheets of stout manilla paper ten inches by four inches. This arrangement became insufficient, and a handsome case of patent American letter files was procured, containing a large number of drawers or files, each with a device for attaching a cord in front with the index of contents.

The subjects are arranged under between thirty and forty numbered heads, each head having lettered subheads.

For example, No. xiii. Geography, has the subheads (*a*) Contents, (*b*) Islands, (*c*) Oceans, (*d*) Climate, (*e*) Deserts, (*f*) Cities and Towns, (*g*) Explorations, (*h*) Children's Stories, &c., &c. When a clipping is made relating, say, to an explorer, it is pasted on a sheet of manilla paper and numbered "*xiii. (g) Exploration*" and placed in its proper file.

Normal Schools at Washington, D.C.

Washington has two Normal Schools, the one for coloured, the other for white students. In the former a "Recitation" on temporary organisation was in progress

N

at the time of my visit; and as it will throw light on the character of the small "ungraded" schools, I will include the substance of the Principal's remarks. After a preliminary discussion on organisation, in its wider sense, which subject had evidently been dealt with before, she proceeded to explain that by temporary organisation is meant the means taken during the first fortnight after the opening of a school to facilitate the work of both teacher and pupil. At the opening of the school on the first day, the teacher should allow the pupils to walk into the school and take places wherever they feel inclined, she welcoming them with pleasant words, and such actions as will make them feel at home. No rules of order should be laid down at first, and no definite instruction attempted; but the time should be taken up with interesting lessons, which will make the pupils like the school. As they begin to feel at home, endeavour to find out what they know, their dispositions, and capabilities, which, with the ages, will form the basis of a proper classification. As soon as the pupils are classified, the teacher should construct her programme, and never fail to remember that it should be a contract between her and her pupils, upon the faithful keeping of which much of her success as a character-builder will depend. I need not deal further with the lecture. Probably few English or Australian training college students have had such advice given them. The students varied in colour and type from the true negro to several who scarcely showed any traces of negro blood. They were bright and intelligent in appearance; and their answers were suggestive of thought and culture. All had graduated in the City High School, and had been selected from a large number of applicants by examination.

The school for white students is conducted in a similar manner. The best forty graduates of the High School, who wish to become teachers, are selected by examination.

These spend a year in the Normal School, in connection with which there are eight practical classes, or schools, as the rooms are oddly called in Washington. These eight classes are taught exclusively by the students under the guidance of practised teachers. No academic work is done. " By way of review, and in order that the pupils may see each subject to be taught as an entirety, so that they may be able to see the relation of every part of the subject to the whole and to every other part, a logical review is made by each student of each subject in the school course. These are constructed from the teacher's standpoint, with the idea of giving uppermost, whereas previously getting had been the object." Considerable time is devoted to psychology, and the science and history of teaching, while the details and methods of school work are learned in con-nection with the practice work, which extends through the whole eight grades of the elementary school course.

This appeared to me to be the best system of training which came under my notice.

CHAPTER VIII.

SUPPLEMENTARY MEANS FOR TRAINING TEACHERS.

TEACHERS' INSTITUTES.

THERE is, fortunately for the progress of the schools, no pupil teacher system in America. Setting children to teach children is now almost, if not entirely, confined to the British Empire. But let them not hastily claim superiority. Speaking generally, the Normal Schools in the various States do not provide more than a very small proportion—in Pennsylvania, about one-fifth of the vacancies are filled with trained teachers—of the number of teachers required each year, although there are large centres, like St. Louis, where nearly all are Normal graduates. This is not at all surprising in a country where such a large number are ladies, many of whom only devote their energies to "keeping school," until opportunity offers for "keeping house"; and where so many teach for a time to accomplish a purpose, which, being attained, they draft off into other work. Speaking of this subject the United States superin tendent says :—"Leaving out the much-canvassed fact tha t about 70 per cent. of the attendance at the Normal Schools of the country are females, and that their assumption of the marriage relation involves their withdrawal from the profession of teaching, we find that with men it is merely used in many cases as an expedient to a better and more lucrative employment, not to say profession. It is evident that a talented lawyer, physician, or theologian, is socially and financially of much more account than a talented schoolmaster. Thus we are constantly reminded that the interest that each has for his own advancement and reward, is not suspended in the case of the profession of teaching ; that ability will not see itself passed in the struggle for reputation and wealth, content because doing good : for that is a celestial, not a business, virtue."

England has 27,000 untrained pupil teachers. America has a far greater proportion of men and women in her schools, who have not had the advantages of systematic training.   Formerly the proportion of untrained teachers was much greater than it is now.   To meet the wants of these, special means have been adopted.   The chief of these is the Teachers' Institute, a purely and distinctly American development; but one which is worthy of consideration at the hands of both English and Australian educators, to supplement the training which the teachers have received, and counteract the tendency to " vegetate," to which teachers with little ambition and a life certificate are undoubtedly subject.   The permanency of the teacher's position in England, and more particularly in Australia, where he is a Civil Servant, and virtually sure of his position—or a better one—for life, unless he grossly neglects his duty, certainly has the tendency to induce a feeling that further efforts in the direction of study of methods and the science of teaching are unnecessary.   It seems to me that an adaptation of the American Institute would be as practicable as beneficial.   The American superintendents are handicapped by the lack of authority; but they do splendid work in promoting the intelligence of the teaching.   The English Education Department, clothed in all the dignity of authority, has not yet thought fit to assume other functions than those of an organisation for the distribution of money.   I know that Her Majesty's Inspectors are gentlemen of wide attainments; but am unable to say whether they usually have the qualifications needed to conduct such gatherings as I have mentioned. In Australia the conditions more nearly resemble those of America; and the plan would be more readily adopted.   In fact, when the new course of study came into operation in South Australia, some years since, meetings of much the same character, and for the same purpose, were held throughout the colony; and one, at least, of the inspectors has continued to hold meetings of a similar character ever since.

Superintendent Draper, of New York, with others, thinks that, however desirable, it is not practicable to obtain teachers trained after the usual plan for the rural schools. At the same time, it is necessary that they should be in charge of only those who have had some definite training. " It is hopeless to expect that the time and money involved in pursuing a Normal School course will be given in order to obtain the salary of a district teacher." He advocates that " normal work of a lower grade, less in extent and nearer the homes of the people, must be had before the needs of the rural schools are supplied." Until this is done, the Institutes must be the chief means by which any special training is acquired.

Professor C. H. McGrew, occupying the Chair of " Educational Psychology, Science and Art of Teaching," at the University of the Pacific, California, is one of the leading advocates of what appears, in view of the special conditions of the country and the long vacations, one of the best plans for improving the professional knowledge of teachers. The custom now is, in most States, to hold the week's Institute during school terms, the schools being specially closed for the purpose. Only in this way can the best men be got to conduct more than a few.

Says the Professor :—" We need a four weeks' Normal Institute system, making the county and county super-intendency prominent factors. . . . Our Normal Institutes should be short-term professional training schools, held during the summer and winter vacations. A professional course of study of three or four years should be prepared by the State Superintendent or State Board, and should be general, and definite, and so flexible that it can be adjusted to the varying conditions and needs in different countries, and at the same time secure a sufficient degree of uniformity. It should provide for a completion of the course by teachers, and some legal recognition of such work by authorities, thus stimulating attendance, and forming a class of teachers for our common schools. Model classes in Kindergarten, primary teaching, and other grades, should be maintained free to the children of the town where the Institute is held, thus furnishing the best illustrations of the new methods."

This is but broadening and extending that present Institute system which is such an important factor in American education. In Dakota, for example, the Department of Public Instruction has arranged for two courses of Institutes a year—one in the autumn and one in the spring, *during the holiday when the schools of the Institute are closed.*

The Department appoints a conductor and assistants, who act as instructors. The Institute is not a school, and academic instruction is a secondary object. The teacher is expected to have acquired the matter. The object of the Institute is to help teachers, especially those of the country, to improve their methods.

" In brief, the object is :—

1. To increase efficiency by giving
    (*a*) A distinct idea of the ends of education.
    (*b*) Elementary knowledge of the science of teaching.
    (*c*) Instruction in methods.
2. To secure greater uniformity
    (*a*) By discussion.
    (*b*) By professional co-operation.
3. To correct prevailing errors."

This latter is a responsible undertaking, since what constitutes an error is usually a matter of opinion.

The Institute is usually held in a hall spacious enough to contain a large number of visitors, whose presence is invited. It was a constant matter of surprise to me, to find the interest which the public took in these assemblies. The far-reaching influence of this fact needs more than a passing notice. It is stated, with truth, that many of those taking charge of small schools, or even receiving appointments as class teachers, have had no professional training in the art of teaching, and to supply this want is one of the purposes of the Institutes. It must not be forgotten, however, that in all probability the lady thus receiving her first appointment has been in the habit of attending Teachers' Institutes—perhaps as a mere idle listener: but she has become familiar with the questions dealt with in the meetings. An "untrained" American teacher must not be compared to an untrained teacher elsewhere. In consequence of these Institutes, the public at large have such an intelligent knowledge of the principles of teaching, that one who has never taught before enters upon her work with a generally correct, concise, and intelligent idea of what to teach, and how to teach it.

In the announcements respecting Institutes, made by one Superintendent, "it is particularly requested that those who have any intention of becoming teachers will endeavour to attend as many of the meetings as possible, and special attention will be given to 'First weeks at School.'" Parents too are able to understand that the teacher is more than a mere instructor; their attention is drawn to the schools; their interest in education is stimulated; while the trustees and members of school committees are the better able to fulfil their duties. Special means are often adopted to enlist the sympathies and support of the people of the towns in which Institutes are held. Morning and afternoon sessions will be held devoted to more purely educational subjects; and in the evening a lecture on some general topic having a more or less direct bearing on education. Often lecturers are brought from long distances to address Institutes; and thus the interchange of ideas between one State and another is promoted.

In consequence of the success of a regular programme

of work in connection with her country Institutes, Indiana has enacted that :—

"At least one Saturday in each month, during which the public schools may be in progress, shall be devoted to township Institutes or model schools for the improvement of teachers." More than four thousand of these were held during the year.

The following principles are laid down as a basis on which Institutes should be conducted :—

For the meeting place the hall of a school-house, if one is available, is better than a court-room, public hall, or church, which have neither the apparatus nor the " atmosphere " of a school.

The meeting should begin promptly on Monday. Two instructors should be employed, and six or at most seven daily lessons of forty minutes each is all that should be given. Certain definite lines of thought should be adopted on Monday, and carried through the week, thus giving opportunity to present a series of connected lessons. It should be understood that the country Institute is a professional meeting, entertainment being incidental, and that it is not a place for academic work.

The professional features are the History of Education, the Science of Education, Methods of Primary Instruction in the various grades, School Management, Moral Instruction, and Psychology.

The paper from which the above is taken proceeds to show in what way education is and is not a science.

" It is not a science in the way that arithmetic, algebra, &c., are sciences, for it lacks the inherent necessity which makes these subjects pure sciences. It is held that education is a science in the view that it is possible to ground all the work of the school-room on rationally determined principles. The processes, and all the concrete work of school instruction, management, discipline, class manipulation, rest on principles.

" These ideas, generalisations, reasons, principles, when brought together and organised into coherent form, constitute the Science of Education.

"This science considers the subjects of study in the

school in three related aspects :— First, the educational value of each ; second, the true order of sequence among the studies of the course ; and third, the methodology appropriate to the different stages of each."

The manner in which it is possible to present the Science of Education before the teachers in a county Institute, so that they shall be able to grasp it, and base their actual work upon it, is discussed. It is held that it cannot be done in the time at the disposal of the Institute. The works of various writers—Locke, Bacon, Rousseau, Pestalozzi, Herbert Spencer, Herbart, and others — are mentioned as having to be studied to accomplish that.

A good deal may be done to induce teachers to read some of these works by drawing attention to them in the Institute.

" The Science of Education does not deal with receipts, prescriptions, and rules; it sets forth ideas, general judgments, reasons, principles. It must do this in the Institute; do it to be sure in the best way, suitable to the conditions existing."

The Michigan State Superintendent thinks that the idea of the Institute is "more to suggest the method than to make an exhaustive study and application."

Considering the Institute is composed of a somewhat promiscuous assemblage of men and women, in a great measure unknown to one another and to the instructors, and that they meet for the space of from one to two weeks, there will probably be little difficulty in accepting his statement.

In New York a plan has been adopted of making the work continuous from year to year for three or four years.

In some States there is a rule to the effect that certificates to teach will not be granted to persons who do not attend the Institutes.

The significance of this statement will be understood

by English or Australian readers, who are acquainted with the peculiar system of granting certificates in vogue in many States, in which, as I have explained elsewhere, the diploma to teach is renewed at periods varying from a year to ten years according to grade.

CHAIRS OF PEDAGOGICS.

Chairs in the Science and Art of Education are now being established in a few of the better colleges and universities in various States. This is considered a hopeful sign, indicating a tendency to raise the art of teaching to a profession—a consummation, which, however desirable, will not be realised until the period of service is very much extended, and teachers take to the work in the same way as members of the other professions, as a life work. It should be the most honoured of professions ; it will be, when public sentiment is further educated, and teachers themselves enforce its recognition by their absolute worth. The advocates of the new Professorships disclaim competition with the Normal Colleges, the aim of which is to train for the practical work of teaching no less than to teach the principles on which it is based. The idea is that the University should train educators, who would in turn create and mould educational sentiment. It should provide trained superintendents and professors for the Normal schools, who, in turn, would provide the schools with teachers.

TEACHERS' ASSOCIATIONS.

Under names as various as their constitutions, teachers in all countries where education has made headway, have formed organisations for their professional, social, or financial improvement. Pedagogical Societies are very numerous and important in Germany, and perhaps hardly less so in the United States; while in the British Isles and Australia they are doing admirable work. The most desirable, and certainly the most general, objects of the Societies—be they Teachers' Associations, Teachers' Guilds, Pedagogical Societies, Clubs, or Round Tables—is professional improvement. They are a recognition of John Stuart Mill's question:—"What does anyone's personal knowledge of things amount to, after subtracting all which he has acquired by means of the words of other people?" and an endeavour to answer it. In a few cases only, as far as I could learn, do they take up questions of educational politics. This is well, although there are times when a decided expression of opinion from those who, next to the pupils, will be most affected by a change of policy may be desirable. Still more necessary is it that practical educators should study the psychological basis of every proposal to effect changes in Educational Legislation. Teachers are as a rule very conservative, and it is therefore likely that the ideas of the few progressive spirits who are usually at the head (or "at the bottom"!) of every educational reform are more trustworthy guides than those of the majority of teachers, who perhaps as frequently retard as advance progressive movements.

In America, each town appears to have its flourishing Association. Sometimes these give prominence to the social aspect, and are known as Clubs or Schoolmasters' "Round Tables." The various towns often combine in a county association, and the counties in a larger organisation comprising the whole State; while the leading educators in every State of the Union have united to form the largest, if not the most important, organisation of the kind in existence.

The National Educational Association has for its objects, "To elevate the character, and advance the interests of the profession of teaching, and to promote the cause of popular education in the United States." It has nine departments, and a National Council of Education :—1. School Superintendence ; 2, Normal Schools ; 3, Elementary Schools ; 4, Higher Instruction ; 5, Industrial Education ; 6, Art Education ; 7, Kindergarten Instruction ; 8, Music Education ; 9, Secondary Education. Additional departments may be formed. The qualifications for membership are very broad. It holds an annual convention in July of each year, which is attended by thousands of members and friends, the largest hall or opera house being engaged for the meetings. Its annual volume of proceedings ranging from seven to nine hundred pages, is a highly interesting addition to current educational literature.

The State Associations are usually organised in departments, the most frequent being the Department of Superintendents, High School Department, and Primary and Grammar Departments. The School Superintendents have an association for the discussion of matters coming more particularly in their sphere of work as directors of Education. I had a volume of their proceedings given me which had been published as a bulletin of the Bureau of Education, and found its contents able contributions to the discussion of the current educational topics of the day.

RHODE ISLAND INSTITUTE.

The largest and best meeting of teachers I attended was the annual gathering of the Rhode Island Institute of Instruction. It differed from the " Institute " proper, which is an official gathering convened by a Superintendent, in being a voluntary gathering of Educators. The nearest approach to it in England, of which I had any personal acquaintance, were the Teachers' Guilds. The nearest Australian equivalent is the Teachers' Association. The subscription is very small, being a dollar for male and fifty cents for female members : but the *State Board of Education supplements the subscriptions by a vote.* The various Superintendents of Schools allowed the teachers to close their schools for two days on condition that they attend the Institute. Superintendent Tarbell, of Providence, informed me that out of four hundred teachers in the city, he only excused eight from attending. There were altogether about eight hundred teachers present, and the attendance varied from a thousand to between two and three thousand— the largest attendance being at the evening meetings.

Believing it will be of interest, I shall quote the programme for 1889, omitting names of essayists, and personal references.

FIRST SESSION.—THURSDAY MORNING.—HIGHER DEPARTMENT.

10.0.   Devotional Exercises.   Music.
10.15. Historical Teaching in Schools.
10.45. Discussion.   Opened by ——.
11.15. Literary Culture in Secondary Schools.
11.45. Discussion.
12.10. Opening of Industrial Exhibition.—While the kindred industrial subjects of Kindergarten, Drawing, and Manual Training will receive thoughtful consideration during one whole session of the Institute, special efforts have also been made to place before teachers and educators a carefully arranged exhibition of such industrial work as is now being done in the various schools of the State. A careful examination of this exhibit will greatly aid every teacher in arranging more systematic and practical work for his pupils.

THURSDAY AFTERNOON.

GRAMMAR AND PRIMARY DEPARTMENT.

2.30. Elementary Science in Grammar and Primary Schools.
3.0.   Discussion.
3.25. Report of Directors of Reading Circle.
3.35. Why do our pupils fail in Arithmetic?
       Illustrative Class exercises from Primary and Grammar Grades.
4.25. Discussion.
4.45. Adjournment.

THURSDAY EVENING.

7.45.   Organ Recital.
      Lecture.   Memories of the English Lakes.

FRIDAY MORNING.

10.0.   Devotional Exercises.   Music.
10.15.   The Recitation.
10.45.   Discussion.
11.15.   Morals in Public Schools.
11.45.   Discussion.
12.30.   Adjournment.

FRIDAY AFTERNOON.

2.30.   Kindergarten, as related to Public School Work.
2.50.   Drawing, as related to Public School Work.
3.10.   Manual Training, as related to Public School Work.
3.35.   Kindergarten, Drawing, and Manual Training as related to each other.
4.0.   Discussion.
4.45.   Adjournment.
5.0.   Social Assembly.—Between the Afternoon and Evening Sessions of Friday, October 25, the members of the Institute will meet in Social Assembly in the Infantry Drill Hall. At 5.45 a collation will be served. Never before have so complete and satisfactory arrangements been made for a social time, and no teacher in the State can, without personal loss, forego the pleasure and enthusiasm of this gathering. The Chairman of the Social Committee will act as Toastmaster.

FRIDAY EVENING.

7.45.   Music.
      Address.   His Excellency Governor Ladd.
      Address.   His Honour Mayor Barker, Providence.
           Music.
      School Legislation.   Commissioner of Public Schools.
           Music.
      Public School Work in Large Cities.—Superintendent of Public Instruction, New York.

SATURDAY MORNING.

10.0.   Devotional Exercises.   Music.

10.15.   The Troublesome Boy.
10.45.   Discussion.
11.15.   Our Profession.
11.45.   Discussion.
12.10.   Reports of Committees and Election of Officers.
12.45.   Adjournment.

The business is carefully sub-divided and in charge of various committees, two of which are, I think, peculiarly American—the Committees on Necrology, and Resolutions. The custom of placing the management of resolutions seems a good one, and likely, not only to facilitate the despatch of business, but to add to the harmony of the meetings.

The custom of delivering orations, preparing extensive, high-sounding resolutions, or memoirs on the death of members, does not commend itself. Like all matters connected with this solemn subject, it is a matter of custom, and its force depends on one's conception of the fitness of things. They are not needed to add to the sincere, loving, and affectionate remembrance of friends. They can do the departed no good, so that it is difficult to conceive of their purpose.

Nevertheless, " Committee on Necrology " sounds well, and, like many other innocent gratifications of the inherent love of distinction in a land where the patronage of nobility cannot be secured, may well be passed over. It, too, will no doubt pass away in time.

I attended all the meetings, and was particularly struck with the remarkably business-like way in which they were conducted. Not once in the three days did the interest flag. Time was rigidly kept. Finished or not, a speaker must give way when his time was up. The value of this rule in inculcating the habit of speaking in the most concise and forcible way, is evident at all meetings. This is *my* opinion comparing with what I have usually seen : but

O

while I admired the precision with which business was conducted, the President thought otherwise, and was annoyed at what he called want of punctuality; and one morning the *Providence Journal*, which reported most of the papers in full, referred to the matter, ironically remarking, "With the customary promptness of the Convention, the afternoon's meeting was several minutes behind the schedule time in starting. Then several moments slipped away after the first rap of the President's gavel, before the last whisperings of the ladies were lost in the remote angles of the building." The American excels in the conduct of public assemblies, and is not satisfied with what pleases another.

The papers and addresses varied considerably in grasp and value; but were almost without exception well read or delivered. The training of children for "commencement," and other fête days ensures that. The clear thought and stammering speech are not associated in America so frequently as in England.

It naturally occurs to one, that with such a variety of diversified subjects, either the most palpable superficiality will be encouraged, or the mind, unable to bear the continuous application for such a time, will be indifferent to much that is said. To a certain extent this is the case; but it will be noticed that there is always an interval between the subjects of like character, and not more than two requiring great application follow one another. Also, that the morning and afternoon sessions are devoted to different departments, and the evening gatherings to subjects of general interest, with indirect bearing on school work.

But while I considered the work of the convention of great direct value in itself, I could not but conclude that its chief value was indirect, and must be sought for in the inquiry the papers would cause the teachers to make at home; the brightening effect of listening to the most enthusiastic men in the various departments of study; the interchange of ideas among members apart from the papers and discussions; the examination of work exhibited, which, while all admit does not represent the average character of what would be seen in the schools, at the same time indicates a possible degree of excellence; the bringing together and affording a bond of sympathy between teachers of all classes of schools, public and private; the training in the forms of public assemblies and general business, which a teacher's occupation, even in America, although not to the same extent as in England and Australia, naturally tends to discourage; and, not less important, the general education of the public in school work. The newspapers publish the papers in full, and find room to report fully the more important discussions.

It may be urged that this attendance on the part of the public at the meetings of Institutes and Associations of teachers, where the object is improvement of the "professional" side of the teacher, is likely to prove a source of injury to the direct object in view. The presence of people who cannot, in the nature of things, be expected to go deeply into the science of education, of necessity proves that as a rule the subjects are treated in a superficial manner. To that it is replied, that in consequence of the frequency of the meetings, and the habit of attending, the public are more interested in and able to follow the principles of teaching than would naturally be expected. A comparison must not be made with other countries, where the District System has not been in operation. In the second place, a constant and general interest by the many in educational questions, is preferable to a deeper knowledge among a few; and thirdly, where the many have a superficial knowledge, there is the more likelihood of a larger proportion having a specific.

O· 2

I am not able to speak as fully as I could wish of the Teachers' Guilds of England. I was only able to attend a few meetings, not one of which was in London. As a rule, I believe they lack the life and spirit of American Associations; and the visitor hears more of the " Interests of Teachers " than on the other side of the Atlantic. As a rule, I understand only teachers attend, there being no wish or attempt to induce the public to take an interest or part in the proceedings. The English teachers have to contend with a difficulty not felt in America, where the public schools are all of one character. There are several kinds of elementary schools which are more or less opposed to one another, and this tends to prevent the free association of the teachers. Then the teachers of the " Better Class Schools," as a rule, take little or no interest in the work of the Board, or Voluntary Schools, which they consider quite different. Of course there are many broad liberal men who act differently, and exercise a wide and powerful influence for good; but, as far as I could learn, what I have stated is true of the rank and file. Apart from the influences I have named, the effects of training, and the character of the school work, influence the attitude of teachers towards organisations of the character under discussion. Teachers have not yet felt so much need for uniting.

There are two very important organisations which must be mentioned here, although not strictly corresponding to those of which I have been speaking. These are the National Association for the Promotion of Technical and Secondary Education, and the National Educational Association. These are powerful organisations apart altogether from the schools, whose objects are to educate the public mind to receive, and the legislative mind to grant reforms —the one in Technical and Secondary, and the other in

Elementary Education. Many of the foremost thinkers and scholars of England belong to these bodies, and to their efforts much of the rapid progress which is being made in English education is due. Their methods of work are very varied; but perhaps the chief are the publication of educational monographs and tracts, the holding of meetings and delivery of addresses, and the constant Parliamentary agitation.

The work of the Industrial Educational Association of New York conducts a very similar work of a more limited character, and in addition seeks to show the result of its theories in practice in its New York College for the Training of Teachers. This is a frequent point of difference in the methods of work in the two countries. In England and Australia legislation is frequently first obtained, the experiment made after. In America it is a more common thing for private enterprise to first show a theory to be practical, and then get legislation on the subject.

The largest Teachers' Association in England, I was informed, is the Liverpool Teachers' Guild, which has a membership of between four and five hundred. Its membership is open to *all teachers and to all others interested in matters of education;* and its objects are as wide as its conditions of membership. Summarised, it may be stated— to promote the interests of teachers of *all grades,* provide opportunities for the discussion of *educational and other matters,* afford opportunities for social intercourse, to diffuse knowledge of means whereby diplomas and degrees may be obtained, *foster a better understanding between teachers and the public,* to interest all in the work of education, to keep an employment register, to form a library of educational books, to encourage teachers to make provision for old age, and to *keep a list of holiday resorts where teachers may pass their vacation on reasonable terms.*

I attended one of the ordinary meetings, held in one of

the lecture halls of University College. There were perhaps one hundred and eighty present, fully two-thirds being ladies. I was struck with this fresh example of the greater average enthusiasm on the part of ladies, especially as the subject for the evening, Technical Education, was one which more particularly concerned men; and there is no such preponderance of female teachers in England as there is in America. Professor Hill Shaw's statement of the present condition of thought in England on the much debated but unsettled question which is known in England as Technical Education, was concise and clear. He said people's ideas may be classified under four heads :—

1. Those who take it to mean teaching of trades.

2. Those who consider it simply to mean a certain amount of manual and science teaching

    (*a*) To give a better training to eye and hand;

    (*b*) As a better preparation for future life.

3. Many hold that Technical Education means the South Kensington course in science and arts.

4. Probably the majority have a confused idea that it includes all these; and, appalled at the magnitude of the conception, wisely say it is impracticable in schools.

After a highly interesting lecture and discussion, it was resolved, "That the teaching of science, manual instruction, combined with cooking and laundry work for girls, should form part of the instruction in all elementary schools; that every facility should be offered for obtaining instruction of all kinds after school hours at the lowest fees; and that boys and girls below a certain age should be encouraged, by a judicious system of rewards, to attend classes voluntarily after leaving school; and that Kindergarten training should be introduced into all elementary schools."

At the close of the regular business, the members adjourned upstairs for refreshment, and social intercourse. One of the most noticeable features of the work of the

Guild is the effort made to induce teachers and friends to travel during vacation. Last summer, between seventy and eighty members joined in an excursion to Florence and the Italian lakes, extending over three weeks.

TEACHERS' ASSOCIATIONS.

Australia.

Teachers' Associations in Australia correspond more nearly to the Guilds of England than the organisations of the same name in America. They vary considerably as to importance and influence in different parts; but generally are but poorly supported by the teachers, and no attempt is made to induce others to take an interest in the proceedings. Unless it be in New South Wales, the teachers of secondary schools do not as a rule join with those of the public schools, notwithstanding the fact that the secondary institutions derive their pupils from the public elementary schools, and are therefore concerned in the work being done. In some of the country districts of South Australia the inspectors make a practice of being present at most of the meetings, which approach in character one session of an American Institute.

The South Australian Teachers' Superannuation and Widows' Fund, being an outgrowth of the associations, deserves notice here. Formerly the Government provided, under certain conditions, retiring allowances for all its servants. This principle was abolished some years since; but the amount due to each civil servant at the time of the passing of the Act was placed to his credit until he should leave the service. A study of the principles of life assurance made it clear to some teachers that, by working in the same way, every teacher could, by having a small sum deducted from his monthly salary, provide himself with an annuity when too old to longer remain in the service; or for his widow, in case of death. It was further found that if the Government would hand over the sum standing to the credit of any teacher who chose to join the fund, that the managers might arrange for the benefits to begin much sooner than would otherwise be possible. The concession was granted, insurance actuaries were employed to calculate sound tables of payments and annuities, and last year the whole arrangements were successfully completed, so that, to quote from the chairman's speech, " After a period which would probably not extend to four years, every member of the fund, in case of any calamity, would know that by the operation of this fund he would be placed beyond the reach of want; and, in the event of death, an annuity would be assured to the wife during her life, to be continued in case of her death till the youngest of his children reached the age of eighteen years. The fundamental idea was that *a man who joined the teaching staff joined for life*, and this fund enabled him at the age of sixty years to retire with one hundred and forty pounds per annum. Though there was no compulsion in the matter, it was calculated that at the age of sixty teachers would most probably elect to retire and enjoy their annuity." Although it would have been impossible to secure equally favourable results but for the action of the Government, whose direct servants the teachers are; yet the fund is the result of sound business calculations, and is supported by the teachers themselves, and has been perfectly voluntary.

TEACHERS' READING CIRCLES.

These are private organisations formed for the purpose of promoting, by mutual support and sympathy, the special reading of the members. They are found in active operation in very many American States. Each year carefully selected books are chosen, having a more or less direct bearing on the teacher's work, and every member procures copies and promises to carefully read them in the course of the year. The books are procured at reduced price on account of the number used. Authorities on the subjects dealt with in the books prepare and issue, from time to time, to all members, general directions, suggestive hints, critical notes, and so forth, which will the better enable them to fully benefit by the reading. At the close of the year, questions are sent out, by which readers may test themselves on the result of their reading. They are expected to send answers to the Council for examination, and—this could not very well be omitted in America—diplomas are issued to those whose papers are satisfactory. The beneficial effects of the reading are considered to be very great. Even careful readers find the moral obligation to systematically study two or three given books thoroughly, to be very beneficial in counteracting the tendency to discursive and purposeless reading. The Illinois Teachers' Reading Circle has between four and five thousand members. The reading is not confined to works on education. Standard literary works are also chosen. Here are several courses taken at random from different States.

OHIO. 1887–8.

I. Pedagogy.—White's "Elements of Pedagogy."

II. Literature.—Shakespeare's *Henry VIII.*, and Hawthorne's "Twice-Told Tales."

III. History.—Any brief history of the United States, to be supplemented by the "History of Ohio. (Barnes's "History of the World" may be taken as a substitute for the "History of the United States.")

IV. Gregory's "Political Economy," or Chapin's "First Principles of Political Economy."

KANSAS.

I. Fitch's "Lectures on Teaching," Bain's "Education as a Science," Goldsmith's "Deserted Village," Kingsley's "Westward Ho!" *Merchant of Venice*, *The Tempest*, Hawthorne's "Grandfather's Chair."

The Iowa Circle publish an elective systematic course of four years' reading. The works chosen are all of a high standard.

The Indiana Circle appears to confine its attention to fewer books each year; but to devote more attention to a thorough study. The critical and illustrative notes which are supplied to members are excellent, and the questions very searching. In 1888, 556 papers were submitted on "The Lights of Two Centuries," and Sully's "Hand-book of Psychology."

The Illinois Circle, with between four and five thousand members, is carried on at an annual cost of about five hundred dollars. For the year 1889-90 the course of reading consists of—"Theory and Practice of Teaching," Page; "Lectures on Pedagogy," Compayré; "Lights of Two Centuries," E. E. Hale.

I might fill pages with quotations from the numerous courses of which I received particulars. The books are almost invariably good, if not standard works. In literature, Shakespeare and Hawthorne are, undoubtedly, the most popular. In the science of teaching, Sully, Fitch, Rousseau, Payne, Compayré, appear very popular; but the reading covers such a wide range in this subject that it is hard to particularise.

Referring to the beneficial effect of the Reading Circles, State Superintendent Edwin O. Chapman, of New Jersey, in his late report says:—"The most encouraging facts to be noted are the increased zeal and efficiency of the teachers, and these cannot be shown by statistics. They are the direct result of the faithful labour of the County and City Superintendents *in the local Associations, of the work done in the Institutes,* and of the honest efforts of the teachers themselves. *The Teachers' Reading Circle has contributed in no small degree to this improvement.* It has opened new fields for thought and investigation, stimulated professional zeal, and made the work of the school-room less irksome to the teacher and more profitable to the pupil."

Possibly the thought may occur to the reader which constantly occurs to me when thinking of the absence of what we in England and Australia call training—To what extent are we justified in considering men and women as "untrained teachers," who have been subject to the indirect influences and means of training which I have endeavoured to describe? To watch them at work, they do not show the great "lack of training" educators speak of. To hear them talk, one would not gather that they were utterly inexperienced. To consider all the points I have spoken of would lead one to believe, that they must have more than a fragmentary knowledge of the proper principles of education. From reading the school journals, and the education reports, an exactly opposite conclusion must be formed. What are we to believe? I will allow each reader to find an answer by analogy. Is the average English teacher as bad as the Educational Reformer would have us believe? Compared with the ideal, yes; on his own merits, no. A consideration of this subject may possibly suggest a modification of the mode of procedure of the said praiseworthy reformers.

SUMMER SCHOOLS FOR TEACHERS.

The Teachers' Institute is an official institution under the direction of the school superintendents, or conductors appointed by them. The cost is defrayed by the authorities, including, in many cases, the whole or part of the teachers' expenses.

Teachers' Associations are voluntary, and are often carried out at considerable cost to the teachers; but although educational, do not profess to have for their object specific study.

The Summer School is quite different. It is usually due to private enterprise, and is carried on as a source of profit by the promoters. It is a combination of health resort, and educational establishment. There are Summer Schools of all kinds : some held in the woods, others on the mountains, some at the seaside. Everyone has heard of that unique institution known as the Chautauqua University, where the holiday keeper may spend his mornings at lectures on any conceivable subject, and the rest of the day at the usual diversions of a popular resort. Work at an ordinary Summer School is carried on in much the same way, but on a less elaborate scale than at Chautauqua. These Schools are perfectly natural under the conditions of American life, where they are an ordinary development to supply particular needs. To try and transplant them to England or Australia full grown, would probably be an experiment of very questionable success. I doubt if they could flourish in any country where the publicity of American life is absent : but they are attended by many thousands of students in many States. American schools and colleges have a vacation of from two to three months. During this time many professors accept engagements to deliver courses of lectures at one or other of the Summer Schools. Arrangements are made months beforehand, and programmes well advertised. The combination of educational, health, and other attractions, is sometimes decidedly amusing to one unused to trans-Atlantic methods of mixing up the grave and gay, and constantly prove the truth of the old adage that "there is but a step from the sublime to the ridiculous." What English summer resort can offer the combined attractions of sea bathing and lectures on laws of health, donkey rides and the study of psychology; an unrivalled promenade, cozy nooks, and an astronomical course ; opportunities for fishing alternating with the study of zoology ; tennis, and a course in civil government ?

Many people who would otherwise not consider themselves justified in spending a month at the sea-side or in the mountains, are quite willing to do so when they can spend a few hours daily at some hobby, or in better fitting themselves for next year's work. At a Summer School, Michigan, in 1888, I was told that more than 100 teachers enrolled themselves in the Kindergarten Classes on the first day of meeting. Lectures and classes were also held in a variety of other subjects. Attendance at Summer Schools is not by any means confined to teachers.

A Summer Normal School has been conducted for several years at Honesdale, Penn. The session lasts for from four to six weeks; the object being "to thoroughly review the common branches taught in the schools of the county; to discuss organisation, and the aims, methods, and means of elementary teaching; to draw the attention of teachers to the study of education as a science, and, finally, to show the use and value of illustrative apparatus." This school of course differs from those of which I have been speaking in having an official standing.

One of the oldest of the Summer Schools, having a large commodious building on a promontory jutting into the Atlantic, is chartered under the laws of Massachusetts. As the course may be taken as typical of many, I will summarise it. One of the departments, in charge of a State educational agent, is devoted to the training of teachers. The *school of method* extends over three weeks, and includes lectures on arithmetic, civil government, drawing, geography, history, kindergarten, language, penmanship, minerals, plants, animals, human physiology, pedagogy and history of education, psychology, reading in primary and grammar schools, school management. The list of lecturers includes many whom I recognise as leading authorities on Education. *The academic department* is open for five weeks, and includes classes in astronomy, botany, drawing, French, English literature, elocution and oratory, geology and mineralogy, German, history, Latin, Greek, mathematics, microscopy, music, painting, shorthand, type-writing, and zoology.

This will probably be considered quite sufficient to prevent the sea air from having a too greatly invigorating effect.

PEDAGOGICAL LIBRARIES AND MUSEUMS.

Germany and France are much in advance in their provision for these valuable auxiliary means of adding to the usefulness of the schoolmaster.   America has paid some attention to the subject; but England and Australia practically very little.   This is to be very greatly regretted. Libraries there are in plenty which contain works on education; but properly arranged collections of the educational literature of various countries, together with educational reports for reference, are almost unknown : and museums of appliances, as far as I know, altogether so.   The largest and best of the limited number I visited was the Musée Pédagogique of Paris.   Excepting with regard to industrial or manual work, I was somewhat disappointed with Parisian scholastic institutions :   and the pedagogical museum and library was no exception.   It is good and valuable, but I had heard such glowing accounts of it that I must confess it did not come up to my expectations.

It was one of the first places I visited.   I found it located in an old convent.   I am unacquainted with the require-ments of convents : but they are evidently very different from the needs of a museum and library—in fact, its un-suitability is probably even greater than that of the costly new museum of Owens College, Manchester.   The differ-ence is, that the Parisian authorities are not to blame, and the Manchester folk are.   The one is making the best of what it could get: the other has apparently solved the problem how best to spend the largest possible sum of money, to secure the least possible convenience and accommodation. It must not be understood that there is any point of resemblance, other than unsuitability of building, between the two museums.

The library of Owens College contains a large collection of educational works and reports in many languages, including a number of volumes by English and American writers. In looking over the shelves I found many familiar names, but missed a number which I expected to find. In fact, I could not avoid thinking that the collection did not represent the best English thought on education, either on its practical or theoretical side. At the various reading tables, which will accommodate about fifty persons, there were some fifteen readers, chiefly ladies. Three or four rooms are devoted to reports and pamphlets. The whole of the walls are shelved with large pigeon-holes, each compartment being devoted to reports on a particular subject; so that confusion is avoided and reference easy, until sets are complete and they can be bound.

The museum is like a schoolboy's pocket: it is not wanting in material; but needs arranging. The building, of course, has much to do with this. The rooms are too small for what they contain, and their arrangement is as confusing as the old portion of Boston, where it is said a street was made along every cow-track. But the building has nothing to do with, for example, the confusion in the rooms devoted to physical and natural science. Here there is considerable variety of material for teaching physics and natural history; but jumbled in a peculiar manner only equalled by the arrangement—or, I should say, want of arrangement—of the excellent collections of common articles in the English Board Schools, where no attempt has been made at classification. In the Board School it is no serious drawback; in an institution such as the one of which I am speaking, it is confusing. I noted the contents of one compartment of a long case extending down the centre of a large room—the skeleton of a frog is surrounded by small shells, piece of honey-comb, a lobster, a quartz crystal, a pair of horns, sample of wool, specimen of mica, silk cocoons, another piece of mica, some shells, beeswax, and specimens of mineral ores. As many of these had no labels, the collection is of comparatively little educative value. Some of the physical apparatus is very good. The diagrams are excellent, as also are the physiological and anatomical models.

The Industrial Education Department is contained in a number of small, unsuitable rooms, but contains a large collection of models illustrative of the work which is done in the various schools of the city. There are specimens of modelling in clay, joinery, chip-carving, turnery, forge work, etc.; but as I have had to speak of this work in connection with the schools themselves, I will not say more here. One of the most useful and suggestive departments is that devoted to home-made apparatus for illustrating the principles of Physics and Chemistry. In several rooms science classes were being conducted, the supply of apparatus affording excellent facilities for such work.

The art rooms contain a good collection of casts for drawing and modelling exercises, and provision is made for work being carried on in the rooms.

Although the perfection of the Musée Pédagogique has, I think, been over-estimated, it is nevertheless well worthy of imitation by all large cities. I will insert a summary of its contents.

First Division.—Library.

Section I.—Works relating to history of education; plans and programmes of instruction in France at different epochs; legislation and organisation of public instruction among different nations; educational statistics in France and foreign countries ; principal journals of education and public instruction.

Section II.—Methods ; tables, models ; charts in general use in the classes ; apparatus for reading, exercises for instruction in reading ; hieroglyphic printing for the blind ; methods and different styles of writing ; globes and apparatus of geography ; charts and maps in relief ; models for linear drawing and ornamental design ; charts and models for primary instruction in natural sciences ; music, and varied apparatus of instructing the blind, deaf, and dumb.

Section III.—The collection of text-books used in the different branches of education in the primary schools of the lower and higher grades.

Second Division.

Section I.—Instruments, apparatus, and models for scientific instruction in primary and secondary schools, in adult schools, normal schools ; instruments used in physics, chemistry, and mathematics.

Section II.—Collection of Natural History specimens used in class-room demonstrations ; anatomy and physiology, skeletons and models for demonstration of the body and its functions ; zoology, botany, mineralogy, industry, agriculture, represented with collections to assist the teacher in the lessons.

Section III.—Models for instruction in drawing ; models in plaster for ornamental drawing ; models for human figure drawing, as well as for linear drawing ; machines and parts of machinery for illustrating and teaching mechanical drawing ; geometric objects in wood, plaster, and wire ; models of building construction, stereotomy, &c. ; models for perspective and shade drawing ; models of an immense variety of manual exercises in wood and iron, including carpentry work, forge work, turnery, &c.

Third Division.—Furniture and Appliances.

Section I.—Here are plans, designs, and models of school buildings, and of different parts of buildings ; plans and models of different systems of ventilation and heating of schools ; of plumbing employed in the most modern and improved buildings.

Section II.—Models and specimens of furniture used in schools and in the Kindergarten ; different systems of tables and benches employed in the boys' and girls' schools ; desks, blackboards, apparatus for hanging charts and maps ; apparatus for the gymnasium and for the playground ; ink-wells, pencils—in fact, every appliance of use in a school.

P

The museum of teaching appliances, models of school buildings, and so forth, in connection with the Bureau of Education at Washington, has already been referred to. It is even more cramped than that at Paris—in fact, the rooms devoted to it are so full that they have become little more than store-rooms to hold the accumulating material until the building for which the Bureau is agitating shall be built. With what is already stored as a nucleus, it would take but a short time to make the collection the best in existence.

There were many interesting exhibits which attracted my attention, but none more than the models of school-houses in various parts of the world. "You can tell a school-house anywhere," I have heard people remark in Australia. If they were taken to America, unless they were told, they might pass three-fourths of the schools never guessing their use. There is only one *best* plan of school-house, *yet every country has it*—or thinks so.

The library of the Bureau is even superior to the museum, and is worthy of special mention, both on account of its size and importance. The admirable system of card catalogues, so generally used in America, but which I have seen nowhere else, is in use, and enables the visitor to refer to the immense number of reports and pamphlets with facility. There are now some twenty-five thousand volumes, and one hundred thousand pamphlets of an educational character in the library.

I found that many of the school superintendents of States and towns have established educational libraries, in which are to be found most of the standard works on the science of education. In some cities where this has not been done, greater attention is paid to this department of the public libraries, and teachers are given special facilities for using the books. For example, the Public Library of St. Louis has a special department for the use of the Kindergarten teachers.

INFLUENCE OF AUXILIARY MEANS OF TRAINING.

I have devoted considerable space to describing what proved to be a very interesting subject of inquiry. It may now be desirable to briefly consider the influence of Associations, Institutes, Reading Circles, Summer Schools, and the various other supplementary means of adding to the sum of a teacher's experience. Pedagogical libraries and museums are too rare to be taken into consideration in a general statement; but they are a means of improvement which it would be well to multiply. Teachers' Associations are so widely recognised as a valuable auxiliary means that little additional space need be devoted to them. They furnish teachers with occasions for comparing their ideas; bring them into contact, companionship, and sympathy with others of their own profession ; and stimulate them to renewed activity with brighter, fresher ideas and firmer purpose.

Of the reading circle there can hardly be a difference of opinion. Its effect is entirely beneficial—that is, if we except the diploma. Summer Schools and Institutes remain. They are distinctly American, and, as I have already stated, can only be criticised in connection with the surrounding conditions of American life. It will, however, be admitted that they have a tendency to cause superficiality. A young lady having listened to a few lectures on psychology or the science of pedagogy—two pet subjects in America—at a Summer School or Teachers' Institute, where the lecturer has been under the necessity of treating his subject in a more or less popular manner, is apt to imagine that she understands the subject. May be she did

P 2

understand what he said; but as he merely introduced her to the threshold of the storehouse of thought, her ideas may be very incorrect. Her knowledge may be compared to the passing view which a traveller in a train obtains of a distant range of mountains illumined by the rising sun, whose towering summits appear as easily scalable as the nearer foothills, which, in the deceptive distance, seem the more important. Rugged gorges and romantic glens; mighty cataracts and charming lakes; great forests or open glades, brilliant with many coloured flowers, may be there but are not seen. The greatest charms, the worst terrors, the glories and the dangers, the grandeur and the quiet beauty are all modified, softened, or entirely hidden. Neither the best nor the worst, nor indeed the true character is visible at all. These are the reward only of those who laboriously conquer the difficulties of passing Nature's barriers. Not a little of the charm of the distant prospect may be foreign to the mountains themselves, and due to brilliant sun and varied sky.

To listen to a brilliant lecture on Herbert Spencer is not necessarily to understand his philosophy. The lecturer may present not Spencer, but himself in Spencerian setting. To hear an enthusiastic Kindergartener speak on Fröbel may not lead the listener to understand the prophet of symbolism, but may shed light on the symbols. But just as a mere glimpse of a new land is better than no view at all, and may awaken a desire to investigate and enjoy its unknown beauties, discover its difficulties or brave its danger, so even a superficial sketch of the principles underlying the practice of teaching may induce the hearer to seek a fuller knowledge. It is sure to benefit the inquiring mind, and the superficial nature is not harmed by increased surface when added depth seems impossible. One hundred acres of a light crop of wheat are preferable to fifty acres of the same, although twenty-five acres of heavy would be better than the whole hundred poor. A little knowledge of many things is better than a little knowledge of a few; but a thorough study of one subject may be more valuable as a discipline in acquiring, no less than in its effect as adding more to the totality of life than a smattering of many.

I nowhere heard it argued that Institutes, Summer Schools, Reading Circles, or Associations, are individually or collectively a substitute for Normal School, or Normal College training; but as auxiliary and supplementary to these proper means, and as the best available way of providing for the lack of such training, their value is very great. To them, I attribute the excellent teaching I had the pleasure of watching in small out-of-the-way country schools, by young teachers who had had no other training. One of the best reading lessons I heard anywhere was in a little frame school-house in the midst of the woods of Massachusetts. It was not to any extent original in method, but the teacher's readiness of resource was remarkable. She did not forget that the object of a reading lesson is *to teach to read;* that in order that a fact may be remembered, there must be a varying but sufficient number of impressions imprinted on the mind; and that the more vivid these impressions the less need be the number. She had had no training, but had been through a high school, and wishing to earn money to go to college, "taught school" and "boarded round" as a means of doing so. I visited a number of these small District Schools, sometimes, as in the case I have mentioned, under guidance, when I presume I was taken to the best available. On other occasions I went hap-hazard into schools I happened to pass. The number of pupils varied from eight, twelve, and fifteen upwards. In every school there was an atmosphere of cordiality between teacher and pupils, an air of business, as though each and all were there for the proper purpose. The teachers were always bright and versatile, and generally appeared quite at ease in the presence of a visitor. I evidently had the good fortune to miss the "green girls and bumptious boys," of which the Editor spoke in a quotation which has been given elsewhere.

CHAPTER IX.

MORE ABOUT TEACHERS AND EDUCATION.

The Teachers' Status in England, America, and Australia.—Proportion
of Male to Female Teachers.—How Teachers act towards Strangers.

Status of Teachers.

A DIFFERENCE is noticeable in the position which the
teacher takes, and the respect in which the work is held, in
England, Australia, and America. I place the names in
this order, because Australia occupies an intermediate
position between her two older relations in this matter. So
many of the public and professional men of the United
States have used the school as a step in Ambition's ladder,
and so many of the wives of her prominent citizens have
either been actively engaged in the work of teaching, or
have graduated in the high or normal schools or colleges
with those who have become teachers, that the pedagogical
profession is held in higher repute than in the mother
country, where the public elementary school is for " common people," and where to make son or daughter a teacher
is more often considered an ambitious aim in itself. The fact
that male teachers in the United States so frequently merely
look upon the work of teaching as a temporary expedient to
earn money to place themselves in an occupation more
remunerative and less irksome, is the cause of much of the
weakness of the male in comparison with the female
American teacher.

In the past men have, to a large extent, taken to teaching
to earn money to go to college ; or, having graduated at

college, teach until they have saved sufficient to commence the practice of the law. Such men will not, as a rule, be first-class teachers. It is only when a man's heart is in his work, that he will do best work. Some taking to the profession with this object, find that they have such a liking for it that they can never leave it. Such are the most successful. As a rule, the door leading to success opens to those having the key of talent and energy. Others, and these seem to be the more numerous, take to teaching as the most available occupation until "something turns up," and continue for the same reason. These men form the drag which hinders the progress of educational reform. The worst teaching I saw in America was by men who were graduates of some of the best universities. They taught as they had been taught when they were boys at school. They are the conservative party at the Association meetings and teachers' Institutes. Their standing as university men gives their words weight, which they should not possess.

This custom, I believe rapidly passing away, of thus looking at the work of a teacher, has been productive of much harm. Except in individual cases, men will always aim at those positions in which it is possible to win the widest reputations, the highest honours, the largest incomes, and the best social position. While the relics of savagery linger to such an extent that the drones of the national hive, the fomenters of quarrels, thrive best—nay, exist at all—in consequence of the barbarism of our natures; while the profession of suppressing crime and fomenting national quarrels and wholesale butchery is more highly honoured than training boys for useful lives; while it is considered an "advance" to leave the education of a child, in order to publicly lie in defence of a criminal who has been allowed to reach his condition of degradation by neglect in early life, it is not to be wondered that the world's progress, though sure, should be slow.

Proportion of Male and Female.

In the United States there are upwards of four hundred thousand teachers, of whom thirty-seven per cent. are men. This statement will astonish the average American, nearly as greatly as the visitor who goes from city to city and finds women reigning almost supreme throughout the public schools. When I further state that of the ninety-six thousand *public elementary teachers* under the English Education Department, only thirty-one per cent. are males, that is to say, according to statistics, the proportion of male teachers is less in England than in the United States, it will be thought necessary to find some explanation for the unexpected result.

In the first place, the number given for the United States includes *all grades* of teachers. If it were possible to find the number of teachers in the primary and grammar schools of the States, the comparison would be very different.

I was fully aware that there has been for some time a decided tendency in England to increase the proportion of female teachers, but I was not aware that it had developed to the extent which it has. Only forty-one per cent. of all certificated teachers, twenty-six per cent. of the assistants, twenty-seven per cent. of the pupil-teachers, and twenty-five per cent. of the candidates for engagement as pupil-teachers, are males.

In London the experiment of employing women teachers for standards I. and II. in the Boys' Departments of a limited number of selected schools was tried a few years since, with such success that the Board decided to continue and extend the principle. There are now nearly twice as many lady as gentlemen adult teachers, while only twenty-one per cent. of the pupil-teachers are males. At the same time women are not found in charge of boys' schools, as in America. There is always a man at the head.

Returning to the consideration of the proportion of male teachers in the United States, some curious results are obtained. Where education is worst, the proportion of male teachers is highest ; while in the centres where it has made the greatest progress, and where the schools are most efficient, it is becoming a curiosity to find a male teacher in the primary and grammar schools.

In New Mexico seventy-eight per cent. of the teachers are men, in Utah fifty per cent., in Arkansas seventy-three per cent., Carolina sixty-two ; while for the whole of the South Central States it is sixty-one, and for the South Atlantic group of States it is fifty-three. I have no practical experience of any of these States except Utah ; but the census shows that illiteracy is increasing at a greater ratio than the population, and it is chiefly for them that the advocates of the Blair Bill wish to devote eighty millions of dollars from the national treasury.

If we examine the figures for the groups of States where education has received most attention, we find that in the Atlantic Division only twenty-two per cent. are men, and in the North Central group of States thirty-four per cent. Taking individual States, the difference becomes still more marked ; New Hampshire has ten per cent. of men in her schools, Massachusetts ten per cent., Rhode Island twelve per cent., New York State seventeen per cent., California twenty-one per cent. Taking a few of the cities and towns, it will be found that in Chicago only four out of each hundred of the primary and grammar-school teachers are men. In Boston there are twelve, Springfield seven, Providence six, Washington nine, San Francisco six, New York City thirteen, Long Island city not three, while there are fourteen smaller cities which employ only female teachers. Philadelphia has three per cent. of men, St. Louis nine per cent., Minneapolis three, St. Paul five per cent.

In Toronto, Canada, there are only thirty male teachers

in the schools, having an attendance of sixteen thousand children, or just ten per cent.

In South Australia forty-five per cent. of all the regular teachers are males. Of the head-teachers eighty-one per cent. are men ; of the assistants and pupil-teachers twenty-nine per cent. are males.

I collected a number of opinions as to the cause and effect of the great and growing disproportion of ladies in the schools ; some of which I will summarise.

The concensus of opinion in England appears to be, that the increase of proportion of lady teachers has been brought about in the first place principally through motives of economy ; but now it is considered that for some departments of the work they are better than men. If this tendency continues, co-education will follow as a natural sequence.

The Clerk of the Liverpool School Board, after watching the result of the gradual increase of the number of lady teachers, is of opinion that except for the higher classes of boys they are preferable to the majority of available men.

The same opinion was given by other School Board and Voluntary school authorities.

The head-master of one of the finest, though not the largest, Board-schools I saw, whose staff of assistants consisted of five female and two male teachers, said he liked female teachers best except for the two upper classes. Said he, " Female assistants are more easily managed, and *I can get a deal more work out of them.*" That reply is characteristic of many I received : " Female teachers carry out instructions better," " Lady teachers are more careful of details," and so forth. On the other hand, there are not wanting a large number of men who predict dreadful consequences if the present tendency is allowed to continue. The work is too hard for women, say some ; and in England there is some truth in the statement, but that is no argument against ability. "Boys need strong management;" "They lose self-respect when they have to remain under women," are remarks often heard.

The principal of the Normal School, Boston, considers that the paucity of male teachers, and the lack of means for training them, is one of the weak spots in the school system of the towns. He greatly regrets that there are not more men in the schools, though under present conditions he considers it a good thing. They have to be obtained where they can, and often are not of the first order: they have had no training, teach as they were taught, and have no grasp of the higher part of the teacher's profession. The consequence is that they are seldom on the progressive side of the education movement, and retard its progress. One of the most difficult tasks of a progressive teacher or superintendent is to fight against the ignorance and prejudice of these men. That they are often college graduates makes matters worse, for they hold up their diplomas as guarantees of capacity, and the people grant their claims.

The same gentleman says that the usual reason assigned for the employment of female teachers is that they are more sympathetic; but after seeing male teachers in Germany teaching junior classes, he is of opinion that men properly trained are more sympathetic than women. "The real reason is economy. We do not pay women more than about 1,750 dollars, and we cannot get first-class men for that."

Among other opinions I sought were those of the managers of the education departments of several large publishing houses. One gentleman who had formerly been a teacher, and afterwards a State superintendent of schools, said: "It is chiefly a question of money. First-class men are, however, looking more to the profession of late since they see that in consequence of the development of the System of Superintendence there will be better opportunities.

At present, it is no doubt true that the men do not show to advantage, and the progressive movements are largely carried on by women."

Another business man, but also having experience of the schools, in reply to my inquiry, said :—

"It is chiefly a question of money. A 1,500 dollars woman is superior to a 1,500 dollars man, and so on down or up the scale. A first-class woman can be secured for a salary which would not secure a second-class man. The women are anxious to take up the work, while the men are equally wishful of finding other occupations."

Questioning Superintendent MacAlister of Philadelphia, who is looked upon as one of the most progressive men in the United States, and who has worked marvels in the improvement of the Public Schools of Philadelphia, he said : "There are fewer men in proportion in Philadelphia than in any other large city in the Union. I think women make better teachers than men ; they are brighter, quicker, more sympathetic, and less conservative than men. We have some splendid women in our schools." There is a magnificent Normal School for the training of women, but no means whereby a man may receive special training as a teacher. I therefore suggested that the comparison between men and women teachers was hardly fair. A man is taken without any preparation, and placed to do the same work as a woman who has had a special training; and because he does not do it as well or better, it is argued that he is not as well adapted for teaching as a woman. They may be educated, cultured gentlemen, but unless the arguments in favour of teaching being a profession are devoid of weight, it is not to be wondered that they are opposed to "New Systems" which, in the nature of things, they do not understand.

He admitted that there was much to be said in the way I had indicated ; but when a man became a teacher, he should read and understand the signification of his work.

A plan was being considered for giving the necessary training to men, who, at present, were often the greatest hindrances to the progress of true education.

I made a number of inquiries in Toronto. One principal said : " Plenty of men could be engaged, but women are cheaper, and the short-sighted authorities will make that the chief consideration. Our boys leave school early because they have to be under female teachers ; boys over ten require a man's force of character. The upper classes of both boys and girls should be taught by men. There are only half a dozen male assistants in the whole of the city, at a salary of not more than seven hundred and fifty dollars, while the maximum salary of a female assistant is six hundred and fifty dollars, and only two or three receive that."

The same statements were repeated over and over again, in a multitude of forms ; but I have no hesitation in saying that the prevalent opinion is that, while women cost less, they are just as effective as men.

How Teachers Act towards Strangers.

In one characteristic, all countries are alike. It seems to be the rule everywhere that as soon as a visitor enters a school the teachers change their work. There appears to be a great reluctance to allow him to see the school in its normal condition. When this desire simply leads to a general brightening-up of both pupils and teachers, while the regular work is carried on in the ordinary way, I am glad that it should be so. I go to a school wishing to see it in its real condition, under the most favourable circumstances. All fine days are not equally bright ; a humorous man is not at all times equally witty ; a poet has not always the divine gift of song. A school may be excellent, but there are times when it is out of harmony, just as there are times when work proceeds with more than ordinary vigour and smoothness. If I am to make but one visit, I do not wish to see it under either of the unusual circumstances, but would choose that which is too good rather than the unfavourable. Even a cipher does not present exactly the same appearance from every point of view. Many objects, having been seen from only one position, are unrecognisable from others; comparatively few people would recognise a side-view of their own faces.

Many teachers find it absolutely impossible to conduct their work in the ordinary way in the presence of visitors. I can, I think, generally detect when this is the case. Some men and women, however, while lacking the power to be natural, have developed to an astonishing degree the power to hide, under a formal bearing and appearance of stolid indifference, their intense excitement and the acute suffering they feel. This is a great misfortune. The children see their teacher is not the same as usual when a stranger is present, and become different too. Both are alike uncomfortable, and both deserve strongest sympathy, and neither get it.

Very different is the lazy teacher, who gathers himself together on such occasions, and adds to the opinion of laziness with which his pupils regard him the further despicable one of dishonesty and hypocrisy. All " show off," and the casual visitor thinks what a fine teacher and well-disciplined class he has seen. The behaviour of children, like that of teachers, varies greatly in different places when a visitor enters a school.

In San Francisco, immediately a visitor enters the room, all rise, step out of the desks with perfect order and quietness, and stand, respectful and silent, until the visitor is formally introduced, when they gracefully bow, and in many schools say, with winning grace, " We are pleased to see you, sir."

Notwithstanding the opinion I shall presently express, I must candidly own that the custom has much to recommend it. Had I seen it burlesqued in even a few of the scores of rooms I visited, I should condemn it ; but I did not. It was performed with greater grace in some than in other schools, but it was only a difference in degree where the worst was good. While it is evidently a result of drill, nothing could be more free from the stiffness one generally associates with drill. The attention, due to the Delsarte System of Calisthenics, must be the secret of the grace of movement. It is essentially pleasing to the visitor ; and while I would much rather have entered without form, I cannot but recognise that the training must have a great influence in producing that courteous, self-contained bearing so noticeable among the Californian people. As anyone who wishes to gain an insight into the schools will not confine his observations to a mere formal visit, the chief objection is thereby removed ; for, after this formal introduction to teachers and pupils, he can pass from room to room while the work is proceeding in the ordinary way. As I proceeded East, I observed, with the increasing conservative tendencies of the people, a gradual lessening of this formality ; but, at the same time, a growing tendency to put the pupils through sets of exercises to show their proficiency. I did not go to hear what the children knew, but to see how they were taught. This weakness was most marked in New York city, whose schools seem to have had great influence in forming the English opinion which I have read and heard of American teaching. There seemed to be so great a desire for me to see what they thought good, with a corresponding apparent disinclination to allow me to see what I wished, that I found it profitable to spend less time in the Empire City than I had intended. I came to the conclusion that there is more system and less education in New York than in any other city of the Union I had visited. In contrast to this, I was pleased to find in many places that, unless I was accompanied by a superintendent or other official, the pupils did not change their positions nor cease work at all, apparently not noticing me; while the teachers politely but silently acknowledged my presence and continued their work.

At one large convention of teachers, the Superintendent particularly impressed upon his hearers the importance of this, emphasising the point that visitors should not be allowed to interfere with the regular work of the school. "Anyone," said he, "who is really interested in the school would much prefer to see it in its normal condition; and anyone not so interested should not be considered." The majority of Australian and English, as well as American, teachers, would do well to adopt this advice.

When the neglect of ordinary work takes the pleasant form I have mentioned in connection with Californian schools, and only less perfectly carried out in the schools of many of the other States, as well as in England and Australia, it is hard to find fault with it; but not when, as is often the case, the regular work ceases, to give place to show-work, and mere efforts to keep order, until the visitor feels the unwelcome nature of his presence and leaves.

In Paris the pupils invariably stood to receive us, and remained standing while we examined the writing, drawing, and so forth. The teachers were very reluctant to go on with their work, and the scholars took advantage of every opportunity to talk and play.

I was very strongly impressed in America with the decorum observable in all the schools. "Boys will be boys, you know," is often the excuse for their being rude, tumultuous young savages. The English boy has this tradition to maintain, and he does it well; so does his

Q

Australian relative. Popular belief led me to expect the American cousin to be the roughest of all. I have come to the conclusion that the smaller the traveller's stock of "expectations," the larger his crop of "realisations." The American school-boy exhibits little or none of that rudeness supposed to be essential to and inseparable from a school-boy. The visitor misses the noisy mode of marching—especially upstairs—with which he is so familiar in Australia and England. The teacher does *not* seem afraid to turn his back or leave the room lest the pupils should take advantage. Perhaps the Americans will be the first to smile at the perfection attributed to their boys and girls; but I speak of my own careful observation. During my visit I only once heard a teacher threaten a boy with a task. Strange to say, this teacher was a man, and his school a small one.

I tested some of the classes severely. In several instances I obtained permission to take charge of classes for a time, sometimes when the teachers were away. I invariably had to make the same note—"The behaviour of the children is most pleasing. They are polite, orderly, and self-controlled." In England, on the other hand, I found the pupils as ready for tricks as the Australians, and had frequently to write—"The children were orderly and quiet when I entered the room; but as soon as the teacher took his eyes off the class they began to talk, copy, or otherwise take advantage."

CHAPTER X.

SCHOOLS AND SCHOOL-HOUSES.

A COMPARISON of the school buildings and accessories by means of which the teacher is enabled to carry on his work is very instructive.

Versatility, readiness, application, continuity, power to concentrate on a narrow field, and frequently repeat a fact in every varying form, are the attributes of the successful instructor. In education more is required. It is intensity, depth, soul—in fact, the man himself that counts. A happy combination of these two sets of attributes constitutes the ideal schoolmaster. When a school system is conducted by a staff chiefly composed of such men, there will be no further discussion as to whether teaching is a profession. The true genius does not assert himself, he works. But a

Q 2

skilful surgeon works in the most perfect operating room, with the best instruments procurable.

Apart from a few exceptions, what we call skill is applied carefulness. The good teacher will give his pupils a good education, with nothing but the sea-beach for a copy-book and Nature for text-books. But he does not wish to be so limited; it is not good that he should be. The learned English professor and eminent scientist who, when asked to give a lesson in a little village school, went and bought a pennyworth of candy, and kept children, who had never heard of chemistry, thoroughly interested in a lesson on crystals, was independent of apparatus; but if he were not an exception, his name would not be honoured the world over. The ordinary teacher needs the best appliances which can be procured, and the welfare of the pupils demands that he should have them. To what extent the school buildings answer the end required of them, with something of the why and wherefore, I shall in this chapter attempt to show.

The counting-house of the American business man is more comfortable, and the office of the professional man more cosy and luxurious, than are those of their English cousins. In the same degree, the American school-house is architecturally more pretentious; and, internally, more elegantly and comfortably finished and furnished than the English, French, German, or Australian *Elementary* School. The difference in furnishing is, however, greater than that of building. Here, again, I must digress. I have made a comparison which, true in itself, is not so in its bearings. In order to give only the proper value to the statement, the scope of the schools must be considered.

The American Public School is for the people as a whole. Theoretically, it is equally and freely open to the children of the poor and the rich—of labourers or professional men. I say theoretically, because while the school is open to them, many in the larger cities, by reason of poverty, cannot attend the ordinary schools, and are either provided with special institutions (chiefly by private liberality), or attend no school. Nevertheless, it is true that the majority of children of all classes, who attend school, are found in the Free Public Schools. Equality is the basis of the social and political structure of the Republic, and the Free Public School is the surest bulwark of democracy. I believe that the majority of pupils attending private schools are sent there from religious rather than social reasons. As far as elementary education is concerned, this is also largely true of Australia, especially outside the few larger towns. At the same time, they are not based on the same broad principle, which is justly the pride of Americans; but the weakness of the American systems has been avoided: and I fancy I can see a tendency towards the gradual growth of their most praiseworthy feature.

Whatever may be said theoretically, however, it is acknowledged that the American schools neglect the children who most need them; or, more correctly, the children neglect the schools, and the schools are powerless to prevent them. What the Americans fail to do was the one special object for which the English Education Act was passed; and the thoroughness with which that nation set about accomplishing their purpose is characteristic. The result may be said to be so far satisfactory. Had the authorities recognised the difference between a railway system, and a system of education, it would have been still more so. A line of rails may be put down, and the locomotive will follow them: a Code of instruction may be drawn up, but it may be quite problematical whether education will follow. The Voluntary and Board Schools of England were established for the special purpose of providing education for the poor. It does not take long to find how strongly the opinion is held that such is still their object, although I was assured—indeed, I met with many instances—that it shows signs of modification. It is still, however, common for poor clerks and small tradesmen to stint themselves to send their children past the fine new Board Schools, with their well-ventilated, well-furnished, well-warmed rooms, provided with modern appliances, maps, and pictures, and taught by the best trained teachers in the country, to attend a " Middle-Class " school, an " Academy for the Sons of Gentlemen," " A Seminary for Young Ladies," or a " High School for Girls "—where the accommodation is not unfrequently poor, if not bad, and the teaching worse ; where, if " gentility " be observed, ventilation may be neglected ; where the useful facts with little education of the Board School gives place to useless nonsense or half-truths with less education ; where the child of the grocer learns to look down on the son of the mason, as in another similar establishment the son of a lawyer looks down on him ; where the books are out of date, and the teaching obsolete enough for a museum of antiquities. Antiquarians abound in England ; Roman remains are at a premium. I commend this kind of relic of the past to English attention.

England has a glorious heritage in her monuments of the past. No American or Australian can appreciate the privileges of his birthright, until he has stood in reverence beneath the lofty arches of England's old cathedrals ; those hoary piles, mellowed and softened by the influences of ages. He can never be the same man again. He has a clearer vision ; he finds that his horizon has leaped back. He sees the ages behind, no less than the future before. He realises the growth of the liberties in which he is apt to be vain-glorious. He watches their struggle ; sees them alternately triumphing as at Runnemede, or trampled under foot by that Cromwell they had placed in power as their advocate and champion ; gaining strength and development alike by victory and adversity, until the dear little island home could no longer contain them, and they escaped across the ocean, into almost limitless lands, beneath clearer skies and in the absence of tradition to bound forward, a Greater Britain nourished in the arms of Democracy.

All this has, apparently, nothing to do with school buildings. What I wished to make clear was that, as a rule, the object of the school being higher, it will follow that the style of the building will be of a better order. No better example of this can be found than the improvement made in the character of English buildings, along with the more liberal interpretation of the object of the elementary schools, particularly in the case of the Higher Grade Schools. It will probably remain a matter of dispute whether the adaptation of the typical American school is better than that of the English ; but the adoption of the former plan for the new Leeds Higher Grade School, which is claimed to be the finest Board School in England, is evidence in favour of the American style. The plan of a school depends on the system of classification it is intended to adopt ; and with the English pupil-teachers, it would be impossible to do as is done in America.

There is more uniformity in the arrangements of the rooms in America than there is in England, where each School Board or Committee of Managers adopts its own style ; but it is significant to find that the London School Board now arrange their schools so that each class shall have a separate room. This, of course, throws more individual responsibility on to each assistant. In Liverpool, however, the opposite tendency is apparent. The newest schools are designed with a special object of enabling the head-master to see as many of the teachers and pupils as possible without being noticed. To such an extent has this idea been carried out that I was shown a splendid school with, I believe, eight hundred pupils, so arranged that from several points the head-master could see all but one or two classes; and yet no more than two teachers are in any one room, and a greater number have a room to themselves. This result is obtained by using folding or rather sliding partitions, the upper portions of which are of glass. "There is no chance for a teacher to 'skulk,'" said the genial and obliging clerk of the Board, who further explained that the head-master was made responsible for the whole of the work and for the order of all, and that the buildings were planned so that he could keep all under his eye. I think this principle of espionage is distinctly wrong, and must tend to lower the standard of morality. It is by giving responsibility and expecting honourable fulfilment that the moral sense on which the performance of duty for the pleasure of doing so depends.

Playgrounds.

In the matter of playgrounds the English Board School, and the Australian Public School, are far before the American Public School. This again is but following the tendency of the country, and is one of the unexpected things which one frequently meets. If we except the older portions of Boston, New York, and a few other towns, the great difference between an English and an American or Australian town is the new appearance of the latter, together with the wide straight streets. One of the noticeable features, too, of an American city is the tendency to construct immensely high buildings, which neutralise the benefit of the wide streets by shutting out light and air.

The Berlin law, which only allows a building to be as high as the street is wide, is not without its merits. As long as six or seven floors were all that was required, the architecture was of the usual European type, and ugly enough it frequently is; but with the wish for structures of from ten to fourteen storeys, came the necessity for a new departure, and the American architect, equal as usual to the occasion, has given the world a new and distinctly American type of building, which towers to dizzy heights above, and descends deep into the bowels of the earth, below the street. Light, graceful, warm in winter, cool in summer, as nearly fire-proof as can be constructed, the electrical appliances and rapid elevators render the fourteenth floor as convenient as a fourth in the old style of building.

This tendency to expand vertically instead of horizontally is seen in the schools, to the great detriment of their playground facilities. The work of the London School Board in providing the spacious playgrounds, to be found in even the most crowded part of the great city in connection with the newer schools, is not the least valuable of the good offices of that great body. When I first visited England, some eight years since, I remember looking over an immense newly-built four-storeyed Board School, which, for want of room, had the boys' and girls' playgrounds on the roof. I saw one or two others this time; but was glad to find that the method of construction had been discarded altogether. A review of the evolution of the English school-house would form an interesting study.

Many strongly object to the high American buildings for girls on physiological grounds; others consider that it causes a waste of time. The fear of fire is another and very strong argument against lofty buildings. That this is a real danger, the recent destruction of the San Francisco High School proves. The following clipping, referring to the fire, may prove of interest, by throwing light on the ideas which Americans have of the requirements of school buildings. The San Francisco schools were the first I visited in America and being unacquainted with the palatial structures found elsewhere, I thought the buildings very suitable. They are certainly well fitted and comfortable, and the city of San Francisco architecturally will compare favourably with most of its size.

OUR SCHOOL-HOUSES.

The Girls' High School has had the good fortune to burn down. Peace to its ashes ! Nothing is perfect in this world ; there is a thorn to every rose—a cloud to every silver lining. [What a mixed-up metaphor !] The Boys' High School did not go too. But there is no need for despondency ; it will go, sooner or later. It used to be said that in every American town the best building was the school-house. If that rule still holds, San Francisco is not an American town. We have none too many good buildings of any kind, but even according to the bay-window, stuccoed front, San Francisco standard of architecture, our public schools are poor relations. . . . We are proud of our liberal spirit in refusing to handle copper coins, and we like to picture to ourselves the thrifty Bostonian reining in his nickel with a string ; but we do not so often consider the fact that that same Bostonian spends dollars in beautifying his city, where we are satisfied to admire ourselves for our lordly magnificence in paying fifteen cents for a ten-cent drink. . . . In architecture of all kinds we have stood still till within the last three years, and in the matter of school architecture we have been stationary down to the present moment. It is to be hoped that in re-building the Girls' High School we shall have a change. With one good building as a model, we should be tolerably safe against any tendency to perpetuate the present system of educational barracks.

The smallness of the playground space in connection with American schools constantly struck me. I do not say the observation is correct, but I could not avoid the conclusion that American boys and girls do not *play* as much as Australian and English children, even when there is sufficient playground. In one or two cases I was given to understand that they were not allowed full liberty to do so. They appeared to stand and walk about in a listless manner, quite different from anything I had been used to during my connection with schools. When the Australian boy quits the school-doors, all the pent-up exuberance of his nature bursts forth, and he flies to cricket or football, if there be room, or tops, marbles, leap-frog, or a dozen other games, according to season, for the Parisian fashions are not more arbitrary than are the games of boys. The English boy's propensity for games is so proverbial that I believe it used to be said that the public school boys played many fine games, and did a little work between times. If my experience is typical, it will afford an interesting problem for some inquiring mind to find the reason why the English character should have changed in this respect in America, and tend to intensify in Australia; but I would caution anyone against taking my observation as correct without corroboration. I believe it to be so, or I would not state it; but I have seen so many good observers misled that I think too much caution cannot be exercised. At the same time, I do not hesitate to state an observation, in the hope that it may assist to a correct conclusion.

Another note, which I find I have put down several times, has a bearing on the same general subject—*i.e.*, the greater decorum of American boys and girls may be mentioned here. It is well known what a trouble the management of boys on stairways in England gives. The banister railing usually has projections to prevent sliding; and gates to prevent running up and down are to be seen now and then. During play-time, and at assembly and dismissal, the stairs are a constant worry to the teachers. In two very large " middle-class " private schools, I found the stairs were completely caged in with three-quarter inch iron bars " to prevent boys from climbing over." Gates of the same strength of material were placed at the foot, and during play-time kept locked. One of the special features of one of these schools was military drill. I watched a company go through their exercises with order, regularity, and precision; but they could not be trusted on a stairway without its being barred like a lion's den.

I found military drill to be practised to a much greater extent in England than in America; but it does not appear to have any pronounced effect in softening the tumultuous natures of the boys. They are simply orderly when under orders. It inculcates submission to authority, and gives a certain amount of exercise, though in this respect it is inferior to gymnastics. As far as I know, I came into contact with no system of schools in America where military drill formed part of the programme of work, and in view of the nature of the teaching staff, it cannot do so, unless a special drill-master visits the school for the purpose. This is, I believe, done in some cities. Calisthenics, or physical exercises, however, receive great attention; and dumb bells, wands, and so forth, are found through the schools in many places. These and the frequency of pianos appear to have a decided influence in the quietness with which pupils move from one place to another without formal marching.

The English school has usually from one to three floors. The latest and most improved of the London Board Schools have only two, with sufficient basement for heating and storage purposes. The infant school in such cases forms a separate building of one floor. When sufficient room is not available for this, the building is made one storey higher, and the infants occupy the ground floor. I was frequently struck with the fact that the girls take the upper floors— "They are so much lighter on their feet, and do not make such a dreadful noise on the stairs." The newly-built schools of Liverpool, which I visited, are of one or two floors only.

The Higher Grade School, of which the Leeds Board are so justly proud, has four floors and a basement. The ground floor contains a large and splendidly fitted gymnasium, eighty by forty feet, after the ordinary plan of the German schools. There are also rooms for demonstration in cooking, and large dining-rooms for both boys and girls, with large gas-stoves for warming or cooking children's dinners. The various floors are arranged on what the Americans call the " corridor plan "—that is to say, there is a corridor ten feet wide running the whole length of each floor, with rooms opening from each side; the partitions between the rooms and the corridor being wood to the height of some five feet, and plate glass above. The rooms are provided with dual desks on terraced floors, and will accommodate from seventy-two to eighty pupils each—in my opinion, about twice the proper number. Instead of blackboards or wall slates, sheets of ground glass with a dead black background are used, and are very effective, but too limited in size. They are of course set in the walls. The boys take the first floor, the girls the second (because they are not so noisy), while the third is devoted to higher science work. There is a lecture hall to hold one hundred and thirty pupils, and a chemical laboratory fitted for about one hundred students. The roof is flat, with asphalt floor, and surrounded with a high parapet. It is used as a playground.

There has been, and to a certain extent still is, a very strong feeling amongst a section of the community against this school, which has cost some forty thousand pounds. The opponents maintain that the Board has gone out of its proper sphere of work in providing from public funds for the education of the children of parents able to pay the fees of private schools; that it is taxing the community for a class, and thereby competing with private enterprise. I have heard other Higher Grade Schools condemned on the same grounds. In themselves, these objections are opposed to the present tendency of thought on education; but, on the other hand, they receive some weight (at all events in this instance) from the fact that, while the school is avowedly, and, in fact, originally was, intended for the higher education of the brightest pupils who had completed the course in the ordinary schools of the city, it has become a "better-class" school, where parents, who would not send their children to an ordinary Board school for social or sentimental reasons, gladly avail themselves of the public provision when the obnoxious term "Board school" gives way to the more pretentious phrase, "Higher Grade school"— where a character of "respectability" is guaranteed, and a distinction conferred by teachers wearing college gowns and caps. When the school was built, it was not intended that children belonging to the lower standards should be admitted. It was intended to continue the work of the various Board schools, not to provide another school for the same work. The object has apparently been changed, for the teachers informed me that it was considered desirable, in order to have good work in the upper standards, that the children should be under their care from the beginning.

The information that several School Boards had provided "Higher Grade schools" gave me unmixed pleasure when I first heard it ; and, although a closer acquaintance with the schools themselves somewhat modified my satisfaction by showing me that a "Higher Grade" school has to a certain extent been allowed to become a school for a "better class" of children, rather than an institution purely for the advanced education of the brighter children from the Board schools, *without reference to whether they are richer or poorer*, I still look upon their establishment as one of the most hopeful signs of the progress towards National Education.

I do not wish to be misunderstood on this important point. All I contend for is, that in connection with a public school system there should be no distinction conferred by a fee. The Leeds Higher Grade School pupil pays a fee of ninepence a week, and threepence for books, etc., while a child attending another Board school may only pay from a penny to sixpence. The one child feels a conscious superiority over the other. When all things are taken into consideration the difference to a large extent vanishes. An ordinary Board school will cost, perhaps, one-quarter of the higher grade school to accommodate half as many ordinary pupils. The salaries, general expenses, and so forth, are higher in the one than the other, so that it is probable that a detailed and accurate comparison would show that the one is as great, if not greater, a tax on the public funds as the other. To recognise that the higher grade school gives a better education than private institutions is to admit that education is better managed by public than by private enterprise, a fact generally admitted everywhere but in England and her Colonies, and there in so far as *elementary education for the poor* is concerned. It sounds very pretty to speak of the same schools for all classes of children ; but practically this has not been realised in any large centre of population, although it has in many places where population is less dense, and where the *very poor* do not exist. In all large towns there are various districts inhabited by particular classes of people. In democratic America, or newer and more democratic Australia, this is seen as clearly, as if some power had taken the people as they landed, and allotted them their locality. There has, in fact, been an authority at work more despotic than any potentate. American schools are provided as much for the children of the wealthy as for the poor ; as much for the son of the famous lawyer as for the child of the pedlar ; and both attend them on the same terms : but a visitor expecting to find these two classes in the same schools will be disappointed. One school is as good as another, but the locality determines the character of the pupils.

I consider the American school-house much more

suitable for good work than either the English or the Australian. During the whole of my visit, I did not find two teachers conducting lessons in the same room. Combined classes for study are often seen in high schools ; and, of course, classes are occasionally combined in the lower grade schools under one teacher, although the system of emergency teachers adopted in all the towns renders this unnecessary to any extent. If a teacher is unable to be in her place, she sends word to the superintendent, and a "substitute teacher" is sent to take her place. Frequently, the payment of the substitute is taken, in whole or part, from the regular teacher's salary. In St. Louis, when the absence is only for a few days, the substitute is sent from the Normal School ; but if it is expected to exceed five days a regular substitute is employed. This question of substitutes is, of course, a much more important one in schools where the rooms will not allow of " double-banking."

Not only is each teacher's attention confined in America to one class, and that a much smaller one than required in England and Australia ; but the combined preliminary and dismissal drill is either absent, or so modified that the worry attendant upon it in the countries mentioned is absent. In several schools where the practice of a general assembly was carried out, I was surprised to find that only the principals and vice-principals appeared in the yard. The pupils filed with great order and regularity into the buildings, upstairs and into their rooms almost without supervision ; the noise (or, as it is expressively termed, "the row") attendant on the like performance noticed elsewhere was absent. I believe the first fifteen minutes of assembly, and the various changes during the day, are more fatiguing and worrying to English and Australian teachers than all the legitimate work of teaching. Frequently, in America, the formal general assembly is dispensed with. Pupils pass into their rooms as they come to school, or at the proper signal, and there is no further change until the dismissal, except for the usual morning interval of ten or fifteen minutes.

The order of the schools generally appeared very good, the most pleasing feature being that it appeared unconscious. I am aware that this may be considered a matter of opinion. What I would praise as good order, another might speak of as a free and easy disorderly appearance. To see children sitting on backless forms, with heels together, hands behind, backs straight, heads set, looking straight to the front, with either an expression of impatient fearful misery, or a dreamy, far-off expression telling of a mind seeking in a distant sphere the employment it should get in school, is, in my opinion, not order, but cruelty. I do not wish to see a class of boys or girls looking like the puppets in a street show, which move simultaneously, and to order, as the showman pulls the string. I did see examples of this modern form of inquisition—excepting the backless seats—in America, but they were few. On one occasion, I was taken to see the " best disciplined school in ————." I did not see what was promised, but I saw much to cause reflection. In this case, there was a look of supreme satisfaction alike on the face of teachers and pupils, as though asking, " Did you ever see anything like it ?" The action on the part of the pupils in thus inflicting inconvenience on themselves—it developed through the application of another sort of infliction—is an interesting phenomenon. Originally obtained by harsh measures, which are always available should the other motive in any individual case fail, the so-called discipline now rests almost entirely on the highly cultivated love of display. The boys and girls take as much pride in the " show off " process as do the teachers. A fitting designation would be " school of hypocrisy," and that surely is not needed.

In bright contrast to this humbug show was an English Voluntary School in South London, under the control of the vicar of a neighbouring church, who is an enthusiastic

R

member of the London School Board.   The happy brightness
of these children, the apparently unconscious courtesy with
which the teachers treated the pupils, and the polite bearing
of the children, was a pleasant change from the brusque-
ness, I fully believe, unintentional, but not the less
objectionable, which I noticed in connection with so many
English teachers.   What is exceptional in the school of
which I speak, is the ordinary condition in the American
schools I visited.   During a conversation with Dr. Harris,
the United States Commissioner of Education, I mentioned
the impression I had formed, and asked whether it was
correct, and if so, the cause.   He informed me that the
system of having separate rooms, so far as relates to America,
was first introduced in Boston, and is the secret of the mild
discipline of American schools.   In St. Louis, when the old
plan was in force, as many as one hundred cases of corporal
punishment were recorded in a week; later, during his
superintendency, it got down to about ten cases in a term
of ten weeks for schools of seven hundred children.   The
average now is about one case per week for two hundred
and fifty pupils.

The schools I visited in Paris and Germany were all on
the separate class-room plan.   I had several very interesting
conversations on this subject with school officials in England,
who, strange to say, usually omitted the only reasonable
excuse they have for clinging to the obsolete method of
long rooms.   The original plan of school-room, many of
which still survive in Voluntary Schools, was to have a long
room with pupils facing the middle.   This, with a partition
run down the centre, formed a long, narrow room, still more
objectionable with frequent back lighting.   This has been
again and again modified, until the best development has
been reached in the London schools, with a separate room
for each class, and left-hand lighting by means of large plate
glass windows.   Still, the pupil-teacher system renders it

necessary to so construct the rooms that the head master can overlook them without undue disturbance or effort.

The argument generally advanced in favour of the plan was that, by having large rooms and a system of general assemblies, teachers become trained to command large bodies of pupils. One gentleman remarked : " Have you considered the training our system gives for head masters ? What power of command does the system you describe as being in operation in America develop, which will be of use to a man on assuming the functions of head master ? " My reply was, that I had evidently mistaken the function of a school. I was not aware that its use was to train head masters, who could act as military officers on a small scale. I had looked at the matter from another standpoint, considering the object was to *educate the pupils*, and every means should be used which would conserve the energies of the teachers so that they might be directed to that purpose ; and that, with the changed conditions, the functions of a head master also changed.

I think that school-rooms in America and Australia present the most cheerful appearance of any I have seen. The construction, or rather the arrangement, of the latter being dependent on the pupil-teacher system, is not of the most satisfactory type, but the inside appearance of the rooms is very pleasing.

Australian school-houses are of one or two storeys only, and are similar in character to many of the English buildings. In arrangement they follow the same model, and same tendency. I do not know that the single class-room plan has been adopted to any extent, but there is a decided tendency thereto. The fittings are also similar. The terraced floor is generally adopted ; and, in the newer schools, dual desks and seats with backs are always found. I regret that many of the old-fashioned and uncomfortable forms are still in use, to the injury of the children. At the same time, I must say that the school-rooms almost invariably present a bright, cheerful appearance; and have none of the oppressiveness which I noticed in the Paris schools.

No doubt the beautiful atmosphere of the sunny South has much to do with this; but the art of the architect and painter has more. The rooms are well plastered, and when they are painted and coloured in bright, well-harmonised tints, the effect is very pleasing. Since my return I have visited several schools in Adelaide, and have been struck with this each time.

By way of contrast to this, I will give my impressions of Parisian schools. When I first visited Paris some years since, during the brightest season of the year, I was delighted with the artistic surroundings of the place, and thought that the Parisian could hardly help his artistic reputation. I have always retained pleasant recollections of my stay in the city of revolutions, and wished to renew my acquaintance. In some reports I have read of frescoed walls, rooms decorated with art treasures, and many other desirable accessories of an educative value not usually found in elementary schools, and I looked forward to my inspection of such model schools with considerable expectancy. Provided with a letter of introduction from the British Ambassador, I called on the Minister of Instruction, and was by him introduced to the authorities controlling the Parisian schools. They kindly provided me with a list of representative schools, some of which I had heard of, and asked to be permitted to visit, while others were suggested by the genial and courteous Director of Primary Instruction for the Department of the Seine. I was unfortunate. I did not find the frescoes; and, although the schools proved very interesting and the manual training more than ordinarily so, the appearance of the school-rooms was nearly always cheerless and depressing.

The first school I visited was a comparatively recent

building of large dimensions. Towards the street it looked like an immense factory or barrack; but this, I knew well enough, had little significance in Paris, where the best view of a pile of buildings is frequently to be had from the courtyard. Facing the street there may be nothing but massive walls and frowning gates, maybe with Liberté, Égalité, Fraternité above, and guards, with fixed bayonets, in front. Pass the symbols of liberty, equality, and brotherhood, and a wealth of beautiful architecture discloses itself, surrounding a lovely court. The reference to sentinels, of course, is limited; but the same change from forbidding exterior to light and ornamental interior is frequent, not only in France, but in Italy and other parts of the Continent. History provides an explanation of the origin of the style; custom continues it, and, indeed, the history of Paris for the past generation does not prove that the necessity for protection against revolutionary citizens has ceased.

On the ground floor of this, as of the other buildings constructed especially for school purposes, there is a large hall, where I saw the children having their dinners. It is also used for purposes of drill, and physical exercises; and, on wet days, for play. In boys' schools part of the hall is devoted to industrial or manual work. The first and second floors consisted of a long corridor or passage, with class-rooms opening on *one side*, with a room for the teachers at the end. The class-rooms were well ventilated, and lighted from the left by ample sash windows. The floors were level, and provided with strong though very plain dual oak desks, sufficient for fifty pupils. This number was never exceeded in any room I visited. The doors had one glass panel to allow the principal, or Inspector, to overlook the class without disturbing it. The teachers were provided with a platform raised some fifteen inches, on which was a combined stool and chair. In nearly every room behind the door a small case about twenty inches square, with a glass front, was fixed on the wall about five feet from the floor. In it were sets of metric weights and measures, always ready for illustrating arithmetic. Instead of black-boards, a long panel, perhaps twelve feet by four feet, was prepared on the wall behind the teacher. Nowhere outside America did I find such ample provision for chalk work; but unfortunately the plaster had been badly prepared and was frequently much cracked.

For all these arrangements and materials, I have nothing but praise; yet the atmosphere of the rooms was de-pressing. Whether I entered a school during or after school hours made little difference; the brightness, light-ness, and joyousness I expected to find in Paris schools were absent. The walls were coloured in a dull buff, without any brightening effects; the furniture looked dirty; and there was an absence of the splendid maps, pictures, diagrams, which I know the French produce better than any other country, and which I have several times seen at International Exhibitions in connection with the French educational exhibit. I found that these are usually, I believe always, available in the building; and, of course, the teachers cannot be always using such things; but the absence of anything to brighten the sombre effect always depressed me. When the pupils were there the result was even worse. I always think that the best ornaments of a school-room are the children; but imagine a gloomy room peopled with teachers and pupils all in black—all wearing very dark or black blouses. I should add that my visits were made in February.

The children frequently began to talk as soon as the teacher's attention was drawn from them, and I saw what I had not witnessed anywhere outside England and Australia —children standing in the corridors for punishment (?)   I sallied forth at half-past eight one Thursday with a long day's programme, but found that all schools were closed, that day being kept as a close holiday, as Saturday is in English-speaking countries. As I had several schools on my list, which I should not be able to visit any other day, I looked over the buildings. In one I found a small class of boys of various ages, at work under a teacher, who informed me that their parents were poor, and had to be away all day at work, so they were cared for at school.

Nothing strikes the visitor to Parisian schools more than the solicitous care which the authorities bestow on the children. The schools are free and compulsory, and no one must be excluded from any school on account of poverty. If their parents have to go to work early, the school is open to receive the children at any hour, and they can be cared for until the parents return in the evening, receiving their meals at the school. If the parents are unable to provide them with respectable clothes, an order is given on the Government contractor, who supplies them at a stated price ; and there is nothing to show that they have not been bought by the parent in the ordinary way. This prevents the saddening sight seen in England—I am glad to believe very rarely—of children attending school barefooted and forlorn. And I am sure the money would be readily provided to clothe all the ragged and poor of English cities, if there could be any certainty that they would not be pawned the next day for drink. How this contingency is guarded against in Paris I cannot say.

Dinners for Parisian School Children.

The paternal care of the French authorities is best shown by the system of school dinners ; and no better illustration can be given of the skill of the French in economical cooking. After the children have worked hard all the morning—and I have reason to believe that they do work hard—a good dinner becomes a necessity for health no

less than to prepare for the afternoon school.   It is of little
use to send the majority home.   Their mothers are either
away, or are too busy to attend to them : besides, *it is more
economical to provide for several hundred than for one or
two.*   Every communal school therefore has its kitchen ;
and at noon long tables and benches are set out in the
large hall which I have mentioned, and all who do not
wish to go home are provided by the Director with a
dinner-ticket.   If they are able, they pay ten to twenty
centimes [from a penny to twopence] ; if not, they get the
check all the same.   In this manner, all appear equal
when they enter the dining hall.   They file down, and as
they pass the kitchen each receives a basin of splendid
soup, and a plate of meat and vegetables.   Each one brings
bread with him ; and, generally, a flask of wine and a napkin
as well.   I understand over eighty per cent of the children
take the midday meal at school.   The average cost per
dish is barely three farthings—that is, about seven centimes.
For a school of five hundred pupils I learned that, during
two months, five thousand two hundred and sixty dishes
were provided, of which one thousand one hundred and
forty were given away.   The total cost was three hundred
and sixty-seven francs eighty-five centimes, of which one
hundred and sixty-two francs had to be provided by the
authorities.

There is no appearance of charity.   In a school held in
an adapted—or shall I say ill-adapted?—old convent, situated
in a poor part of the city, I witnessed the serving of a penny
meal.   The food was excellent, all the arrangements were
orderly, everything was very clean.   The majority of the
pupils had very cheap but clean *serviettes*, in which the
bread they had brought had been wrapped.   The children
were chatting, but were not noisy ; and they partook of their
meal in as deliberate a manner as can be expected from
boys.   There was none of the ravenous, wild-beast-feeding

character, which I have seen in connection with dinners
for the poor elsewhere.

The French Infant School.

"Every commune of a population of two thousand, where
an aggregate of at least twelve hundred are congregated in
one locality, is bound to build and maintain an infant
school." The schools are usually limited to about one
hundred and fifty pupils. No child can enter the school
without a certificate that he has been vaccinated, and is in
good health; and a doctor, appointed by the mayor, visits
the school once a week, and enters his report in the school
register. The schools are divided into two departments,
which we may call the juniors and seniors. The work may
be somewhat loosely classified under six heads:—1, Exercises
in language and recitation; 2, play, including marching
accompanied by singing; 3, manual or physical exercises;
4, first principles of moral education; 5, chats about
common objects; 6, elements of drawing, reading, writing,
and arithmetic. I have put play second; as a matter of fact
it should be first so far as the juniors are concerned. Mat
making, plaiting, building with bricks, and such busy work,
form an important part of the earlier occupations.

Instead of slates, I found the children using a substitute
made of two sheets of ground glass, with a sheet of white
paper between, set in a neat frame. One side of the paper
was ruled in small squares of about one-third of an inch,
and the other had parallel lines also about one-third of an
inch apart. They write with an ordinary lead pencil.
Numerous devices are provided for interesting the little
ones, who may be at school from seven a.m to seven p.m. in
summer, and from eight a.m. to six p.m. in winter. This is
to take care of the children during the absence from home
of the parents—indeed, this was one of the primary reasons

of their being first established.   A mid-day meal is provided at a cost of one penny for those able to pay, and free fo others.   The schools as nearly as possible are intended to provide a substitute for a mother's care, and are called "Écoles Maternelles."

VENTILATION, LIGHTING, AND HEATING.

In the newer buildings in all the countries I visited, the most careful attention has been paid to the proper ventilation, lighting, and warming of school-houses; and, probably, no one can be more conscious of the defects of the older structures than the authorities themselves, who have often spent large sums in trying to adapt to modern hygienic requirements buildings which, when opened, were no doubt considered as nearly perfect as possible.   One generation is lauded for what the next condemns.   I have already stated that I consider the American school-house best adapted for teaching purposes, on account of its arrangement and fittings.   To this I must add that it also appeared to me to be the best lighted, ventilated, and warmed.   I, of course, am speaking generally, but I imagine that the cost per head of accommodation is greater in America than elsewhere.   It is difficult, if not impossible, to compare one country with another in this respect, the purchasing power of money varies so greatly.   I have not been able to satisfy myself sufficiently to insert comparative figures, which, at the best, are unsatisfactory: there are so many considerations influencing the comparison which cannot be summarised. For example, the genial mild climate of Australia renders it unnecessary to make any elaborate provision for warming schools; and proper ventilation can be secured without the application of machinery.   In the southern portions of the continent, open fires or stoves are used, more or less, for two or three months, or from June to August, but frequently during this season no fire is necessary after the first hour or two in the morning. The problem how to keep the rooms cool during December, January, and February, is a much more difficult one, and is still open for solution.

In England, open grates and stoves are still frequently seen; but all the newer buildings are fitted with hot-water, steam, or hot-air pipes. Machinery is not usually provided for supplying fresh, or exhausting vitiated air. That is usually left to natural means, provision being usually made for the free admission of fresh, and egress of foul air. In one or two of the schools I found elaborate ventilating apparatus at work.

More attention is paid to this of late in Germany, and I was somewhat amused at the pride the rector of an older building, which had been lately fitted with an engine and ventilating fans, took in showing and explaining their working to me. The genial old gentleman was very visibly astonished when in reply to his question, " Had I seen any-thing like it before ? " I had to say that all the approved American schools were provided with far more elaborate machinery. I was sorry he asked the question, because it lessened the pleasure which my genuine expressions of appreciation of the benefits of his apparatus would otherwise have given.

The elaborate and apparently complicated machinery for heating and ventilation used in America requires the attend-ance at the school of an engineer. The engine room, con-taining a battery of boilers, a powerful engine, and supply and exhaust fans, always proved an interesting sight. I think steam pipes are most frequently used, hot water taking second place; while in a limited number of newer schools, air warmed by passing over coils of superheated steam pipes is forced into the rooms. Each room is invariably furnished with a thermometer, and teachers are expected to keep the rooms at an even temperature—between sixty-five and seventy degrees Fahrenheit; and to their credit be it said, that I did not once notice in a school the uncomfortable overheated atmosphere so prevalent in American rail-road cars, public buildings, and so forth. I invariably found the rooms mild and comfortable. As I left America at the end of November, I cannot speak of the severe winter.

SCHOOL FURNITURE.

I think it is no libel on the American character to say that much importance is attached to appearances ; but they must be associated with comfort. The American is fond of " elegance," a term used in various connections not usual elsewhere. It at first sounds odd to hear of " an elegant dinner " or a " real elegant luncheon "; but I will not digress, for after the novelty has worn off the fresh significations of certain words appear quite natural. An American's house must be handsomely furnished, but it must be comfortable. He has no use for a chair which does not fit his back. He was not made for a chair, and so insists that the chair shall be made for him. He prefers rockers, but anyhow it must be easy. The extent to which this principle is carried into every grade of school is noteworthy. I did not see a form without a back in the course of my wanderings, from the Golden Gate on the west to Sandy Hook on the east. The Kindergartens are provided with small nursery bent wood armchairs. I did not see any other kind of seat in dozens of these institutions. Small kindergarten tables take the place of desks. They are usually about four feet long and twenty inches wide. Chairs and tables are all movable by the children themselves, and the operation of shifting them to the walls to make room for games is itself an interesting sight. Each little child lifts his chair, and then all march round the room to the sound of the piano and deposit them where told : then every second pupil steps out to carry the tables. The kindergarten rooms are invariably as bright and cheerful as money and care can make them, but as I have already spoken of them more particularly, I omit further reference here.

The primary and grammar grade rooms vary considerably, as might be expected in such an immense country. Some are new and, of course, more elaborate; but the worst I saw were quite as comfortably fitted as the best English schools. The furniture was not so new, for they do not use dual desks to any extent now, neither perhaps was it quite as strong; but as it probably is not subjected to such rough usage it will last as long. More frequently the rooms are fitted with single desks, in the construction of which American ingenuity, stimulated by competition, has succeeded in providing a combination of comfort, convenience, and elegance unequalled outside of America. The teacher is provided with a platform, on which is a convenient office table or desk, and two or three armchairs. These teachers' desks are often quite elaborate. All round the room, extending from two feet six inches from the floor to a height of six feet, is a continuous "blackboard." This is prepared in various ways. Slate slabs are frequently used, but are expensive; wood is objected to because it becomes glossy; plaster properly prepared and blackened is common, but a prepared surface of paper appears to be very popular and satisfactory.

Neither in Canada nor the United States did I see a room without this continuous blackboard; and an exceedingly valuable addition to the teaching facilities it is. It is another of the reasons why American untrained teachers take so readily to the work. They are perfectly familiar with the use of the blackboard. It is no uncommon sight to see a whole class engaged at working problems in arithmetic on the blackboards. The teacher can see what each one is doing, and check a wrong method or inaccurate calculation when the error is made. I need hardly say that the blackboard writing of American teachers is of a character unequalled anywhere. The blackboards are used a great deal, in many schools, for drawing. Some drawing teachers like to have the pupils take every second lesson on the blackboard. Pupils, as well as teachers, consequently become adepts at sketching; and it is no uncommon sight to find the blackboards half-covered with splendid sketches from life, or freehand drawings. In some schools it is customary to devote a portion of the board to an elaborately bordered imitation tablet, on which are written the names of the most praiseworthy pupils. This is known as the " Roll of Honour."

The private rooms for teachers are much more comfortable in America than in England or Australia. I cannot speak with confidence with respect to Paris or Berlin; but I think the same comparison will hold good to a considerable extent.

All the newer American schools are fitted with electric bells, communicating with the principal's room; and the signals for change or dismissal are given simultaneously throughout the building by pressing a series of electric buttons : or the principal may ring for a messenger from any particular room. Speaking tubes are to be found in a few places. These conveniences have been introduced into a few superior buildings in Germany.

The principal's office and teachers' retiring rooms are always comfortably if not handsomely furnished. All these things must be considered when comparing the salaries of teachers.

One almost invariable article of " furniture " to be found in American school-rooms is Webster's Unabridged Dictionary, known as " Webster's Unabridged." These are not there solely for ornament. Every boy and girl is trained and practised in the use of a dictionary; consequently, one does not hear the abominable spelling drill which announces to the otherwise unconscious passer-by that an elementary school is nigh. Spelling books are still used in some parts of the States; but I did not find a class "sitting up" like rows of emotionless, expressionless automatons, singing in loud tones, "o-f, of; t-e-n, ten— ŏf'-fn;" "c-o-l, col; o-u-r, our—kŭl'-ér;" or such contradictions, from twenty to fifty times, while performing mental rehearsals of intended bargains, games, or pranks, when school is over. In one London school, I heard a class of sixty infants repeat "c-a-t, kăt," thirty-three times, using the names of the letters, not the sounds.

It struck me, after seeing a few of the American rooms, that their plan of having flat floors and single desks made "copying" from each other a less easy operation. I afterwards paid attention to this point, and found that my observation was correct. With terraced floors, the pupils behind can easily see the slate or book of the pupil one place to the right in the next row.

I have not space here to enter at any length into the philosophy of copying; but I believe that the absence of the temptation, or unsought opportunity, will remove much of the evil. With the terraced floor, the pupil may absentmindedly raise his eyes while thinking; and as he looks round, without intending to do so, catches sight of the solution of the problem which is puzzling him. The first time he starts, blushes to think of what he has done, and bends his eyes to his own slate; he makes no attempt to copy, but in that momentary glance he has received a hint which enables him to work out his problem. If this be repeated several times, his moral sensibility becomes deadened, and accompanying his loss of moral sense is the loss of power to work on his own account. His mind becomes atrophied, necessity now compels him, and he becomes the shameless confirmed copier. With a level floor, single desks, and pupils properly seated, a boy must exercise more direct effort to benefit by his fellow-scholar's work.

I do not speak of the few boys and girls who will exercise patience, effort, and ingenuity over copying sufficient, if properly directed, to do the work twice over. Such cases are, happily, comparatively rare, and as difficult to account for as kleptomania. Generally speaking, copying is the result of bad teaching, or unsought opportunity, or a combination of the two; and consequently, not the pupil, but the architect and teacher are to blame.

CHAPTER XI.

ORGANISATION OF SCHOOLS.

Position of Teachers in the States Schools.—Teachers in English Schools.—
Number of Pupils under one Teacher.—Proportion of Boys to Girls in
America, England, and Australia.—Compulsion in France, Germany,
England, and the States.—Attendance and Compulsion.

ORGANISATION, a complex and difficult task in connection
with English and Australian schools, where two or more
classes have to be taught in one room, and where a portion
of the staff consists of inexperienced boy and girl apprentices,
is a simple matter in American schools. There all teachers
are at least eighteen years of age (generally a year or two
older); and each, whether trained or not, has to take charge
of a class, and be responsible for it. The classes, too, are
small, it being an exception to find more than fifty in a room.

The general plan is for new teachers, if inexperienced, to
commence with the primary grade, and work up as they gain
experience. In one or two places, however, I found an
excellent plan in force for securing the best teaching where
it is most needed, and the poorer in grades where it can do
least harm. This system is in force in the St. Louis
schools, being, I believe, one of the many reforms introduced by Dr. W. T. Harris when he was Superintendent of
the city. There are no Result Examinations in the city; promotion is continually taking place. As soon as a child is considered capable of the work of the next class he is put into it.
It is considered that *the best teaching is required when a child
first goes to school*, because then the foundation for all after-
work is being laid; and during the *last years* of school life,

S

because he is then receiving the impression with which he will go into the business of life. The majority do not enter a higher school. If poor teaching is to be tolerated, let it be placed where it can do least harm, say these authorities; and that they consider to be in the intermediate grades. The pupils, having been under skilful teaching previously, have had a good foundation on a sound basis of reasoning, and will again come under the best influences later on. A new teacher is therefore first placed in the highest primary, or lowest grammar grade. A knowledge of the adaptability of the teacher will decide whether she will be promoted towards the upper or lower grades. It makes no difference to the status of the teacher whether the promotion be towards the senior or junior departments of the school. The plan seems a satisfactory one, especially in connection with the very fine gradations of classes existing in these schools.

In a few cases I found an attempt being made to have the teachers move from grade to grade with the majority of their pupils. I believe the same plan is in operation in a few Board Schools in London. One head mistress spoke of its merits in very high terms of praise. In brief, her argument was an application of the principle " System and method are in themselves only empty forms; to the teacher is reserved to breathe into them the life-bringing spirit." It was the success of the method in giving a particularly high moral tone to this school, which led to my discovery of its application.

The order of the English schools I found to be almost invariably good; very often, according to my ideas, much too good for the welfare of the children. In schools where two or three classes are in one room, it is necessary to have this objectionable quietness and soul-destroying order; and it has become the standard by which the teacher's power of government is judged. It is intimately connected with that roughness of treatment, both as to speech and manner, which so grated on my senses in most of the English schools. When I became used to it, I of course understood that it is custom, mannerism, habit, and not the objectionable assertion of superiority which it at first appeared.

In the particular school of which I have just spoken—I have no doubt it is one of many, although still the exception —there appeared to be an entirely different atmosphere. Pupils moved—glided would be a better term—from one place to another in a perfectly free, but orderly, manner. There was an absence of that military regularity about the movements, which were, however, not the less rapid. The pupils did not have to sit during a lesson as though they had all been cast in the same moulds, and joints had been forgotten in the manufacturing. In wording, the orders were very similar to the ordinary; in expression, very different. The simple words, "Come here," may mean anything, from the domineering command of a narrow-minded despot, wrapped in a little brief authority, to the polite request of one gentleman to another. I have heard the words used with every shade of meaning between these two. The actual utterance of such words as "please," "thank you," makes no material difference; it is the tone of voice, the expression of the face, the whole bearing of the one giving the command or making the request ; and in the best schools all commands are merely requests. Authority must be felt, not uttered. This is the beauty of the American discipline ; and the same thing impressed me before I had been long in the school which has called forth these remarks. After spending a considerable time watching the work, I ventured to express the pleasure my visit had given me ; and was informed that all attributed their success to the personal influence of the teachers, which was the result of the plan of allowing them to remain with the same pupils from year to year. The teacher of the fifth standard, for example, had had the greater number of her pupils under her care for five years. I would not require anyone to tell me of that lady's power for good. It was seen in her pupils. Her character was written on her class.

It is this sort of education which will regenerate the people. Could we but have the whole of our schools —I say "our" without reference to country—under such management, all our children under such teachers, then in the great mass of humanity there would be a realization of the beautiful conception, "And God breathed into him the breath of life, and he became a living soul," and the mythical Eden of the past would become a reality in the glorious Eden of exalted man. I have often thought that this same principle is the secret of the greater proportion of splendid men who are produced in small country schools, with poor appliances, whose teachers either have not the learning or the power of command sufficient for a city school. They do not produce the brilliant superficialities of towns; but they imbue their spirit of trust, inquiry, and thoroughness. The pupil knows not that he is clever; but in his slow way he grows, and, as is beautifully idealised by Hawthorne in his "Great Stone Face," is honoured by that portion of mankind which is always seeking for the best men to lead and teach it.

Number of Pupils under a Teacher.

Few statements are more deceptive than averages; but averages are frequently the easiest—if not most correct— form of comparison. So difficult is it to prevent misconception, that it is only on account of the strong and general interest I have found everywhere on this point, that I have decided to insert notes on the subject of the quota of pupils to a teacher. I will first quote figures from reports or averages drawn from official sources, and then give a few of the numbers which I jotted down when visiting different schools. The average number of pupils in daily attendance to a teacher in England is twenty-nine, in the United States twenty-four, in four chief colonies of Australia, twenty-seven. There are so many conditions affecting these averages peculiar to each country, that the similarity is somewhat remarkable. I am, unfortunately, unable to give the average attendance per teacher in France and Germany.

A more suggestive comparison can be made between the number of pupils allowed as a basis on which to calculate the staff required in a school. This varies very much, so that I shall take two or three centres in each country which I think may be considered fairly typical.

The London School Board count thirty pupils in average attendance for the head master, sixty for each assistant, and thirty for each third and fourth year pupil-teacher. Candidates on probation, and first and second year pupil-teachers, are not counted in calculating the staff required in a school ; but as they assist in teaching, and are paid, they lighten the work of the other teachers, and must be taken into consideration when making a comparison. The average number of pupils to a teacher in London is forty. I have not taken any account of the difference between pupil-teachers and pupil-teacher probationers.

The Huddersfield School Board allow twenty-five for the head teacher, sixty for each assistant, and twenty-five or each pupil-teacher. The average number of pupils in average attendance for each teacher employed is thirty. This result proved so much less than I expected, that it caused me to go over the figures a second time. Even then I could not at first understand the great difference between the two places. I certainly did not notice any difference in the size of the classes in the schools under the two Boards, except that in London there are many schools without pupil-teachers. This led me to examine the figures again, and I found that in Huddersfield forty-one per cent.

of the whole body of teachers are pupil-teachers, while in London—counting the probationers and first and second year apprentices who are not included in fixing the staff, only twenty per cent. of the total of teachers under the board are pupil-teachers. I state this as another example of the deceptive nature of averages.

In South Australia the Department allows a pupil-teacher for every thirty, and an assistant for every sixty pupils in average attendance. The average number per teacher is twenty-five. The number of small schools in the country under provisional teachers makes this general average of no value for comparison with the schools of London or Huddersfield, where all the schools are large.

In Massachusetts the average number of pupils to a teacher is thirty; in New York, twenty-seven; in Missouri, thirty-two; in the District of Columbia, forty; in Dakota, twelve. These numbers illustrate the principle, that as soon as the schools of thinly-peopled territory are taken into consideration the average number of pupils to a teacher falls. In the District of Columbia, for example, there are only a few small schools where it cannot be arranged so that each teacher shall have her requisite number, from thirty-five to forty-five being usually found in a room.

In Boston the newest schoolrooms have seating accommodation for from fifty to fifty-four pupils. I usually found from forty to fifty in charge of a teacher. For the year 1889, taking all grades of schools for the year, the average attendance per teacher was forty.

I will now give a few examples, which will, I think, be typical of the larger centres in the United States.

The rules and regulations of St. Louis state that, " In the assignment of teachers there shall be an average of at least one assistant for each twenty pupils in the Normal School; one assistant to each thirty pupils in the High School; one assistant to each fifty pupils in the fifth, sixth, seventh, and eighth years, and one to each sixty pupils in the first, second, third, and fourth years in the District School Course. In schools in sparsely settled districts, where it is necessary to assign pupils of more than two grades to one room, an assistant shall be allowed for each forty pupils additional, after the number has reached forty. In each case there may be allowed an additional assistant in case of an additional number of pupils greater than one-half the quota defined in this rule. In a Kindergarten, sixty pupils shall entitle the director to one paid assistant, and an additional paid assistant for each thirty pupils over sixty.

" In the coloured schools, having eight rooms or more, fifty pupils shall constitute the proper quota for a teacher. In all other coloured schools, a teacher will be allowed for every forty pupils."

The average number for the year 1889 was forty-seven for each regular teacher. This is exclusive of the special teachers, and the large number of unpaid assistants in the Kindergartens, who are from seventeen to twenty years of age, and are gaining experience for taking positions as Kindergarteners. In the Kindergartens, counting those who are equivalent to the English pupil-teachers, but more matured, there is a teacher for each sixteen or twenty pupils.

It may be interesting to give further details. The average number belonging to each English teacher:—in the Normal School, thirteen ; in the High School, twenty-eight; in the District Schools for white children, forty-nine; in the District Schools for coloured children, forty-one.

I have a record of the numbers of the pupils I saw in a number of rooms ; but as I was there during the first and second weeks of the school year, they are, probably, not fair examples. They vary from thirty to sixty, and the average is forty-five.

In New York city, the average number of pupils to

a teacher, in male Grammar Schools, is thirty-seven; in female Grammar Schools, thirty-six; in mixed Grammar Schools, thirty-three; in Primary Departments, forty-nine; in Primary Schools, forty-six. I saw larger classes in some of the New York schools than anywhere else, although I am given to understand that the New Jersey schools have the unenviable leading position in this respect. I cannot say, but the report of the superintendent seems to confirm the statement, for he says there are ninety-two rooms, having over eighty pupils in them, and very strongly urges that such a state of things be no longer allowed to exist. Of course he does not infer that the eighty are usually under one teacher—in fact, they are not. In Chicago, I found the rooms fitted with seats for sixty to sixty-three pupils; but it was not usual for that number to be present under one teacher.

In connection with this, it may be interesting to quote the Superintendent of Schools for Chicago, who says in his report for 1888: " There seems to be a somewhat prevalent opinion in the community that many children are permanently excluded from the benefits of school, owing to the want of school accommodation; that there are some fifteen or twenty thousand children, of school age, roaming our streets and alleys unable to obtain admission to any school. Never was an opinion more unfounded; none are thus cut off from the training and culture of the schools. Our rooms are seated for sixty-three pupils, and usually contain, in the primary grades, from fifty to sixty children. As new pupils are received—as they are almost daily—the number is increased to sixty-five or seventy, when a class is doubled. For instance, with a room of seventy pupils, forty can attend both sessions, and of the remaining thirty, one half come in the morning, and the other in the afternoon. With eighty pupils, a division is doubled, with two teachers, some forty-five in the morning and the rest in the afternoon. These half-day pupils, with two teachers alternately hearing classes and doing individual work, make as good progress, as I have often expressed the opinion, as those who attend all day with a single teacher. We have eighty schools, and with the lowest or youngest division doubled, there might be eight thousand half-day pupils with no detriment, but rather in the interest of the teacher and pupil."

Speaking generally of the very large number of rooms I visited, and leaving out, of course, the small schools, it may be said that the number of pupils in one room and under one teacher ranges from thirty to fifty, the number most frequently being about forty-five. In Paris, Dresden, Berlin, and Hamburg, I found that the rooms were seldom provided with more than fifty seats, and the attendance usually ranged from forty to forty-eight. There are exceptions to this, how frequent I cannot say ; but several schools were very unevenly divided, in one of which I have made a note. Some rooms would only accommodate twenty-eight, and others as many as seventy. The average per teacher was the same as in other schools, but the numbers were very unequally divided, and consequently the work fell more heavy on some than others. The average number of pupils to a teacher in England compares very favourably with other countries ; but this result being due to the number of pupil-teachers conveys an erroneous impression. The same may be said of Australia. The construction of the rooms is such that even when the staff consists largely of assistants, or, as in some cases, entirely so, an equitable division of the pupils is rarely practicable. The difficulties caused by classification are formidable enough, but when the additional one of ill-adapted rooms is present, a just distribution of the work among the staff is impossible. One great feature of the American schools appeared to me to be the evenness with which the work is distributed.

Proportion of Girls and Boys.

In the schools of the middle and western States I was struck with the comparatively small proportion of boys in the upper classes of the Grammar Schools, and all the classes of the Higher Schools, the proportion being smallest, however, in the graduating classes. In the eastern states the proportion, although still unevenly balanced, was much better maintained. In large schools with both primary and grammar departments, for example, I frequently counted boys and girls in the lower grades, and found that not uncommonly there were more boys than girls. As I passed upwards this equality decreased until, in the classes composed of children from ten years and upwards, there was an increasing preponderance of girls. It is stated that over fifty per cent. of the children who ever enter school leave before the age of ten. If this be so, a much larger proportion of boys do not attend school after that age.

This result is, of course, due to a variety of influences. Some attribute it to the great preponderance of lady teachers. This, no doubt, must be taken into account; but I would rather say that the great tendency to employ—or rather the necessity of employing—female teachers is but another effect of the same influences which have such an undesirable result on the attendance of boys at school. Another reason not unfrequently assigned was that the character of the work was too bookish, too theoretical, not practical enough for the average American boy, who wished to be doing something of which he could see the use.

This naturally leads to the prevalent opinion, which I think the correct one. The cause of the boys leaving school early is chiefly due to economic and business reasons, and points to a condition of things which is anything but satisfactory ; and which, if allowed to continue, will have a great and undesirable influence on the welfare of the Republic.

I sought opinions on the point from three sources— teachers, superintendents, and other officials, and business men. The business man does not usually take a very wide view of education, and is not impressed with its importance. The consensus of opinion appears to be that the modern development of business and city life has created a demand for a vast army of boys for employment, in ways which were not known but a short time since. With how much truth I cannot say, but it is stated that the employment of boys in mills is not nearly so great as formerly, because machinery requires more skilled labour to attend to it ; but the progress of the nineteenth century inventions, while shutting out boys from old employments, has opened new and more extensive fields of work. The chief of these are telegraph messengers, telephone boys, elevator boys, and bell boys. The elevators alone in any of the large cities of America require a regular army of boys, whose work is light, but hours long. The extent to which these conveniences are used in the United States is surprising to one used to the English idea of a "lift" being a luxury, not an absolute necessity. The telephone, again, necessitates the employ ment of a host of attendants.

Not only has the development of the age drawn on the supply of boys in the ways I have indicated ; but there is a tendency for the sons of well-to-do men to wish to go to business early, so that they may pass through the various gradations of office or business work at an early age. When for a boy to remain a few years longer at school may mean that he will have to take a place in his own father's office below a boy who started school with him at the same time, but left a few years earlier, it is not to be wondered at if he prefers to go to work himself. The nation will have to pay the penalty for this sacrifice of education and culture to business smartness. Were it not that other influences diminish this effect, the evil would be greater. Principals and superintendents with whom I conversed on this subject recognised the danger, and said it was one of the problems constantly before educators. This is one of the minor arguments used by the advocates of manual training.

After spending a morning in a large, splendidly conducted, mixed grammar school in Chicago, where some twelve hundred boys and girls were taught entirely by lady teachers under a lady principal, and where I had been pleased to observe that the number of the boys equalled that of the girls, I mentioned the fact that I had not found it usual for the boys to equal the girls in numbers, and wished to know whether there was any special reason for the different state of things in that particular school. The supervisor of drawing for the city was present at the time, and the manner in which these ladies discussed the question, clearly indicated that it was no new one, but that the principal took very considerable pride in having succeeded in maintaining the equality of numbers as she had. She said it was only done at the expense of hard work in continually impressing the boys, from the time they enter school, with the idea that a few extra years at school will pay them in the end, and by making the work of the school as interesting and practical as possible. She said: "Boys are more thorough than girls, look for reasons more, seek novelty, and dislike details, and if they are not satisfied in these respects, they leave." If manual work were put into the schools, she thinks that besides its value in itself as a means of education, it would have a tendency to make the boys think they were doing work which would be of practical value to them in after-life, and they would remain at school.

To realise the force of these observations, it must be borne in mind that the American boy himself has much more to do with determining how long he shall go to school than does his English or Australian cousin. Money, that is, school fees—no small item in either of the two places mentioned—has no influence in America, where the schools are free. The young people in the United States begin to think of the realities, the business of life, at an age when those elsewhere have few thoughts for anything but play; consequently the boys wish to go to business as early as possible, while the girls for the same reason remain at school, that they may fit themselves for earning a living by one of the many occupations open to them. As a gentleman in San Francisco, the father of three lady college graduates, remarked, "It costs no more to keep a girl at school and college than at home —in fact, less; were she at home, she would be entering into all sorts of expensive amusements, for which she has no time while at college. Then if she does well and cares to take up a profession, or if there should be need for her to do so, she is provided for; and if she has no need, she is still the better woman for her educational training."

To test the accuracy of my observations, I have made a careful study of the figures relating to High Schools in the State of Illinois. I find that there were in 1888 five thousand four hundred and four male, and nine thousand nine hundred and twenty-four female pupils; that is, thirty-five per cent. only were males. I then took the figures for each year, and found that for every hundred girls there were, in the first year, sixty-four, or thirty-nine per cent., boys; in the second year, fifty-three, or thirty-four per cent.; in the third year, forty-seven, or thirty-two per cent.; in the fourth year, forty, or twenty-eight per cent.; and in the fifth year, only thirty-nine, or twenty-eight per cent., were male pupils; while for every hundred girls who graduated, only thirty-two, or twenty-four per cent. of boys completed their high school course.

After leaving the United States, I found the following confirmation of my observations in the October number of the *Century Magazine* :—

"American boys usually leave school before they are

fourteen years old. Boys find the utilities lacking in the schools, and they are tempted to leave them as soon as they are able to understand the dominant conditions of society. . . . Less than twenty per cent. of American boys enter high school, and less than half this percentage complete the course. Not one-twentieth graduate."

In connection with this fact, and being, if not largely due, certainly considerably influenced by it, is the position women take in the United States. There is no doubt but that they take a place in the nation not accorded to them in any other country. This is not a case of usurpation on the one hand, or gracious permission on the other. It is as much the working of a natural law, as that in any time of crisis the strongest man, whatever his former position, surely gravitates to the head, and becomes the controlling spirit.

I did not come to this conclusion at once ; but it followed on the gradual conviction that, as a body, the women of the United States are better educated than the men, and therefore better fitted to take many positions elsewhere filled by men—positions which, by a natural adjustment of conditions, are handed over to their charge. This confirms what I have often read and heard stated, that in no other country are women as a whole treated with such universal respect as in the United States, and nowhere do they maintain their position with greater dignity, and conscious yet unpretentious, power.

Compulsion.

In all countries where elementary education has made great progress, *except the United States,* instruction in the elementary branches of knowledge is compulsory ; and in America those States which have made the greatest progress in public education have affirmed the same principle.

In France attendance at school is compulsory from the time of leaving the infant school until the child is thirteen years of age; and he cannot go to work more than six hours a day until he is fifteen, unless he has passed the compulsory test. If, however, he has his "compulsory certificate" he may be free at eleven.

In Germany the law varies. In Hamburg, attendance is compulsory from six to thirteen years of age; in Saxony, the same. In Baden, Zurich, Bavaria, and other provinces, boys and girls leaving school at twelve, thirteen, or fourteen, are required to attend the evening "Continuation Schools" several years more. The essential principle in Germany is that a child shall attend school as many years as possible under good teaching, rather than that he shall be prepared for an examination. Much of the superiority of the German education is attributed to this fact. The German authorities endeavour to ascertain how the children are taught, the English what they are taught. The German inspector pays more attention to methods, the English to results.

In England a child must attend school at five; when he has passed the fourth standard he may work half-time; after passing the fifth standard he may leave altogether. In manufacturing districts, the majority of children are said to commence work in the factories for half the day at ten years of age; but, although only attending school half-time, make equally rapid progress in the compulsory subjects with those who are at school the whole day, so that at eleven years of age the larger proportion of children are exempt from attendance at school. There is a growing feeling in favour of extending the school age, and adopting the German plan of evening Continuation Schools. Attendance is compulsory to the age of fourteen, unless the fifth standard is passed before.

The State of Massachusetts' compulsory law makes

attendance obligatory for twenty weeks in the year between the ages of eight and fourteen, under a penalty not exceeding twenty dollars; but if the parent neglecting to comply with the law "was unable by reason of poverty to send such child to school, or if he has attended a private school, or if his physical or mental condition renders it impracticable, such penalty shall not be incurred." (All these reasons are valid in England except poverty.) That does not relieve the child from the need of education or the parent from the obligation of allowing him to have it. The authorities then find a home for both in the poor-house. The minimum of attendance is just half that of England, where four hundred half-day attendances are necessary to comply with the law. The law, as far as I could learn, is well carried out, and the proportion of children who do not attend any school in Massachusetts is small. With reference to the law, one of the superintendents says, "The means for compelling the attendance of pupils are as complete as they can well be made. . . . But with all these appliances for securing school attendance, the chief reliance is the influence of the teacher in making the exercises of the school profitable and pleasing; and the influence of the parents who desire for their children the best that is within their reach."

All the North Atlantic division of States except Pennsylvania; all the North Central except Indiana, Iowa, and Missouri; all the Western, except Colorado, Arizona, Utah, and Oregon, have compulsory laws. None of the Southern States have legislation in this direction. The laws are in a large degree inoperative, owing to the want of accommodation, and the absence of a public opinion. The children most in need of education consequently receive none.

The law of Idaho requires that children between eight and fourteen shall attend school for at least twelve weeks, eight of which shall be consecutive, under a penalty of from five to fifty dollars; but the Superintendent said he had not heard of a fine having been collected. He believes the law is of no benefit. In Nebraska the law is more recent, and appeared to be supported by public opinion. It enacts that school must be taught by a qualified teacher for at least three months in a district having less than thirty-five children, six months if there are from thirty-five to one hundred pupils, and nine months if there are over one hundred pupils. It appears that nearly four thousand schools are open over six months, five hundred from four to six months, and nine hundred from three to four months.

The New Jersey law requires school to be open at least nine months, but I did not ascertain the number of days children have to attend. I was informed that over one-fourth of the children of school age do not attend school at all; but I cannot say whether this refers to the age for free attendance, which is from five to eighteen, or the age for compulsory attendance, which is from five to fifteen.

New York has a compulsory law embracing children between the ages of eight and fourteen, but such a law is of necessity inoperative when in many of the cities there is not sufficient accommodation for the children. I was informed that in September of 1888, three thousand eight hundred and seventy-three children were refused admission to the schools of New York City alone. If there be such a number of children who wish to attend, there must be great numbers who do not. In cities such as New York the difficulty of providing school accommodation is considerable. I saw a number of schools nearly empty which were too full a few years since. The city is long and narrow, and the population moves northwards as the city grows, leaving the schools in the south empty, while there is an outcry for room in the newer districts.

In Rhode Island I was informed that about one-fifth of the children between seven and fifteen do not attend school. Nevertheless, the law says all must attend for at least twelve

T

weeks, the school age being from seven to fifteen. The school regulations of the town of Newport direct that "the Truant officer shall endeavour to procure the attendance at school of all the children of the city who are required by law to attend school, and especially such as are not members of any school, visiting them at their homes or places of employment, or looking after them in the streets for this purpose; and he shall, by persuasion and argument both with the children and their parents, and if possible by other means than legal compulsion, strive to secure such attendance; when he is unable to do this he must report to the School Committee, who have power to order the arrest of the offender."

Pennsylvania has no compulsory law, and the Superintendent says, "After making all due allowance for those who attend private schools, this (increase) still leaves a large number of children of school age who attend no school." The length of the school year in Pennsylvania, exclusive of Philadelphia (which is ten months), is a little over seven months.

Attendance and Compulsion.

The President of the Board of Directors for the city of St. Louis, in his last report, says :—

"A careful inquiry was made by the Board from all available sources of information to ascertain the number of children between the ages of six and twelve in the city who were not in attendance in any school. The principals of the schools made investigations in their respective localities, and the police authorities cordially co-operated with investigations of their own. Averaging the number of estimates thus reported, we obtain what may be deemed a fair approximation of the number, to wit, about 9,500, between the ages of six and twelve, who were not attending any of the schools

of the city. So impressed was the Board with the import
ance of remedying this evil, that it urged the General
Assembly to enact laws prohibiting the employment of child
labour, and for the enforcement of compulsory attendance
at school."

The principals of the schools joined in the recommendation, but neither of the laws was enacted.

" The recommendation of the compulsory education law
was not unanimous. Several members of the Board, including myself, believed that it was wiser first to enact a law
regulating child labour and ascertain its results, before
attempting *so radical an interference with parental authority;*
and, furthermore, that such a law would be futile without a
sustaining local public opinion which could render its
administration a success."

I found considerable feeling in Illinois respecting compulsion. In the neighbouring State of Missouri, I was
assured that any attempt to pass a compulsory law would be
futile. That it was opposed to the idea the " imported
Americans " had of liberty. They had come from every
country in Europe to be free, and are giving Americans a
bad name for not being able to distinguish between liberty
and licence. Said one gentleman to me, " If the right
thinking and more intelligent people would take but a
portion of the trouble and interest in politics which the
ignorant hoards of foreigners, who cannot even speak the
language of the country, are made to do by unprincipled
designing politicians, the power of the latter which causes
all the frauds and chicanery would be gone. In times of
danger these men lose their vocation, but it requires so
much to rouse the best people to do their duty that the land
is often not ruled by its best men. At the same time the
publicity of life in America, and the sensational nature of
press writing, undoubtedly gives outsiders a wrong impression of the country." I fully agree with this statement.

T 2

In Missouri, however, they have adopted an even greater reform than a compulsory education law. In future, elections are to be conducted by the secret system of ballot, known all through America as the Australian Ballot, thus giving honour to the country which first adopted it. In view of this I shall not be surprised at any time to hear that the State has affirmed the principle of compulsory education: but it will be a long time before it can be carried out in a satisfactory manner as under the English and Australian laws.

But to return to Illinois. A compulsory law has been in force for some years ; but, as might be expected, it was to a large extent inoperative. Still it affirmed a principle, and last year a new law was passed, which, it is believed, will be properly enforced throughout the State. The importance of this step, in the interests of the States, cannot be exaggerated. When one reads all that is said about it, he is apt to conclude that a piece of Russian despotism has been transplanted ; but this is all that is required : " 1. Every person must send his children to school for at least sixteen weeks during the year, provided they are between the ages of seven and fourteen years. 2. He must send them consecutively (regularly) for at least eight weeks. 3. The time for sending such children to school shall commence with the beginning of the first term of the school year. For every neglect of such duty the parent may be fined, or sent to jail until the fine is paid."

This law which " infringes the liberty of the subject " provides for about half the compulsion which public opinion so freely supports in equally if not more democratic Australia. It is difficult, when considering such aspects of American life, not to misjudge the whole people.

Referring to this law, a writer in *Education* says :— " Chicago people are trying to be very wise in executing the Compulsory Education Law. A committee of women from the Women's Club, presided over by Mrs. Tuley, wife of Judge Tuley, have undertaken to clothe the children who otherwise would be kept from school on account of insufficient or unsuitable apparel. Where the family are in need of the child's earnings, attendance at the night school is accepted. The Board discard the name Truant Officer and use Attendance Agent ; and these officers are instructed to use friendly methods in their work ; and avoid, as far as possible, any needless compulsion. About one-half of these officers are women, and are proving themselves very efficient in winning the children to the schools. Suffering and worthy families are thus discovered that probably would not be found by the charity organisations."

There can be no doubt but that the United States are very greatly behind other nations in allowing a large number of children to grow up in ignorance. I have spoken in warm terms of praise of the pleasing features I noticed, and which cannot fail to attract the attention of an inquirer. The expenditure is liberal, though the money is spent more freely on buildings than in payment of teachers. The former are not a bit too good; but the latter should be better paid. It is gratifying to find how large a proportion of the children attend because of their appreciation of the advantages of school ; but the poor beings who, more than any others, need teaching, receive no benefit from the Public Schools.

In England it is different. The rich pay for their children, and educate them as they like. Good, cheap schools are provided for those of limited means, and poor children who would never know the inside of a school are made to attend, and the effect of the law on the mass of people is already seen. Whether their clothes are ragged or whole, whether they have boots or are barefooted, the law says they must attend school, and the School Boards insist on their doing so. It presses heavily at times, but it is the hardship of kindness. The authorities of Liverpool collect such into special schools, where provision is made for regular baths and meals. The schools are open early in the morning and do not close until late in the evening, so that the poor children, who would otherwise be confined to miserable dirty homes, or running wild in the cold streets, are gathered in warm schools, taught the virtue of soap and water, and are not only instructed in ordinary lessons, but are provided with nourishing food and taught to use their hands in useful employments.

One additional point deserves consideration here. To some extent it has received attention in the extracts I have quoted. It frequently occurred to me that the efforts to make the schools popular and attractive increased as the means for enforcing compulsory attendance decreased. Lacking compelling power, the authorities have used the force of attraction. I also almost invariably found that one of the strong incentives to attend punctually and regularly was a rule to the effect that a few days' absence would entail suspension from school. Thus the rules for St. Louis state that, "cleanliness in person and clothing is required of every pupil ; and repeated neglect or refusal to comply with this rule will be sufficient cause for suspension from school."

"Any pupil who shall be absent four half-days in one month ; or who is repeatedly tardy and without giving an excuse satisfactory to the teacher, may be suspended from the school by the principal.   .

"No pupil shall be allowed to be absent more than one day to attend any picnic party, and *only* when previous request for the same has been made to the teacher by the parent of the pupil. Any violation of this rule shall be deemed sufficient cause for suspension.

"Any pupil guilty of disobedience may be suspended."

I might quote from the rules of many of the cities I

visited in illustration of the same principle. The right to force a parent to send his child to school is denied by many who consider that they have the power to prevent him from doing so unless he conforms to their opinion as to the frequency of his attendance. To say that it is an interference with the liberty of the individual to insist on the education of every child, when not only the well-being, but the safety of the nation as a free self-governing Republic depends on the intelligence of the people ; and at the same time to adopt a rule whereby a pupil may be suspended from membership of a school for attending more than one picnic a year, involves a nicety of distinction of which I am not capable. As the majority of the people are willing to conform to such rules, it must surely be a very forced sentiment which causes them to object to a compulsory law. Indeed, I strongly suspect that it is a combination of indifference and cringing to an ignorant minority, which prevent the adoption of the needful reform.

English Estimate of American Education.

I believe that the average Englishman forms far too low an estimate of American education. Particularly is this true with regard to the Universities. For this he, or rather his insular character, is not more to blame than the American's love for high-sounding phrases and titles, which have caused the misconception. This love of effect has prompted him to use, in trivial matters, expressions which, to English minds, convey a much higher meaning. For example, the term "graduate" conveys to an English mind the idea of one who has taken a college course, and received the hall mark of a university degree. When, therefore, he hears an American boy or girl of fourteen talking about having "graduated," his notions of propriety receive a shock. It is an innovation, and he does not like innovations except when brought in with proper decorum and powerful patronage. As a matter of fact, the American boy thinks no more of "graduating" than the Leeds lad does of passing his seventh standard; but his appropriation of a term used only in the higher exclusive sense seems to give him an air of presumption.

Again, one hears of the teacher in charge of an ordinary public school spoken of as the "principal," a term which, in England, designates the head of a more pretentious seat of learning: "head master" being used in elementary and middle class schools. Then, the terms "faculty" and "alumni" are used with great deference in the older land. To the conservative Britisher, with his decorous respect amounting almost to reverence for the old associations of expressions connected with profound learning, it seems undignified and little short of ridiculous, to hear the teachers of a high school spoken of as "professors," the staff as the "faculty," and the pupils, boys and girls of from fourteen to eighteen, "alumni." These are but small matters, and with American associations are perfectly natural, but afford a field for the satirist. On the other hand, they are quite as important as many of the points which give the American equally false ideas of England.

The official statistics show that an immense number of untrained teachers are taken into even the city schools of the States each year; and the reader unacquainted with the country draws a reasonable inference that the teaching must be very poor. But what would happen if the English Board schools were practically staffed each year with raw untrained material of the same character as the present teachers, but without their special experience, throws little light on the American condition of things. A group of Arabs looks picturesque in an oasis of the desert; but place it in Ludgate Circus, with lamp-posts substituted for palms, and London fog for sunshine, and a scarecrow has charms as great. Things can only be judged in their environment.

Another source of misconception is the supposed character—I am not in a position to state what foundation now exists for the opinion—which many of the institutions called colleges or universities have for rapidly transforming working men of ambition into graduates with LL.D., Ph.D., D.D., etc., tacked on to their names, leading to the statement that it is a greater distinction to have no degree than to be an American doctor of laws. When talking of this, a gentleman of exceptional ability said: " Fools enough in all conscience manage to obtain degrees in England, with all the exclusiveness of our Universities ; what must it be where the strictures are absent?" I will not answer the question; but may it not be that the fool is in the same position on both sides of the Atlantic?— he does not differ greatly the world over—but that after the degree has been won the man has still to prove his worth for practical purposes of life, or there will be no use for him any way, whether he be in one or the other country. I have not found it to be a cardinal doctrine of belief among the University men of England that undergraduates always make study their *chief purpose* at college. In some way, and with various aids, they "get through." Many of these afterwards settle down to work, and carve out names for themselves. They are not the " fools " my friend spoke of, and yet they did not deserve the degree at the time they received it. Now if this can be, it is possible that a man— although he has been but a carpenter and lacks that indescribable bearing, nowhere acquired as at the great Universities, which marks the English gentleman — by his natural ability, wide reading, and much seclusive study, in the course of three years' hard work such as a physically strong man, urged by ambitious motives, can endure, may actually earn a far higher degree than those who have done the compulsory work of Cambridge, and who, by being well coached up, at the end of the term "got through," may be, fairly well. Were I to judge the English University-man by the young men, not a few, with whom I have travelled; and the American by the Doctors, Masters, or Bachelors who commenced life as tradesmen or farmers, first earning the money with which they paid their expenses at college, I should not hesitate long in deciding that the latter were the better men. But I would be doing equal injustice in each case. Yet the ideas held of each other by the average subject or citizen of the two great divisions of the English race is not any more correct than the absurd example I have given. Did each understand the other, much ridicule on each side would be turned to admiration.

CHAPTER XII.

EXTRA-OFFICIAL EDUCATION WORK.

Natural History Societies :—Huddersfield School Board. —Worcester,
Massachusetts. —The Agassiz Association.
School Museums.—Arbor Day. —School Libraries. —Pupils' Reading Circles.

NATURAL HISTORY SOCIETIES.

In connection with the Huddersfield School Board there is a flourishing Natural History Society. Its origin and vigour, as is usual in such cases, are due to the work of a few enthusiasts. During the summer the members meet for country rambles on alternate Saturday afternoons, and in winter on alternate Saturday evenings for botanical and entomological study. Each member is supposed to provide himself with a notebook in which to record observations made in the country walks, such as the first blooming of flowers, the first appearance of migratory birds and insects, etc. It is enjoined on members that they shall not wantonly kill or injure any living creature ; shall not take birds' eggs from a nest unless they are really needed for a natural history collection, and in that case shall not take more than half of the eggs found in any nest ; and that members shall consider it their duty to provide a wooden trough, into which all the crumbs of the household shall be transferred, especially in winter, for the use of wild birds.

The following extract from the report of Mr. S. B. Tait, the School Board Inspector, indicates the character of the work of the society :—

"The Huddersfield Board Schools Natural History Society, which owes its existence to Mr. S. L. Mosley, has been reorganised during the past year. Last year, as pointed out in my report, the numbers had become too unwieldy, especially in the summer rambles, to be successfully managed and instructed by any one person. With fewer members, the work has been more thorough. The meetings, instead of being held for six months only, as was formerly the case, are now held throughout the year. The Society has been divided into two sections, one for the study of insect life, under the direction of Mr. Mosley; the other for the study of botany, under Mrs. Rawlings, who kindly volunteered her services. The consecutive class-lessons which have been given on these subjects are more likely to be productive of permanent benefit than the lectures of former years, which, extremely interesting as they were, did not form a connected course. Excursions of the two sections have taken place on Saturday afternoons in the summer months, and there was an enjoyable picnic of members and friends. The flower show which took place in July was the most successful, both in the number of exhibits and the attendance of visitors, which has yet been held.

"In addition to his work in connection with this Society, Mr. Mosley has visited each of the Board schools during the winter evenings, and given a lantern lecture on some natural history subject. These lectures have been attended by two thousand five hundred children, who have been invited to write accounts of the lecture, prizes being offered for the best accounts. A number of these papers have passed through my hands, and I have been pleased at the evident signs of the close attention that the writers must have paid to the lecture.

"The disinterested work which Mr. Mosley has been carrying on for five years, in a quiet, unostentatious manner, among the children attending the Board schools, is deserving of recognition. Of the importance of the study itself, Mr. Ruskin truly says, 'The study of natural history is one of the best elements of education ; there is no child so dull or so indolent, but it may be roused to wholesome exertion by putting some practical and personal work of natural history within its range of daily occupation ; and, when once aroused, few pleasures are so innocent, and none so constant. But we must *show* them things, not tell them names. A deal chest of drawers is worth a hundred books to them, and a well-guided country walk worth a hundred lectures.' It is in this spirit Mr. Mosley has worked ; and there are children now passing out of our schools, who will remember with gratitude in after-life the direction which he has given to their tastes, and how he has taught them to see the beauty in the world about them, which the unobservant eye lets pass unnoticed."

The evening meetings of the society are held in the Grove Hill Board school, one of the best situated, handsomest, and best finished Board schools I have seen in England during two lengthy visits. It is built on a plan which I do not think will become general on account of the expense, even if it were desirable. There is a large central hall, capable of holding about eight hundred children, which is lighted from the roof, and is surrounded on three sides by class-rooms to accommodate about sixty children. Those on the ground floor open directly from the floor of the hall, the doors having glass panels for easy supervision. The upper rooms open from a gallery running round the room. From one end a door opens on to a small outside balcony, from which the eye of the observer ranges for miles over a scene the like of which is probably not to be found out of England. To the right the view extends for miles up a valley, through which, in years gone by, a crystal stream meandered its peaceful way through the Pennine hills.

The stream has been enlarged and straightened ; the limpid water is now a black decoction of logwood and other dyes ; for, as far as the eye can reach, its course is marked by an avenue of tall chimneys, each indicating a woollen mill. This view in the heart of the " Backbone of England " is not without a weird grandeur, particularly just at dusk on a clear winter's evening, when the mills are illuminated with thousands of lights. Even in the day-time, despite the destruction of natural beauty, and the substitution of the sameness and smoke of mills, the scene is fascinating. But it is the thought which the sight brings to the visitor's mind which holds his attention, as his eye wanders over this hive of restless industry. Each of the immense ugly piles of brick and stone, with its scores of windows, encloses a scene rivalling that of a beehive for system and wonderful manipulative skill. No wonder Yorkshire and Lancashire are rich, when one can travel for days and find every valley, every stream similarly guarded.

But to return to the hall, the walls of which are decorated with a great variety of pictures and specimens illustrative of natural history, some of which deserve a detailed notice.

Miss E. A. Ormerod, F.R.S., has shown her appreciation of the work of the society by presenting it with a series of large hand-drawn and painted diagrams illustrative of the life-history of some insects injurious to agriculture, including greatly magnified drawings of the onion fly, pea and bean weevil, American blight, turnip moth, and bean aphis, in their various stages.

An equally striking series, also drawn by the same lady— whose work in connection with proving the practical value of entomology to the agricultural community is so well known—but printed and published by the Royal Agricultural Society, includes large diagrams and illustrations of such pests as the beet fly, cabbage butterfly, wireworm, hop aphis, wish ladybird, crane-fly or daddy longlegs, and others.

Each illustration is accompanied with a boldly printed description of the life-history of the insect depicted. For example, the sheet devoted to the beet fly gives greatly magnified illustrations of the female fly, eggs, larva or grub, pupa, and a natural-size illustration of the leaf injured by the grub, together with the following notes :—

"The eggs are laid under the leaves, and produce grubs. The grubs eat their way into the substance of the leaf, where they live about a month, causing large blisters, which turn brown, or the skin of the leaf dies. When full grown, the grubs change to pupæ either in the leaf or about three inches beneath the surface of the ground, from which (in the summer) the flies emerge in about ten days. Flies first appear from March to May, to produce several later broods.

"*Remedies.*—Keep up a vigorous growth by dressing with mineral superphosphate, guano, or soot, and give applications of paraffin. If plants are attacked young, the injured ones should be thinned out and destroyed before the grubs can leave them, thus preventing a second attack."

The value of such information being diffused in agricultural districts cannot be over-estimated.

The room also contains cases of the moths, butterflies, and beetles *of the district*, properly named. One set of cases contain typical specimens or species of insects, with directions how to identify. There are also illustrations of British birds, with letterpress giving food, habits, etc., besides many other objects which speak of a very valuable work among the young people.

A Recreation Society in connection with the York Place Higher Grade School, Brighton, deserves mention because it again illustrates the fact, too frequently unnoticed, that boys are as willing to engage in the more profitable recreations as in the too prominent—so far as Australia is concerned—football and cricket. The society which I have mentioned has branches for cricket, football, literary work and chess, natural history, and swimming. The Natural History Club, as usual, owes its success and vigour to the enthusiasm of two or three of the teachers. It matters not whether it be in Europe, America, or Australia that the inquiry be made, the same answer is received. The only successful teachers of natural science are the lovers of it. Children like natural history, and will always follow one who can introduce them to her secrets; but these appear to be exceptional. Mr. E. B. Lethbridge, F.R.G.S., the head master of the school, appears to be one of the few enthusiasts able to infuse his spirit into the boys. The school is a perfect storehouse of treasures for illustrating all branches of natural history; and the specimens are so catalogued that every teacher can readily refer to any object, from a human skull to a piece of flint, with which to illustrate his lesson. Not only are the means of illustration provided, but their use is insisted on. Three-fourths of the benefit of having specimens are lost when a teacher uses them under compulsion; but it is advantageous to have the remaining fourth. Work is carried on indoors during the winter months by means of lectures, conversaziones, and so on; while, in summer, rambles take place every fortnight. Time would not permit me to remain in Brighton in order to attend one of the meetings; but I saw enough to convince me that the club must be doing a valuable work.

The description I have given of these two societies, selected because I think they are typical, will be sufficient to indicate the character of the supplementary work being done by many similar organisations all over England. Their existence is probably unknown to the Education Department; but they are exerting a quiet and unobtrusive, but not the less valuable and permanent, influence on the welfare of many hundreds of young people.

Worcester (U.S.) Natural History Camp.

The object of the Worcester Natural History Society in establishing their summer camp for boys, was to afford a pleasant and profitable place for boys to spend a part, or the whole, of their summer vacation.

The first camp was pitched in the summer of 1885, under the direction of the president, Dr. W. H. Raymenton, and, since then, has grown in numbers, efficiency, and resources—until it has attracted the attention of many of the foremost educators, literary men, and scientists of the United States.

The camp is situated on the west shore of Lake Quinsigamond, on the old camping and fishing grounds of the Nipmuck Indians. The spot is one of great beauty, and is all that could be desired from a sanitary point of view. The tents are pitched on dry, gravelly soil at the foot of Wigwam Hill, where the afternoon sun throws the shade of the wooded hillside over the camp. The whole region is a " haunt and nesting-place for birds," a tract of wooded hills and upland pastures, clear streams, and lakes, which offer every variety of occupation to boys who love outdoor life.

Boys of the school age, from ten to twenty years, can join the camp at any time during the season, for one day or for the eight weeks it is in session, provided application is made in advance.

The tents used are of the " army-wall " pattern, with substantial wood floors and waterproof fly. Each tent will accommodate four persons, and is provided with straw mattresses, wash-basins, a tin dipper, pail and broom. Campers furnish blankets, pillows, towels, etc. Meals are provided in spacious dining tents; and there is also an enclosed pavilion, and large workshop for the use of members. The rules provide for every care of the boys; and during its existence no casualties have occurred.

The daily routine is varied. Boys are expected to take

U

care of themselves, to be clean and tidy in person and dress; and keep their quarters neat and orderly. Each must air his bed and bedding, make his bed, sweep his floor, hang up or fold his clothes, etc. He may do these things after his own fashion, but he must do them effectively, regularly, and punctually.

Sufficient drill and light military discipline are enforced as an admirable camp tonic; and, without being burdensome, have proved very advantageous and popular. Fifteen minutes per day are also given to gymnastics.

A variety of occupations are provided for members. Lectures are given by specialists in different branches of science. Specimens, drawings, the microscope, stereopticon, and so forth, are all used in illustration. The boys are not compelled to attend; but it has been found by experience that many of them do so voluntarily, and nearly all such become interested in one or more of the subjects.

The large, well-lighted, and well-appointed workshop is fitted up with benches, lathes, and other appliances, and is well supplied with tools. In connection with the workshop is a laboratory, where those engaged in collecting specimens can prepare them under the direction of experienced naturalists.

There are practical outdoor lessons to teach boys how to fish, the habits of game, how to pitch a tent, make a camp fire, handle a canoe, and so on. Swimming and rowing are carefully taught; and provision is made for healthful games, such as base-ball, lawn tennis, football, and athletic contests; but it is curious that the English and Australian summer game, cricket, is not played any more here than elsewhere in the United States. A graduate of the University of California mentioned, when speaking of this subject, that they used to have a club in connection with the college; but the leading players were generally young Australians.

Each week one or more evenings are devoted to camp-fire stories, when the members gather round the central camp fire to listen to the personal experiences of hunters, soldiers, naturalists, woodsmen, and others. There are also evening entertainments in the pavilion; and every effort is made to make camp life free and buoyant.

I have purposely omitted to mention the excursions, which are one of the most prominent features of the camp. There is no doubt that the best way to enlist the interest of boys in the study of natural history is to take them out into the woods and fields. Pupils and teachers meet on a new and different footing, and are much nearer together than in the school-room. There is no better way for a boy to learn the arts of collecting and preserving specimens, than by acting as a sort of jackal to a collector. This may or may not be associated with an elevating study of natural history; but although there are many collectors who are not naturalists, it is necessary for the naturalist to be, to a certain extent, a collector. The leader of an excursion is on quite a different footing from a teacher in the ordinary sense. He carries on his investigations, which his companions are permitted to share, or repeat the process of his own growth, carrying them through the same.

The Agassiz Association.

The Agassiz Association is a society for the observation of nature. The organisation is peculiar to itself. It may be best described, by saying that over ten thousand lovers of nature, of all ages, in many countries, have formed over one thousand small societies, varying in numbers from two or three to over one hundred; and, although not knowing of one another's individual existence, are yet bound together in one common organisation by kinship of work and the personality of the president and founder, Mr. H. H. Ballard, of Pittsfield, Massachusetts, U.S.

Each incorporated society is known as a Chapter; and, apart from the common name and constitution, is free to follow its own peculiar pursuits in any way thought desirable. The smallest number recognised as a Chapter is four; but after a branch has once been admitted, and has continued alive for six months, it is not then cut off though its membership should decline below four.

Chapters are to be found in Canada, Japan, Great Britain, Russia, and Australia; but their chief home is in the United States.

Family Chapters are formed by the parents and children of a single family, who unite for joint study and research. There are very many of these, and their effect is very beneficial. Somewhat more extended in scope are the School Chapters. There are many teachers able and willing to devote their energies to fostering a love for study and inquiry out of school hours. Such find the Agassiz Association of great assistance, and they have done and are doing much good to many hundreds of pupils. These Chapters correspond to the Natural History Clubs and Societies in connection with English schools of which I have spoken.

Very interesting and profitable Chapters are sometimes formed by boys and girls alone, who thus give themselves a training in other things besides the study of Nature, for they learn to conduct meetings, and generally are benefited by the feelings of independence and self-reliance which are fostered. Some of these junior Chapters, which conduct their own affairs although seeking the advice of older friends, have formed attractive and useful museums illustrative of the natural history of their districts.

All societies for the promotion of the study of natural history with which I am acquainted have originated through the energy and love of nature of one or two men or women, who have infused their spirit into the ever-ready and receptive minds of children. The Agassiz Association is no exception. It was first a small society without a name, in a country school. What it has become I have already indicated.

Much of its success is due to the handbook of the association, known as "The Three Kingdoms," which is intended as a guide for young people in making collections, preserving and mounting specimens, and giving advice on everything in connection with a small natural history society.

School Museums.

Collections of objects, such as specimens illustrative of industrial processes, natural history specimens of various kinds, be they minerals, woods, or, under certain conditions, representatives of the animal kingdom, and even curiosities, may be made very valuable additions to the more ordinary equipment of schools. Indeed, rightly selected and used, they may be made the most highly educative and interesting of the auxiliaries of a teacher's personal influence. I am aware that there is probably no part of the belongings of a school with regard to which the visitor needs to exercise greater caution in forming an opinion of its usefulness. They may be the means of adding life and interest to the teaching; or they may, like false jewels, simply serve to impress the superficial observer.

When they are the mutual work of the teachers and pupils, their appearance may be largely depended on to show what value may be attached to them. Where they are provided by school authorities more care must be exercised. It is by no means the finest collections of specimens which are the most useful—or, rather, which may be best utilised. The old blunderbuss of the Crimean War type may be more effective in the hands of a skilled marksman than a Winchester repeater in the hands of a raw recruit. Mind is superior to matter, although it needs matter to promote its growth; and the poor means with the capable head are better than the most perfect appliances without the interest or skill to use them.

The desire to have a " School Museum " appears to be increasing among progressive teachers in the three continents, and I think there are signs of distinctive and varying tendencies on the two sides of the Atlantic. The movement has not made sufficient progress in Australia to warrant generalising. If my observation be correct, the tendency in the United States is to collect natural history specimens, especially stuffed birds and other small animals, minerals taking an inferior second place, and industrial articles being seldom seen. In many schools I saw some small but good collections of stuffed birds; but they were frequently ill provided with suitable receptacles, and often showed signs of ill-usage. They were apparently frequently provided without definite purpose, beyond fulfilling the indefinite desire for a school museum to make school life more attractive and encourage the study of natural history. They are of little use in promoting the latter purpose unless there is some method in the selection of specimens. If one specimen of each order of birds be included, a foundation is laid for systematic study. The names of the orders may or may not be taught; but the way in which the birds are classified can be clearly shown, and the need and basis of scientific classification will be imparted to the pupils.

On the whole, I was pleased to see them, because they indicate a tendency to recognise that the love and study of nature is increasing; but, on the other hand, I could not help sometimes feeling that they were, as used, the reverse of educational, because they tended to lower the standard of reverence for the sacredness of life.

In one large school, where I had been pleased to notice a good and varied collection of specimens, after I had given an address to the senior classes on Australia, I was asked if I could place them in communication with some one who would send some bird-skins for their museum; and apparently introduced the teachers, no less than the pupils, to a new line of thought when I replied, that until they had studied all that was knowable about the living birds around them, they, as well as I, would be guilty of sinful cruelty in encouraging the destruction of Australian birds for the mere purpose of gratifying their curiosity or seeing what they are like. I not only have no objection, but would assist in the killing of birds for genuine scientific research; but I have nothing but disapprobation for destroying life for the purpose of having specimens in one's collection. It is only less barbarous than doing the same thing to decorate one's hat. The life-history of the Platypus of Australia (*Ornithorhynchus paradoxicus*) is only imperfectly known; but, owing to the curse of the professional collector, it is rapidly being exterminated.

The museums of American public high schools are often useful and creditable collections; but the same defect noticeable in the grammar schools is often present. The specimens are badly classified, and frequently not named.

I found that in several of the cities I visited in England the School Boards have recognised the value of school museums, by providing large and convenient cabinets or cases for the reception of specimens, and in some instances providing specimens as well. I believe the same thing is done in many towns which I did not visit. The collections are usually of a very miscellaneous character. Natura history predominates in the United States: in England specimens illustrative of the industrial arts, articles of com merce, and collections of minerals, fossils, and shells are most common. Where no proper provision has been made for the preservation of specimens, it is not uncommon to find a collection of different kinds of grain, spices, tea, coffee, and such readily procurable articles, in bottles on the mantle-shelves or window-sills.

Occasionally, the visitor to the schools finds a case in which a serious attempt has been made to systematically arrange and name specimens; but usually they are mixed up in a very promiscuous fashion.   In such cases it is probable no one knows just what the cabinets contain, and cannot find what is wanted when he does.

The best type of school museum I saw was at the York Place Higher Grade School, Brighton.   The collection was large, varied, and comprehensive. Specimens were well arranged and named; and a convenient catalogue had been prepared for easy reference.   I will give an example of its use.   The head master had carefully prepared a reading book for each teacher, marking on the margin various instructions with reference to the facilities for illustration to be found in the school.   Thus S.P. means Show picture, S.S. Show specimen, D.D. Draw diagram. Each teacher has a catalogue of pictures, indicating where each is to be found; and a catalogue of the museum arranged alphabetically, with the room, case, shelf, and number of specimen indicated, so that if a reference to mica, for example, occurs in the lesson, the teacher will have a specimen ready to show the children.   The intention is not that the reading lesson shall be interrupted to give a lesson on mica; but that the thing itself and the quality mentioned in the lesson may become realities.   Too much importance can hardly be attached to a museum, used in this way to develop the observing and reasoning faculties; and to add general interest to otherwise unmeaning and largely mechanical work.   There are other schools with museums as well provided and used as York Place; but it will serve my purpose of showing how useful they may be made when properly arranged and systematically used, even by teachers who themselves may not have any other motive in using them other than that the principal insists on their doing so.

A large business is done in Paris in providing specimens for school museums. Most schools have one or more cabinets known as "*musée des écoles.*" This museum for schools is a large chest or cabinet of ten drawers, each drawer being divided into sixteen compartments. Each drawer is devoted to a class of related specimens. Textile plants, minerals and metals, casts, fossils and coals, products of vertebrate animals, products of invertebrate animals, products of the forest, indicate the contents of some of the drawers. Generally, each compartment is devoted to one material under different forms, or in different stages of manufacture. Thus the department devoted to flax has the seed, the flax-plant matured, pressed specimen of the flower, the raw fibre, each stage of manufacture, and the finished linen. In the drawer devoted to products of invertebrate animals would be found a compartment devoted to silk, including models of the silkworm in various stages, dried mulberry leaf, different sorts of cocoons, silk in its various stages of manufacture. In the drawer devoted to minerals would be a compartment for copper, containing the common forms of copper ore, sulphides, oxides, and carbonates, native copper, ore dressed for smelting, the "regulus" or "matte" in its different stages, the pure copper, sheet copper, copper wire, bronze, and bell metal.

The plan of these school museums is, for convenience, economy of space, ease of reference, and completeness, the best I have seen anywhere. The enthusiastic teacher would in addition have his specimens accessible to the children; but for some time to come, at all events, it is hopeless to expect more from the average teacher than that he will conscientiously use the specimens provided. For the upper classes, the Parisian authorities provide cabinets or museums containing the most important apparatus for teaching chemistry and physics. In fact, everything is done by those controlling education to make it worthy of the name; and although disappointing in many respects, perhaps, taking all things into consideration, their efforts may be said to have succeeded as well as those of any I have examined.

Arbor Day.

The great "treeless region" of the north-west of the central valley of the United States has changed its character and its people. Boundless prairies are now cattle ranches and cultivated fields; treeless areas have become landscapes diversified with groves, woods, and clumps of trees; the bison has disappeared, and his place is taken by uncounted herds of cattle; and the savage Indian has given way to industrious, thriving settlers. Instead of an occasional trapper's camp, are frequent towns and cities rivalling those of the East in size and prosperity. The savage, barbarous West, with its lawlessness and terrors, becomes wonderfully civilised by the time one reaches it. The bloodthirsty ruffians are always "further out." The "noble savage" appears to have lost his nobility, and become a sort of disreputable mixture of the traditional gipsy and tramp; the terrible cow-boy becomes a somewhat rough, but nevertheless a jolly free-and-easy fellow; and one comes to the conclusion, not that people lied who wrote all the idea-forming literature of the West, but that things have changed; and that he has failed to understand that the events of many years and of large areas have been focussed into one spot, and one brief period of time. An incident which is remarkable and exceptional enough in a land of stirring life to be considered worthy of special notice, must not be considered an ordinary incident of daily life. Probably, more revolvers than umbrellas are carried "out West"; but to a large extent it is mere custom. When a case of shooting does occur, by the time it has undergone the usual exaggerations by word of mouth to the local correspondent, who sends his account, which is duly "written up" and printed, and then transformed and transferred from one journal to another, it is as difficult of recognition by those who took part in it, as the incidents of English life which the Western people read in their papers, would be by those to whom they refer.

In so far as the planting of trees has aided in the transformation of the treeless region, the result is largely due to what is known as Arbor Day, which is a happy combination of a pleasant holiday and one of the most profitable school-days of the year. I believe that the State of Nebraska—once a vast undulating prairie, but now a prosperous State—was the originator of the idea, to which, since 1872, is attributed the planting of 355,560,000 trees, and which has since been taken up by more than three-fourths of the States and territories. It is usual for the State Governments to establish the day by a short special enactment, making Arbor Day a public holiday, for the purpose of affording teachers, children, parents and friends, time and opportunity to engage in planting trees, shrubs, and vines about the homes, the schools, the public highways, and public grounds of the State. I have no space, if it were my wish, to give the arguments to be met with in nearly all school reports, in favour of thoroughly carrying out the spirit of this holiday. The usual method of celebrating the day is for the children to assemble in the morning, and either have lessons on the trees and their uses, or to meet and carry out a programme of recitations and singing, interspersed with speeches, all having a bearing on the value and beauty of trees. In some States, programmes of suitable exercises for the occasion are issued by the superintendent, and it is made the duty of the authorities of each school in the State to assemble the pupils in the school building or elsewhere, and to provide for and conduct such exercises as shall tend to encourage the planting, protecting, and preserving of trees and shrubs, and an acquaintance with the best methods to accomplish such results.

During the last few years, Arbor Day has been observed in South Australia, and bids fair to take its place among the permanent institutions of the Colony.

School Libraries.

In England school libraries are rare, in Australia an exception. Authorities insist on the mechanical power to read, but take little pains to utilise it as a means of education. By it, the pupil must educate himself when he leaves school, but no attempt is made to introduce him to his instructors. The Sunday-schools have set a worthy example in this matter, which it is a thousand pities the authorities of day-schools have not followed; the more so that the Sunday-school literature, written for a purpose which it is not my intention, were it my inclination, to discuss, is not usually of very high literary merit, is untrue to the realities of life, and does not tend to broaden, stimulate, and prepare a man for the struggles which he will have to encounter, any more than it leads him on to the best literature of the language.

The majority of the children have few books at home. If they develop a taste for reading, it is in spite of, rather than in consequence of, their opportunities. This will be disputed by many of my readers who live beneath the shadow of Free Public Libraries. Let such remember that, before any resident uses the free library, he must have the taste and inclination for reading. The library gives him the means of gratifying and intensifying a desire which already exists. What proportion of citizens use a public library? I am speaking of those who have not yet developed the love for reading, to whom it is an undiscovered paradise. Some have not, and probably could not be given, the taste—more is the pity—although I admit if they are thinkers it does not so greatly matter. But there are tens of thousands whose time at school produces but a fraction of the good it might, were an honest effort made to give them a knowledge of and love for good books. True, they leave school too soon ; but much could even now be done, were the authorities actuated more by a desire for the good of the children than by political motives. The training of good citizens must be thought more important than party feeling, or the wish for public notice. The public must recognise that it provides the money, and insist that it shall be spent to fulfil to the best purpose the end for which it was raised. This requires, first of all, that the people shall be intelligent enough to understand the process and aim of education ; and the teachers wise enough, far-seeing enough, to detect the tendency of the present plan, which, nominally educational, is largely political and financial. Many do, and resolve that while performing that part in politics which it is the duty of every citizen to take, they will leave the rest to the people ; and as long as they are law, will do all that regulations demand; but, in addition, without reward other than the consciousness of duty done, endeavour to make each school a centre from which shall radiate good, intelligent citizens, more capable of self-government.

By enlisting the aid of those whose money and whose time is ever at the disposal of all who show they are actuated by unselfish motives, and wish for the good of the children, it is easy to establish school libraries of the best books, adopting in the selection the motto " Few but Good," rather than " Many and Cheap."

The work set by the department, for doing which they

receive their small salaries, would then become all that it is fit to be—a skeleton round and on which a strong body of ideas is built. The library would be an invaluable help to them. People do not read, because they do not know sufficient to create the inclination for reading. Knowledge of lack of knowledge is at the root of love and desire for knowledge; the understanding is at the root of love for books. He whose knowledge of human nature does not extend beyond that depicted in the penny dreadful, will read that literature; anything higher would not be intelligible to him. We learn by doing. To get the young people to read, give them power to grasp a book; and then, by a judicious talk, give them a desire to obtain what the book will give. A great deal cannot be done at once. Too much should not be expected. It is always a problem of indefinite solution to decide when a thought will germinate, and still more uncertain when it will flower and bear fruit.

The first aim should be to get the majority of pupils to become so absorbed in one or other of the many optional and supplementary means of indirect education, of which school libraries are but one, that they will continue to remain associated with school after they leave its walls. Where there are free public libraries, the school libraries would naturally lead up to them; where there are none, they would in a measure supply their place, and be the means of their establishment.

While I know this is practical enough if there is the right spirit combined with tact and energy, I am confronted with the fact—I had almost said law—that, as a rule, people do not work for a higher aim than that which is set them; and often enough fail in reaching that, however low it may be. The attainment seems so easy, that they take a " short cut " for it; and a short cut is apt sometimes to prove a difficult road.

I cannot give details of any school libraries in English

schools. I saw several excellent ones, but find I have failed to make notes of them. Where they exist, they were due to the enthusiasm of individual teachers or members of School Boards, and are not part of a comprehensive plan. I have since learnt that every school under the School Board for London has its Lending Library.

There is a useful plan in operation in a number of towns which may be better mentioned here than elsewhere. The custom of awarding prizes to pupils is frequent in England. It is a natural associate of examinations. The difficulty of selecting suitable books in quantity is very great, so that the School Boards frequently publish lists of books adapted to the various departments, from which selections can be made when ordering.

In America, I found that City or State Boards of education frequently make provision for school libraries. In California, the law provides for a yearly appropriation of fifty dollars to each school district for library purposes. In the cities, it is fifty dollars for every one thousand children between the ages of five and seventeen years. The libraries are all free to all pupils, and to residents on payment of a fee. The appropriation may be spent in school apparatus, and books for supplementary work. The School Board does not always have sufficient money for all its purposes, and the regulation is read very liberally, so that the library money is not always used to add books. Still, all the schools have libraries, many of which contain comparatively extensive collections of books, showing careful selection and signs of good use.

Chicago provides for school libraries in all her schools. The school law of Illinois allows boards of directors to appropriate any surplus funds to the purchase of school libraries. There are now one thousand two hundred and thirty-nine districts, having libraries containing one hundred and sixty thousand volumes.

In the State of Rhode Island there are thirty-eight free libraries, containing about one hundred and forty-four thousand volumes. It is estimated that eighty per cent. of the population are within reach of a library; and when a few more shall have been established, the State will be able to claim the distinction which possibly no other can claim, that free schools and free libraries have been placed within the reach of the entire population. The public libraries serve the very important purpose of harmonising and unifying the heterogeneous mass of people gathered into the State.

In Dakota, one of the States just admitted into the Union, it is thought worthy of report that over three-fourths of the schools have an unabridged dictionary, and two hundred and seventeen have school libraries which are rapidly increasing.

In Minnesota, "according to the provisions of the law, a careful selection of suitable books for the different grades of the Public Schools was made, and, after advertising, the contract for supplying the schools was awarded to the lowest bidder. So far the experiment has proved a decided success.

"The test of one year fully sustains the claims urged for the passage of the law. When the people have been interested and have ordered books for their children, the effect has been wonderful. I am informed of counties, largely Scandinavian, in which the districts are generally supplied with libraries. The effect of all this is that these children are rapidly becoming interested and informed in American history and literature. That means they are becoming Americans."

In New Jersey there are eight hundred and forty-two school libraries, the appropriation for last year being two thousand eight hundred dollars. In Wisconsin, a new and sparsely peopled State, thirty-four per cent. of the towns have provided school libraries; while in Colorado the law authorises the School Boards to levy a tax of one-tenth of a mille for library purposes.

I have given sufficient instances to show the influence of these supplementary provisions for education in the small out-of-the-way schools, where the difficulty of obtaining books would otherwise be great. I believe country people as a rule are better read, though not so versatile as those of the city. They are like the sailor's parrot—they think more, but talk less, than their town cousins. Their minds, like their bodies, are more vigorous; but are not so highly strung.

In South Australia the need for the school library, though still urgent, is not so much felt, on account of the number of Public or Institute libraries, which are to be found in nearly every township of a few hundred people. Sometimes, indeed, in driving through an agricultural district of South Australia, a plain substantial building like a meeting-house will be seen on the roadside, with no house near. If the visitor is uncertain as to its use, he may be fairly sure that it is either a Methodist Church or an " Institute." The church will almost certainly have some ecclesiastical feature. Either there will be a dedication tablet, or the windows will be of the long, narrow type, with frosted glass, which is considered correct in a church— every house of worship is a church in Australia—or a graveyard, to denote the use of the structure.

These Institutes have been built half by public subscription, and half by subsidy from the Public Treasury. The Government also subsidised—pound for pound—all money spent in books and general expenses. The subsidy has been reduced lately, owing to a tendency of the local committees to spend the money on a large hall for concerts and entertainments, instead of for more purely educational purposes. Some contain well-selected libraries of considerable extent, for the use of which a nominal quarterly subscription has to be paid.   In connection with most there are free reading-rooms, in which the leading magazines of England and America, and other current literature, together with books of reference, are open to all.   While acting with great liberality in this way, the Government have done nothing in the way of providing school libraries.   Individual teachers have established a few, raising the money by subscription and by school concerts.

The following extract from a lecture delivered before the Keighley Teachers' Association, by Mr. T. G. Rooper, on Elementary Education at the Paris Exhibition, deserves mention here :—

"My attention was next attracted by an exhibit of a seemingly useful local society called the Society for Providing a Circulating Library for use in the Public Elementary Schools in the Canton of Lizy-sur-Ourq.

"The statutes approved by the Préfet in 1881 are worth noting : (1) An association is formed of all persons subscribing to the present statutes under the name of the 'Society for the Establishment of a Popular Circulating Library for the Public Schools in the Canton of Lizy-sur-Ourq ;" (2) The object of the Society is to establish and maintain a library of useful and instructive books for every school in every parish. The books are to be renewed annually.   All books of a polemical description, and all religious works, will be excluded. The books will be chosen, as far as possible, from the catalogue of reading-books published by the Minister of Instruction."

Pupils' Reading Circles.

The inadequacy of the ordinary school work for the education of the pupils is becoming more clearly recognised each year.   It is not long since the popular idea of education embraced little more than being able to read, write, and

work the simple rules of arithmetic. With the growth of
the conception of the scope of public-school education, is
the wish to make the best possible use of every possible
means, whether they be within the ordinary range of school
work or not.

In the United States, but I believe more particularly
in the middle and north-western States, one of the latest
devices is the Pupils' Reading Circle. It is organised on
similar lines to the Teachers' Reading Circles, of which I
have spoken, and is said to be very popular, and productive
of much good. The following report of one of the organisations will give a clearer idea of their work than a mere
general statement.

THE ILLINOIS PUPILS' READING CIRCLE.

At the meeting of the Illinois State Teachers' Association held in
Springfield in December, 1888, a resolution was adopted, requesting
the directors of the Illinois Teachers' Reading Circle to organise a
Pupils' Reading Circle. In accordance with this resolution, the
directors proceeded to organise the Circle on the following plan :

1. That the first year's work should consist of the two following
grades :

INTERMEDIATE GRADE.

SEASIDE AND WAYSIDE.   STORIES OF OUR COUNTRY.

ADVANCED GRADE.

HEALTH LESSONS.   ANIMAL MEMOIRS.   STORIES OF THE PATH
FINDERS.

The time for the completing of the reading of either of these was to
be one year.

2. It was determined that at the close of each year's reading (for the
first two years) a certificate will be issued to all members who pass a
satisfactory examination in the recommended course ; and upon the
same evidence, a diploma will be issued at the close of the third year, a
seal at the close of the fourth year, and a seal at the close of the fifth
year, which will show that the member has completed an entire course
of reading in the Illinois Pupils' Reading Circle.

The first twelve months of the history of the Circle closed January 1, 1890, and the records show that about thirty-five hundred copies of the books have been sent out during the year. No one anticipated such a demand for the books. It shows that the Circle meets an actual want of the schools.

At the late meeting of the directors, it was determined to provide for three grades at the beginning of the second year. It was also ordered that the manager should issue a certificate to every pupil whose teacher would certify that the books prescribed for any grade had been carefully read. Teachers are respectfully requested to inform their pupils upon what condition certificates can be obtained.

CHAPTER XIII.

PRIVATE MUNIFICENCE IN AMERICA.

General Remarks—The Rindge School—Mr. Williamson's Trade School —The Pratt Institute—Cogswell Polytechnical College—New York Trade School—Leland Stanford University—Clark University.

IT is not an uncommon thing, to hear people of intelligence speak seriously of the American as though his chief end in life is the accumulation of dollars. As is usual with popular fallacies, there is enough of truth to make the lie plausible. However great his propensity for getting may be, his freedom in spending is correspondingly great. Whatever may be the average American's vices, those of the miser are certainly not among them. When we misunderstand, we often misjudge. How often this result is due to indifference, how much is culpable ignorance, how frequently to lack of opportunity, or how much to the spirit which actuated the old lady who when asked to attend a lecture on the French, replied, "What do I want to know about the French? They are a wicked, light-headed, sensual people, who eat horses, dogs, and frogs, and have no respect for Sunday or anything good," I will not attempt to decide. I know of no people to whom it would not be a blessing, could every notion which nine-tenths have of foreign lands and people be blotted out, and the whole bundled off under the guidance of the remaining tenth to gather new ideas more in accordance with fact. I insist on the preliminary erasure of old notions, because, otherwise, the result would be similar to what frequently does happen in the case of those who do travel, and effectively prevents their learning anything, by their incessant tirades against the people with whom they come in contact for not being in the same enlightened condition as they modestly consider themselves, or for actually presuming to think their way of doing things as good as that of the traveller. The tourist who, when on an excursion, was indignant at being considered a foreigner, informing the natives that she was English and they were foreigners, was not more absurd than many others ; but as one bird builds her nest to be seen by every passer-by, while another hides hers away, so that it can only be seen by those who, wise enough to understand her actions, seek in the recesses of the hedges for it, so the folly of one nature may be small in amount but very evident, innocent in character but exceedingly laughable, while another, though still more foolish, has yet wit enough to hide his folly from the unthinking.

Were this to be done, I would further advise that the American should start with England, and the Englishman with America, because they are essentially one and the same people, but are given to exercising their imaginations in thinking themselves different. So they are, and rightly so ; but frequently in a very different way from what is imagined. I think I may safely say that it is characteristic of the American that he does not look to the Government to do much for him. He is thoroughly self-reliant. The same reaction against monarchism, which gave him his system of district government, has produced this result. He wants money—not because it is money, but because it often gives him the power which position gives to an Englishman ; and one of the uses he makes of it is to relieve distress, which in England or Australia would have to be dealt with out of the poor rates or by the authorities for the purpose. This comparison is general only.

But the object of the present chapter is to show some of

the results of private liberality in providing education in a land where the Governments provide free education from the primary grade to the university, and in some of the Western States in the university itself. I had not seen it stated, and was quite unprepared to find, how frequent and large are the sums given to found or support educational establishments. I do not think another country can show a like record in this respect. I cannot mention many, and I have not particulars of some of the largest and most important, such as the Sohns-Hopkins, Cornell, Vanderbilt, and Vassar Universities.

I did not see all of the institutions I shall describe. Several, indeed, are not yet provided with a local habitation, being in course of organisation. References to some will be found in the chapters devoted to the work they are carrying on. When I did visit them it was usually to see the result of the development of an idea under the most favourable circumstances. An enthusiastic body of teachers, supported by ample funds, often with selected material in the shape of picked pupils, and unhampered by the meddling of busy-bodies and politicians, who are often the curse of public systems, are able to do work and accomplish ends unattainable under less favourable conditions.

My purpose in giving the particulars of private bequests is the consideration that the donors were—or are—usually such as we are used to hear described as " practical, hard-headed, business men," generally men with one strong predominating idea to which they attribute all their success ; sometimes even men who give their fellows little of their sympathy during their lives, but freely, generously, leave what has engrossed all their energies, sympathies, and time to the custody of others, who, often lacking the faculty of accumulating, have highly developed powers of dispersion. The predominating idea of these men usually finds exact enunciation in their deeds of trust; and on this account these documents are always of very great interest to me; and, if to me, by inference, to others.

When the gift is made during the lifetime of the donor—for the purpose, according to their contemporaries, whose criticisms are, however, not always prompted by the most charitable motive, of gaining some coveted honour, title, or position—the object to which the money is devoted is still often determined by similar influences.

The Rindge School.

Mr. Rindge has lately presented to the City of Cambridge, Mass., a fully organised industrial school, with funds for its maintenance. In his deed he says:—"I wish plain arts of industry to be taught in this school. I wish the school to be for boys of average talents, who may in it learn how their arms and hands can earn food, clothing, shelter for themselves; how after a time they can support a family and a home; and how *the price of these blessings is faithful industry, no bad habits, and wise economy, which price, by the way, is not dear.* I urge that admittance be only given to strong boys who will grow up to be able working men. Strict obedience to such a rule would tend to make parents careful in the training of their young, as they would know that their sons would be deprived of the benefits of the said school unless they were able-bodied. I think the Industrial School would thus graduate many young men who would prove themselves useful citizens." This is not only interesting as showing the value he attaches to a trade; but that it requires other qualifications besides being a good workman to ensure success.

Mr. Williamson's Trade School.

Mr. G. V. Williamson is providing some two and a quarter millions of dollars for the purpose of establishing a great trade school in or near Philadelphia. "The great object to be attained," he says, in his deed of trust, "is to board, lodge, clothe, educate, and instruct in mechanical trades those who, when arrived at manhood, will be obliged to labour with their hands for their support." Later on he continues, "I *especially direct* that each scholar shall be taught to speak the truth at all times, and I *particularly direct* and *charge*, as an imperative duty upon the trustees, that every scholar shall be thoroughly trained to habits of *frugality, economy,* and *industry,* as, above all others, the one great lesson which I desire to have impressed upon every scholar and inmate of the school is that in this country every *able-bodied* healthy young man who has learned a good mechanical trade, and is *truthful, honest, frugal, temperate,* and *industrious,* is certain to succeed in life, and to become a useful and respected member of society."

Here, again, is a "practical" business man emphasising with £450,000 sterling his conviction that even able-bodied, healthy young men, with good trades, need to be truthful, honest, frugal, temperate, and industrious, to ensure success.

The Pratt Institute.

One of the grandest institutions of its kind in the world, is the Pratt Institute, Brooklyn, founded after careful study, to put into practical form the governing thought of its generous founder, Mr. Charles Pratt, that the first essentials to success are *self-helpfulness and self-respect.* Its aim is to aid those who are willing to aid themselves. He says, "The need of manual training as a developing power is scarcely less than that of industrial education—such education as shall best enable men and women to earn their own living by applied knowledge, and the skilful use of their hands in the various productive industries. Accordingly, the Institute seeks to provide facilities by which those wishing to engage in mechanical or artistic pursuits may acquire a thorough practical and theoretical knowledge thereof, or may perfect themselves in that occupation in which they are already engaged.* The Institute, alike in the magnificent buildings, beautiful equipment, and the splendid work being carried on, is a fitting fulfilment of a noble and generous conception.

Cogswell Polytechnical College, San Francisco.

This institution, founded by Dr. H. D. Cogswell, at a cost of 180,000 dols., to which he has promised to add another 100,000 dols., is for the purpose of "giving boys and girls of the State of California a practical training in the mechanical arts and other industries. The design is *not to teach trades*, but to fully prepare the student to enter successfully on any line of life. The aim is to fully develop the boys and girls, mentally, morally, and physically, thereby producing self-reliant and self-helpful men and women." The school gives a literary education corresponding to a High School, with the addition of manual training—half the time being spent at each kind of work. In fact, it corresponds with the St. Louis, Toledo, Chicago, and Philadelphia Manual Training Schools, and for the present, is being worked in conjunction with the public schools of the city. The building and furnishing are of the usual fine character adopted in scholastic institutions, the "drawing room" being one of the best I have seen. The equipment of the workshops is also of that handy and neat character which characterises the American "Manual School" as compared to the English "Technical School."

---

* Tuition fees are charged, but are devoted to the enlargement of the free library, for the general use of the city, as well as for the Institute, so that the sole cost is borne by the founder.

New York Trade Schools.

The founder, Colonel R. T. Auchmaty, in the prospectus of the school, for the ninth session, says :—"The New York Trade Schools were established eight years ago, for the purpose of giving young men instruction in certain trades, and to enable young men already in those trades to improve themselves. Commencing with thirty members, during the last seasons we have had over four hundred and sixty-nine (469). They are conducted on the principle of *teaching* thoroughly how work should be done, and leaving the quickness which is required of a first-class mechanic to be acquired at real work, after leaving the school."

The proprietor has the school carried on as though it were a business concern, except that he has laid out some £30,000, for which he gets no interest, and provides the large deficit in the working expenses. He has now built a large house, where pupils can secure rooms at eight shillings a week ; but in connection with this, he says, " The proprietor does not assume any control over the young men after they leave the workshops. Those who are strangers are warned what to avoid, and thus far have conducted themselves like earnest young men, who have come to New York to learn a trade and not to amuse themselves." Here we have a man spending many thousands of dollars a year, teaching trades to young men, who, as they pay fees, probably consider the whole in the light of a business. This, I believe, is the owner's wish ; in order not to interfere with ideas of self-reliance.

North Bennet Street Industrial School.

This institution, situated in one of the poorest parts of Boston, is one of the most interesting I visited. Attracted by the school-like aspect of the building, I called, in a

casual way, during the dinner hour at a neighbouring
public school, which I have mentioned elsewhere, on account
of its work in teaching so many foreign immigrants to speak
English.   Finding it to be the centre of an organisation, in
its totality unlike anything I had seen elsewhere, although
organisations for the accomplishment of one or other of its
individual parts are to be met with frequently enough, I
paid a number of visits, each time becoming the more
impressed, as much with the greatness of the work done as
with the quiet, thorough, unassuming methods of organisation and work.   It would be almost as easy to say what is
not done as to enumerate the branches of work, carried
on at an annual cost of some £5,000 sterling.   Though
carried on by an association, its benefactors are not known:
"in deference to the wishes of the contributors, no list of
names has ever been published."

So deep-seated is the habit of estimating all things by a
short-sighted economic standard, that it seems sometimes a
hopeless undertaking to make an intelligent answer to the
question, "What is this school for?"   If one could be made
here, it would be something like this: "The chief aim
of the school is identical with that of all other good
schools—to give education; a difference being the use
of both manual and intellectual work for educational
purposes.   A prime object of the school is also to show
what results may be expected from the manual training
which rests on an educational basis, and to hasten its
introduction into the Boston public schools."   This explains
the fitting up of work-rooms for Kindergarten, clay modelling, drawing, Sloyd, carpentry, printing, shoemaking, cooking, millinery, and dressmaking, where pupils from the
public schools attend for free instruction during the day,
and in which classes are held in the evenings for those who
are employed during the daytime.   Over one thousand
pupils attend the day classes, and about three hundred

the evening. The above statement does not, however, account for the provision for free baths, game clubs, social clubs, drill, gymnasia for boys and girls, library, and a number of other departments, not forgetting a day nursery where over one hundred little ones, nearly all the children of foreign immigrants, chiefly Italians, Polish Jews, French, and Hungarians, are cared for while their mothers are away at work.

One of the chief supporters of this association is Mrs. Quincy Shaw, daughter of the great American naturalist, Agassiz. Either by her unaided effort, or together with the above association, she established in close connection with many of the public schools of the city free Kindergartens, which she supported for years. The pupils were passed into the primary grades of a school as though the Kindergarten were part of the establishment. The value as an educational preparation for the public school was thus demonstrated, and so impressed have the School Board been, that they have taken them over as part of their system, and are now establishing them in connection with other schools.

This illustrates how most of the reforms in educational procedure are brought about in America, and is analogous to the experiment of the City and Guilds of London Technical Institution, which I have described under Manual Training.

Leland Stanford, Junior, University, California.

California has been well supplied with facilities for higher education in her several Universities, the foremost being the University of the Pacific, endowed to the extent of about five million dollars. Senator Leland Stanford, however, is organising one to be named after his son, on a scale of magnificence never before known. It is situated at Menlo Park, and is intended to carry out Senator Stanford's ideas of fitting men and women for honest self-support.   In one of his addresses he said : " I am particularly anxious that the young men who by thousands are graduated from the colleges of the land and sent forth weaponless, so to speak, shall find here an opportunity to take up some speciality.   We shall teach the classics, and in fact everything, beginning with the Kindergarten ; but we shall also teach the specialities, so that young men and women will not be without a knowledge of a speciality on graduation.   We shall fit all the students for some active calling in life.   I hope the University will have a standing from the start.   Eventually, I hope that it will have several thousand students.   The real problem is, *How to realise the possibilities of the Students.*"

The Senator's ideas may not be very well defined, but with an endowment of from fifteen to twenty million dollars there should be scope for realising possibilities ; but it will require the influence of that great equaliser Time to say just how.

Clark University.

Jonas G. Clark is a "self-made man."   A native of Massachusetts, a carriage maker by trade, a successful Californian gold digger, a more successful investor in New York city, an American millionaire, he yet has found time to develop a great and grand idea as opposite to money-gathering as can be imagined.   It is " to promote science for its own sake and not for its marketable aspects, to extend the frontier of human knowledge that the world's store of wisdom may be increased, and next, in order that the new facts brought to light may contribute to the advancement of the race, that as all civilised communities are in the hands of experts, that the man who has special and extensive knowledge on any given subject, is the man whose verdict decides important points at issue, and sways the opinion of the multitude, the provision of a home for the training of experts and where investigators may carry on original research is a necessity." Imbued with this idea, Mr. Clark spent eight years studying into the history and working of the universities of Europe and America, and on his return set to work to prepare a home for the consummation of his ideas. The result is a pile of buildings of brick and granite almost as plain—though more substantial—as a factory outside, but inside fitted without regard to expense in the most handsome and convenient way. In this it is typical of American educational establishments. They are not architecturally as handsome and costly as those of Europe ; but in so far as convenience, adaptability, and comfort go, they are as great an improvement as a Pullman car is on a third-class European railway carriage. In State capitals, court-houses, and post-offices in the United States, there is often as great a waste on architectural ornament in dressed stone, with as little adaptability to the purposes for which they are built, as in the museum of Owens College, Manchester, or the University of Adelaide in Australia; but in buildings intended for school purposes, what I have said of Clark University will generally apply. There are exceptions, of course, generally in the case of high schools built at public expense. That at Denver, Colorado, for example, has a central hall and staircase suitable for the palace of the Czar, altogether out of place in a public school.

I might add many more accounts of institutions, practical embodiments or dominating ideas ; but I think I have given sufficient to illustrate my purpose. There are many noble instances of similar appropriations in England ; but they are not nearly so numerous or so liberal as in America.

www.ingramcontent.com/pod-product-compliance
Lightning Source LLC
Chambersburg PA
CBHW021726110726
47902CB00005B/1363